GRIM GAMES
THE THORNHILL VAMPIRE CHRONICLES
BOOK FOUR

LUCIUS VALIANT

THORNHILL PUBLISHING

"It is true, we shall be monsters, cut off from all the world; but on that account we shall be more attached to one another."

—— MARY SHELLEY, FRANKENSTEIN

GRIM GAMES

THE THORNHILL VAMPIRE CHRONICLES BOOK IV

LUCIUS VALIANT

ONE

V illa Graves stood out stark and glowing white against the dark, winter-bare branches of Queen's Wood. Frost-kissed ivy clung to the ornate Grecian marble columns at the front of the main building, lending an eerie, almost gossamer beauty to the scene. The broad white marble steps and the griffins guarding the black lacquered double doors were all frosted over with the thinnest layer of crystalline ice.

It was early January, and this had to be the coldest night in England in about a hundred years. I was aware of the cold, but the below minus temperature didn't bother me. I was undead; I could sleep on the ground out here in the woods if I wanted to and I wouldn't even catch a cold.

This was my third visit to Villa Graves, and the first time I'd come here both alone and completely voluntarily. Tonight, I was neither here to save anyone, or to test out a powerful lycanthrope sedative on an unsuspecting lab rat. Or lab octopus, if you really want to get specific.

I was here because I wanted to find out what Gabriel Graves knew about my family history between 1861 and

1970. He'd hinted that he knew things, including things that my undead cousin, Lyrica, either didn't know or wasn't willing to share with me. I wasn't sure why he'd agreed to share the stuff he knew, but that didn't matter.

Gabriel had promised me this months ago, but then he'd been gone all of November and half of December, apparently off to Europe. Something to do with his funeral business, Deep Graves. And since he'd been back in London, it had been my turn to be busy. I was back to hunting vampires and because of my suspension and the recent death of a prolific hunter, I was facing a huge backlog of vampires that needed staking.

I was about to ring the intercom next to the double doors when they opened on their own.

I stepped through into the vast hall. The floor was solid black marble, the walls white. The air carried a subtle scent of lilies and a hint of something aromatic, like a note of cologne or a trace of incense.

"Harlan Thornhill," Gabriel greeted me as he descended the solid marble staircase from one of the building's upper floors, trailing a floor length jacket in emerald velvet. The jacket was paired with a crisp white shirt, tailored black trousers and footwear that would not have been out of place at someone's funeral. Go figure.

His hair, long, straight and the palest shade of gold, hung loose over his shoulders, framing his elegant angular features and bright citrine green eyes.

Like all vampires I'd come across, Gabriel refused to use my legal surname in favor of the family name I'd only learned about five months ago. At this point, I'd given up on correcting anyone and decided to just roll with it. Harlan Thornhill didn't sound so bad. Even the Van Helsing Society - the secret organization of vampire hunters and supernatural scholars that had employed me since my eighteenth birthday - had updated my documents to reflect my new name, without asking my permission. A Harlan Thornhill file now existed in the Society's archives, under the section labeled 'Known Vampires,' which included vampires they were aware of and monitoring from a safe distance. Of course, I wasn't at a safe distance - I was one of their own.

Plunging down the stairs ahead of Gabriel were two massive dobermans, both of them growling. In a matter of seconds the marginally bigger and more manacing looking of the two had reached the bottom of the stairs and started leaping up at me, snapping and trying for my right hand.

"Meet Faust and Mephistopheles," Gabriel introduced the twin beasts. "They already seem to adore you."

If by 'adore' he meant 'want to maul,' then he was clearly right. Something was definitely wrong with the dobermans - their movements were too fast, too agile, and their teeth were too long and too damned sharp.

"What the hell are they?" I asked.

He reached the bottom of the staircase, not in any particular hurry, and stopped there to watch as the dogs kept leaping up on both sides of me, snapping and growling while I held my hands out of easy reach. I was armed, as I usually am, but I wasn't about to get my knives out and slaughter Gabriel's new pets. If I pissed him off, where else would I find the answers to those last hidden family secrets?

"They're gifts," he explained, "from my dear friend Dolores. But don't worry, they're entirely harmless. Harmless to you, at least. They sense you're of the blood. Their training in this regard is impeccable."

I frowned. Living or undead, don't all dog owners give you a similar line?

Faust leapt up at me again, trying for my left hand this time. Mephistopheles, meanwhile, pressed his nose against the back of my calf while emitting a low growl, not biting but clacking his teeth ominously close as if to tell me that he was at least considering tearing out my Achilles tendon.

"Faust, Mephistopheles, enough now." Gabriel finally took mercy on me and waved them away. The dogs immediately backed off with their heads lowered, their ears back and their teeth still barred. As they slinked off to the corner of the hall, one of them let out a whimper.

"I am pleased to see you," Gabriel said. He tilted his head slightly to the side and his eyes narrowed, as if he were at an art auction trying to decide how much the piece he was looking at might be worth.

"Did everything go well with your business plans in Europe?" I asked, striving for the politest tone I could manage. I still wasn't sure where Gabriel and I stood. We weren't friends, I didn't think, but I had nearly let go of any resentment over him ending my life.

On some level, I suppose I was hoping that easing up on Gabriel for killing me might somehow alleviate my guilty conscience over Ramsay.

Ramsay Fairweather had been a rival for a long time, but I'd never wished him any harm - until he showed up at Sebastian's comeback photography exhibition last October, intent on either killing me or making me believe he would. It was never clear which intention he really harbored, deep down. Regardless, I'd thrown him under the bus. I wasn't proud of that. Two and a half months later, I was still trying to shake the nagging feeling that I'd acted in a panic and missed the mark.

"Beyond expectation," Gabriel replied, bringing me back to the moment. "But you're not here to hear me talk about the plans I have for Deep Graves - fascinating as I assure you they are. You're here because you want to uncover the parts of your family history that remain shrouded in mystery."

"Well, yeah. I appreciate you agreeing to do this."

"It's no trouble. However, before we get sidetracked, you must promise me one thing." His tone sharpened, and the temperature in the room seemed to drop several degrees. "The next time you plan to unleash a werewolf in the mansion, I expect advance notice. That's not the kind of attention we need. As a hunter, you understand the cost vampires pay for indiscretion. I've had the cavern beneath this villa reinforced. If there's someone or something I wish to contain down there, they simply will not escape until I decide otherwise."

"That's... really reassuring, Gabriel. Thanks." I made a mental note to never set foot in the cavern below Villa Graves again. Not that I had any plans to - that place was riddled with too many bad memories.

"Well then, follow along."

Gabriel turned and led the way up the extravagant marble stairs to his office on the second floor. As we ascended, I kept an eye out for his little sister, Elizabeth, hoping to run into her.

She had managed to inject Eli with a powerful sedative, finally bringing him down and saving me from seriously hurting him, or vice versa. She also stitched up the deep claw marks I'd sustained. Though I'd insisted I was fine after Eli had slashed me, the cuts were deeper than I'd realized, dipping below my ribs, and I must have lost more blood than I thought. Still new to being a vampire, my supernatural healing wasn't as instant as I expected. As soon as I made it back to the grand hall, I collapsed and passed out in front of everyone.

I awoke in my coffin the next night, fresh stitches pulling at my skin and a guilty conscience lingering from the whole Ramsay ordeal. But at least I was alive, Eli was alive, and none of my vampire family had lost their souls. Venedict had returned, and we had a truce with the Graves. Things could have been worse.

Gabriel's office was magnificently expansive, its windows framing the villa's grounds and the dense Queen's Wood beyond. Fires danced and crackled in two white marble fireplaces, one at each end of the room. Amber-glass lamps hung at varied heights from the lofty ceiling, casting a warm glow that shimmered off the Persian rugs blanketing the floor. These rugs featured intricate patterns of leaves in deep green, purple, and blue. Near one fireplace was a collection of leather-upholstered Chesterfields, while at the other end, Dante and Faust curled up on the rug beneath a table, seemingly content now that they had shown me their intentions.

At the center of the room stood a desk crafted from polished black wood, topped with a solid slab of gold-veined marble. Gabriel gestured for me to take the chair overlooking the woods as he moved toward a wood-paneled shelving unit built into the wall. With a press of a hidden button, the panel slid aside quietly, revealing rows upon rows of black, leather-bound folders, each meticulously labeled.

"What's in all those?" I asked curiously.

"The dirt I have been collecting on everyone of interest for centuries," Gabriel revealed, his back turned to me as he rifled through the shelves. 'Everyone' probably meant other vampires that he wanted to hold some kind of sway over.

"Indeed. You never know when you might need to dig up someone's old secrets - or family history - to use against them. Or in this case," he added with a hint of cordiality, "simply to share it."

Gabriel returned to the desk carrying one of the black leather-bound folders. He slid into the chair facing the room and placed it on the table between us. "Everything I have on your family is here. Keep in mind it's mostly a paper trail. It'll fill you in on some details, but not all. The dead have taken many of their secrets with them to their graves, as they are wont to do."

He opened the folder and retrieved a document. "Perhaps this might interest you."

It was a birth certificate. My birth certificate.

The name on it was Harlan Thorne, and the date was March 27, 1997. The location was Vienna General Hospital in Austria. Until now, I had never known my place of birth or exact birthdate. The date on the falsified papers provided by the Van Helsing Society had always been January 1, 1997. It was a close estimate but not entirely accurate. It meant I was still 27 when I thought I had just turned 28. Not that I would ever turn 28.

At the Van Helsing Society, there had been a long-running bet among my colleagues about how old I'd be when I met my end. Most seemed to think I was a prime candidate for the infamous 27 club, and when I died in August of last year, everyone who had placed their bets on 27 had cashed in, including - completely shamelessly - my two best friends, Jed and Carmen.

As I continued scanning the birth certificate, my eyes snagged on my mother's name: Vivian Thorne. The field where a father's name should have been listed was conspicuously blank.

"Did you ever meet or see my mother?" I asked Gabriel, who shook his head. "I lost track of the Thornhill family's whereabouts in 1969. Your mother had not yet been born. I never saw her."

Gabriel went on, his tone shifting slightly, "Your birth certificate is the very last tangible relic of the Thornhill bloodline's mortal lineage. I acquired it not too long ago."

A spark of irritation flared within me. "How did you get it?"

"Jeremy Gently," Gabriel replied casually.

"Jeremy Gently had my birth certificate? And he just, what, handed it over to you?" My voice sharpened. I was unable to suppress my annoyance. Wasn't Jeremy, the Thornhill family solicitor, supposed to protect our interests rather than sell them off to someone who, until recently at least, could be considered an enemy of the family?

"And why would you want my birth certificate anyway?" I demanded.

Gabriel offered an innocent smile. "Merely curiosity. Surely that's permissible?"

I suspected that obtaining someone's birth certificate through their family solicitor wasn't exactly legal. But questioning how Gabriel had gotten my birth certificate, along with likely other private documents in his Thornhill file, felt futile. I stayed silent, shooting him a moody glare instead.

"Let's move on, then," Gabriel suggested smoothly. "Where did Lyrica leave off in her recounting of the family history? I can continue from there."

"She stopped at October 1861," I replied, my tone slightly clipped.

"Did she mention Augustine?"

"Octavia's and Clyde's illegitimate son, born on the night they were turned? Yes, she did."

"Octavia's and Clyde's son?" Gabriel raised a pale eyebrow. "Oh, no. She must have wanted you to believe that out of a sense of family loyalty. But Augustine was Octavia's and Algernon's son."

I frowned. "No way. That would be incest."

"It would be," Gabriel agreed, "and it was. This wasn't public knowledge, of course, but Venedict shared quite a few of his family's secrets with me that he probably shouldn't have. Including this. If you want more detail, you'll have to ask Octavia - though she may not wish to speak about it. She might not want to recount being violated by her own father. And isn't that quite understandable?"

Was this the real reason why Venedict killed Algernon? Not just to avenge his mother, or at least not only that. Not to claim the family fortune, as Algernon had insisted to me. It was to protect or avenge Octavia.

"As for Octavia's and Algernon's son, Augustine," Gabriel picked up, "he was, as you know, born on All Hallow's Eve 1861. Lacking any other mortal family, he was raised by Lyrica's parents, Harold and Emma Hartenbrook, believing them to be his parents, despite sharing no genetic link with them. He grew up without any awareness, it would seem, of the family he truly belonged to. Some might say that was for the best."

I could feel my jaw tighten, but I managed to hold my tongue.

"And yet," Gabriel continued breezily, "he was never entirely free of the looming shadow of the Thornhill legacy. Not only was he raised in Kentish Town, just a stone's throw from the ill-omened mansion, but he also ended up living there for a few decades leading up to his untimely death. But let me return to that. Before madness claimed Augustine at Thornhill Mansion around the turn of the century, he harbored creative ambitions and traveled to Paris around 1885, hoping to establish himself as a poet. Despite his talent, he never achieved commercial success."

Gabriel produced a small hardback poetry collection titled *Folie à Deux* from the papers on the table. He held it out toward me. "This is some of his work. Take it and read it when you can. I assume you don't read French, but much of it is in English."

I took the book. Its antique leather cover felt smooth and worn. "Augustine's Parisian pursuits may have been fruitless, but he didn't return to London empty-handed. In 1889, he came back with a son, Alastair. The identity of Alastair's mother remains a mystery, but the boy couldn't have been adopted - he had those distinctive amber eyes that you share." Gabriel glanced over at me while I flipped through the book, the aged paper printed with my ancestor's poetry.

"Another enigma," Gabriel continued, "is who invited Augustine to reside at Thornhill Mansion, which by then was falling into disrepair. It's clear someone must have extended an invitation because that's where he spent the rest of his rather abbreviated life. Augustine seemed to wage a private battle against the allure of the bottle and a myriad of unspecified inner demons. It's not far-fetched to imagine that he might have felt haunted by one or more of the mansion's resident ghosts. And although he never stumbled upon Venedict locked away in his casket in the basement, the mere presence of such a secret might have cast an unsettling pall over his stay."

I couldn't help but interrupt with a question that had

been gnawing at me. "Gabriel, be real with me for a sec." I leaned over the table, locking eyes with him. "Why didn't you ever just head over to Thornhill Mansion to cut the chains and let Venedict out of his casket? He was confined in that box for over a century and a half. It would have been such an easy thing to do. I thought maybe you loved him."

Gabriel surprised me with a candid answer. "I did love him. Terribly. That is precisely why I left him there. For my own peace of mind and, truly, for his safety. You could say I was a little disappointed by how things ended between us."

His eyes met mine, revealing no guilt or remorse, though maybe there was a trace of old hurt lurking beneath the surface.

Surrounded by these Victorian vampires, with their penchant for veiling things in secrecy and innuendo, this was the first time anyone had explicitly clarified that the relationship between Gabriel and Venedict was romantic - not that I hadn't been able to work that out.

I appreciated Gabriel's candor, but not how he'd treated Venedict, whom I had come to see as a sort of little brother from another era.

"Leaving someone you claim to love locked in a casket for over a century seems pretty toxic to me," I said, folding my arms across my chest and leaning back in my chair.

Gabriel's strange, cat-like green eyes met mine, a slight smile playing on his lips, as if daring me to push the issue further.

When I didn't, he continued recounting the Thornhill family history. "Augustine's son visited the mansion only occasionally, mostly to care for his father, who, according to rumors, was losing his grip on sanity. From what I observed, this was indeed true. He seemed deeply troubled."

"Troubled?"

"Haunted, perhaps." Gabriel paused for dramatic effect, lowering his voice. "He died, in 1903, aged 42. Fell from the third floor gallery - the very same one from which Helen Thornhill, Venedict's mother, fell to her death approximately half a century prior. Perhaps, something startled him."

"One of the mansion's ghosts," I suggested, to which Gabriel merely raised an eyebrow.

"By then, his son Alastair was already a lecturer in literature at the University of Oxford. Tragically, his life was also cut short. In 1918, he enlisted to fight in the Great War, leaving behind a young widow, pregnant with a child who would never know him - Amelia Hartenbrook, your great-grandmother."

Gabriel lifted an old sepia-toned photograph from the table and held it up for inspection. It showed a young Alastair Hartenbrook in full military regalia. Despite the uniform, his expression was more poet than soldier.

"Dashing," Gabriel remarked as he returned the photograph to the file. "As for your great-grandmother, Amelia, she became a governess for the children of the recently widowed Viscount Frost. According to the newspapers, the Viscount's household was in 'dire need of a woman's touch and tender presence.'" His tone held an edge of sarcasm.

Sensing where this was headed and feeling defensive of my ancestor, I interjected, "The Viscount was probably just lonely after his wife's death. They didn't have Tinder back then - what was he supposed to do?"

"Regardless," Gabriel continued, unfazed - he probably didn't even know what Tinder was - "Amelia answered the Viscount's call, and predictably, their relationship spiraled into a whirlwind romance that culminated in a rather brief marriage. Soon enough, the Viscount grew tired of Amelia and divorced her, leaving her to live in a humble home on the outskirts of his estate, where she could only watch as he remarried multiple times."

My opinion of the Viscount plummeted dramatically within those few sentences.

"Their marriage," Gabriel continued, "produced one child: your grandfather, Alastair Frost, born in 1942 and named after his maternal grandfather. Although Alastair inherited nothing from his father's estate, he built a moderately successful wine-importing business with one of his half-brothers. Later, he married Christabel Flint, a journalist from London."

"And what happened after that?" I leaned so far over the table that I nearly pushed some of the papers onto the floor. With an elegant sweep, Gabriel rescued them just in time.

"That is as much a mystery to me as it is to you," he said. "I suggest you prod your cousin Lyrica. It's peculiar how soon after her awakening in 1969, all traces of the Thornhill descendants seemed to disappear, wouldn't you agree?"

Our conversation was abruptly interrupted when a door next to one of the fireplaces swung open with a bang. A woman half-stormed, half-stumbled in. She was small and very pretty, with disheveled brunette hair and bare stockinged feet, wearing a short, champagne-colored dress. Her eyes were wild as she slammed the door shut behind her and sank down against it, trembling all over like a leaf.

CHAPTER
TWO

Gabriel didn't seem particularly thrilled to see the new arrival, but she lit up with obvious relief at the sight of him.

"Gabriel!" She scrambled to her feet and started moving towards us.

"Nina," Gabriel said with a deep sigh, "Can you not see I have company?" He gestured toward me and, without waiting for her response, pressed a button under his desk and spoke to one of his employees, "Rita, I'm aware it is late, but could you drive a guest home? Yes, come up to the front. She'll be down in a few minutes. Thank you, I appreciate it."

Nina attempted to interject, "I- but there's something-" Her words tumbled out in a frantic rush as she gestured wildly over her shoulder, her eyes wide with fear as she pointed back towards the shadowed corridor she had emerged from. "Gabriel, please. There's something in there, in Thomas's wing. In the bedroom. It's... you won't believe me, but you have to. Please, it must have come up from the lake!"

"I understand you're feeling unsettled, Nina, but try to take a deep breath." Gabriel's tone was smooth and velvety as usual, but there was a subtle shift in its cadence. It had taken on a faintly hypnotic quality, and I could almost see the invisible undertow, pulling her under.

Nina stopped her approach, standing rooted to the spot, her breathing gradually slowing. Her eyes glazed over as the tension seemed to drain from her, down through the floor where she stood.

She stopped trembling and nodded as she walked over to the cluster of Chesterfield sofas in front of the fireplace. Here, she let herself sink down onto the plush leather in a near slump. "I'm feeling really drowsy." Her voice was barely even a whisper. "And heavy."

Gabriel rose gracefully from his chair and moved towards Nina. "Yes, and isn't that much better than that awful feeling of panic?" He sat down next to her, placing his palm against her forehead, likely to amp up his influence.

"Uh-huh. Much better," she murmured, her voice sounding weak and distant as she closed her eyes.

"You haven't seen anything particularly disturbing here tonight, have you?" Gabriel asked softly.

"No. No. Just an octopus monster from the lake."

"An octopus monster from the lake is hardly worth worrying about, is it? Certainly not worth mentioning to anyone. Just a fleeting shadow in the grand scheme of things," he coaxed.

"You're right, Gabriel, it's not a big deal. Not worth talking about. Not worth panicking about," she echoed.

"You understand me so well. Now that you're feeling much better, don't you think it's time to consider taking your leave?" Gabriel suggested.

"My Louboutins are still in there," Nina protested, her

eyes popping back open. She was hypnotized, positively tranquilized, but she wasn't prepared to leave without her designer heels. I'm not saying she had her priorities in order, but she at least knew what her priorities were.

"And you are very welcome to go fetch them before you see yourself out," Gabriel offered.

Nina shook her head under his hand, dispelling some of the fog that had settled over her mind. "I can't go back in there. There's a monster in there," she protested.

"Speaking of." Gabriel turned to glance over at me, his eyes gleaming. "Harlan, have you eaten?"

It took me about a second to realize what he meant. I shook my head and he just made a light shrug.

"What about my Louboutins?" Nina interjected. She was completely oblivious to the fact Gabriel would have been perfectly happy for me to drink at least some of her blood right here in front of him. "I also left my jacket in there."

"Let me get them for you," I offered, rising from my chair. Gabriel watched me with an expression that was half amused, half condescending. He wasn't running any errands for any mortals, but what gave him the right to judge me for doing this girl a simple favor?

I could understand why Nina was in shock. Thomas Graves in his usual lycanthrope form was a shocking sight. I knew that he shifted back to his original human form on the full moon, like a werewolf in reverse, and this was probably when he found his opportunity to bring women home. Clearly, though, he wasn't in the habit of getting them out the door again before he shifted back into his tentacled, Lovecraftian self.

"Straight on down to the end of the corridor," Gabriel instructed.

Nina was still slumped over on the Chesterfield with Gabriel beside her, her hand dangling limply over its edge. She glanced up at me with a hazy smile as I walked past.

I felt a little uneasy about leaving her with him. I wouldn't come back to find her drained of blood, would I? He'd called one of his employees to pick her up at the door. He wouldn't have if he was going to kill her. They seemed to know each other, so she was safe. Right?

I opened the door that Nina had burst through and started down a long marble-floored corridor. Villa Graves seemed to be full of them.

I walked past several rooms, some closed and some open. This was Thomas's wing and the style of decor was markedly different to Gabriel's, which fluctuated between classic, somber and ostentatious. Thomas seemed to like modern art, bright splashes of color and animal prints. There were old-fashioned paintings too, all of them of ships and of the sea. I'm not exactly an art history buff, but I think I spotted a few original Turners.

Here and there stood old and weathered wooden chests with painted lids. It was tempting to go and open one of them, but I'd better not.

Before I reached the end of the corridor, the door was opened by a single tentacle and a pair of spike-heeled Louboutins were ejected from the bedroom along with a cropped tan leather jacket. I caught them before they hit the floor.

"That was super quick, thank you so much!" Nina beamed at me the second I stepped back into Gabriel's office with her rescued clothes. Gabriel hadn't touched her, but he had poured her a whiskey on the rocks, which she was sipping from now with obvious relish. She seemed way more alert, too.

"Don't mention it," I gave her her things and she wiggled into them. With her outfit now complete, she downed the remainder of her drink in a single, graceful gulp and left, in a better mood and more composed than she had been in minutes ago. The only sign that she had even been here was the lipstick stained glass she left on the coffee table.

Gabriel sighed with obvious annoyance. "I really need to get that door sealed off," he mused, more to himself than to me. "This is a regular occurrence in the wake of the full moon, and it is truly starting to irk me."

"Who is she?" I asked.

"Thomas's current paramour. Every full moon, it is the same scenario. After three and a half centuries of me picking up my brother's slack, running the business, and raising his son for him, you would think he might at least handle his own dalliances without relying on my intervention - which, alas, he knows he can count on."

Gabriel griping about Thomas was an unexpected glimpse into their dynamic. Honestly, I found it slightly amusing and had to keep myself from looking too gleeful.

"But enough about Thomas," Gabriel declared as he rose from the Chesterfields we had migrated to and started rummaging around a globe bar crafted from wood, steel and glass. "He has already encroached sufficiently on my plans for the evening."

When Gabriel returned, he offered me a glass filled with a liquid that looked like wine but definitely wasn't.

"Don't fret," he said, reading my mind. "This comes from a hospital. No karmic calories to worry about, or at least not many. Like you, Elizabeth has her qualms about going to the source. We have found that this is the best alternative."

When I was still mortal, the thought of drinking human blood would have made me gag, but now the subtle metallic scent was overpoweringly delicious.

I eyed the glass of blood with suspicion, then glanced over at Gabriel. "How did you get this from a hospital?"

His smile broadened. "Private health insurance."

I waited for the punchline, but apparently, that was it.

Gabriel set the glass on the table and settled into the Chesterfield across from me, crossing one leg over the other with a casual air. "Tell me," he said, "when did you last have blood? I am, of course, referring to real blood, not the tragic animal substitute Venedict tells me you have been procuring from a butcher."

"I haven't."

"Surely," Gabriel said, his tone now dripping with both pity and exasperation, "you're aware that bloodlust has a way of overpowering you at the most inconvenient times if you try to suppress it? Elizabeth had a recent ordeal with it - she accidentally killed a boy, a rather charming one from the neighborhood she was quite fond of. The poor little darling was inconsolable, despite my assurances that guilt was entirely unnecessary. And I should know - I may have killed a few boys in my time. Or," he paused, eyes gleaming, "if I'm perfectly honest, perhaps more than a few."

Gabriel threw his head back and let out a peal of rich, velvety laughter.

"It's guys like you that keep the Van Helsing Society going," I observed wryly. "And it's why so many of my colleagues don't trust me now. But I'll prove them wrong, because I know how to control the bloodlust."

"Oh, you do?" Gabriel shot me a look of amused disdain. "If that is true, having human blood just once and then never again should not be a problem for you, should it?"

With a push, he sent the glass of blood gliding across the table. It stopped perfectly in front of me, the overhead light making the deep red color appear all the more vivid.

"If I drink this, it isn't some kind of slippery slope, is it?"

"No, surely not," Gabriel's green eyes gleamed as he watched me intently to see what I would do. "Not for someone as... in control as you."

He was clearly egging me on - I wasn't stupid; I could tell that's what he was doing. But it was still working on me because now not drinking the blood would feel like backing down to him, and I just couldn't do that.

I took his dare and lifted the glass.

What harm could one glass of blood do, anyway? I'd successfully managed to repress my bloodlust for months, and I'd repress it again after this.

I took a hesitant sip, expecting resistance from my conscience. What I felt instead was an electrifying sensation, a surge of pure, raw energy cascading down my throat and radiating throughout my body. I downed the rest in one gulp. It was almost like an echo of what the turning itself had felt like. Animal blood, by comparison, seemed hopelessly lackluster and dull.

"Was that so awful?" Gabriel asked, watching me with a sly smile.

"It was alright," I responded. It was a dramatic understatement of my reaction.

"I personally prefer the fresh variety, but I suppose this will do in a pinch, or as a temporary stepping stone while you are still coming to terms with your condition. So, forgive me if I don't join you in drinking, but would you like another glass while we discuss the Grim Games?"

Not waiting for an answer, he plucked the glass from my hand and disappeared from my field of vision.

"The Grim Games," I repeated, the name rolling off my tongue with a hint of irony. "Sounds exactly like your idea of fun."

"Indeed. The Grim Games are a competition among friends, a vampire-only event by invitation only. They're hosted by Lord Evander Eve - I suppose I should use his full title since he's technically a count and, as you might expect, rather full of himself because of it."

Gabriel returned with the glass refilled to the brim with blood and set it down in front of me without a word. But I caught the subtle arch of his pale eyebrows when I immediately picked up the glass to take a sip.

"Evander Eve is a vampire count?" I asked, unable to mask my skepticism. "Who came up with that?"

"The irony is not lost on him," Gabriel promised, settling back into the Chesterfield. "Much like your undead family, Evander has been around since the 1800s. His family owns an indecent number of properties here in London and throughout the south. Plus a few in Italy and France. And, much like the Thornhills, the Eves were involved in trade. They were also involved in smuggling for about a century, though they hardly needed the money, given their existing wealth." He paused briefly before adding, "Evander has a few undead relatives, including a nephew, Roderick. Very fetching, if slightly unhinged."

Gabriel didn't seem to think that any other members of the Eve family were worth highlighting and moved on briskly, "The Games are set to take place at Eve Hall, the ancestral home of the Eve family, on the last weekend of this month. They start on Friday and conclude on Sunday, with each evening featuring a distinct game. Four blood-lines, including ours, are invited."

"We're not part of the same bloodline" I began protesting.

"Oh, but we are. The vampiric spark in your blood comes from me. I am the master of your bloodline - the progenitor, the furthest upstream. The Sire."

"You can't be. Elizabeth told me you became a vampire in 1665. There have to be vampires in this bloodline that are much older than that."

"I don't see anyone else stepping up to claim the title, do you?"

I couldn't argue with that. According to what Elizabeth had told me, Gabriel's maker, Isadora, had been struck by lightning in a recent, unfortunate turn of events - at least unfortunate for her. And it seemed quite possible that Gabriel was unaware of Isadora's maker or any of the lineage beyond that.

Gabriel responded with nothing more than a satisfied smile.

"The Games themselves consist of three distinct games, or challenges, if you will. There is a conjuration game, which I will leave to Csilla, who, as you know, has rather impressive gifts in that regard. The hypnosis game I will handle myself. I have challenged Evander specifically, and I am very confident that I will succeed in putting him under my influence."

That I could believe. I had just witnessed a clear demonstration of Gabriel's hypnotic abilities - and I'd seen him wield them over several people at once during the aftermath of Sebastian's catastrophic exhibition.

I'd experienced a more subtle version of them myself, the first time I was here. As a hunter, I knew about vampiric hypnosis, and I'd been careful to not look him in the eye. Even so, he had done something to my mind using only his voice and it had put me off my guard. When he led me to the underground lair beneath Villa Graves - a hundred feet or so below where we were right now - I had followed right along to my death, like an idiot.

"As for the remaining game, Evander has been somewhat reticent about sharing details, but from what I gather, it involves retrieving a trophy of sorts from the depths of Eve Hall's smuggler's waterways. This seems to cater to the kind of rough-and-tumble activities that are your specialty." Gabriel let out a sigh, "Scrambling around in the mud is not really my preference, but I'm sure you'll find it entertaining."

Gabriel didn't seem to think I was very sophisticated, so I made an extra effort to restrain the urge to lick every last drop from the inside of the glass I'd just drained. The rich taste of blood still lingered, sending a shiver through me.

"And what's in it for you if we win?" I demanded.

"Officially, it's merely the honor. And, I suppose, the very trophy that you will be competing to retrieve during the final game. But unofficially," he leaned forward slightly, lowering his voice, "I'm eyeing a greater prize."

Of course he was.

I found myself leaning forward, too, "What prize?"

"I am making quite the confession by telling you this. But I want to see if I can trust you," he said, his gaze intensifying.

"You have no reason not to trust me."

He frowned slightly at this. "Did you not turn up on my doorstep, pretending to be a client the first time we met?"

"That was under exceptional circumstances," I countered.

"It certainly was. Well, my true agenda for the Games is to persuade Evander to sign over a number of properties to me that I have coveted for decades. He has always been resistant, despite my offering generous sums for each of them. Once I have him under my spell at the Games, he will be signing these properties over to me with a smile on his face, in front of everyone."

"That's gutsy," I commented, a note of admiration creeping into my voice despite myself.

"I dare say," Gabriel smiled. "But here's the rub; my plan hinges on your willingness to compete in the final game. I am certainly not doing it, and there is no one else in the bloodline who would be capable."

"I'll think about it."

"How might I persuade you?" Gabriel asked, his tone both challenging and persuasive. "Blood, money, anything you want."

"I'll think about that, too." In light of recent experiences, I'd promised myself to never immediately agree to anything a vampire proposed - as well as to never sign anything, or promise any souls as payment.

"Very well," Gabriel said, his attention momentarily shifting to the silver Rolex with a green quartz dial on his wrist. Then, he stood up in one smooth motion. "I would like to keep you longer, but you should start thinking about leaving. Sunrise is in an hour."

I glanced at my own watch, a habit I had picked up since my turning; when sunrise means certain death, keeping track of time just becomes more important. It was 6:25 AM. Like any vampire, I could feel when dawn was approaching, somewhere on a deep instinctual level. But the watch, and my iPhone, were extra assurance against any mishaps.

Gabriel escorted me to the front door, with Mephistopheles and Faust descending the stairs behind us. Their claws clicked softly against the marble, echoing in the grand hallway.

"You're certain you don't want a ride home?" Gabriel had already offered to call up his mortal assistant Rita again, but I felt bad for her having to run errands for her undead boss all night long so I declined. Besides, Thornhill Mansion was just a short walk from here.

"I'll walk."

"As you wish. I do hope you will give serious thought to attending the Games. I would consider it a great personal favor."

"Got it. I'll call you by the end of the week."

Gabriel pressed a Deep Graves business card into the palm of my hand, with two direct numbers scribbled on the back in emerald ink. "Please do."

I slipped the card into my pocket. Augustine Hartenbrook's poetry collection was already tucked securely inside my jacket. Then, turning on my heel, I stepped out into the chill morning air.

THREE

I'd gotten my hunting license back in mid-October, but the Van Helsing Society's elders hadn't let me get back to work right away. First, they had dragged me through numerous long-winded meetings and mountains of paperwork. It was the first time the Society had ever taken a chance on a vampire as a hunter since its founding in 1899, and the elders were determined not to screw it up.

I took getting my license back just as seriously. So, I sat through all the mandated meetings with uncharacteristic saint-like patience, signed every form shoved in front of me, and even went along with the psychological evaluation they insisted on.

In my sessions with Malcolm, the Society's resident shrink, I kept things toned down. I knew exactly what he was up to - one slip, and he'd be reaching into his bag of tricks and pulling out a bunch of labels, pasting them all over the character report he was compiling.

So, I didn't tell him anything I thought might sound too alarming. I left out my recurring nightmares and my tendency to black out during intense moments while hunting - incidentally, the real reason behind those overkill accusations that had inspired Ramsay to suspend my license. Staking vampires ten, twenty, even thirty times instead of just once isn't something I ever plan to do, it's just what ends up happening before I can stop myself.

I also skipped over the part where the only time I really feel at peace is right after an orgasm or a kill, and that killing is way more effective. And, of course, I never brought up the fact that, since arriving at Thornhill Mansion, one of the resident ghosts had occasionally started talking to me inside my head. I figured those were the kind of revelations Malcolm could feel tempted to frame as problematic.

In each session, he'd hit me with his probing questions. One of them was whether I had healthy strategies for handling negative thoughts, emotions and experiences. I told him I like to visualize locking them in a reinforced box and sinking it to the ocean floor, never to be looked at again. I found it effective, but Malcolm didn't seem impressed as he furiously scribbled in his notepad.

Another of Malcolm's questions was whether I thought Eli, my mentor and only real parental figure, had set a good example for processing emotions as I grew up. I answered honestly that, yes, by following Eli's lead, I'd learned to channel inconvenient emotions into hunting, so there was rarely a need to talk about them.

What I didn't tell Malcolm was that Eli's method never quite worked for me. My temper was far more volatile than his seemingly built-in stoicism. I felt things intensely, and it was hard for me to keep it from showing. Up until my death, it had taken a lot of hunting just to keep me balanced on a knife's edge.

When we were still together, I'd sometimes help Aubrey practice her ballet moves that required a partner. Thanks to my martial arts training, I picked it up quickly, and she'd half-joke that I should ditch being an assassin - no matter how many times I insisted I worked for a private security firm, that's what she believed I was - and become a dancer instead.

But the truth was, I had to hunt. Without it, I probably would've become the assassin Aubrey suspected I was, taking out crime lords, cheating husbands, and politicians, not for the money, but just to feel something strong enough to drown out the restless shadows in my mind.

Of course Malcolm wanted me to talk about my early childhood - but I couldn't. My earliest memories were shattered fragments from the night my parents were killed by a vampire, or vampires. I was six, nearly seven. Everything before that was a complete blank, a gaping abyss of nothingness. No matter how I tried to reach down and grab hold of something, anything, I always came up empty-handed. Or at least, I never came up with anything concrete, anything I could describe. Just sadness and fury.

Malcolm really gave it his all, peppering my report with buzzwords like repressed trauma, unresolved anger, poor impulse control. He claimed I believed the rules that applied to everyone else didn't necessarily apply to me, and that I deflected uncomfortable topics with sarcasm. But in the end, he couldn't dig up anything solid enough to convince the elders to keep me from hunting. By mid-December, they caved and let me return to work.

It had been about a month now, but they were still only comfortable assigning me execution warrants. Execution warrants aren't issued lightly - a vampire always gets three warnings within the same century before it comes to that. But you probably won't be shocked to hear that the kind of vampire who kills recklessly and draws the attention of the Van Helsing Society isn't the type to heed those warnings. In other words, a fair number of cases do end up with an execution.

Tonight's warrant was for one Mr. Nolan Clark, born 1912, married to Valentina Clark (née Volkov) in 1945. Their address was on the south bank of the Thames, almost directly across from Csilla's river-facing mansion on the north bank. The Clarks were probably her closest undead neighbors.

According to the Society's files, Nolan Clark wasn't exactly a sympathetic figure. He had long periods where he kept a low profile, only to erupt into violent month-long sprees, leaving young women dead or nearly dead in the streets of central London, like a bloodsucking Jack the Ripper.

My team tonight consisted of Jed and Carmen, which was perfect. We'd worked together countless times before. Ramsay had once mockingly dubbed us the "Three Muske-teers," but we took it as a compliment.

The residence of Nolan and Valentina Clark was a well-proportioned detached house enveloped by a high, ivy-clad wall.

A weathered plague informed us that the house had been built in 1923. The main entrance featured a heavy, ornate wooden door with iron detailing and a heavy cast-iron door knocker in the shape of a ram's head. There was no doorbell. The glow of electric lights behind the tall narrow windows indicated that we would find the couple home this evening, which was just our luck.

Sometimes when you have an execution warrant it can take several attempts to actually locate the vamp you're after, which is why the warrants are usually good for two weeks before you need to worry about getting them re-issued.

The three of us went up to the door. I raised the ram's head door knocker and knocked three times.

If I'd still been a mere mortal I would have picked the lock and let myself in. But being one of the undead now made me feel as though I ought to arrive with a little more courtesy. I was here to drive a stake through a fellow vampire's heart (and then to sever his head, before setting both the head and the body on fire), that was a truth we couldn't get around, but there was no reason why I shouldn't be civil about it.

Besides, if I could keep the rush of adrenaline that tended to flood my brain under some kind of control, I could sometimes narrowly avoid the moments of blacking out that tended to make me overdo it a little with the staking.

And I really had to tread carefully, because I was being both watched and recorded. As I stood on the stairs outside waiting for Nolan or Valentina Clark to answer the door, four of the Society's obsidian-winged ravens circled over-head, the little cameras in their beaks rolling as they captured the scene.

I'd willingly agreed to let the ravens follow me on hunts for the foreseeable future, but to be honest, I found them irritating. Their presence was a constant reminder that the elders didn't quite trust me. And they reminded me of Ramsay, who had been involved in training them.

After a prolonged silence, the door was opened from within. We had heard no steps on approaching on the other side of the door. Vampires tend to move silently like that.

The door swung inward and there stood a gorgeous woman, undead of course, her long butter-yellow locks swept up on top of her head in a shimmering fountain. She was wearing a floor-length midnight blue gown, high heels, pearls and elbow-length gloves. It was only a quarter past midnight and Valentina Clark looked like she might have just returned home after a concert or perhaps some kind of ball.

"Yes, can I help you?" she asked in a resonant voice, still with a touch of a Russian accent.

"Valentina Clark? My name is Harlan Thornhill and these are my colleagues, Jed and Carmen." I didn't give her their last names - it might not be wise. "We're here on behalf of the Van Helsing Society."

Valentina's expression shifted from mild skepticism to clear hostility. "Why are you here on behalf of the Van Helsing Society? Are you a negotiator?"

"Not exactly. We're hunters."

"Nolan will not be happy about this!" Valentina said in a sharp, warning tone. "You will have to leave. All three of you."

"I'm sorry, but we've got a warrant," Carmen spoke up. "It's only for your husband, Mrs. Clark. Step aside and let us through, and you won't come to any harm."

"I am not stepping aside and letting you walk in here to kill my husband!" Valentina protested. She turned around to look back down the long corridor behind her, clearly hoping that Nolan would have sensed the commotion.

"Yes, you are." In a rapid move, Carmen had her Glock 17M trained on Valentina's collarbone. The Van Helsing Society's hunters always use the same guns as the police. It just makes the cleanup afterwards that much easier to deal with. "Please take us to see your husband. After you. Walk slowly or my finger might slip."

Carmen was tough and direct - she had to be. At just

around 5'3", her small stature and classically feminine beauty didn't always earn her much respect among the vampires we dealt with. Many of them hadn't been born in this century, and more often than not, their mindsets were as archaic as their wardrobes. They tended to underestimate her, a mistake they rarely lived long enough to regret.

Her long black hair was tied back in a tight bun, a length she had painstakingly regrown after I'd once had to chop it off. A banshee - a type of vampire you really don't want to know more about - had grabbed it and tried to drag her down into the crypt beneath an abandoned, banshee-infested castle. But that's a story for another time.

Jed, towering next to her at 6'2", had broad shoulders and a powerful build. His long, deep brown hair fell freely around his face, despite both Carmen's lesson and the Society's regulations. Since the night I turned, he had sported a wildly staring glass eye.

Valentina slowly turned around and started down the corridor. Carmen walked behind her, her Glock aimed between Valentina's bare shoulder blades. The ravens followed us, their wings flapping almost silently as we moved through the corridor.

"Nolan? Nolan, the Van Helsing Society have sent some of their bloodhounds!" Valentina called out. She led us upstairs and down another shadowy corridor and finally into what turned out to be a very large bedroom overlooking a large shadowy garden.

Nolan Clark was tall and gaunt, and with his long black hair and the all-black ensemble he was wearing - and which included a cape, a silk top hat and even a silver-tipped cane - he was every bit the quintessential vampire.

"Haven't I told them that I am not prepared to entertain their nonsensical demands?" he asked in a haughty, educated voice as he turned around from the vanity table upon which he had just placed his tophat. "Oh, hello. And who are you?"

Nolan's eyes, powder blue, shifted between me, a fellow vamp, and Carmen who was still holding a gun pointed at his wife.

"He says his name is Harlan Thornhill. He says he's an executioner," Valentina answered for me in a disdainful tone. She didn't even deign to mention my colleagues. Vampires tended to do that, act dismissively toward mortals as if the only people in the room were the ones who didn't have a pulse.

"A hunter, technically," I explained. "But tonight, I'm here because we have an execution warrant."

Nolan snorted. "I refuse to believe it. The Van Helsing Society has never been able to threaten me, so now they start turning my own kind against me? There seems to be no end to their attempts to deter me from simply doing as I please." After a brief pause he added, "This is my city. I have lived here, in this very house, for nearly as long as that miserable little Society has existed. They cannot tell me what to do. They're mere mortals, cowards, buffoons."

"Sure, there are a few cowards and buffoons among them, but they've got the right idea of protecting mortals from guys like you," I pointed out.

"You do not know what you are talking about," Nolan replied dismissively. His tone was relaxed, conversational, but I could tell from the way his eyes were gliding around the room, seemingly casually, and by the way his white-gloved hands still clutched the tip of the silver-tipped cane, that he was considering his next move very carefully. "I am sure that's why they have recruited you. You're too young to understand that they will one day send someone to put you down, just as they have now sent you to, supposedly, eradicate me."

"So you acknowledge that you have received the Society's repeated warnings," Jed observed.

"Of course I have!" Nolan's calm, superior facade was starting to crack and a hint of nervousness was bubbling up to the surface in both his voice and in his demeanor. "They have warned me to stop hunting on my own hunting grounds! They have warned me to leave the theater troupes and the bars and haunts of the West End alone. Well, I have notified them in writing that I will do no such thing!"

Very thoughtful of him.

"Valentina, would you like to leave the room?" I offered, "You don't have to see this."

"Leave and let you murder my husband?"

"Execute, Mrs. Clark." The bedroom had a door, other than the one we'd entered through. I opened it now and held it for Valentina. "If you please."

"I am not leaving! You will not do this!"

Suddenly, in a coordinated rush of movement, Valentina flung herself at Jed and Nolan pitched himself at Carmen. They'd both avoided me - as a fellow vampire, I'd be less fun to fight. They were saving me for last, probably so they could descend on me in a shared effort and with double the fury.

In a split second, Jed had his gun drawn and he fired it, planting several shots in Valentina's arm. Valentina hissed with anger and pain, and by the time she was back in focus, Jed had a stake aimed at her chest.

Nolan collided with Carmen and the two of them were crashing to the floor, her gun firing off into the wall. Before I could think I'd planted one of my own stakes through the small of Nolan's back. It was one of the impact-activated ones and it went right through, piercing the vampire's chest from the back.

The tip of the stake appeared on the other side of Nolan's chest a split second later and I pulled back sharply on the handle before it went through Carmen, too, nailing her to the floor.

I'd been quick to react, but Carmen's dark eyes were nearly black with fear as I lifted the vampire off of her by the stake's handle.

A red pinprick in the tender skin above her heart suggested that it had been a close call. A single drop of crimson blood welled up in the indentation. That drop of blood was the only color in the room, the only thing I could see.

I could feel my eyes glaze over.

"Tell me you had complete control over that move," Carmen said in a voice that was faint with shock.

I was probably imagining it, but I thought I could hear her blood rushing in her veins. A vivid image flashed through my mind - pinning her to the floor and sinking my fangs into her neck.

"Harlan, snap out of it!" she said sharply.

I did. I swung Nolan around and then used both hands and all my weight to thrust the stake down and nail him to the floor next to Carmen, who recoiled.

I wrenched the stake out of his chest, blood spraying as it came free, then drove it down again with brutal force.

Out of the corner of my eye, I saw Jed frantically slicing his hand across his throat. It was the signal we'd agreed on for me to stop immediately and move on to the next step.

I glanced down and realized I'd driven the stake so deep into Nola's chest cavity that only a few centimeters of its handle were visible above his shoulder blades. His entire chest was a mangled mess, dark blood and bits of tissue seeping into the cream-colored carpet. I was drenched in his blood.

I quickly released the stake, sprang up from the floor, and severed his head in one clean sweep with my Japanese steel blade.

Nolan's head rolled across the floor, unfortunately stopping at Valentina's feet, prompting her to scream uncontrollably. The sight of Nolan's lifeless body seemed to drain all the fight out of her, at least for now.

Jed turned on the flamethrower, and within seconds, the intense heat reduced Nolan's body to smoldering ashes. I opened a window to let out the ravens, and the acrid smell of burning vampire.

CHAPTER

FOUR

About ten minutes later, the three of us settled into my black Chevrolet Corvette Stingray, parked a few streets away from the Clark residence. I didn't know the first thing about cars and had chosen this one after paying off my flat when I finally had some money to splurge, purely because it looked great and could fly down the road.

Since bringing the Stingray to London, it had mostly languished on the corner of Pond Square in Highgate, a spot famously haunted by a headless medieval chicken. There, it had accumulated fallen leaves and the occasional parking ticket until I realized I was fed up with riding the tube.

In London, driving can seem more hassle than it's worth - finding parking is a nightmare, Ubers are abundant, and the tube bypasses all of the traffic jams that tend to clog up the city's arteries. But over the past couple of months, it had dawned on me that the way people stared at me now, the double and triple takes if I passed them anywhere with bright lights, wasn't going to change. Vampires may look human at a glance, but the subtle differences - the poreless skin, the pallor, the fangs, the unnaturally vivid eyes, and that instinctual feeling of alarm, like glimpsing a beautiful but deadly snake slithering through the grass near your ankle - are hard to ignore.

I was in the driver's seat, Carmen in the passenger seat, and Jed in the back, surrounded by our considerable stash of stakes and knives.

"That went fairly well, didn't it?" I asked.

"Eight out of ten," Jed offered his encouraging verdict before adding, "though you did go a bit overboard."

"I'm practicing," I replied, "Give me a chance."

Carmen was silent for once, a pensive mood enveloping her as she seemed to fall into herself. Then she finally offered her thoughts. "This could have gone catastrophically wrong, Harlan. Look." She pulled down the front of her top to point out the mark left by the stake that had skewered Nolan. Even dried, the sight of blood was a faint, alluring whisper. "If it'd gone in just a few centimeters, I might be dead."

"You're not, though," I pointed out, "And I had complete control."

Close enough, anyway.

I could tell from the look in Carmen's eyes that she didn't quite believe it. She hadn't quite believed anything out of my mouth since Ramsay's disappearance. There were moments when things felt normal, but then there were moments like this, when an edge of suspicion would cut in.

"If anything were to ever happen to either of you while we're out on a job together," I promised, "I'll turn you."

Carmen and Jed exchanged a disturbed glance.

"Don't," Carmen said firmly. Her bluntness was usually something I appreciated, but this time her words stung. "I know you're trying to reassure us, but I don't ever want to be a vampire. No, thanks. If it comes down to it, I'd rather you just let me die."

Jed nodded in silent agreement.

"It's really not so bad," I said, a bit hurt.

"But there are so many things you can't do now," Carmen pointed out. "Not to put too fine a point on it, but you'll never see or feel sunlight again. And if this hadn't happened to you, I'm pretty sure you'd be going to see Aubrey at Sadler's Wells this week and probably patching things up with her."

"What's happening at Sadler's Wells?"

Carmen and Jed exchanged another furtive glance. "Aubrey mentioned she invited you," Carmen said in a quieter voice.

Maybe she had. Aubrey had messaged me several times over the past couple of months. I hadn't been able to bring myself to block her, but I'd deleted every message without reading it. Algernon, Thornhill Mansion's resident poltergeist, had probably read them all, despite my telling him not to.

Aubrey was the only girl I'd really loved - or, as Eli had unhelpfully tried to assure me, just the first. It had been almost six months since she'd broken up with me, this time with a sense of finality, but I still felt tethered to her. I missed her, but what could I do? Hiding my real job from her had been hard enough when we were together - how was I supposed to explain becoming a vampire?

"Aubrey's performing at Sadler's Wells with her ballet company all month, and she mentioned something about auditioning for the Royal Ballet," Carmen said, her voice cautious. "I haven't told her what's happened to you."

"She wouldn't believe it anyway," I muttered, crossing my arms and sinking deeper into the car seat.

"Maybe," Carmen suggested carefully, "you should try to see her anyway. What's the worst that could happen?"

The worst? Oh, I don't know. Maybe I'd give in to the dark fantasy that had been haunting me - draining Aubrey's blood and feeling her die in my arms. For some disturbing reason, my vampiric instincts told me that killing her would be extremely hot. But those weren't the kind of thoughts I could share with anyone, not even with my closest friends. I used to be able to tell Jed and Carmen almost anything. But that was before vampirism.

And definitely before I drank that damned glass of blood Gabriel had offered me. Ever since then, the blood-lust had only gotten worse.

I shouldn't have accepted it, but there was no going back now. I just had to deal with the consequences.

"Never mind," I said gloomily, turning the key in the ignition.

∼

THORNHILL MANSION IS HAUNTED by several ghosts. Helen Thornhill is the most prominent, the one most likely to make a public appearance.

But the spirit drawn to me - the one who showed up uninvited when no one else was around - was her husband, Algernon, the long dead tyrant father of Venedict and Octavia.

Algernon had been so quiet lately that I'd almost been able to forget about him. After his struggle against Csilla, the vampire medium, he had been laying low. As he'd put it that night, after I'd swapped his soul out for Ramsay's in the bargain I'd made with Csilla, he had needed some time to recuperate and regain his strength. The endeavor had apparently taken him a few months, but here he was.

I'd come back from the hunt with Jed and Carmen about half an hour earlier and had just stepped out of the shower after washing all of Nolan's ink-black vampire blood off my skin and out of my hair.

I slipped into black silk pajamas and a matching kimono before opening the ancient windows to disperse the lingering shower fog.

As the mist began to clear from the gilded antique mirror above the sink, I noticed a shadow moving within it. At first, it was just a flicker, but as I stepped closer and wiped the damp mirror with my palm, the shadow became distinct, manifesting Algernon Thornhill's features.

A shiver went through me, but despite the abruptness of his arrival, I managed not to show any sign of surprise. I guess I was getting used to living with ghosts.

My ancestor's face hovered in the mirror, right next to my own reflection. We didn't look much alike, except for the strange amber-golden color of our eyes. And I suppose the light caramel shade of his hair wasn't a world of difference from the deeper cinnamon shade of mine.

"Indeed," Algernon agreed, and I could hear his voice distinctly, although his lips in the mirror hadn't moved. "We are undeniably family. And yet you have spurned me these past few months. Much against both my interests and your own, I might add."

I've spurned you, have I?" I chuckled at his Victorian jargon. He wasn't wrong, though. After the Ramsay incident, I'd decided it was best to avoid Algernon. He was a bad influence on me. If it wasn't for his persuasive whispers, promising boundless power and insisting that Ramsay would be a perpetual problem if I didn't get rid of him, I might not have signed off on Ramsay's death. Or maybe it was just convenient for me to have someone else to blame.

"I am merely making an observation," Algernon stated, his disembodied voice seeming to sound from the back of my skull as much as from his image in the mirror. "At the risk of seeming a little forthright, have you thought about the proposition I made some time ago? I trust that you have had time to consider it."

"What exactly are we talking about?"

"Have you thought any further on the possibility of helping me take possession of Venedict's body?" His query hung in the air with a sense of hopefulness, as if he actually expected me to say yes.

"Oh, that," I said flatly. "Yeah, I'm still not interested. I thought I made that clear."

"Who knows?" he continued, undeterred by my resistance. "I believe Csilla could be persuaded to assist us. I have something she wants."

"There is no 'us' in this. I've already caused one soul to be expelled from its body, and I'm not about to do it again. Particularly not to Venedict. Can't you just try to be a normal poltergeist and possess a random stranger instead of pestering your own family? Not that I'd want you to do that, but you get my point. Leave Venedict alone. That's what I'm saying."

"As I've told you, Venedict is my son, and Helen's son. That would make it easier for me to walk in and take over."

A shiver went down my spine, like a trickle of cold. "Are shared blood and DNA really that helpful when it comes to possession?"

"Yes," he replied. Silence fell between us before he

added, with a touch of wistfulness, "I suppose you wouldn't let me have yours?"

"I'd rather step out into the sun," I replied, my voice chilly. I was suddenly uncomfortably aware that he might have been waiting in the bathroom mirror for several minutes while I had been getting showered and dressed, waiting to have this little chat about possibly taking over my body. Something about that seemed a little gross, like he was window-shopping for a new skin to wear.

"How can you be so heartless?" he asked, though his tone was more resigned than accusatory. "But I understand - you have only lived a quarter-century. Venedict has had his body for a century and a half without fully appreciating it."

Algernon knew as well as I did that Venedict had spent most of that time locked in a coffin in the mansion's basement, so I didn't bother pointing it out.

"If it weren't for me," Algernon mused, "Venedict would not even exist. It's only reasonable that I reclaim what I created. The cemetery would be the ideal setting for my ritual of rebirth to take place."

"You can forget about that," I said sharply. "I'm not helping you with any of this. Never."

My words made him fade away, as if in disappointment or disapproval. I doubted I was in Algernon's good books anymore.

CHAPTER

FIVE

I arrived at the Van Helsing Society's southern headquarters just after seven PM the following evening. Built into the historic foundations of the Old London Bridge, near Fishmongers' Hall Wharf, the Society masqueraded as a cultural and historical exhibit.

The areas off-limits to the public were accessible through a discreet side entrance and extended deep beneath the bustling streets of central London. As soon as one of the Society's butlers - essentially just a polite term for a bodyguard - buzzed me through the obelisk-flanked, steel-plated door, the city's noise vanished behind me.

I was here to meet Carmen and Jed, and to pick up the execution warrant before tonight's hunt. We needed to make our way down to Folkestone, a coastal town in Kent, and it was good we were getting an early start.

I headed straight for Godfroy Rosebery's office. Rosebery, one of the Society's elders, was overseeing the experiment of letting me back into the fold despite my turning. He'd spent decades lobbying for the Society to open its doors to undead hunters. Now, he finally had the majority on his side, willing to take that leap of faith - if only because I'd proven my loyalty to the Society's cause long before I ever grew fangs.

It's safe to say that not everyone shared Rosebery's enthusiasm for the concept of an undead vampire hunter. A number of the more conservative members, led by Edna Adler, were hell-bent on getting me ejected.

So far, they hadn't succeeded, but walking down the corridor, I'd gotten used to the reaction. Often a door would be opened, a head would poke out, only to be quickly retracted.

I couldn't really blame them - vampires aren't popular around here. If I were still mortal and one of my fellow hunters had joined the ranks of the undead instead of me, I'd take it as badly as the worst of them. That's just a fact.

I stopped outside the heavy wooden door to Rosebery's office and knocked twice. It wasn't long before it swung open, revealing a short, rotund, and cheery elderly man dressed in a black-and-peach pinstripe suit. Rosebery always favored these elaborate, tailored suits, and he usually topped them off with a hat. Tonight, it was a black-and-peach flat cap.

"Ah, there you are. Just on time. Step on in, Harlan." Godfroy had long since dropped the formality of "Mr. Thorne" in favor of calling me by my first name.

He waved me into his office, which was cozy but elegant, with high mahogany-paneled walls and tall, narrow windows that overlooked the darkened courtyard. Outside, the old stone fountain with its lone cherub holding a monstrous-looking oyster splashed water softly into the basin below. In summer, the courtyard would bloom with colorful flowers, but now only the ivy still seemed alive out there.

I was surprised to see Carmen already seated in one of the chairs facing Godfroy's leather-topped desk. She smiled, but there was a hint of unease in her expression. I moved to take the chair beside her as Godfroy walked around the desk, resting his hands on the surface but not sitting.

"As I've just explained to Carmen," he began, "tonight's hunt is going to be delayed. We may even push it until tomorrow. The reason being, we are conducting another round of interviews regarding Ramsay Fairweather's disappearance. It has been nearly three months, and we've had both the police and private investigators hired by the Fairweather family involved. As you know, Harlan, we've already carried out our internal investigation, but now everyone will need to undergo a second round of interviews."

"Jed is in the boardroom now, being interviewed by the elders," Carmen added, glancing meaningfully at me.

Godfroy's dark eyes shifted to me. "It's no secret that you and Ramsay had something of a rivalry, and it's also known that you were among the last people to see him prior to his disappearance."

I was doing my best to stay calm, but my mind was racing. Of course there was going to be another internal investigation. I should have seen it coming. But in a typical act of hubris, I hadn't.

Right now, I was especially grateful for my vampiric inability to blush or sweat, otherwise, I was sure I'd be doing both. The only thing that might have given me away was the sudden thudding of my heart, which had been still in my chest just moments before, and the way I shifted in my chair before I could stop myself.

"Now," Godfroy said, pausing to let his words settle,

"you will both have to excuse me while I join the other elders in questioning Jedesh. Once we've finished with him, I'll return for one of you. In the meantime, make yourselves comfortable."

"Sure. No problem," I said, trying for a breezy tone as I sank deeper into the chair. I didn't want to have to lie to the elders again, telling them that yes, I had seen Ramsay on the night he vanished, but no, I had no idea where he went after leaving Thornhill Mansion.

Carmen's expression was hard to read.

"Very well," Godfroy said, clapping his hands together. "I'll be back in about half an hour, maybe forty minutes."

With that, he exited, his footsteps fading down the marble corridor toward the boardroom. I turned to Carmen as soon as he was out of earshot. "Really, this again?"

She sighed heavily. "They're still trying to get to the bottom of it, of course. And the elders are under a lot of pressure from the Fairweathers."

Of course they were. The Fairweathers were one of the wealthiest and most influential families involved with the Society. Their history was so intertwined with the institution that the two were practically synonymous.

"Harlan," Carmen began, her voice softer now, her eyes focused on the window across the room instead of on me. "I've been meaning to ask you something. Be honest with me. Tell me you really don't know anything about what happened to Ramsay."

Carmen had been there that night. She knew most of what had happened, except for the ending. She and Jed had left amid a cloud of the Society's trained ravens, before I'd made the decision to let Csilla feed on Ramsay's soul.

An idea came over me with irresistible force. My recent conversation with Gabriel had reminded me of my first attempt at vampiric hypnosis. I'd managed to compel a hotel receptionist to give me the key to a room that wasn't mine. Perhaps now, it was time for my second effort.

"Carmen?"

She turned her head to look at me. There was something in her eyes, an uncertainty, a flicker of mistrust. But her faith in me, in who I had been before, outweighed her suspicions, and that's how I caught her.

With the Langham's receptionist, I'd fumbled through several attempts before managing to reel her in. But with Carmen, it was surprisingly easy. I felt the sensation of an invisible cord of energy forming between us, latching into place almost immediately. It felt like an etheric fishing line going taut the moment the fish bites the hook.

Carmen balked, pushing back in her chair, her pupils dilated, her body stiff. But then the tension faded as quickly as it appeared, and her posture relaxed.

"Yes, what is it?" Her voice was distant, sluggish, as if she'd had one too many drinks.

"You don't really think I had anything to do with Ramsay's disappearance, do you, Carmen?"

She hesitated. Her head bobbed in confusion, first nodding, then shaking, then nodding again. "I... don't know. I don't *want* to believe you did, but I know you must have been angry with him. I'm mad at myself for leaving him with you. Maybe I trusted you too much."

The word, spoken in the past tense, stung.

"I hate that I mistrust you now," she said in a small voice. "I feel guilty about that, because I love you. Not romantically, but it's still love, you know?"

"Yeah, I know. I love you too, Carmen." I leaned in slightly. "I'll tell you what happened after you left. Are you with me?"

I still wasn't too sure how this hypnosis business worked, but so far, things seemed to be going well. Keeping eye contact with Carmen, I shifted both of our chairs so they were facing each other directly, our knees nearly touching.

Carmen nodded, even more sluggish now, her long ebony hair brushing her arms. "I'm with you. I'm there. On the roof, and it's raining."

As if on cue, raindrops began splashing against the window overlooking the courtyard behind us, its rhythmic patter shutting out the rest of the world. The timing almost felt too perfect.

On impulse, I decided to try something I'd seen Gabriel do when hypnotizing Nina. He'd placed his hand on her temple, as if directly accessing her thoughts. That seemed a little invasive, so instead, I reached out and gently encircled Carmen's wrist with my fingers, feeling her pulse beneath my palm. It was as if I could push my perspective into her bloodstream, weaving my version of events through her very pulse.

"This is what happened, remember?" I made my voice as soothing as possible, willing myself to speak slower than I normally would. "After you and Jed left, Ramsay admitted to manipulating Eli and turning him against me out of jealousy and spite. He confessed everything, and promised to turn himself in to the elders." All true, up to this point. Then I added, "I believed him. So I let him go. But instead of turning himself in, I guess he fled, went underground. He knew the elders would expel him permanently if he admitted everything. I don't think he could face it. Are you still with me, Carmen?"

Her eyes fluttered, her breath shallow, almost syncing with the rain outside. I felt her pulse quicken under my fingers. "Yes," she whispered, her voice soft, barely audible.

Her dark, unfocused eyes held a rare vulnerability, a trace of trust that made me want to protect her, even as I was twisting her memories. I leaned in closer. "Good. Do you remember how Ramsay looked when he admitted it? The guilt in his eyes, the fear in his voice?"

Carmen nodded more assuredly. "I remember. He was scared."

I gently squeezed her wrist. "Exactly. He was terrified, and that's why he disappeared. He couldn't bear the thought of being cast out."

Suddenly, Carmen slumped forward in her chair, giggling softly. "Oh, I'm so drunk. I've had too much."

"That's okay, Carmen. Don't worry about that." I kept my tone steady, soothing. "Just tell me you understood everything I said."

"I've understood everything," she mumbled.

"That's great. Ramsay went underground, don't you think? It's nothing to be concerned about. He'll turn up when he's ready."

She slumped further, her forehead resting against my shoulder. "Sorry, Harlan, what were you saying?"

"Carmen, focus," I said, struggling to concentrate myself. Having her this close was distracting. The blood in her veins, so close, seemed to emit a magnetic field compelling me to bite her.

"Carmen, please sit up." I placed both hands on her shoulders, gently pushing her back into a sitting position. She resisted, suddenly wrapping her arms around me.

This wasn't going as I had hoped. I glanced at the clock hanging above Godfroy's desk - it had been twenty minutes since he left us. He could return at any moment.

"I'm sorry," she mumbled, her voice muffled against my shoulder. "Ever since what happened to Ramsay, I've been a little afraid of you. It's confusing."

"Please don't be, Carmen. There's nothing to be afraid of."

Or was there? My throat felt dry. I could almost taste the warmth of her blood, feel the rush it would bring.

Maybe a little distance would help. I got up from my chair and started pacing the floor. Carmen slumped in her chair, and I worried she might slide all the way to the floor. What would Godfroy think if he walked in on that? He had been with the Van Helsing Society longer than I had been alive. He'd know instantly that I had used my still-amateurish vampiric hypnotism on Carmen.

And to make it worse, the desire to bite her, to drain her, pulsed through me, growing stronger.

I needed to do something.

Venedict or Octavia might be able to help me with this, but trying to contact anyone at Thornhill Mansion through electronic means was like asking for the moon on a stick. Lyrica was off on her so-called Grand Tour of Europe, and Sebastian was in New York with his ex-fiancée-turned-girlfriend, Irene, so there was no point in trying to get him to wrangle one of our undead cousins for a call.

Carmen slid all the way down onto the floor, collapsing like a ragdoll, and that's when a thought struck me - Gabriel could fix this, couldn't he?

He'd given me his direct number. Technically, I could call him. But would he help if I asked?

I hated the idea of owing him anything, but I hated the idea of getting kicked out of the Society over something this stupid even more. So I swallowed my pride and dialled.

Gabriel answered on the second ring. "I assume you

have a compelling reason for disturbing my evening at the opera," he said, his voice like silk, laced with just the right amount of annoyance.

"I don't have a lot of time to explain," I jumped right in, skipping any snide remarks I felt tempted to make about opera. "But I need you to do me a favor. Will you?"

"Will I? Oh, that depends." Gabriel sounded both unhurried and slightly condescending. "That depends entirely on the nature of your predicament. What seems to be the matter?"

"I accidentally used hypnotism on one of my colleagues, and now she's completely out of it. I need you to bring her back around."

A pause followed, long enough to make me grit my teeth. Then, "I could help, yes. There is only one problem. It is not entirely clear to me why I should."

So much for thinking we had some kind of tentative friendship.

Gabriel's voice took on a gentler tone. "Suppose I handle this little mishap. Would it make you more amenable to my invitation to the Grim Games?"

"Fine. Done."

I could practically hear the smile through the phone. "Excellent. And you will, of course, adhere to the dress code I specify."

"Why?" I asked, not liking the implied insult.

My question was met with stony silence. Clearly, Gabriel believed he had superior taste and wasn't interested in discussing it.

"Fine," I relented. "Whatever."

"Very well. We have a gentleman's agreement."

Feeling a mix of irritation and relief, I held out the phone. "It's for you - Gabriel Graves."

"Carmen, do you remember me?" Gabriel asked, his voice slipping into that smooth, hypnotic tone that seemed to dissolve all resistance. With my vampiric hearing, I could effortlessly pick up both sides of the conversation.

"I do," Carmen replied, clutching the phone. "You're one of the vamps who showed up at the exhibition the night Ramsay disappeared. We've got a big, fat file on you at the Van Helsing Society - centuries worth of fascinating stuff."

"That's truly fascinating, Carmen. Perhaps, one night, you could be persuaded to bring me that file, along with a few other items of interest."

I itched to snatch the phone from Carmen and shout, "*Over my dead body!*" at Gabriel for even daring to think he could worm his way into accessing the Van Helsing Society's archives. But I held back.

"For now," Gabriel continued, his voice like velvet, "aren't you starting to feel that fog lifting? Simply drifting away."

"I am," Carmen said. She sounded clearer now. "I'm noticing that." Slowly, she began to prop herself up, looking more alert as she listened to something Gabriel whispered so softly that even I couldn't make it out. She nodded, murmuring, "Yes, I understand."

Finally, she took my hand, allowing me to pull her up from the floor. Still speaking to Gabriel, she sank back into her chair, her usual alertness returning to her eyes.

Then the doorknob twisted, and as Carmen said goodbye and hung up, Godfroy re-emerged in the room. These three events unfolded nearly simultaneously, but in a way that seemed so seamless and natural that Godfroy didn't notice a thing.

"I am sorry it took so long. There was quite a bit of ground to cover. Carmen, could you please come with me?"

"Sure, I'm ready." Carmen stood up and handed me my phone. "Thanks for lending me this. Sit tight."

I nodded, watching as Carmen followed Godfroy out of the room. Relief washed over me, though it was tainted by the awareness of owing Gabriel something. But all in all, I felt like I'd just managed to step from the fire into the ashes.

CHAPTER
SIX

When I stepped into my quarters at Thornhill Mansion a few nights later after work, Octavia was standing in front of the oval, floor-length mirror - Algernon's favorite - in what was now my bedroom. She was framed by the mirror's ornate edges, almost as if it were a portrait frozen in time.

As part of the recent restoration work on the mansion, Octavia's and Venedict's former rooms had been combined into adjoining quarters consisting of a bedroom, which overlooked the garden and cemetery, and a wardrobe-slash-weapon-storage room that faced the back garden. The two were connected by the tiled Victorian bathroom with its copper pipes, claw-footed bathtub and recently installed shower.

Octavia, the youngest of my newfound undead family, hardly looked the seventeen she had been when she was turned. She was perhaps 5'1", with the small rounded features of a porcelain doll and large amber eyes swathed in dark lashes. In true vampire fashion, she was stunning and unreal.

She wore a short, rose petal-colored silk dress that complemented her dark cherry-red corkscrew curls cascading down her back. The soft, feminine look seemed oddly at odds with the leather knife sheaths she was strapping to her arms and calves, not to mention the harness across her back holding my crossbow.

"Harlan?" she said, turning as she caught my reflection in the mirror.

"Octavia, you can borrow anything you want from my wardrobe," I replied - though I knew none of it would fit her - "but steer clear of the weapons, especially the stakes. You could injure yourself."

"I'm not likely to injure myself," Octavia insisted, fumbling with a stake in her hands. Suddenly, she pressed a button, and the sharp end shot forward with surprising force.

I rushed over, quickly snatching the stake from her grasp and tossing it onto the bed, where it landed with a muted thud. "What's this all about, Octavia?"

"I, too, am becoming a hunter," she announced proudly, beaming up at me as if expecting applause.

"Oh yeah?" I replied, unconvinced. "I'm not sure that's such a good idea. Who or what are you planning to hunt?" I started loosening the straps on her arms. The harnesses were too big for her and would slide down the second she began to move.

Her answer came promptly: "Men."

"Great. Just men in general, or is there someone specific?"

"Men like my father."

A brief silence followed.

She broke it by saying, "You know, don't you, that Clyde was not the father of Augustine? Clyde and I were never romantically involved. I am not merely saying that," she underscored, "because a relationship between cousins would be considered inappropriate from your modern perspective. It is simply the truth. Venedict arranged our wedding to save me from social disgrace. Being pregnant and unmarried was a very big, bad deal at the time."

"I figured," I said while removing the badly secured crossbow from her, placing it on a shelf higher up in an old wardrobe, which I had repurposed into a weapons cabinet. I deliberately placed it out of her reach. Of course she could easily leap up and get it, but I hoped that a bit of psychological distance would deter her.

"You can likely guess who the real father was."

I didn't answer - I sensed she didn't really want me to.

"There was only one man it could have been," she said, her expression souring, her small button nose wrinkling as if something nearby was emitting a foul stench. After a moment, she fixed her gaze on me and lowered her voice to a whisper. "My father. I think you already know, so I might as well tell you."

"You don't have to tell me any of this. You don't have to go there," I said.

She shook her head, her curls bouncing with the movement. "I want to. Some men scare me, but not Venedict, Sebastian, or you. I feel comfortable with you."

I knew that. Since moving into the mansion, Octavia had unexpectedly become the undead relative I spent the most time with. Most evenings if I was home, she'd drift into my quarters, settle on her old four-poster bed, and insist I play The Sisters of Mercy or Marilyn Manson - a problematic choice, as Sebastian pointed out when he once stuck his head through the door to admonish us. We didn't necessarily talk. I'd busy myself sharpening my knives or typing up a report for the Society if I had to, while she listened, sometimes reading.

I wondered if she missed her old room and had offered to give it back - the mansion was more than big enough for me to move my things to another part of it - but she had declined.

Now, Octavia moved away from the mirror, as if worried the ghost of her father might be listening - and in this house, who knew, he might be.

She crossed the room and sat on the edge of the four-poster. She looked small and fragile against the towering bedframe as she took a deep breath, clearly bracing herself for what she was about to say.

"Father always claimed he wanted to marry me off quickly to some wealthy suitor - said he needed to rid himself of the 'temptation' I posed, as he so delicately put it." Her tone was full of bitterness, and she gritted her little pearly white teeth. "The truth is, Father had absolutely no intention of finding me a husband. Had he not died, who knows how long his charade would have gone on. Perhaps forever."

She paused, her eyes flicking briefly back towards the mirror as if she expected to find her father lurking in its glass with a disapproving stare, admonishing her to stay silent. But the only reflection there was her own, pale and impossibly young.

"Venedict decapitated him," she said softly, her fingers nervously tugging at a loose thread in the bedspread. "But it wasn't easy. I had to help restrain Father and move the body afterward. Venedict used one of those old swords from above the fireplace. It's still there, you know. He sharpened it for the occasion, but even then, it took a lot of hacking to finally take Father's head off. Neither of us had ever killed before. We were entirely unprepared for the sheer volume of blood, the harrowing screams, the pungent smell, the terrible thrashing."

A chill passed through the room, though whether it was from her words or the mansion itself, it was hard to say.

Octavia's face twisted into a grimace. "All in all, killing our father was more traumatic than we'd imagined. The body was exceedingly heavy, too. Venedict managed the arms while I took one leg and Lyrica took the other."

"Wait, Lyrica was involved?"

"Not by plan," Octavia answered. "I cannot recall why she came to the mansion so early that morning, only that she walked in on everything. And that turned out to be a great fortune, because once she grasped what was happening, she immediately pitched in to help. At the time, she was betrothed to Father, and I must say, I think she felt relieved. She was free of him, free from her commitments. We decided to leave Father's body on the front steps, to make it look like he opened the door to his attacker. His head, we buried at the garden's edge, facing the cemetery."

She smiled faintly at the memory. "Venedict wanted to put Father's head on a spike by the garden gate, but Lyrica and I managed to talk him out of it, in case such a statement could be interpreted as personal."

I raised an eyebrow. "It must have worked - you got away with it."

"Indeed, we did." Her smile widened slightly. "Helping Venedict kill our father was the most terrifying thing I've ever done. Yet, in retrospect, it was also strangely exhilarating. It felt freeing." She paused. "Now, I know I can't kill Father again - at least not in a physical sense - but I can destroy the reflection of him I see in other men."

She gestured toward my red iMac on the desk behind

me. "I have already lined up my first targets, I will have you know. I used your communication machine to lure in mortal predators. I tell them I am fourteen, and yet, they still invite me to their homes and hotel rooms. There seems to be no shortage of men who would jump at the chance to take a fourteen-year-old girl to bed, if offered the opportunity. But the ones who invite me to theirs are going to be met with dire consequences."

A dark glint sparked in her eyes as she said that.

"I like your idea, Octavia. But if that's what you want to do, at least let me teach you how to do it properly. I can show you how to use the weapons, how to clean up after a kill. I've never killed a mortal or made one disappear - but I'm sure some of the skills transfer." I paused, letting my words settle. "Will you let me? And promise me you won't start hunting until I'm sure you can do it without getting yourself killed."

For a moment, she studied me, her head tilting slightly as if weighing my offer. Then she smiled, a genuine, soft smile. "Certainly."

"Good." I exhaled in relief. "We'll need to get you some gear that fits you properly. I can get it from the Society."

"Will they approve of my intentions?" she asked, glancing at me with a sense of hopeful expectation.

I hesitated briefly. "Not exactly. They're not vigilantes, and they don't like vigilantes. Honestly, they barely even like me. So it's best if we don't tell them."

"I know you've never had siblings, but you're adapting quite well to being a protective brother. And I will protect you, too."

As if she could see straight into my thoughts, Octavia narrowed her eyes and added, "You don't seem to think it's necessary, but I think you might need me to, sometime."

As if they had coordinated this, Venedict appeared almost the moment Octavia left, just as I was stowing away the pile of stakes that she had removed from the weapons cabinet.

At 5'6, Venedict was a few inches shorter than me, and lithe in a way that complemented his otherworldliness. His hair was cut straight across and just shy of brushing his shoulders, a light shade of caramel with the ends tinted violet. His high cheekbones, sharp chin, and small nose were all finely carved, an echo of my own. I'd always thought my features were too delicate, teetering on androgynous, but with vampirism they finally seemed to fit.

Venedict was rocking the whole New Romantic look that he seemed to have pioneered about a century before anyone else thought of it. Tonight's ensemble consisted of a Victorian-style shirt, calf-length lace-up boots, and a profusion of antique jewelry inherited from his mother.

Apparently, Helen had appeared to him on a recent stormy night and led him to a jewelry box hidden away in a crawlspace beneath the parlor floor. Now, he wore a rotating selection of her necklaces and earrings on a nightly basis, and always her wedding ring, a silver band beset with flashing sapphires.

"I hear you've accepted the invitation to the Grim Games," Venedict remarked as he entered the room. Word certainly traveled fast.

"I have," I said. "I decided it'll be an experience."

Venedict gave me a skeptical look as he walked past me to the window.

"Nonsense!" he declared, levitating into the windowsill and sitting there with his legs folded under him, facing the room. "I know Gabriel backed you right into it. Ah, don't look so stunned. I promise you, I'm not reading your mind. He told me."

"I thought you said you weren't on speaking terms," I pointed out.

"We don't speak frequently, but, well, it does occur."

It did. Just last night I'd seen Venedict down by the wrought-iron gate, talking with Gabriel through the bars. They'd paced the length of the garden, then back, fingertips trailing along the bars, now and then touching. Then suddenly, Vendict seemed to have either changed his mind or gotten mad about something and had abruptly turned and stomped back up through the garden to the mansion, slamming its front door in a way that caused all of the glass in the building to shiver.

Even my computer screen had shivered. I'd been up here, typing up a report about the execution of Nolan Clark at my desk by the window. I hate doing paperwork and have always possessed an almost supernatural talent for wiggling out of it, sliding it onto someone else's desk. But I didn't always succeed.

"And so I know you didn't simply decide to go to the Games." Venedict concluded smugly.

"Okay," I admitted, "so he twisted my arm a little. He helped me out of a situation and in return, I had to promise to compete."

"Well, I hope you have exquisite fun at the Games." Venedict's tone was a little sharp.

"You make it sound both like you're jealous and like you're not going. I know you won't be competing, but couldn't you just come along?"

"Oh, no," Venedict replied with a dismissive wave. "I simply cannot. A whole weekend trapped in the countryside, sandwiched between Gabriel and Csilla? There may have been a time when the idea would have thrilled me, but I have my reasons for not wanting to be anywhere near Eve Hall if it means being in their company."

"And what are those reasons?" I prodded.

Venedict's jaw tightened. "You can well imagine."

"I think I can, but why don't you tell me instead? You've never really told me much about Gabriel. Or Csilla."

"I told you Gabriel is vain and vicious. What more could you possibly need to know?"

"The story," I challenged. "My entire existence has been turned upside down, and as far as I can tell, it can all be traced back to Gabriel showing up in your life sometime around 1860. He must have given you the immortal blood for a reason. Right?"

Venedict fell into a sullen silence while I put the rest of the stakes away. But then he said, "Surely Lyrica has told you everything you could want to know, and then some. Even locked away in my casket like I was, I could hear her upstairs in the library, prattling away to you and Sebastian for nights on end. It gave me quite a migraine, if you want the truth."

"She only implied he was influencing you in some way. And then, suddenly, you were a vampire. I think there's a lot she left out, I guess out of some sort of Victorian sentiment that your secrets are your own to share. So tell me. What went so wrong with Gabriel? It must have been pretty bad since you've both been mad about it for 164 years. I can't imagine holding a grudge against anyone for that long."

Venedict scoffed. "You think holding a grudge for 164 years is difficult? You simply haven't lived long enough."

I took a seat on the edge of the bed and waited for him to continue. Eventually, he spoke.

"Gabriel and I first met in 1860. It was early October, shortly after what was to be my last stay at Bedlam."

"Bedlam?" I repeated.

Bedlam, or Bethlem Royal Hospital, was only the most infamous and longest-running insane asylum in Britain's history. During the Victorian era, I think it had already been going for about a century and had become synonymous with the worst excesses of psychiatric care, notorious for its awful conditions and the inhumane treatment of its patients.

"As you can probably imagine, my father was the one who sent me there." Venedict elaborated.

"How long were you at Bedlam?"

He gave a casual shrug. "Oh, it wasn't a continuous stay. I was admitted several times between 1857 and 1860." His expression turned wistful as he added, "I never stayed long, and they never did manage to cure me."

"Cure you of what?"

"Oh, a myriad of things - melancholia, mania," he began counting them out on his fingers, "morbid thoughts, moral insanity, sexual inversion, and a very persistent case of what they called," he paused for dramatic effect, "general lunacy."

"General lunacy? Fuck, that could apply to anyone."

"Don't I know it," Venedict gave me a thin smile. "Each time my father sent me there, he conjured up some new and alarming diagnosis. The doctors either believed him or were too eager to accept his substantial donations to question his motives. Essentially, whenever my father wanted a break from me, Bedlam became my reluctant sanctuary."

Venedict's gaze grew distant. "Some of the treatments

for my supposed ailments were quite dreadful, if I'm honest, but not every moment inside was terrible. I actually have a few fond memories from there, and I made some friends. In fact, you will meet one of them at Eve Hall - Roderick Eve, the count's nephew. Unlike me, he was at Bedlam for a real reason. He had killed a man whom he felt cast a slightly too lingering glance at his fiancée. Actually, this was not the first man Roderick had maimed or killed for a similarly flippant reason - but because Christopher Crawford was an Earl, it was the first time Roderick got in any trouble over it. Still, thanks to his family's wealth and connections, he avoided prison and was sanctioned to a six-month stay at the asylum."

Venedict shrugged, "I found him very personable. He was gentle as a lamb while he was on the inside with me, great sense of humor, and he never once attempted to carve me up. Although, come to think about it, he did on one occasion hold a knife to my throat and threaten to castrate me if I ever looked at his fiancé in a way he did not appreciate. They were mere words, of course, spoken in jest."

"Huh," I commented. "Sounds like maybe it was good for him to have a little break from his fiancé."

"I suppose so," Venedict agreed. Then, he sighed. "Truly, my stay at Bedlam is a whole saga unto itself, but tonight, I think I will stick to telling you the full, cursed history with Gabriel. And it has to include my history with Csilla, since they overlap. I might as well be upfront from the start: that overlap was part of why everything went so disastrously awry."

CHAPTER

SEVEN

In October of 1860, I accompanied my father to a board meeting of the London Funeral Company one evening. Naturally, he was a board member, having donated the land on which Highgate Cemetery was built, and he wanted to stay involved in its oversight. You're aware of that part, aren't you?

My presence was necessary to take notes and keep things on track. My father was in one of his phases at the time. He managed, for the most part, to stay sober for most of his business meetings and official commitments, but outside of those, he was often inebriated, and the rest of the time, he was nursing a vile hangover accompanied by a foul mood. Without me there to keep everything together, he might have squandered our fortune much sooner than it eventually happened.

Gabriel was also on the board of directors, as a representative of the funeral trade, and I believe he had had something to do with planning the layout of the cemetery. Regardless, he was there, at that meeting.

This was the first time I was introduced to Gabriel

Graves, but he had a reputation that preceded him. He was quite a mysterious figure in Victorian society. He was wealthy, but had no title. He was unmarried, but appeared to have a son, or at least a small blond-haired, green-eyed boy who lived with him and shared his last name. This, of course, was Dwight Graves, his nephew.

Society naturally speculated about the existence of a Mrs. Graves, presuming she must have been a remarkable beauty to have caught Gabriel's eye. It was widely assumed that she had died, most likely during childbirth, or due to some tragic illnesses.

All of these perceptions played in Gabriel's favor. There was no shortage of women who found the notion of a handsome, wealthy widower devotedly raising his bereaved son utterly irresistible. Gabriel's aloofness, his apparent indifference to the numerous beautiful women vying for his attention, only heightened his allure.

Beneath the surface, however, other rumors swirled about him - and these rumors turned out to be true. Whisperings suggested that Gabriel's romantic interests were exclusively men, always young, always phenomenally gorgeous and often sons of nobility, as if he got some sort of kick out of that. There was even one scandalous occasion when he pursued a young widower he met when said gentleman entrusted him with arranging his late wife's funeral. More ominously, it was said that those who caught his eye sometimes mysteriously vanished.

I'd never encountered a vampire before, so I didn't know what Gabriel was when we first met. Of course I could tell he wasn't like anyone else. He was a little frightening. You know what I mean, the way vampires are. That simultaneous stillness and intensity. The dark aura.

In a sense, I feel like that moment I stepped through the

door and into that board meeting, set a whole avalanche of events into motion that defined everything from that moment forward.

Nothing about Gabriel's behavior at the meeting implied that he had even noticed me. But I could tell that he liked me from the moment he laid eyes on me. I knew from the way he was acutely aware of my presence in the room. I've always been good at picking up on such things.

When the meeting was over and it was time to leave, Gabriel slipped his business card into the palm of my hand. On the back he'd scribbled his home address and a time to come and see him the following night.

I knew what it was about. I knew the rumors, and assuming they were true, it followed that I was his type. Besides, I was eighteen and not completely naive. I'd had a few experiences. Gabriel wasn't the first man to be interested in me. Merely the first vampire.

I went to Villa Graves the following night. You know how close it is to the mansion, and yet I'd never noticed it before. It's rather well secluded in the woods. It looked pretty much the same then as it does today - of course without so many outbuildings and with stables and horse drawn carriages instead of cars.

It was evening, of course. The sun had just set, and its orange glow had faded behind the lacework of branches overhead as I walked up the allele to the villa. There must have been servants around, but they knew how to make themselves invisible.

Gabriel answered the door himself and held it open for me as I stepped inside. He seemed pleased but not surprised that I had accepted his invitation.

I never told my father where I went, and I'd decided not to tell Octavia on this occasion. No one knew where I was.

Gabriel could easily have killed me either that night or on any number of nights that followed, and then just put me in one of his caskets and buried me. Have you considered that? He has the ideal setup for a vampire. While many he buries are undoubtedly clients by choice, others, countless young men over the centuries, might not be so fortunate.

Something set me apart, however, something that kept me from being just another stupid boy who crossed Gabriel's path only to end up in a casket, buried in the cemetery or in the woods without a trace.

It wasn't merely the fact that I came from a notable family and wouldn't have disappeared unnoticed, nor was it solely my looks. Although Gabriel certainly appreciated my appearance, he also liked my personality. The very traits that others found unacceptable or too much - my mood swings, my brazenness, my sharp edges - were qualities he inexplicably adored. His response was a refreshing deviation from the norm, and it made me lower my guard, perhaps all too quickly.

On that first evening, he brought me upstairs and there were all of these refreshments. He didn't touch any of them, of course. His poise terrified me, and something about him sent my senses into high alert for danger. I had the feeling that perhaps, he might want to hurt me badly. He might even make me disappear. It was all terribly exciting.

At first, I think he was careful not to scare me off, something he might have done if he'd been too forward too soon. Only when he was sure I was at ease, and not about to bolt, did he gesture for me to come closer.

I didn't have to, but I slipped into his arms right away. I wanted to prove I wasn't afraid, even though I was trembling all over. My instincts were in turmoil, urging me to both run to him and run from him as fast as I could.

I asked him while looking directly into his eyes, "Are you going to hurt me?" to which he responded, "Is that not why you are here - because you think you might want me to?"

He did not offer me immortality that night, nor did he tell me what he was. When I left, I left not knowing what that pin prick feeling against my throat had been. He had not even broken my skin. He was very careful with me, at first.

He would bite me later, countless times. Over and over and over. It was fortunate that cravats were all the rage at the time - it made it a little easier to cover up the bruises and puncture wounds he marked me with.

Were there moments with Gabriel where I panicked, where I felt I might have gotten in over my head? There were plenty of such moments. A vampire is a vampire, no matter how you spin it. I don't need to explain to you that vampires are faster and stronger than mere mortals and that they are encumbered with some rather intense desires. On occasion, I could sense that only a thin line of control kept him from doing me serious harm. More than a few times, I ended up losing so much blood that I lost consciousness - and who knows if, on these occasions, he ever toyed with the idea of draining me to the brink of death and perhaps beyond it? I bet he did.

I recall one time waking up alone in the enormous four poster bed at Gabriel's villa late in the afternoon, absolute panic setting in at the thought of him emerging as soon as darkness fell outside the windows. By then, I was already accustomed to his mysterious nocturnal habits, and usually, if we were spending time together, I would head home at dawn when he vanished off to... wherever he went during the day. But on this occasion, I must have been so deeply unconscious that I'd slept through the entire day. It was nearly twilight.

The thought of him biting me again was unbearable. Rationally, I knew that I could simply tell him not to bite - that I couldn't take anymore right now. I had had to say that a few times, and so far, he had always listened, though admittedly he had a tendency, and a real knack, for coaxing and pushing me a little further than I wanted to go.

But he had assured me that I was safe with him. Even if that were true, that didn't matter now. An instinctual fear clouded my thoughts, screaming at me to run.

I couldn't run. I could barely walk, my legs trembling beneath me as I made my way to the front door, my vision blurry and my heart pounding. Crossing the driveway to the stable was a Herculean effort, but once I got there, I ran upon one of Gabriel's servants and demanded that he drive me home at once.

As the gleaming black carriage rattled away from the villa, the servant's eyes kept darting back to me, filled with something that was either pity or fear. I was aware that my white shirt was dyed red with my own blood, but it was only when I reached home and saw myself in a mirror that I fully realized the state I was in.

Octavia looked crestfallen when I ran into her in the hallway. She knew about Gabriel and sensed that he must have done this, despite my being too exhausted to even attempt to explain anything to her.

I caught my reflection in the bathroom mirror before getting in the bathtub to rinse off all the dried blood. My neck was absolutely covered in puncture wounds. My bottom lip had been bitten through. I also had similar puncture marks on my wrists, in the crooks of my elbows, and scattered liberally all over my buttocks and thighs. I could not conjure up even a trace memory of what might have taken place the previous night. I certainly hoped that whatever we had gotten up to had been worth it.

At this point, I still didn't understand what Gabriel was or why he took such pleasure in hurting me. It was overwhelming, to be honest. Gabriel could easily be the death of me - I sensed that on an intuitive level. But now that the panic had subsided and the warm water eased the sting of the many tiny wounds, I already knew I was going to come back for more.

After the bath and changing into nightclothes, I crawled into bed and slept for nearly forty hours. When I woke up, I learned that Octavia had paid Villa Graves a visit, toting a knife and apparently threatening Gabriel to leave me alone. Gabriel later recalled the incident from his perspective, his eyes gleaming with delight as he described Octavia's fury and how she had been stabbing at the air and finally planted the knife in a priceless painting to underscore the gravity of her threats. Gabriel felt that the painting had been improved with the addition of the knife and had decided to leave it in the canvas. For all I know, it might still be there.

Truly, what have I done to deserve a sister like Octavia? Anyone should be so lucky. Octavia was always fearless when it came to standing up for me - it was when it came to defending herself that she wavered. But let me return to that.

Gabriel gradually disclosed to me what he truly was, and about six months into our... dalliance, our relationship, he presented me with the idea of turning me into what he was. He didn't make any promises about it, not yet. I believe he wanted to gauge my reaction. And perhaps he wanted to give himself more time to decide whether he would prefer to keep me or kill me.

Had I rejected the idea of becoming a vampire, would he have simply let me go? I doubt it. I believe he would have ended me, if only to spare himself the discomfort of watching me age.

Fortunately, I did want to become a vampire. Once I found out what Gabriel was and what powers came with it, I never looked back. I figured I could easily live with being a predator and a killer if it meant I would remain young and drop-dead gorgeous forever. That's just the truth. I have been entirely honest with you throughout this conversation - I might as well continue in that vein. By the end of it you may like me less, but you'll know me better.

Gabriel turned me on my twentieth birthday, at his residence where we were least likely to be disturbed. If it were up to me it would have happened sooner, but in retrospect I am glad he made me wait instead of condemning me to living out the rest of eternity as an immortal teenager.

Come to think of it, I condemned Octavia to that very fate. All I can say for myself is that it struck me as a marvelously great idea at the time, and I really don't think she holds it against me. She certainly hasn't complained.

The transformation itself was a horrible, messy ordeal, as you know from experience. Gabriel sat with me on the marble floor of his conservatory while it was happening, stroking my hair and wiping my tears while I shivered and cried and threw up black bile and cursed him, utterly convinced that something must have gone horribly wrong and that I was dying, never to return to life.

If you were to ask Gabriel, I am certain he would claim that I was never in love with him at all, only with myself, and with the power and immortality he represented. And while he may feel justified in holding that opinion, it isn't true.

I accepted Gabriel's invitations into his home and into his bed long before I accepted his invitation to immortality, months before I knew what he was. These are undeniable facts. But he would like to conveniently leave that out of his estimation of me now, simply so he can frame me as the bad guy, and there is nothing I can do about that.

Would I have played along if it meant he would make me immortal? Admittedly, yes, I would have. I would have let him do anything. But I didn't need to. I wasn't merely being opportunistic. My feelings for him were real.

The trouble, perhaps, was that my love for him was intertwined with fear, with a hunger for immortality, and with something within me that has always been there - something that compels me to seek out the edge and stare into the abyss. Gabriel was both the abyss and the devil on my shoulder, inviting me to jump.

EIGHT

N avigating my relationship with Gabriel had its challenges, and it became no less complicated when I also met and fell in love with Csilla.

The context of my path crossing hers was that both Lyrica and I were being rather relentlessly haunted by the spirit of my dearly departed mother. I was on a quest to find a medium who could facilitate communication with her, but most of the mediums I encountered were disappointing frauds, not to mention, old and frumpy.

Then there was Csilla. At that time, Csilla wasn't yet a vampire, but her formidable powers gave her an unsettling presence. The contrast between the power she exuded and her delicate beauty was so striking, it made me want to cry. The first time I watched her fill a room with dark tendrils of energy, it was nothing short of a revelation. I had never known a woman could be so intimidating. It felt as if a magnificent secret had been kept from me.

Don't get me wrong, it wasn't news to me that I was capable of finding a woman attractive. Despite my father's relentless commentary to the contrary, I was well aware that I liked girls too. But before Csilla came along, I had certainly never found a reason to take one seriously.

The young women that occupied my social strata tended to be excessively sheltered and hopelessly naive, which of course made them easy targets for my teasing and penchant for stirring up drama. Capturing the affections of the prettiest ones and pitting them against each other was a sport for me.

And you cannot believe how easy it was. A stolen kiss behind a rose bush, followed by a seemingly innocent touch as I passed her in the corridor, was often all it took for a girl to believe we were madly in love. Then, doing the same, or more, with her best friend ensured they'd eventually compare notes, stirring up a cloud of jealousy and confusion. It was marvelous fun, tearing through entire friend groups in this manner.

Despite conflicting evidence, Father had labeled me a nancy boy long before I was old enough to have any concept of what that meant. I could only tell from his tone that it had to be something bad. Of course he never believed that his perception of me was only partially true. I didn't care that he thought me a deviant - by Victorian standards, I was. What stung was his refusal to see me for the deviant I truly was.

Father claimed to tolerate my so-called sexual inversion, but that never stopped him from making cutting remarks or trying to undermine me with barbs like barking at me from across the hall to "walk like a man." He seemed determined to remind me of his disdain at every opportunity. Naturally, my deviance was something he made sure to note on my Bedlam admission forms as well.

As I've implied, Father was frequently intoxicated, and when he was, it wasn't unusual for him to do things like grab my chin, pull my face close, and hiss that it was disgusting how much I looked like my mother. He had chosen her as his bride for her beauty and presumably because he loved her, so how he could look at me and see her reflection with such contempt was something I'll never understand.

On one memorable occasion, he barged into my room clutching my mother's wedding dress in one hand and a revolver in the other. He aimed the revolver at me, threw the dress at me, and told me to put it on. I was cold with fear, but I refused. I told him I wouldn't let him disrespect my mother's memory like that as I picked up the dress and carefully hung it in my wardrobe. After that, he mumbled some vague apology and stumbled out, slamming the door behind him. I had no idea what he intended to do - probably humiliate me in some degrading manner.

These are just a few examples of my father's unreasonable behavior. If I listed them all, we'd be here until dawn. I could write an entire book about my difficult and bizarre relationship with my father, and perhaps, one night, I will.

I will admit that Father's willful ignorance worked in my favor on one occasion when the parents of a girl I'd fooled around with showed up at the mansion, insisting I'd gotten their daughter pregnant. They demanded my father force me to marry her posthaste. My father laughed in their faces, declaring that such a thing was impossible. In the end, I believe he paid them off to make the problem disappear and arranged for their daughter to have an abortion. Tragically, she developed an infection from the procedure that killed her. But at least I didn't have to marry her, and that was quite frankly a relief.

But I digress.

Csilla was nothing like the naive girls I was accustomed

to - and of course, that was part of my instant fascination with her. She wasn't someone I could easily wrap around my finger or whose heart I could break for fun.

At twenty-six, Csilla was uniquely unburdened by ordinary obligations. She was independently wealthy, childless, and a spinster by choice. Her adoptive parents, Maximilian and Forthilda Fairweather, had disowned her about a decade earlier, so she had no parents to worry about disappointing. Consequently, she lived as she pleased, touring Europe and the New World with her seances and hosting lavish, scandalous parties whenever she was in London. She even had a pet cheetah named Lord Byron, imported from somewhere in South Asia, and would take him for walks around Bloomsbury on a leash encrusted with diamonds while her neighbors watched in fear from behind their curtains.

Naturally, rumors about Csilla abounded - some undoubtedly true, others born from the fevered imaginings of London's gossip circles. One rumor she particularly loved was that she had obtained her powers from the devil himself. Whenever this was mentioned, she would throw her head back and laugh uproariously.

Another rumor claimed she had her reproductive organs removed so she could be as free and promiscuous as any man. This one was true - she proudly showed me her battle scar, as she called it. Considering the surgical methods of the time, she had risked her life for this level of independence.

The surgery, she explained, her eyes alight with glee as I winced at the vivid description, had been performed while she was fully conscious, albeit high as a kite on laudanum. The surgeon had cut her abdomen open with a long, sharp knife and meticulously removed the treacherous organs that might trap her into unwanted motherhood. Then, he had stitched her back up and covered the incision in several layers of seaweed and bandages. She kept the removed organs in a jar of formaldehyde on her shelf, like some sort of macabre trophy.

Despite her somewhat scandalous reputation, Csilla had plenty of suitors - but none of them were lucky. Csilla wasn't impressed by the usual tricks one might employ to charm a woman, such as flaunting wealth and social clout. She had her own fame, her own fortune, and unlike many of the hopefuls trailing after her, she had built it all herself.

I was in thrall with Csilla. I had never fallen as fast or as hard for anyone before, Gabriel included. I found it impossible to stop thinking about her. The power of it was disorienting - like being picked up by an enormous tidal wave and carried away beyond my control. It was both exhilarating, frightening and inconvenient; I knew it was in my own best interest to keep my focus on Gabriel. After all, I wanted immortality. But I was drawn to Csilla as helplessly as a moth to a flame.

It was a shock to me when she didn't take my fascination with her very seriously at all. She was undeniably attracted to me - she flirted back, invited me to her parties, and let me accompany her and Lord Byron on walks along the Thames. She even summoned the spirit of my dearly departed mother for me. But she was stubbornly resistant to falling in love with me. She said we could be friends, and then some, but she had made a promise to herself to protect her independence by never falling in love with anyone, never truly belonging to anyone. And while on some level I could admire that decision, it was also infuriating.

Gabriel was aware of Csilla, but he arrogantly underestimated her. Instead of viewing her as a rival, as you might expect, he had the nerve to find my efforts to win her affection amusing.

Had Csilla been a man or had she shown genuine interest in me from the start, I can assure you his attitude would not have been so cavalier. But as it was, he felt he could dismiss my attraction to her as a fleeting obsession, a passing phase of confused puppy love, and either way, as something I would soon have moved beyond.

Even when I bluntly stated that I intended to overcome Csilla's resistance to falling in love with me by taking her to bed, Gabriel remained unfazed. He even encouraged me to go right ahead, suggesting it might help me get it out of my system.

I suspect he doubted I would follow through - perhaps thinking I would hesitate out of loyalty to him, or because he believed, as he does, that women are ultimately unexciting in sexual matters. No doubt he imagined my encounter with Csilla would end in disappointment.

Well, he was entirely wrong on both counts. Not only was I more than capable of following through, but Csilla and I were like fireworks. Once our relationship became physical, her emotional defenses began to crumble. Slowly but surely, I was making her fall for me, though of course, she did not give in without a fight.

I knew she was seeing other men, so I retaliated by sleeping with other women - mostly married ones, for the sheer novelty and the thrilling possibility of being caught. Anything with other men was out of the question - Gabriel would kill them, he had made that perfectly clear.

By this point, Gabriel's patience with my antics was wearing thin, and fast. He had precious little sympathy for the fact that, instead of growing tired of Csilla after finally consummating my attraction to her, I found myself even more entangled in my feelings, sinking deeper into the mire than before. It was finally dawning on him that she was a true rival.

I'm not entirely proud to admit it, but I may have used this to my advantage, trying to hasten his decision to turn me into a vampire. I implied that vampirism would create an irreparable gulf between me and everyone else, especially Csilla, making it easier for me to belong solely to him - something he could clearly see I was having a bit of trouble with. I did everything I could to crank up the pressure, pushing him to give me the blood sooner rather than later. Once I was immortal, I figured, I would have all the time in the world to navigate this feeling of being trapped between Gabriel and Csilla.

As if my life wasn't already sufficiently complex, it was around the same time that I uncovered the grim truth that my father had been abusing Octavia for years. Octavia confessed this to me despite our father's threats to end her life if she ever dared tell anyone.

She was full of guilt and remorse for not having confided in me sooner, and I shared much the same feelings for not having noticed. But this discovery did shed new light on my father's attempts at carting me off to Bedlam. Whether I was suffering from various maladies of the mind was of no concern to him - he had simply wanted me out of the house.

I should have known. But Father had only ever beaten me, insulted me, threatened me, never Octavia, and I had stupidly believed that she was in no danger from him.

The final tragedy in this regard was that Octavia had fallen pregnant.

She went through multiple failed abortion attempts. Lyrica attended most of the procedures with much more stoic calm than I was able to muster, even though I was always banished to a nearby parlor to wait.

Octavia was quite willing to swallow mercury compounds and other experimental substances, and she even threatened to cut the fetus out of her womb. I had all of the servants watch her like hawks, lest she attempt it.

There was one instance when Octavia slit both of her wrists from wrist joint to elbow, and I found her in the claw footed bathtub on the second floor. I only found her because I could hear her thrashing in the bathtub - I believe she must have regretted her suicide attempt moments after putting down the razor blade. But she had locked the door from the inside, and by the time I had managed to get it open, she was seemingly already dead, floating in the bathtub like Ophelia. She had strewn rose petals in the water and the water was red, saturated with her blood.

She was so heavy, impossibly heavy, as I lifted her out of the tub. I thought it was too late, that she was already gone. But then she started gasping, breathing again. We were both crying by the time the servants began milling around us, lifting her away.

Gabriel would have been able to salvage the situation, but you know how it is with vampires - this happened in the late morning so there was simply no point in even attempting to reach him.

It was a morning of sheer panic while a doctor - the same one who had performed Octavia's most recent failed procedure - stitched up her wrists, wrapped them in gauze and when she finally came to after an hour or so of dipping in and out of consciousness, admonished her never to misbehave like this again. I will never forget the look on her face as this kindly-faced doctor scolded her.

I suppose it was Octavia's near suicide that made me

realize that everyone I loved could die at any moment, but also that I, once I had immortality, could make sure that never happened.

It was also this experience that made Octavia decide to resign to the cruel twist in her fate that the pregnancy was. And you probably have to consider that a good thing, since you wouldn't be here if she had succeeded in destroying the fetus and possibly herself along with it.

You already know how I chose to deal with Father's transgressions. And I must say, I think I did the right thing. I made plenty of bad decisions in 1861, but beheading my father wasn't one of them.

Turning all my remaining relatives (with the exception of my aunt and uncle, who seemed hopelessly old in my eyes) into vampires against their own wishes may have been a bad one, or at least, not entirely good. I am willing to acknowledge that now.

I would have turned Csilla, too, had it not been for Lyrica and Clyde's intervention. As you're aware, they decided to restrain me by locking me away - a rather clumsy solution to a family crisis, I might add.

Still, in retrospect, this likely shielded me from a darker fate, considering Gabriel's furious reaction to my reckless distribution of the blood. But it was not only that. It was my intention towards Csilla that made his blood boil. In fact, I daresay it was primarily that.

Perhaps I shouldn't have told him, almost immediately as I awoke with new vampiric senses, that I intended to immortalize her, that I wanted her to see like I could see now.

Interestingly, Gabriel never blamed Csilla for my infatuation with her or for indulging it. He held me solely responsible, placing all the fault squarely on my shoulders. In a twisted way, that was probably for the best. If Gabriel had sought revenge on Csilla because of my feelings for her, our conflict would have escalated to unimaginable heights as soon as Sebastian freed me from my casket in the basement.

I'd like to pause here to underscore Gabriel's astonishing hypocrisy. Shortly after Lyrica and Clyde had locked me away, he turned Csilla into a vampire when he would most likely have killed me for doing the same.

He might claim that his only motive was to procure the ectoplasm that he realized would allow him to travel through time. But I am convinced part of his reason for turning her was knowing it was what I wanted - to grant her the immortal flame - and he did it purely to spite me, to plant his flag in my territory. If you knew him as well as I do, you would understand this is precisely the kind of thing he would do.

The rest of the story is familiar to you. Fast forward 164 years, and I emerge from my casket in my crumbling mansion, only to discover that Gabriel and Csilla are both still around, and nothing has truly been resolved, at least not for me. It all still feels open-ended, like an open wound.

Of course, not everything remains unchanged. The family has expanded to include you and Sebastian. Whatever became of your two sets of parents and any siblings you might have had remains a mystery. Perhaps we'll never know.

Gabriel, Csilla, Lyrica, and Clyde - they all knew precisely where I was the entire time. Any of them could have changed their minds at any moment; they could have decided enough was enough and come to release me. But did any of them do that? No! They were all perfectly content to leave me to decay, likely for the rest of eternity.

Lyrica has accepted my return to the family with stoic calm - yet she hasn't so much as apologized for locking me away. And Clyde? Who knows what has become of him.

Gabriel and Csilla seem to have developed a peculiar friendship based on mutual admiration and shared history with me. Perhaps they even see a reflection of themselves in one another - it wouldn't surprise me. They both come from nothing but have clawed their way up, driving by self-ish, greedy ambition. In another reality, I might even say they deserved each other.

What is abundantly clear to me is that they have both moved on, while my afterlife has remained suspended for much longer than anyone could claim is reasonable.

I'm uncertain of where I stand with Csilla. I wish I could forget about her, at last, but how can I when our story remains unresolved, abruptly interrupted by the events that unfolded in the autumn of 1861? Would she have accepted immortality from me? Did she ever love me?

I know she did - but I also believe that I did not get the time I needed to cement it. In the summer leading up to my twentieth birthday, I threw an elaborate, Shakespeare-themed party for myself. It was one of those rare occasions when my father was away on business without me, and I could commandeer the mansion for the week. The idea was for the party to go on for three days and three nights, like something out of a fairytale.

Anyone who wasn't dressed up as a Shakespearean character was turned away at the door. Among those who were turned away was my own dear cousin, Clyde, who thought that turning up in a suit with his hair combed for once would suffice.

Clyde, arguing with the two servants I had appointed to guard the door, managed to catch Octavia's attention. She had been in one of the downstairs parlors, trying to drown her sorrows in absinthe. This was all shortly before she revealed to me that she was pregnant, shortly before it started to show, and shortly before I beheaded Father with a little help from her. And of course, shortly before I became a vampire.

Clyde explained the situation to her and insisted on being let in. Octavia fetched me, and I took mercy on Clyde, ushering him upstairs. There, I transformed him into Hamlet by draping one of Father's long black theater capes over his shoulders and giving him a skull I'd found in the cemetery and brought home.

Cousin Clyde was always a little gloomy, so when he finally bothered showing up to one of my parties - the last one running during daylight hours, at that - I felt obliged to let him in.

At dawn on the last day, only a few guests remained - the rest had long since given up and crawled home. I was in the garden with Csilla and just a few others. She was dressed as some sort of Shakespearean fairy queen, and I honestly can't remember what I was supposed to be at that point. Lord Byron, Csilla's pet cheetah, was chasing something down through the garden to where the cemetery begins. The sun was just starting to bleed through the horizon.

Suddenly, Csilla put her arms around me so tightly I almost couldn't breathe and whispered, "I love you," in my ear. "I'm terrified, but I love you."

We were both halfway out of our minds on a heady combination of opium and absinthe, but I knew she meant it, because I could feel it - a warm energy bleeding from her chest into mine.

"I love you too. Why are you telling me now?"

"I cannot let you die without knowing."

She must have had a premonition, but she didn't explain what she meant, and the next day, she left to tour Europe. By the time she returned to London a few months later, Gabriel had taken my life but given me another, and Lyrica and Clyde had put it on hold by locking me away in the mansion's basement.

Since my return to the surface, so to speak, Csilla has kept her distance. Whether it's because she feels guilty for not freeing me, or because her feelings for me have faded and her armor has slipped back on, I do not know. Or, is it precisely because she does love me and is afraid of what it would mean if she were to admit it?

To be perfectly honest, it is driving me out of my mind. I wish she would visit me here at the mansion and talk to me. For someone so brave, she is being a coward. Or perhaps she is just being cruel. She may have healed and moved on, but I have not. I need answers. I still love her, as much as I did when she confessed to me in the garden and I felt the energy of her words. I can still feel it now when I talk about it. But I am also angry and resentful. Why did she not simply come here with a pair of bolt cutters and let me out? Is she really that terrified of loving me? Would that really be such a terrible fate? I would have rather liked her to be my knight in shining armor.

Gabriel, for his part, is wary of me, but will he allow me to forget about him? No, absolutely not.

He knows I've been isolated in that accursed casket for the past 164 years, and he can well imagine how lost and lonely I must feel, how starved for touch and attention. He has hinted that he can provide all the attention I can possibly handle, and while I have no doubt that he would like to do that, he is deluded if he believes I will take him up on it.

I have agreed to bury the hatchet, but I have not forgotten the past. I have not forgotten Gabriel's significant role in robbing me of 164 years of my immortal existence, among other transgressions, including your death.

And yet, sometimes - I'm not proud to admit this - I am tempted to let go of the past, to let it float away as if it were weightless. In moments of dreadful weakness, I feel an urge to run to him, to renounce Csilla, who refuses to love me, and agree to be his, on his terms, as he wishes. Sometimes, I long for him. Despite everything that went wrong, despite all he has done. Only a bit of stubbornness and a sliver of self-respect prevent me from doing something so spineless.

Of course, Gabriel senses my wavering and expects me to come crawling back. Whether or not he would reject me if I did such a thing is another question entirely.

CHAPTER
NINE

"I do wish-"

The rest of his sentence was abruptly cut short by the reverberating boom of the lion-headed door knocker being lifted and slammed against the mansion's front door.

Venedict, still perched on the window sill, turned to look over his shoulder, a flicker of surprise in his eyes. "Well, speak of the devil."

"Gabriel?"

"No, Csilla. Did you expect her?"

"No." I hadn't seen her since she trotted off with Ramsay's soul. I stifled a shiver as I walked over to the window and looked down into the mansion's darkened grounds. Down on the front steps stood Csilla, moonlight glancing off her mahogany hair. It was as if his talking about her had drifted across London and summoned her here.

Venedict opened the mansion's creaky front door for Csilla about a minute later. "Csilla," he said, his expression wavering slightly as the door swung open. After everything he had just told me about their complicated history, it was easy to see why. "Do come in."

Csilla stepped through the door, accompanied by a waft of spiced perfume. She wore a crimson biker jacket over a stunning red dress with thigh-high slits that would have gotten her arrested in 1861. The tips of her hair, styled into a sharp Cleopatra bob, brushed against her cheekbones.

"I see you have had the place spruced up again after that foul werewolf incident," she remarked, her large hazel eyes, flecked with copper, gliding around the hall as she walked deeper inside. Her whiskey and honey voice was so delicious, it felt almost criminal that it couldn't be bottled.

"Yes, that was quite a mess," Venedict agreed, shooting me an amused look.

Csilla's gaze followed his until her eyes locked on mine, her expression darkening. "I daresay. Harlan, I'm sure you didn't intend it, but when you offered me Ramsay's soul, you fed me the spiritual equivalent of poison." Her voice caught in her throat, and she blinked rapidly.

Then, she burst into tears.

I stood there, stunned, as Csilla's usual bravado crumbled before me. It caught me completely off guard. I should've been angry - she'd made me put my name in her book of souls to collect - but her tears were so disarming I had to fight the impulse to promise her everything would be fine, even as my mind raced to find a solution.

Venedict couldn't restrain himself - he rushed forward, arms open wide. His face was so distraught that for a moment I worried he might start crying too. "Csilla, please, don't cry. It's too distressing, I cannot bear it. We'll find a solution, no matter the cost."

Csilla allowed herself to be enveloped in his arms, and as I met Venedict's eyes over her shoulder while he gently stroked her lustrous dark hair, his expression had changed. He now looked quietly ecstatic. I guessed he had just realized she might finally need something from him.

"Since I took Ramsay's soul," Csilla confessed, not noticing this, "my powers have vanished."

"But didn't you say that any spiritual consequences would be mine if I signed your book and took responsibility?" I asked. That's what she'd said - I'd heard her loud and clear.

"I know what I said!" Csilla's voice was a little sharp, a little defensive. "But it seems what I said would happen and what actually happens are not always one and the same. Normally, I feed on souls just as well as I feed on blood. But taking Ramsay's has, to use a modern phrase, completely fucked me up."

Venedict continued to stroke her hair with obvious tenderness, and slowly, her agitation began to ebb, her clenched jaw loosening and her eyes softening, albeit reluctantly.

"What about the Grim Games?" I asked. "Gabriel seems to expect you to summon some kind of spirit for him."

"Yes," Csilla admitted, wiping the last crimson tears from her cheeks. "I'm aware."

She took a shaky breath. "Lately, my only contact with the spiritual realm has been through your father." She glanced at Venedict, searching his face for a reaction. "Since my visit here in October, he seems to have been following me around. He was the only spirit to appear at the few séances I conducted before I had to call off all my engagements indefinitely. Of course, he acted like a complete menace - throwing my spirit board against the wall and frightening my audience. I cannot say why, but Algernon seems to have grown in strength, enough that even those without the slightest glimmer of psychic ability can see and sense him when he wills it."

"Oh, that explains rather a lot," Venedict said, his eyes sliding over to me. "Father appears and converses with Harlan all the time. At any given moment, I'll hear them chattering away."

"You're exaggerating," I said, more defensively than I intended. "We barely speak, and not much since October."

"That could be because he's focusing more on me," Csilla said with a grimace. "He's been appearing not only at my séances but also in my home, in my mirrors - always, I might add, when I'm in the shower or getting dressed. Tonight, he showed up again, hinting that he could help me. He also mentioned something rather strange: that Ramsay Fairweather is his guest."

"Ramsay is Algernon's guest?" I asked, incredulous. "*Where?*"

As if wanting to answer the question, the chandelier flickered overhead.

Csilla shrugged, disentangling herself from Venedict's embrace. She seemed to be regaining her composure, her usual confident demeanor slipping back into place. "That I don't know, but I suppose-"

"Why don't you leave it to me to explain?"

Algernon's voice reverberated through the hall with a sudden force. We turned as a dark cloud of mist began seeping from one of the portraits on the grand staircase landing, swirling and pooling below it.

Gradually, Algernon's familiar outline began to materialize in the mist. At first, it looked like a hazy, billowing shadow, but soon it took on the nuanced hues of his favorite three-piece suit, the one he wore in the portrait hanging on the paneled wall behind him. The light brown of his hair, graying at the temples, emerged along with the amber glow of his eyes.

"Venedict, Harlan, and Csilla. What a perfectly horrible little posse of traitors," he drawled. "Have you all gathered here solely to converse with me? I am truly flattered - although I know neither of you are really here for my sake."

"It's always a pleasure Father," Venedict aimed a frosty smile at the spirit.

Algernon's gaze drifted almost lazily from Venedict to me, then to Csilla. "Ah, the little succubus couldn't wait to rush here the moment she realized I hold the key to restoring her lost powers."

Csilla glanced down, clearly embarrassed.

Algernon turned back to Venedict, his tone patronizing. "She has no love for you, son. You realize that, surely? She only loves herself and those dark, dark powers of hers. That is the only reason she is here. I would certainly hate for you to gain any false hopes about her motives."

"With all due respect, Father, you don't know that. You've no right to meddle."

"Oh, it stings, doesn't it?" the ghostly figure mused. "They say even a broken clock is right twice a day, but the one time you show interest in a woman, it's this beautiful yet defective one."

"Csilla is not defective, Father. Watch your tongue."

"Oh, but she is. A fine display of your warped instincts."

Suddenly, Venedict charged toward the staircase. "Enough, Father," he declared. "I've had it with your perpetual insults."

He rushed up the grand staircase, stopping in front of his father's spirit, which lingered calmly on the landing in front of his own portrait, its semi-transparent mouth curled into a mocking grin. "You were always a terrible embarrassment to me, Venedict."

Venedict lunged at the apparition, but passed right through it - it only wavered slightly at the interruption. He spun around, eyes ablaze with frustration as the spirit's laughter echoed down the staircase.

Venedict's fists clenched at his sides. "What about you, Father? Do you not think you embarrassed me when you got so drunk and high in public that no one could fail to notice? When you stumbled around, crashing into furniture and slurring your insults and curses at our business associates? I kept it all together for you. I was always mopping up the damage. Those last few years before your death, I ran the business, even if you took the credit. And everybody knew."

The chandelier flickered again.

"And everybody knew about your messy private life," Algernon's voice was thick with disdain. "You were anything but discreet, a complete disgrace. Always so busy dragging our good name through the mud."

"Father, this is like having an argument with you in 1860 all over again. Can't we move past it?" Venedict's anger seemed to waver, his tone becoming pleading. "Please."

"That is easy for you to say, son," Algernon responded dismissively. "You may be undead, but you are vividly alive. You have the luxury of moving past things. I, however, am simply dead, and I cannot. So forgive me if it seems I am a little stuck in my ways. Yet, I always tolerated you, far more than you deserved." His tone softened deceptively, almost ironically as he added, "When I left you at Bedlam, did I not always come back for you?"

"No, Father, you did not! But you were probably too

drunk to remember whether you did or didn't. I still have the release forms, and only one bears your signature."

"Oh, well." Algernon flashed us all a grin, as if to say, *Silly me.* "Perhaps I had more sense back then than I give myself credit for. I should have left you there to rot, where you belonged. You will never be the lord of this manor, irrespective of what you may call yourself these days."

Venedict stood frozen for a heartbeat, breath caught in his throat, as if his father had slapped him. Then, he turned and practically flew down the stars, a rush of cold air as he crossed the great hall. The door leading into the parlor slammed shut behind him with a resounding crash.

"Regrettably," Algernon sighed, a note of faux apology in his tone as he turned his attention to Csilla and me, "Venedict has always been overly sensitive. I fear he's inherited his mother's frail nature. Mixed with my fiery temper, it is an unfortunate combination, indeed. Now, shall we turn our attention to the business at hand, the reason for your visit?" He directed this question at Csilla, who gave a quiet nod.

"Then I will reveal the secret behind your evaporated powers and how to restore them." Algernon paused, his ghostly form rippling slightly as he stepped off the landing and descended a few stairs. His hand-stiched leather shoes seemed to hover just above each step, never quite making contact. "As I have already mentioned, Ramsay Fairweather is currently a guest in my realm. And I do mean *my* realm. It's quite a place. I have had ample time to make it my own. Every spirit that passes away in this house, under my roof, passes through it on the way to the underworld, the great beyond, or whatever we might call it. Sometimes, I permit one of them to, well, linger for a little while."

A vivid image flashed in my mind of Algernon and

Ramsay munching scones, sipping tea, and comparing notes on me in some shadowy afterlife realm. Algernon's eyes shone with enjoyment as he sensed my discomfort. "What you are imagining is not too far from the truth," he chuckled. "We have certainly had ample opportunity to discuss you, Harlan, and what is to be done about you."

"What do you mean?" I demanded. I didn't like the sound of that at all.

"I have rather enjoyed young Fairweather's visit," Algernon continued, ignoring my question. "But at this point, I have no need to keep him any longer, and that is why I have come to you now. I am prepared to let him return to this realm, and when that happens, Csilla, it will be like unplugging a drain. You will have access to the spirit world again and to your source of confidence."

He paused, his expression brightening and becoming almost cheerful, as if we were finally arriving at the part of the conversation he had been anticipating. "That being said, if you expect me to offer my help out of the goodness of my heart, you are sorely mistaken. I recall the two of you conspiring to do away with me, planning to banish me from this mansion. I remember my name inscribed on the pages of your book, Csilla, in the barely legible scrawl of my last descendant."

Csilla's eyes narrowed. "What do you want in exchange for your assistance, Algernon?"

"I want him," Algernon waved a semi-transparent hand at me, the motion causing a ripple in his ghostly form, "to visit my realm. He will have to come and retrieve Ramsay Fairweather himself."

"Should I not do it?" Csilla asked, her eyes quickly flickered to me. "Harlan has no experience with the spirit realm or how to navigate it."

"My invitation," Algernon bit out, "only applies to one of my own blood. I will not tolerate some little gypsy succubus rummaging around in there, no doubt with some insidious agenda. Harlan will retrieve Ramsay, or Ramsay stays, and your powers remain bound up. Forever."

Algernon's ultimatum hung in the air, heavy and oppressive like a thundercloud, as the door creaked open and Venedict reentered, his expression sour but noticeably calmer. He sauntered over to the grand staircase, sitting on the bottom step, positioning himself halfway between Csilla, me, and Algernon's shadowy outline on the stairs above.

"Wait a minute. I'm not sure I like the idea of Ramsay being alive again," I admitted, feeling a knot of resistance tightening in my mind. If he wanted to, he could make my life hell once he was back. He'd despised me before - he'd absolutely loathe me now after what I did to him, and who knew what he'd be capable of then?

"You're not sure you like him dead either, so why wouldn't you do this - for Venedict, for Csilla?" Algernon prodded, his voice turning into soft, persuasive treacle.

Venedict and Csilla both looked at me, their expressions tense, silently pleading. I sighed, finally nodding. "Fine," I said. "I'll do it. But, Algernon, if something goes wrong, I swear I'll haunt you to the ends of the earth."

Algernon didn't comment on this. Instead, he stipulated, "Well, there is another thing." His voice lowered. "A request I'd like to make. Consider it payment for my considerable generosity. You can probably imagine what it is. I want one night of living again, experiencing, tasting, and touching the things I miss. For this purpose, I require a body, and either of yours will do."

I hated that Algernon had complete control over the

conversation, the bargain tightening around us like a trap. But what could I do? He held all the reins. This was why I'd always dismissed dealing with any of the poltergeist or other more esoteric cases that came across the Van Helsing Society's desk - they irritated and unsettled me. When you're dealing with a non-physical entity, you can't necessarily just drive a stake through it and be done with it.

Venedict's posture was tense as he processed his father's demand. "And what if we refuse?" he asked, his voice quiet.

The room seemed to grow colder as Algernon's smile widened. "Refusal is not an option," he replied, quite calmly. "Not if you wish to see Ramsay returned and Csilla's powers restored. One night is all I ask. A humble request, all things considered."

Venedict's jaw was set, and his eyes were wide with determination. "Very well, Father, you can have mine. For one night. If it means Csilla gets her powers back. I do not care what happens to Ramsay."

"Venedict, no," I said sharply. "You're not responsible for Ramsay ending up in the afterlife, that's on me. Much as I hate the idea, if Algernon has to go careening around the earth plane in a borrowed body, it should be mine."

"No, I insist." Venedict rose from the stair he had been sitting on and walked over to me. "Harlan, this is one of those times when you cannot contest me. I will do this for Csilla, and you will not question my decision. You will back off."

His eyes met mine, both commanding and imploring. "I am the lord of the manor. Show me that you understand." Then he added quietly, "Please."

Algernon chuckled. "Well, this is a most fascinating exchange."

I hesitated. I shouldn't let Venedict get into this agreement with Algernon. I didn't trust him as far as I could throw him.

"Okay, I'm backing off." For now. I'd think of an alternative solution later on.

"Very well!" Algernon declared, his tone triumphant.

"One condition, Father; you will receive your payment only after Csilla's powers have been restored."

"Of course. That is understood. For this, I, too, need Csilla's powers to be restored. For this to be guaranteed to work, I require her assistance. And in the meantime, I shall be holding Ramsay Fairweather in escrow." His eyes gleamed with satisfaction, as if he were in on some private joke the rest of us weren't. "I've always known how to handle business."

"You said you wanted me to visit your realm and retrieve him," I said. "Tell me how I can."

"In the same manner you have seen Csilla reach into another realm - via a portal. Only in your case, you will have to step all the way through. But don't worry, you will have me to guide you. And when you visit, you will see that the surroundings are much more familiar than you might expect."

"Without my usual abilities to produce ectoplasm, I cannot create a portal," Csilla interjected.

"No, you cannot. But I can, using a mirror," Algernon replied. "And I intend to do so at Eve Hall, during the Grim Games. Retrieving young Fairweather's soul during the event will make quite the impressive display, sure to earn you some points in the competition. Besides, a few old friends will be in attendance that I'd quite like to visit."

"That would mean I won't have my powers back in time for the Games," Csilla pointed out.

"But only we will know that," Algernon countered. "As far as anyone at Eve Hall is concerned, *you*, Csilla, will be the one performing a spectacular feat - transforming my mirror into a portal. Harlan will disappear through it. Only to re-emerge, of course, with the soul of Ramsay Fairweather." Algernon accompanied his last sentence with a wink that I didn't exactly trust.

"How do I know that you won't shut the portal once I am on the other side?" I asked.

"Well, don't you think I want my reward for helping Csilla? I don't believe it will be forthcoming, unless I let you return to the surface."

He had a point, but everything about this deal he was dictating and putting together made my skin crawl. The last thing I needed was to be stuck on the other side with Ramsay. If there was a hell, that had to be it.

"Well, it seems we have all reached an agreement," Algernon declared, "I would shake your hands, if I only could. But I shall see you at Eve Hall. Bring me a mirror, my favorite from upstairs in Octavia's bedroom, and bring Ramsay Fairweather's body. Once his spirit returns to the physical realm, it'll need somewhere to lodge. And if you have rid yourself of it, you must bring an alternative vessel, preferably one that is genetically related, or otherwise familiar or equivalent."

In an instant, Algernon transformed into a void-black mist and retreated down through the floorboards, leaving the air trembling in his wake.

CHAPTER
TEN

Tonight, for the first time since Ramsay suspended my hunting license five months ago, the elders had decided to trust me with something more than just an execution warrant. In my satchel, I carried a folder containing a first warning for none other than Evander Eve. Yes, that Evander Eve. The vampire count, the host of the Grim Games.

Godfroy Rosebery had briefed me on the vampire count, on whom the Society had an extensive file. Evander was the proprietor of Nightside Of Eden, a nightclub that had become a fixture of the night scene for over one and a half centuries. Recently, the establishment had garnered unwanted attention from the Society due to a disturbing pattern: a significant number of its patrons were disappearing without a trace.

Godfroy had read aloud to me from the file, and from the tidbits he'd shared, it seemed that Evander Eve, born in 1829, had led a privileged but seemingly conventional life initially - marrying Tessa Blagrave in 1853, with whom he fathered a daughter, Emmeline, in 1860, and two more,

Victorine and Felicity, in 1862. Then, his life took a dark turn when he was suspected of the double murder of his wife and younger brother, Everett, in 1868. This event cast a long shadow and marked the beginning of several mysterious decades. Evander vanished from public view, with only sporadic sightings in Paris, Berlin and Rome suggesting his continued existence.

What was known for sure was his dramatic reappearance in London in 1899, transformed into a vampire. This new chapter in his existence was crowned by the opening of Nightside Of Eden, which threw open its doors with a grand celebration on New Year's Eve in 1900. Godfroy showed me the illustrated flier for the event. Csilla was featured on it, touted as 'the Queen of the Spiritual Realm, the High Priestess of the Mysteries of the Underworld.' I'm sure she relished that title.

Nightside Of Eden occupied a three-story mansion on the Strand, just a stone's throw from the Van Helsing Society's headquarters. Its windows were tinted, revealing only faint glimpses of light and movement from within. The muted echoes of laughter and music occasionally drifted out into the night. I couldn't help but wonder if this was one of the properties Gabriel intended to have Evander sign over to him. I had to push that thought aside while inside, in case Evander possessed that all-too-common vampiric ability to read minds.

Why didn't I have that gift, by the way? Whenever I tried to tap into people's thoughts, all I got were what seemed like scrambled radio signals. But hey, at least I had a knack for hypnosis - I just needed to learn how to hone it properly.

A bright red neon sign above the door displayed the name of the club in a dramatic, swirly cursive font that I guessed might have been modeled on Evander Eve's own handwriting. The entrance was guarded by two stern-faced bouncers dressed in sharp suits. Both were unmistakably vampires - their pale skin and luminous eyes were dead giveaways. "Do you have a reservation?" asked the hostess at the door.

"I'm here to see Evander Eve. Please tell him Harlan Thornhill is here on behalf of the Van Helsing Society."

Evander would know exactly what this was about. This might be Evander Eve's first warning this century, but his record showed he had received one in the 20th century and two in the 19th. If these warnings didn't reset every hundred years, I'd be here with a warrant of execution.

I used to think vampires shouldn't get warnings, just a stake through the heart and their throats slit. It's not like vampires tend to warn their victims, either, is it? I'd admittedly softened my attitude a little since joining the undead - but ultimately, I still felt the Society was quite lenient, all things considered. If I ran it, we'd run a tighter ship. Three warnings in total, if I was feeling generous.

This made me think that I should check the records for everyone I knew in the vampire world to see if and how many strikes they each had against them. Just so I could keep an eye on things.

"The Society?" The hostess's brown eyes narrowed. She turned and spoke to someone on the discreet headset she was wearing. After a brief exchange she turned back to me. "You can go in. Lord Eve will see you in his office. But first, if you're carrying, you must leave your weapons here."

Lord Eve - did he really expect people to address him that way? How pretentious can you get?

"I'm unarmed," I said. It wasn't true, but it would take a particularly diligent bouncer and a sensitive metal detector to uncover the razor blades stitched into the structured collar of my leather jacket and the razor-lined straps wrapped around my arms and legs. The thin layer of copper-threaded fabric kept them concealed, making them almost undetectable. Not foolproof, but reliable enough.

The Society's official policy was showing goodwill by going unarmed when requested. But whoever had thought that one up had clearly never contented with a furious vampire dead-set on tearing out his collarbone, that's all I'm saying.

One of the bouncers stepped forward to conduct a pat-down. He immediately confiscated my jacket, handing it off to the hostess without a word and without indicating whether he had detected the razors or was simply taking routine precautions. He missed the rest of the blades, though.

Then, he did something else that I didn't particularly appreciate.

"Show me your fangs."

"Why?"

"It's Lord Eve's policy. No entry without a fang inspection."

Clearly there was no way around it. I pulled my upper lip back in a snarl, but he grabbed my whole chin and leaned in with a flashlight, like some kind of heavy-handed vampire dentist.

"Hm," he commented, knitting his brow.

Was this good or bad? He let go of my chin and I snapped my teeth shut with an audible clack.

"Better be on your best behavior in there. If not, Lord Eve might ask us to remove them before you leave. Wouldn't be the first time."

A vivid image of being dragged off to some back room to

have my fangs extracted flashed through my mind. An involuntary shiver went down my spine and both bouncers chuckled menacingly, probably seeing the image as vividly as I was.

"Lord Eve will meet you on the third floor," the hostess said as she stepped aside, "Use the lift."

I stepped through the door, which was draped in red velvet curtains, and into a black-and-white tiled foyer. It reminded me a little of the one at Thornhill Mansion, except the stairwell was lit by neon signs and there were no haunted portraits.

Through a double-wide doorway the opulent, neon-lit scene of the club itself could be glimpsed. The marble-topped bar, gleaming under the soft lighting and plush red velvet-upholstered booths were scattered along the periphery of the spacious room. A DJ dressed in a long slinky black silk dress and wearing elbow length lace gloves, was blurring harpsichord with electronic beats, and somehow it worked.

The restroom signs were a humorous touch - both the male and female pictograms sported fangs and capes. Nearby, a wardrobe cubicle stood adjacent to frosted glass doors labeled 'Staff' and 'Crimson Room'. Both were backlit by bright red light. The staircase was declared off-limits by a thick golden rope stretched across it, but an old-fashioned cage lift offered another way up.

I stepped into the lift and pressed the button for the third floor, the two middle levels marked by simple Xs. As the lift rattled past them, I found myself wondering about the activities on those floors. I tried pressing one of the X's, but the lift sailed past without stopping. Could this be where the unfortunate souls who disappeared from the club downstairs were taken, never to be seen again?

The lift's doors rattled open with a metallic groan on the third floor. There was no hallway and no other rooms; instead I had arrived in the middle of a very large study filled with dark, polished wood furniture.

The walls were lined with bookshelves that reached towards the high ceiling and in the far corner of the room stood a grand, mahogany desk cluttered with stacks of paper and a laptop. Behind the desk, large windows looked out over the Thames and the city's myriad twinkling lights. The floor was covered by a deep blue Persian rug.

Evander wasn't behind his desk but seated on a dark brown leather sofa at the other end of the room, an antique-looking book open in his lap. The rattling sound of the lift had alerted him to my arrival and he had stopped reading.

Count Evander Eve, the host of the Grim Games, was as all vampires, timeless. From his file, I estimated he'd been turned in his mid forties. Stocky and impeccably dressed, he wore a tailored black suit with silk lapels, a black tie and shirt, accented only by a glittering ruby tie pin. His dark brown hair, streaked with a single silver strand, was pulled into a ponytail. His eyes were the cool gray of London skies.

"Good evening," he greeted in a deep, pleasant voice that sounded like it belonged in a luxury chocolate commercial. "Harlan Thornhill, representing the Van Helsing Society. I am Count Evander Eve. Under different circumstances, I would say it's a pleasure to meet you. Nonetheless, you are welcome to join me."

He rose from the sofa and motioned for me to come closer. Like me, he was about 5'8", moving with surprising grace and an air of easy authority.

My eyes landed on a large-scale black-and-white framed poster on the wall behind him from the original

Dracula movie featuring Bela Lugosi. I skimmed part of the poster's blurb: 'Dracula will haunt you... he will thrill...and yet amuse.'

Evander gave me a nod but didn't offer a handshake, which seemed fair, given the reason for my visit.

I settled onto the sofa across from him.

"I appreciate you taking the time for this meeting," I said, maintaining as polite a tone as possible, before adding, "Why did your staff check my fangs downstairs?" I couldn't hide my irritation with that.

"Oh, that's just a bit of fun they have with new vampire patrons. It isn't really necessary," Evander replied. There was a definite trace of amusement in his voice. He leaned back against the sofa's backrest, a teasing smile playing on his lips as he casually crossed his ankle over his knee. "But why deny them their little amusements?"

The count seemed good-humored, but getting into an argument with him about how he ran this place probably wasn't going to set us up for a constructive meeting.

"You a Dracula fan?" I asked instead, nodding towards the large poster behind him.

"Very much so," Evander replied, his entire demeanor sparking with enthusiasm. "Perhaps I might invite you to one of the spontaneous movie nights I host here at Nightside. The black-and-white classics, like Dracula, truly come alive on a stormy night, especially when enjoyed in the company of friends who understand why they are such enduring classics."

When I didn't respond with anything but a laconic smile, Evander smoothly transitioned the conversation, leaning forward slightly. "For now, shall we proceed with the formalities? I believe you've brought me a little message from your superiors?"

I extracted the written warning from its manila folder and handed it to Evander, who skimmed it quickly. He then looked up with an overbearing smile. "What a load of smart-sounding nonsense, if you don't mind me saying."

"I don't mind," I said. "I'm not in the admin department."

The truth was that I completely agreed with him. I'd suggested to the elders several times that warnings didn't need to be so clunky and formal that the wording almost obscured the meaning. But had they listened to me? No.

"Still," I added, "you're a smart guy. You understand why the warning was issued."

"Of course," Evander replied, raising one dark eyebrow, a hint of amusement playing at the corners of his lips. "Quite a number of young women, and a few young men, have indeed been disappearing from my club. No one disputes that. The real question is whether or not I am in any way responsible."

"The Society seems to think so," I pointed out. "It doesn't really matter if you're directly orchestrating it or not, the fact is, these disappearances keep happening at your club. And that's a problem. It's *your* problem, Evander."

The count spread his hands in a gesture of innocence. "Well, what do you expect me to say? Nightside is an inclusive establishment. I welcome my fellow undead with open arms. As long as my patrons adhere to the club's rules, what they might do afterwards with anyone they meet here is neither my concern nor my responsibility. Isn't anything between consenting adults fair game in this glorious age?"

"And what about any activities on the premises?" I prodded, leaning slightly forward. "For instance, on the two floors below this one. Does anything ever happen there?"

"I'm not sure what you could possibly be alluding to," Evander replied with a playful wink, his eyes twinkling mischievously. It was clear I wasn't making any headway with him.

"Do you have any questions about the warning that you'd like me to answer?"

"Not at the moment. For now, all I can tell you is that the Van Helsing Society will be hearing from my lawyers. I fully intend to make them retract this... ludicrous piece of paper," Evander replied as he let the warning slip from his hand and drift to the sofa beside him.

"In the meantime, will you agree to stop any activities that could lead to more disappearances?" I asked. I wasn't exactly holding out any hope, it was a box that had to be ticked.

"Perhaps, perhaps not." Evander gave me an affable smile, but the mischievous glimmer in his eye didn't fade. We both knew he had no intention of changing his ways or his business model, whatever it was that led to the problematic disappearances.

The room briefly fell into silence before Evander smoothly shifted the topic. "I have to admit, meeting you is rather intriguing. I've known the Thornhill family for quite some time, and I'm quite familiar with Lyrica. That, and recently, your name's been circulating. The vampire community in London is small, and news travels fast, especially when someone new joins the blood. But you? A vampire who hunts other vampires? Now that's a novelty."

His smile broadened as he watched for my reaction, before continuing, "The idea of barring you from the Games has, of course, crossed my mind. I've even been encouraged to do so. But as long as you follow my rules, I see no need for such drastic measures. Besides, Gabriel has made it clear that he would consider my doing so a personal affront."

Evander rose from the sofa as he concluded in a confident tone, "In other words, I look forward to welcoming you to Eve Hall next weekend, along with everyone else."

"Appreciate it," I replied, gave him a curt nod and rose to leave.

Evander walked me back to the lift. His cloud-gray eyes locked with mine through the lift's ornate bars as I stepped in and pressed the button for the ground floor. The ancient lift rattled into motion, the gears and chains creaking with age.

"Harlan, would you extend my most sincere regards to Lyrica when you see her? And send her my love?" he asked. His voice seemed to carry a hint of something deeper.

"Why would I do that?" I asked as the lift started its descent.

His smile was a strange blend of mischief and nostalgia, his eyes glinting in the dim light. "Oh, trust me," he said softly, his voice almost a whisper as it echoed after me, "she will understand."

CHAPTER
ELEVEN

earing Venedict recount his tangled saga with Gabriel and Csilla had inspired me to resolve my own romantic entanglements as they arose, rather than letting them linger for a century or more. Carrying that much baggage just seemed excessive.

My love life could be summed up as a series of short-lived, chaotic flings, with only one significant relationship in the mix.

In a way, it was surprising I'd managed to have even one real relationship in the 27 years I'd been alive, because since I was eighteen and officially started hunting (unofficially, I'd started a few years before that, assisting Eli on his hunts), I'd been so obsessed with my career that there almost wasn't space in my life for anything else. If there was an execution warrant or a possible vampire problem to be handled anywhere at all, I'd get it done. The Van Helsing Society kept chiming me down, knowing they could count on me to take on even the most dangerous or uncomfortable cases because I had absolutely no fear, or at least the fear of what would happen if I didn't keep moving was always much greater. Whenever freelance work found its way to me, I took that on, too.

I met Aubrey while we were both working, just under two years ago. A couple of other hunters and I had been sent to Festival Theatre in Edinburgh to shadow, follow, and slay a vampire known to specifically target performers.

Angus Stewart had been stalking theaters throughout the UK for decades, selecting his prey based on some obscure mix of talent and personal taste. He had a predilection, as so many of these centuries-old fiends do, for the classical arts, and of course, ballet was one of his favorites. Enjoying the thrill of the hunt and the selection process, Angus would often go to see his victims perform for nights, weeks, or even months on end before he suddenly struck. That night's show was *La Sylphide*, performed by the Scottish Ballet.

Angus Stewart had been in the front row, and I had been in the box diagonally above him that the Van Helsing Society had hired out for the occasion, flanked by Jed and Ramsay. This was a few months before Ramsay had had his mysterious hunting accident, which ended up transforming him into a dhampir, a half-vampire, and resulted in his hunting licenses being permanently revoked and him really hating my guts.

I'd been watching Angus through a pair of ornate theater goggles, but then I had noticed Aubrey. She was the most gorgeous girl I'd seen, but it wasn't just that. It was subtle, but she moved differently from the other ballerinas, more animated somehow, with a deeper sense of surrender to her art. It gave me chills, and I didn't even give a damn about ballet. It was the one time at work I'd been so distracted that I gladly entrusted the vampire-watching to the others without a second thought.

After the show, I'd had a vampire to kill and dispose of, but I returned to the theatre the following night, which happened to be my night off. It was also the final night the Scottish Ballet performed *La Sylphide* in Edinburgh before touring other major UK cities. To be fair, if Angus Stewart hadn't met his end the night before, that would likely have been the night he'd struck. And who knows, maybe Aubrey would have been his chosen victim.

The whole theatre had been buzzing, and all the planets seemed to have aligned perfectly because I was able to walk right up and find Aubrey in the theater bar after the show. She turned around as I approached, lighting up as if she already knew me.

There were a lot of things I'd never told Aubrey the truth about, mainly to do with what I really did for a living. It was too late to save our relationship, but not too late to give her the answers she'd always wanted, and on second thought, always deserved. And maybe then I'd finally get a sense of closure. I'd exorcise Aubrey from my life like a demon - except I was the demon, but you get my meaning.

It was just after 10 PM, and the crowd in the brightly lit, modern foyer of Sadler's Wells Theatre was thinning out. The show had started at 7:30, while I'd been at the Van Helsing Society to collect the warning intended for Evander. I knew the performance would last about two hours, and Aubrey would take at least another half hour to change, maybe longer because she always had to make sure she left the character behind on the stage, or at least in the dressing room. It was a whole thing with her, and I sort of got it because, after a hunt, it was similar for me. It'd take me a moment to get back down to earth.

Three of Aubrey's colleagues, Alice, Georgina and Douglas, stood over by the broad white stone staircase and had already spotted me. I could feel the sharp pings of their attention as they leaned in closer together and whispered.

As I walked toward them, their conversation stopped, and they tensed, like they could feel the dark aura surrounding me. To be fair, they probably could. Whatever animated me now wasn't the usual vital energy of a living body; it was darker, more intense, like raw electricity.

I should've at least worn tinted glasses or something. But as long as I didn't let them see my fangs, it might be okay.

"Harlan, what are you doing here?" Douglas's voice was defensive, tinged with nervousness. He was slight, pale-skinned, with short, tightly curled deep-brown hair, eyes that couldn't decide if they wanted to be blue or grey. As Aubrey's best friend and frequent dance partner, he was the colleague I'd been around the most. Once I'd accepted he wasn't interested in Aubrey that way, I'd grown to like him. But now, there was no hint of friendship between us. Something around his eyes and mouth tightened when he looked at me - whatever Aubrey had been telling him about me lately wasn't good.

"Aubrey doesn't want to see you," Alice added sharply, sweeping her blonde ponytail back over her shoulder with a clearly dismissive gesture. Like her movements, her features were all sharp and narrow. I had never been able to figure out whether Alice was Aubrey's friend or rival, and when I'd asked Aubrey about it, she admitted she wasn't sure either.

As if summoned, Aubrey appeared at the top of the stairs. She stopped abruptly, her eyes widening in surprise.

She was in her civilian mode, dressed all in black - a short, fitted skirt, long-sleeved top, lace-up boots, and a cropped, glossy black puffer jacket. Her ballet gear was slung over one shoulder in a black athletic bag.

I hadn't seen her in nearly six months, but the only thing that had changed was how she wore her ink-black hair. It had been shoulder-length with a short fringe, but now it was cropped into a short pixie cut that accentuated her large gray-green eyes and how delicately her face was sculpted. Apart from a sprinkling of tiny freckles, her skin was impossibly porcelain-like for a mortal's. With my heightened senses, it was all too easy to sense where the blue veins ran close to the surface at her wrists and neck, even from a distance. She was so beautiful. So alive. The pang I felt wasn't just from missing her - it was something less innocent than that.

"Harlan? You've been ghosting me for months."

"I know, but can we talk?"

"Aubrey..." Georgina placed a hand on Aubrey's arm, giving her a pleading look as if to remind her to stay strong. "Don't go with him. He's just going to draw you back in, and then it'll start all over again."

I didn't even glance at Georgina. My focus was entirely on Aubrey, who looked torn.

"I'll tell you everything," I said, "if you still want to hear it. About my work, all the things I was hiding from you."

"You're really going to tell me everything?" she asked, her voice wavering, as if she found it hard to believe I was finally and suddenly willing to open up after nearly two years of stubborn secrecy.

"Everything," I promised.

She descended the staircase slowly, stopping in front of me on the marble floor.

"You better mean it," she said, her eyes searching mine.

"I mean it. But you'll have to trust me." I reached out,

my hand hovering in the space between us. I wore black leather gloves, a trick I'd known for ages that vampires use to avoid people noticing the coldness of their touch. Now, I used it too.

Aubrey still hesitated, her eyes flickering with doubt. Then, slowly, she placed her hand in mine. I could sense the others behind her on the staircase tensing up. But they didn't matter.

The moment our hands touched, even through the gloves, an electric tension crackled between us like static, sending a shiver down my spine. I could feel her pulse quicken.

"I trust you," she said, "at least a little."

"Then there's a place I need to show you."

I'd walked in here thinking we might just go for a walk or head into one of the many bars dotted around the area. But a different idea had seized me and struck me with absolute conviction. I needed to show Aubrey Thornhill Mansion. She'd be much more likely to believe me then.

Thornhill Mansion is a half hour drive from Sadler's Wells in light traffic, and with my penchant for driving fast, we got there in just over twenty.

There was a lot of ground to cover so I started on the story on the way there, starting with the death of my parents when I was six, and my being raised by Eli, who had a bit of an unusual profession. Aubrey had met Eli several times and knew that he was my mentor and a sort of father, so starting with something familiar seemed like a good segway before we descended into even stranger territory than secret societies, werewolves and vampire hunting.

As we drove uphill, I'd occasionally shoot Aubrey a sideways glance to gauge whether or not she was shutting down and closing her mind to what I was telling her. So far, that hadn't happened.

I killed the engine once we had come to a stop in front of the mansion's frost-encrusted wrought-iron gate. The air was cool and stung as we got out of the car. Aubrey left her bag in the backseat.

I unlocked the gate and pushed it open with a distinct creaking sound that rang out in the frosty night. I held the gate open for Aubrey, who stepped through. Her breath turned into ghostly clouds in the frosty air - mine didn't, but she hadn't noticed, yet.

Thornhill Mansion rose grandly above the ice-glittering garden, its silhouette the bluish black of a bruise, save for the colorful stained-glass dome covering the vast hall, which was softly illuminated from within.

We'd just gotten to the part of the story where Jeremy Gently showed up at Eli's home in Scotland with Lyrica's invitation for me to come to Thornhill Mansion. Now as Aubrey could see, at least the mansion was a real place, not some figment of my imagination. Whatever she might be thinking of the rest was anyone's guess at this point. She hadn't said much, only listened with a pensive expression, now and then knitting her eyebrows, or frowning or flinching at my words, but she hadn't interrupted once.

We made our way up the winding garden path, which was really just a narrow trail of flattened grass until we reached the imposing front door with its peeling, lion-head door knob. I unlocked the door, too, and opened it as quietly as I could. Much as I wanted Aubrey to know that everything I was telling her was true, introducing her to all of my undead cousins within fifteen minutes of having introduced her to the reality that vampires really do exist might be a bit much.

Aubrey stood very still beside me, taking in the grand hallway with its black-and-white marble floor, its many Victorian-era portraits and the stained-glass dome far above.

"This place is really something," she commented with a note of awe. "Like a Hammer Horror movie set."

"Pretty much," I agreed. "When I first stepped through this door, the entire place was dusty and overgrown with vines."

"So what happened in this place, and how come you live here now?"

"Lyrica Hartenbrook," I said, crossing the hallway and indicating that she should follow me, "turned out to be a long-undead cousin, and she wasn't the only one. There were a few more in the basement."

"Harlan, do you know how crazy all of this sounds?" Aubrey's tone was bemused. But she followed me up the creaking wooden staircase, past the portraits of Algeron, Helen, Venedict, Octavia and Dorothea. I introduced each of them by name as we passed them before adding, "Yes, I know. It sounds crazy to me, and I've known about vampires since as far back as I remember. I'm still processing all of this, believe me."

I turned to glance over my shoulder. Aubrey had stopped a few steps behind me and stood, seemingly mesmerized, in front of a gilded-framed painting of Venedict, Octavia and Dorothea that must have been painted shortly before they became vampires. The painting captured each of them so perfectly, the soft brushstrokes bringing such a haunting quality to their gazes that you half expected them to follow you with their eyes. Of course, the only portrait that ever did that was Algernon's.

"How many of them are still alive, or I mean, undead now?" she asked.

"Just Venedict, Octavia, and Lyrica."

"Venedict looks a lot like you," Aubrey commented, her head tilted to the side. Then she turned to look up at me, then back to the painting. It struck me that taking her here had been exactly the right decision. There was no more convincing argument I could give her than letting her see everything for herself.

"Aubrey?"

She turned towards me, the moonlight filtering through the stained glass overhead gleaming in her hair.

"I'm sorry it's taken me this long to just tell you the truth. I'm not sure why I took the Society's NDA so damned seriously. I should have taken you more seriously instead."

The Van Helsing Society and their damned rules. I'd never truly thought to question them before, not really. I'd bent the rules, sure, but I'd never actually breached them. Not the fundamental ones. Algernon might be a poisonous influence in many ways, but it was his whispered words in my head that made me wonder how much I'd let the Society shape every aspect of my life. The Society had been my whole life - because I'd let it.

Aubrey's conflicted approach to the meds she took for bipolar disorder had sometimes made our relationship challenging, but it was my secrecy that had messed everything up. I knew that; I'd just never been able to admit it before.

"It's... I want to say it's okay. But I wish you had been honest. It would have saved me a lot of speculation about which crime lord you were probably working for, and where you got your scars from."

"Come, this way."

I showed her the library, describing how Lyrica had told me and Sebatian the family history, or most of it.

Then, I led her down the carpeted hallway to what was now my living quarters in the mansion, consisting of Octavia's and Venedict's old rooms adjoined by the bathroom with its copper pipes and claw-foot tub.

Aubrey took it all in with wide-eyed fascination. While the rest of the mansion's interiors were essentially antique, my quarters were a mix of original features, like the haunted, black-stained floor length mirror in its ornate frame and the elaborately carved four-poster bed, and modern details like the backlit display unit I'd had installed along one wall to have more space for my weapons, and my red iMac perched on the antique desk below one of the windows.

She let her eyes glide around the room. At least some of my things were familiar to her, including my extensive collection of weapons. My flat in Edinburgh had a narrow walk-in wardrobe. I had always used one side for my clothes and the other side for stakes and knives.

"Now I finally know what those are for," she said, nodding towards one of the spring-activated stakes in the cabinet.

"Remember throwing about twenty of these out in the street?" I asked, referring to one of the tumultuous times Aubrey had broken up with me. She had forbidden me from going on a hunt that would disrupt our planned weekend together, threatening to lock me out of her flat if I joined what she called my gang when they came to pick me up. Determined to disrupt our planned weekend, I infuriated her to the point of giving me an ultimatum: if I left, she wouldn't let me back in. I told her I was still going.

Her kicking me out hinged on my cooperation, but it felt

unfair to resist, so I let her usher me out without even gathering my things.

As I stood on the street waiting to be picked up, Aubrey appeared at the window and dramatically began tossing the contents of my weekend bag into the street. At first, it was mundane items like clothes, a toothbrush, a razor, the keys I'd given her to my flat. Then she grabbed my second bag and turned it upside down. A cascade of about two dozen impact-activated stakes rained down, clattering onto the pavement and springing open. I caught some before they hit the ground, but a few rolled downhill - Edinburgh is a steep city, and the street Aubrey lived on was particularly steep.

The drama drew the attention of a few passersby, who looked on in confusion and mild alarm until one of the Society's sleek black cars pulled up to the curb.

Aubrey walked over to the desk by the window, pulled the cord to turn on the antique lamp atop its polished dark wood surface, and slid her puffer jacket off, draping it over the chair.

"Sorry. I'm already forgetting that you mortals need light to see properly at night," I said with a hint of a smile. I switched on a few more lamps, and the room came alive with the added illumination, the rich, dark wood and elegant furnishings taking on a warm, inviting glow.

Aubrey frowned softly. "Do you have night vision?"

"There have to be some perks to no longer being alive."

"But you are alive," she said, a little hesitantly. "I mean, aren't you?"

I hadn't even gotten to the part of the story where I lost so much blood that Venedict decided to turn me. But she knew. I could tell by the way she looked at me in the soft glow that now filled the room, as if she had just noticed something she hadn't seen before. Everything I'd said, the changes she sensed in me—they were all clicking into place in her mind.

I could see the conflict in her eyes, but still, she moved closer. I'd taken off my gloves, and when I reached out, letting my fingers trail lightly up her arm, she could feel the coolness of my touch. Her skin prickled with gooseflesh under my fingertips. Her eyes widened as they lifted to meet mine, but she didn't flinch or pull away.

"I don't know whether I should be afraid."

"You don't have to be. I'm still me. Almost."

The uncertainty in her eyes lingered, but there was also a hint of something else - curiosity, maybe, or longing.

Our eyes locked, and that familiar current of energy passed between us, an electric hum that had always been there, though now it felt sharper, more dangerous. Probably because we were alone.

"Would it be okay if we kissed?" she asked, almost shy.

"A goodbye kiss?"

"It's just a kiss. Don't overthink it."

She stepped into my arms, and our lips met softly at first, tentative, as if testing boundaries. But we must have missed each other. The kiss deepened, and Aubrey winced when she nicked her tongue on one of my fangs, the metallic taste of her blood seeping into the kiss, darkening it.

I worried the blood - and my reaction to it, how it heightened the thrill for me - would frighten her, but it didn't seem to.

I pushed her against the wall, and she let out a sound that was half startled laugh, half gasp. I'd meant it playfully, but the moment I did it, it wasn't just that. The impact pressed her body against mine, and I felt the rapid beat of her heart through her chest. I already knew this was a bad idea, but it was already difficult to care.

The rush of her pulse thundered in my ears like the onset of a migraine. I should've had my fill of animal blood before heading off to work earlier, but when I'd opened the fridge downstairs and taken a few sips of yesterday's pint of pig's blood, it had tasted like chalk, and I'd given up on it after just a few gulps. Now, I regretted it. But not quite enough to stop. I wasn't about to let the bloodlust control me or spoil the moment.

She arched her back, allowing me to slide her top over her head, revealing her small breasts, more decorated than concealed by black lace. Her skin was warm and smooth beneath my fingers, her pulse steady and hypnotic.

My fingers continued up, tracing the line of her neck, sliding to her chin, tilting her head to the side. She watched me with those gray-green eyes, her lips stained with her own blood. She knew what was happening, what I was thinking. Her eyes widened slightly, but there was no real fear. Why would there be? I'd never hurt her before, and I wasn't going to now. Definitely not. It was just that her blood was so distracting, calling to me from just under her skin.

"You should go," I said. But my voice sounded distant, like it didn't belong to me, and the words didn't mean anything.

"What if I won't?" she replied, breathless and defiant. "You can't bring me here, throw all of this at me, and then just send me away."

"Maybe you're right," I murmured, still in that distant voice. I guided her head to tilt further, exposing the tender curve of her neck. Her pulse, the faint blue line of her artery, throbbed just beneath the surface.

I closed my mouth over it, carefully. I just wanted to feel her lifeforce beating against my tongue. What was wrong with that? Her heart raced wildly in her chest as she went very still, holding her breath.

My control slipped, just for one second. But that was enough. Before I could stop myself, I was sinking my fangs into her neck, breaking the skin and rupturing her artery as easily as a hot knife sinking through butter.

Her body tensed against mine and every muscle went rigid, the sensation making me clamp down harder. Her hot, metallic blood poured into me like liquid fire, igniting my own blood along the way. This was almost as good as the turning itself had been, before the pain.

As I sank my fangs deeper, I let her slide down onto the floor, cradling her as she shivered in my arms, her body responding to the pull of her lifeblood flowing into me.

I was lost in the overpowering need to consume her entirely. Nothing else seemed to matter. The tang of her blood, her body against mine, and the pulse of her life force flowing into me were perfection.

I knew I should stop, but I wasn't sure I could.

CHAPTER

TWELVE

My grip on her tightened as I fought against the bloodlust. Her pulse weakened, and her shivers grew more pronounced. I had to stop, to pull back before it was too late. But I struggled to remember why it mattered, why I couldn't just let go and let it happen.

With monumental effort, I lifted my head, breaking the connection. I pulled my fangs free at the same angle I'd sunk them in, trying not to cause more damage, but the harm was already done - her artery was badly torn.

Resisting the urge to sink my fangs back in took everything I had. I bit into my own wrist to stop the temptation from crushing me. One more little slip-up and I'd kill her for sure.

She looked up at me, paler than I'd ever seen her. Blood stained her mouth, tracing a vivid line from her neck, cascading over her collarbone and down her chest. Her gray eyes, with their rings of emerald, shimmered with pain, fear, or maybe love. The thought crossed my mind that she had never looked more beautiful than she did right now.

I felt doomed as I pressed my hand over the puncture wounds, trying to stem the flow. Her blood was warm and sticky. My pressure slowed it but didn't stop it completely.

I reached for her top, found it, and pressed it over the wounds, guiding her hands to hold it in place. "Here, keep pressure on it. Don't let go." My voice was tight with anxiety, despite my best efforts to sound calm and reassuring.

"What happened?" She sounded faint, the words slipping from her lips in a daze as I lifted her and carefully placed her on the bed.

"I bit you. I need to find a first aid kit."

"It's okay," she whispered. "Don't go."

"I'll be back in a minute."

If there was a first aid kit in the mansion, it'd be in Sebastian's living quarters in the recently converted attic. I used to keep one around, but since I'd become a vampire, I hadn't bothered getting one for my bathroom at the mansion, and I'd arrogantly binned the one I kept in my car.

I bolted down the hallway and up the rickety stairs to the attic, which had been little more than a dumping ground for old daguerreotypes and antique diaries when I first saw it. Now it was a snazzy loft apartment with abstract black-and-white art on the walls, many of Sebastian's own large-scale photographs among them.

Sebastian was nowhere to be seen, and I couldn't ask him for assistance - he was still off somewhere with Irene. The last time we'd spoken had been on New Year's Eve, and I'm pretty sure he'd mentioned something about going to Florence in mid-January to shoot something for *Vogue Italia*. I couldn't keep track.

Sebastian's newly installed bathroom looked like it had yet to be taken into use. There was not even a shampoo bottle, let alone a first aid kit. *Fuck, fuck, fuck.*

I made my way down through the mansion and back out to my car. The night air was cold, biting into my skin as I fumbled for the keys. I grabbed Aubrey's bag from the backseat. She always sustained little cuts and bruises from dancing so I knew I'd find plaster and bandages among her things.

I returned to my bedroom where Aubrey, to my relief, had dutifully kept the top pressed against her wound. But she was nearly as pale as me, her eyes fluttering closed.

"Aubrey?" I said sharply.

"I'm here," she whispered hazily without opening her eyes.

I knelt beside her and rummaged through her bag.

As I sifted through her cosmetics, a pill bottle rolled onto the floor, the lid popping off, and her bipolar meds scattered across the rug. Aubrey's approach to her prescription was inconsistent, to say the least. She'd sometimes decide to ditch the pills, holding out for as long as her resolve lasted. Her unmedicated periods had always coincided with the most tumultuous times in our relationship. Of course, when I'd pointed it out, she had outright refused to consider that there could be a connection. But shortly after, she'd started taking her meds again. She was stubborn and proud - nearly as bad as me.

When she was up, her lust for life would kick into overdrive. Aubrey was exhilarating to be around when she was flying high - except when that energy turned confrontational. We'd had some explosive fights during those times, but the equally intense makeup sex that invariably followed had usually made it all seem worth it.

When she was down, everything around her fell apart. One particularly bad depressive episode had lasted a couple of months. I'd go to work at night, come home to clean up, catch a nap if I had time, and then swing by her place to wake her, make her breakfast, and get her showered and dressed, with almost no participation from her. After that, I'd drive her to rehearsal, and once we arrived, a flicker of her own fire would start sparking, just enough for her to take it from there.

Eli had been stunned that I could show that kind of care for a girlfriend, especially when I'd never managed to keep a single houseplant he'd given me alive. I was just as surprised - I hadn't known I had that instinct in me. But taking care of Aubrey had felt effortless, something I didn't even need to think about.

I hadn't exactly enjoyed her depression, but it was the closest we'd come to living together, and I liked that part of it. It made me wonder what actually living with her might've been like. The only person I'd ever lived with was Eli, and then it had just been me, on my own, cutting girl-friends off the moment they got too attached.

In a parallel reality - one where I hadn't gone to London and turned into a damn vampire before we could reconcile - maybe there was a whole life with Aubrey I could've had. Not for long, maybe just a few years or even a decade before I inevitably died in the line of vampire-hunting duty.

Neither of us wanted the full traditional setup, but we could've had our own version - moved in together, maybe even gotten married. Aubrey had made it clear on one of our first dates that her body belonged first and foremost to ballet, and she wasn't willing to sacrifice it for kids she had no interest in raising. That suited me perfectly. I didn't want kids left behind when I died young. I'd always thought I didn't want to leave a widow either, but Aubrey had made me wonder.

Not that there was any point in thinking about that now.

I sat next to her, carefully applying the bandages I'd found. Her blood was still warm and beckoning, seeping through the gauze as fast as I could layer it, but the flow was slowing. The metallic scent hung in the room like a cloud of dark conscience.

She reached out, her fingers brushing against my cheek.

"Aubrey, I'm so sorry," I said, my voice breaking.

"I know. Stay. Just five minutes." Her voice was weak but clear. Somehow, she still wasn't afraid of me. Or maybe she was just in shock.

"Okay, five minutes," I agreed.

Promising myself that the danger had blown over and that there wasn't even a sliver of a chance of me biting her again, I laid down next to her. She nestled into my arms and curled up against me with her head tucked under my chin.

Aubrey's small frame fit perfectly in my arms, and her warm breath against my cool skin made me feel nearly human. But I was so far from human I could cry. I managed to clamp down the urge.

After a few minutes the rhythmic rise and fall of her breathing slowed and I realized she had fallen asleep. How could she just peacefully doze off in my arms after what I'd done to her?

I was wide awake, mind racing. This had come so close to ending in disaster. I should've stayed away. But at least now, she could never claim I hadn't been brutally honest with her.

I awoke with a start.

Aubrey was still asleep in my arms. I checked my watch; it was 5:47 AM - dawn was only about an hour and a half away. How careless was I allowed to be and still get away with it? The room's blackout curtains weren't even drawn. If the sun had risen I'd be dead.

Carefully, I extricated my arm from under her. She didn't stir.

The room was a mess, her toiletries and meds scattered all over the blood-spattered rug.

There was also blood on the bed's sheets and pillows, and even, somehow, on the headboard. No wonder she was sleeping so deeply; she must have lost a lot of blood. Some of it had gone down my throat, but I'd wasted just as much of it on the floor and on the bed, and it seemed like a crying shame to let something so amazing go to waste.

I found some makeup wipes in her cosmetics bag and, standing in front of the haunted floor length mirror, used them to clean her blood off my chin. The sight of myself in the mirror, wiping off her blood and in the background, Aubrey sleeping peacefully on the bloodspattered bed struck a macabre chord.

I sat beside her and gently wiped away the smudges of black mascara that had run down her cheeks, as well as the blood from her hands and neck.

A single drop of crimson seeped through the makeshift bandage. The sight of it sent a twinge of craving through me. But the bloodlust, now partially sated by her blood, was just a faint call in the distance rather than a deafening roar in my head.

I let my fingers trail up her leg. Right now, all I wanted was to wake her up, unwrap her like a gift, and erase every trace in her mind and body of whoever else she might have been with since me. But I'd just come dangerously close to killing her - this wasn't exactly the right moment for that.

Reluctantly, I got up from the bed, leaving her to sleep peacefully. Her expression was serene, her chest rising and falling in a steady rhythm. I needed to get a grip on this bloodlust, to stamp it out completely, before I even considered waking her up.

She needed to be in an Uber before dawn so she wouldn't have to see me die with the sun. After everything else she'd gone through tonight at Thornhill Mansion, that would only add more trauma to the nightmare.

I didn't really think any of my undead family were likely to swoop into my bedroom and finish what I'd started, but just in case, I left a handwritten note on my door: *Don't eat Aubrey.* Below the words, I drew a drop of blood crossed out with a big X. That should make it clear.

I closed the door quietly behind me and made my way down the hall, descending through the mansion to the barely-used kitchen.

Like much of the rest of the mansion it had been restored, with black marble countertops and a full array of copper pots and pans hanging above the new stove - which had been used by Sebastian to cook pasta approximately twice.

Sebastian had been gone with Irene for about three weeks now, and I found myself wishing he'd come back soon. I felt a little less unhinged with him around. I felt like I needed his human presence to help keep me anchored to a vague sense of normal perspective on the world.

I sent him a quick text saying something to that effect as I walked over to the fridge and let its door swing open.

The fridge was predictably empty except for two pints of blood in the door, one labeled with yesterday's date and the other with the date before that. I brought them both over to the sink and emptied the older bottle into it. Once blood gets a few days old it's just not worth having. I'm not sure exactly what goes wrong with it, but the enzymes must stop working, or something like that. Either way, the vital energy fizzles out. The fresher, the better.

I screwed the top off the other bottle and poured myself a mug full. Could I just pretend this was coffee? Drinking it from a mug made it seem somehow less morbid.

I grimaced. The cold pig's blood, or whatever the hell this was, tasted like dank, chalky water. I had to force myself to drink all of it down, finishing with a shiver of disgust. This was vile. How was I supposed to drink this shit every night for the rest of eternity?

When I turned around to head back upstairs, Octavia stood right behind me.

Tonight, she wore a short ivory white satin dress that was completely at odds with the wintry temperature. For aesthetic reasons more than because she needed to, she wore a white fox fur draped over her bare shoulders, fastened with a white diamond brooch that looked like a sparkling, oversized snowdrop. The fur and the brooch looked like something a little girl would find in a wealthy old aunt's closet and play dress up with. She would resent me if she picked up on that thought, but luckily, she didn't.

"I glimpsed the two of you in the library," Octavia informed me in her clear silver bell voice. "She is just as beautiful as Father insisted."

I furrowed my brows. "Algernon has told you about Aubrey?"

"Several times since you joined the family. He is quite enamored - or enraptured, as he put it. He has been wondering when you might bring her here and introduce her to the family."

"Huh." That wasn't really surprising. "Once I'm back from the Games, we've got to figure out how to banish Algernon from the mansion for good."

Octavia nodded, "I agree - Father's departure is already long overdue." After a beat of silence during which I placed the empty mug in the sink to let it soak in soap and water, Octavia demanded, "Are you and Aubrey engaged to be married?"

"No."

I left the kitchen and started walking down the corridor towards the grand hall. The air was cool, and the light from the chandeliers cast a warm glow on the black and white marble tiles. Octavia, burning with curiosity, followed me. Her footsteps made no sound as we crossed the hallway, but I could clearly sense her energy, buzzing with inquisitiveness.

"Did you break off the engagement, or did she?" she prodded.

"We were never engaged," I replied, my tone clipped.

"But do you not love her?" she pressed, her eyes boring into the back of my head.

"It's complicated," I said. Had Octavia ever been in love? Her life had ended at seventeen, she had spent most of the intervening century and a half detached from her body, and there was the whole awful, incestuous situation with her father. So my guess was, probably not.

"Are you going to bestow the dark gift upon her?" Octavia's voice lowered with intrigue.

"No," I answered firmly.

"Are you going to kill her?"

I spun on my heel to fix her with a stern look. "I'm not, and neither are you. Is that clear?"

"Perfectly clear," Octavia agreed, her tone deceptively innocent. As I started to turn around again, she added, "But what will happen if I *do* kill her?"

"Then," I replied, "I'll be mad. I'll probably wrap your

casket with chains and put it in the basement for a century or two. Maybe three."

"So you do love her."

As we reached the grand staircase, Octavia's questions didn't cease. She followed me up the stairs, her voice a constant stream of inquiries. While she bombarded me with questions, I ordered an Uber to take Aubrey back to the Strand Plaza Hotel, where she had mentioned she was staying for the month.

"You are not paying me any attention," Octavia complained.

Hadn't Carmen mentioned something about Aubrey trialing out for the National Ballet? What if she got accepted - then she'd be moving to London. Not that it mattered. When I woke her up in just a moment to get her sent on her way, that would probably be the last time she ever wanted to see me.

"Stay here," I told Octavia when we reached my door at the end of the second-floor hallway.

She wrinkled her little button nose, a sign of her impending protest. "But I wish to be formally introduced. Indeed, I insist upon it."

"Maybe later."

I stepped into the room and closed the door behind me, leaving Octavia to sulk in the hallway. I guess this was what it was like, having a little sister. An undead one, from the 19th century.

I started gathering Aubrey's scattered belongings from the floor, placing each item back into what I hoped were the right compartments of her bag. As I worked, I checked my phone - the Uber I'd ordered was ten minutes away, and sunrise was looming just under an hour from now.

Behind me, I heard Aubrey stir, as if my thoughts had

nudged her awake. I remained seated cross-legged on the floor next to her bag, my back to the bed, but I could sense the shift in energy as she woke.

My muscles tensed - I had no idea in what state of mind she would be, and I braced myself for the possibility that she might panic at the sight of all the blood - or of me. Venedict's description of waking up in Gabriel's bed and panicking at the thought of being bitten again rang vividly in my mind. I never wanted to make Aubrey feel like that.

But instead of reacting with fear, she quietly slid off the bed and wrapped her arms around me from behind, resting her chin on my shoulder.

THIRTEEN

Hampstead in North London was shrouded in stillness and darkness.

I still didn't know how Jeremy Gently had managed to track me down in Scotland back in August - anyone had yet to give me a damn explanation, and who better to do it than the guy himself?

As far as I could tell, my grandparents's decision to change their last names and to go underground in 1969, had coincided with Lyrica rising from her tomb (or actually from the Thornhill family tomb, but you get the picture) and making Jeremy Gently her familiar.

Jeremy, as well as being Lyrica's familiar, was also the Thornhill family's solicitor. He had worked tirelessly for Lyrica since the summer of 1969, and since Octavia and Venedict had sprung back to life, he had been working tirelessly for them, securing the documents they needed to pass as fully fledged 21st century natives.

But despite his seeming loyalty and dedication to my family, Jeremy had either sold or given my birth certificate to Gabriel, and that was something I needed an explanation for. Why would he do that, instead of giving it to me? Why Gabriel had wanted my birth certificate in the first place was a mystery I could probably forget about ever getting a direct answer to.

I could have dropped by Jeremy's office months ago, but I just hadn't gotten around to it. But better late than never. Tonight, I was determined to finally speak with Jeremy directly. As well as telling Aubrey the truth about everything, speaking with Jeremy and trying to glean the last mystery-shrouded pieces of the puzzle of my family's background and how and why I'd been drawn into it was one of those loose ends I wanted to tie up before the Grim Games, which were looming at the end of the week and approaching rapidly.

Gently's office premises were located near Hampstead Heath and were overlooking it. Hampstead is just a stone's throw from Highgate, and instead of driving I'd cut across the wintry heath on foot.

The law practice, Gently & Daughters, had apparently been rebranded from Gently & Sons, the law practice Gently and his brother had overtaken from their father. Neither of the Gently brothers had any sons, but Jeremy's two daughters were the next generation of Gently solicitors. I'd met one of them, Ariella, when she came by Thornhill Mansion a few weeks ago, carrying Venedict and Octavia's new passports (Claiming the birth years 2004 and 2006, respectively) in a leather briefcase.

Gently & Daughters was on the first floor of a well-kept Victorian-era terrace and looked reassuringly normal compared to most of the places I visited or spent time in these days.

I could have made an appointment like a regular client, but I didn't want Jeremy to be prepared with any canned answers. I wanted to catch him off-guard and was hoping that showing up just before he turned off the lights and went home for the night would make him more likely to be honest with me. I remembered Lyrica mentioning that he always stayed until midnight one evening every month, which was typically when she held her meetings with him.

Despite having been around Lyrica for decades, I got the clear sense that Jeremy was very uncomfortable around vampires. Now that I was one, it could absolutely work in my favor. I wasn't planning on threatening him, of course - but simply showing up to speak with him alone while having fangs might be enough to inspire him to talk.

It occurred to me that I might attempt to hypnotize him if he was reluctant - though maybe I shouldn't try it, considering how my last attempt had gone.

As I approached, the gentle glow of indoor lighting escaped into the night from the first floor window's office, which stood ajar, as did the faint strains of jazz.

I rang the buzzer labeled 'Gently & Daughters,' but there was no response, despite Jeremy clearly being up there, with the lights and music on.

After waiting a few moments without response from the buzzer, I decided to take a more direct approach. The front door of the building was sturdy, a polished dark wood that spoke of the building's Victorian heritage, but I knew from past escapades that old doors like this often had vulnerabilities.

I slipped a set of lock picks from my pocket - just one of the handy little tricks I knew, because not all vampires are eager to let you in when you show up with an execution warrant or even just a few inconvenient questions.

I didn't need to see what I was doing, so I turned my back to the door as if I was just casually standing in the doorway looking out over the street and the heath while I worked the tension wrench and rake pick into the keyhole, feeling for the click of the tumblers. The night was quiet, but the soft snicks of the lock yielding were barely audible.

With the door unlocked, I spun on my heel and slipped inside the building's dimly lit foyer. The decor was tastefully old-fashioned, with floral wallpaper, a few elegant chairs standing below a dark-framed mirror, and dark wood paneling that absorbed the soft light from overhead. I made my way to the staircase leading up to the first floor.

Ascending the stairs, I listened out for any signs of movement from Jeremy's office. There weren't any but the faint jazz music grew clearer with each step, as did the slightly musty smell of old books and leather that permeated the air.

I reached the top of the stairs and found myself in a narrow hallway with a few doors on each side. Jeremy's office was easy to identify; it was the one at the end of the hall, and the only one with light and the soft sounds of late-night radio jazz seeping out from under the door.

I knocked softly at first, then more insistently, ready to confront Jeremy with or without his invitation. And clearly, I wasn't about to be invited in - there was no response from the aging solicitor.

So, I pushed the door open. It swung inward with a faint creak.

Jeremy's office was a grotesque mess, everything in disarray like a blizzard had swept through. Papers lay scattered like fallen autumn leaves, spattered with dark, drying blood. Filing cabinets and drawers stood open. Some of the drawers had been ripped out of the furniture that held them and overturned on the thickly carpeted floor.

At the heart of the tumult was Jeremy Gently. He was

slumped over in his chair, his upper body draped over the desk, his face hidden by his outflung arms. He was dead for sure. I could tell instantly from the blue-tinged color of his skin.

The tangy, cloying scent of his blood hung in the air, and because it wasn't fresh, it made me feel queasy. Jeremy must have been sitting dead like this in his warm, toasty office for hours, and whatever mysterious process of decay took place in the human body after death was clearly already in full swing.

I stepped into the room with the sinking feeling that the pieces of a puzzle I was only beginning to comprehend lay scattered around me. And now Jeremy couldn't help me assemble it. Damn it.

I picked my way through the mess until I was standing beside Jeremy's desk. When I grabbed the back of his shirt and gently hoisted him up from the desk and let him lean back in the chair, his head lolled back. His face was contorted and all of the color of life had drained out of it.

It was pretty obvious where it had gone; the poor guy had been split open from neck to belly button, though not, as far as I could tell, by a knife. It looked like someone had torn him open with his bare hands. The edges of the long wound were jagged and messy. Whoever had done this must have gotten a lot of blood on himself - or herself, I guess, but let's be honest, that probably wasn't the case. It would take one particularly sick, malicious fuck to do something like this - and I felt pretty sure it would take someone with greater strength than a mere mortal. When I was still just human, I doubt that I would have been able to tear someone open with my bare hands, even if I had wanted to.

Everything was hanging out; Jeremy's trachea, heart,

lungs and other innards were all on the floor or on the desk, and a very long coiled intestine that I didn't have a name for was laying slick with blood in his lap. The thick carpet around his chair was so soaked through with blood that it squelched under my boots. You'd think it had been raining in here for hours on end.

I placed my fingertips on Jeremy's eyelids and closed his eyes. I didn't need to worry about leaving fingerprints; since becoming a vampire, I no longer had any. No lines, no pores, no fingerprints.

I knew that I needed to call both an ambulance and the police - and the Van Helsing Society; this was the work of a supernatural killer-, but I also knew that if I needed anything from Jeremy's office, this was my only chance to get it.

And so I set to work, rifling through Jeremy's papers and drawers, with him still sitting gutted and dead in the chair behind me, as if in silent judgment.

In the top drawer of an archive cabinet, I found a thick manila folder. Its labeling read "Thornhill" in stark, bold letters. When I lifted it, it was disappointingly light - and when I opened it to have a look inside, it was empty. Whatever it had contained, someone had taken it.

But why, and why now? I hadn't told anyone that I was planning on paying Jeremy Gently's law practice a visit tonight. It didn't make any sense.

Jeremy's killer was someone he had invited in; I was pretty sure of that. There were no signs of struggle or of Jeremy having attempted to escape his attacker.

The realization hit me like a sledgehammer, filling me with a bitter cocktail of anger and frustration. That folder might have contained crucial information about my lost parents. Now, it was gone, and with it, any immediate hope of uncovering the secrets I'd been chasing.

I slammed the drawer shut, the sound echoing in the office. I ran my hands through my hair, trying to calm down. The anger was a raw, pulsating force, much stronger than the sadness of Jeremy's brutal death and the sickness in my gut from the violent scene.

Then, something on the floor caught my attention - a photograph. I knelt and picked it up. It was a mid-80s school photo of a teenage girl with the same large, expressive amber-colored eyes as me, delicate features, cinnamon-colored hair falling in soft waves around her shoulders, and a small button nose exactly like Octavia's. I knew who it was before turning the photograph over and reading the text scrawled on the back in blue ink - Vivian Thorne, Danube International School, Vienna, 1986.

Whoever had murdered Jeremy and taken the contents of the Thornhill folder had either been so careless or in such a rush that he hadn't noticed or cared that he had dropped this, the only photograph I'd ever seen of my mother.

My eyes stung as I slipped it into my jacket.

Standing around here, trying to puzzle it all out, wasn't going to help Jeremy. And it wasn't going to help me. I disappeared back into the night, seething with frustrated anger.

BACK AT THORNHILL MANSION, I was greeted by Venedict, who was clearly in a strop.

"How," he demanded as soon as I stepped through the door, "am I supposed to excise Gabriel from my life when you are accepting his gifts?"

Venedict was sharply dressed in a slim-fitting aubergine-and-silver pinstripe suit, paired with one of his voluminous Victorian-esque shirts, and the usual profusion of his mother's antique jewelry. A leather briefcase hung on the navel post of the staircase behind him, indicating that he had just returned from whatever business night class it was he attended. He gestured irritably, if not downright accusingly, towards a clothing rail laden with covered garments, and several high-end branded cardboard boxes and paper bags stacked beside it just inside the door.

"I'm not sure what you mean," I responded, making no attempt to hide my annoyance. "I've just been to see Jeremy Gently, and I found him dead. Gutted, to be specific."

Venedict waved a dismissive hand and wrinkled his nose. "Do not attempt to distract me from the conversation I wish to have," he said. The tragic fate that had befallen the family solicitor clearly did not concern him right now. "Gabriel knows when I am likely to be back from class, and he must have timed his assistant's arrival perfectly to coincide with it. Thus, Hyacinth manifested right here in the doorway where you are now standing, just a few minutes ago, with all of these for you. He said it is 'the dress code.'"

Now it dawned on me what had to be in the bags and boxes - whatever outfits Gabriel deemed necessary for the Grim Games. I'd expected a few pointers to help me blend in with the old-money crowd. But judging by the sheer number of bags and boxes, he had seized the opportunity to replace my entire wardrobe. There was so much of it that, unless Gabriel expected seven costume changes a night, there was no way I could wear it all in a weekend. Who did he think I was, Madonna?

I sighed, half in exasperation and half in resignation.

"These aren't gifts," I explained to Venedict. "It's just

Gabriel being a bit of a control freak. I agreed to go with whatever dress code he specified for the Games. He clearly doesn't think I know how to dress myself."

Venedict furrowed his brow, arms folded defensively across his chest. "He is doing this to irk me, I am perfectly aware. He believes he knows precisely how to provoke a reaction from me, but I am not so easily manipulated."

For someone not easily manipulated, Venedict seemed a little flustered.

"If you want any of this," I gestured to the clothes and bags, "you're welcome to it."

Venedict shook his head. "All of this will have been picked or tailored to fit you perfectly."

"I don't see how it could be," I said. "No one's asked for any measurements."

"Gabriel can work these things out by sight. He always could with me." Venedict whipped around so fast I could feel the air move. He started ascending the stairs, his usually silent footsteps deliberately loud and reverberating on the old wooden steps.

He paused when he reached the first floor landing and turned back towards me, fixing me with a direct stare, very much like the one I'd seen him pull in an old daguerreotype. "You should not be accepting any more gifts from him."

"I wasn't exactly planning to."

I carried everything upstairs - clothes draped over hangers, a tower of eight Alexander McQueen shoe boxes - just to get it all out of Venedict's line of sight. I could practically feel his annoyance radiating through the mansion's thick walls, pulsing like an electric charge from his distant turret at the opposite end of the house.

There were so many packages that they nearly filled my

bedroom, making it feel like Gabriel's presence hung over it, overwhelming, excessive, and cloying.

Upon closer inspection, the clothes turned out to be predictably lavish: silks, premium cotton, and brocade, mostly in tonal black with splashes of white and crimson. The styles were modern and slim-fitting, with only the faintest nods to Victorian-esque influence - a high-necked collar or a whisper of lace at the hem of a sleeve. There were no cravats, no lace-dripping horrors that would have made me throw up a little in my mouth. Everything was surprisingly respectful of my own tastes and 21st Century origins.

I tried on a pair of steel-capped Alexander McQueen Chelsea boots. I wanted to hate them, but I didn't. I loved them.

That fact alone irritated me. Gabriel had twisted our agreement about the wardrobe into a weapon against Venedict. And something about him sending me all these beautiful clothes unsettled me. If I didn't know any better, I'd think he was making a pass at me. Of course, being a pawn in his endless drama against Venedict was bad enough.

I sat at my desk, pulling out the only thing I'd brought back from Gently & Daughters - the photo of my mom.

"A remarkable beauty, your mother. She looks so much like my Octavia."

Algernon's voice startled me, but I refused to let it show. I glanced around, scanning the shadows in the room. He wasn't anywhere, not even in the haunted mirror. His voice was just there, in my head.

"Algernon, didn't expect to hear from you again so soon. I figured you and Ramsay would be busy planning my welcome party on the other side."

His only response was a deep, resonant chuckle, reverberating inside my skull.

"Look at you, trying to piece together your history, searching for the parents you feel you never had." There was something mocking in his tone, but it was subtle. "But you will never find them, you know - they are gone. They disappeared forever that night. You know the one I mean, the night that set you on your path. The night you keep dreaming about."

"You eavesdrop on my nightmares." It wasn't a question, just a resigned acknowledgment.

"You have a lot of those. Sometimes they're too much, even for me. But I also eavesdrop on your more pleasant dreams."

"Great. Enjoy the show."

"I wish you wouldn't take such easy offense. I am only trying to get to know you. Glancing into the corners of your mind is much easier when you're asleep."

"I bet. But as I've told you before, stay out of my private life. That includes my dreams and my mind. In case it isn't obvious, you don't have my permission to bumble around in there."

"But I've discovered so many interesting things in your mind," he persisted. "You'd be amazed. There are many locked rooms in there, many doors that are bolted shut. Some of these have been sealed off by others, others you have deliberately shut yourself. Fascinating, is it not? What do you think lurks behind those locked doors? I could tell you, but you wouldn't like what I have seen."

I hated the way he said it, as if he knew me better than I knew myself. "Whatever's behind those doors, I'm sure it's none of your business."

"On the contrary," Algernon said, his voice a low

rumble in the back of my skull. "I consider everything about you my business."

I stood, stepping back from the desk, wanting to create some distance from the invisible presence, even if the distance was an illusion. "Not everything."

A brief pause, then, almost gently, he replied, "Oh, but it is. You've invited me into your life, even if unintentionally. Our fates are intertwined now, like it or not. You are Dorian Gray and I am your picture in the attic - though I have no intention of remaining just that."

With those words, his voice and the pressure in my skull vanished as abruptly as they had appeared.

FOURTEEN

Great, here we go again. I was back in the damned
corridor.

For all I knew, the corridor in my early childhood home might have looked completely different to the
one I was standing in now. How was I supposed to know?
The half-sunken memory that inspired this recurring nightmare had long since subsumed any actual memories I
might have had either of the place or of the night when my
parents died.

I'd spent countless nights over the past twenty years
and nine months making my way through this warping,
burning dream-corridor with its peeling and coiling,
branch-patterned wallpaper. The length both of the dream
and of the corridor tended to vary, but the way it ended was
always the same.

The corridor, seemingly endless, would suddenly turn a
corner, and there would be the staircase, and the silhouette
of a man blocking it, flames dancing and writhing behind
him as they rose from the ground floor. This was no regular
man, of course, but a vampire.

Much as I'd try, I never could see him clearly. My only impressions were glimpses, the outline of his shoulders, a marble-white hand, a narrow chin, fangs stained with crimson. Dark hair.

The otherworldly laughter that seemed to have emanated from the very walls of the building seemed too deafening to have come from just the one vampire standing at the top of the staircase, but if others had been involved, I didn't know, didn't remember.

I had been six years old that night, but whenever I visited this place in my dreams, I was always my current age.

Ever since my turning, my subconscious had kept stubbornly showing me myself as a mortal. But tonight, after a four-and-a-half month lag, there in the corridor's only mirror was my newly vampiric reflection, deathly pale, the vivid amber of my eyes nearly the same color as the flames rising behind me. When I smiled at my reflection, my fangs showed. I wondered what the nightmare vampire was going to think of this. Would it make any difference?

Unearthly laughter billowed around me as usual as flames fanned out from the walls, from the ceiling, and from the wooden floor below me. The flames themselves were like ghosts, faintly warm as I stepped through them, but not searing or burning.

The burning corridor dream used to scare the living crap out of me. I'd wake up shivering and cold-sweating, but now some of the horror seemed to have gone out of it. In the distance, I could already see the outline of the vampire.

What usually happened was that I'd try to confront him and demand to know who he was. Sometimes I'd run at him with the intention of shoving him down the staircase.

But invariably, before I could reach him, he would envelop me in an intense static, electric sound and sensation, as if the air around him vibrated with raw, unbridled power. The sensation, almost like a forcefield, always overwhelmed me before I could get a word out or lift a finger to attack him, and then the dream would end.

Tonight, as I approached, I felt a shift in the dynamic; the atmosphere between us was different. The anticipation of discovering whether my turning had granted me any semblance of power over him made my heart race.

"Who are you?" I demanded, my voice echoing down the flaming hallway as I advanced. "You have to tell me this time."

The vampire's eyes glowed with an unearthly light as I drew closer, their intensity piercing through the haze of smoke and fire. He seemed to think he could break my resolve with a mere glance. I stopped mere feet away from him, closer than I had ever been before. The realization sent a thrill through my veins

"You've changed," he noted, his tone a strange mix of surprise and sorrow. His voice resonated with a hollow echo, as if emerging from the very depths of the inferno surrounding us. "I had so hoped that the darkness would never touch you. But of course, it was inevitable."

"Is that why you wanted me to die all those years ago - to prevent this?" I demanded, the flames casting erratic shadows across my face.

"Why, yes, as a matter of fact. It was better that you die than become one of us."

His admission hit me like a punch to the gut, but at least we were finally getting somewhere.

"You still haven't answered my first question," I pointed

out, my frustration boiling over. "Tell me who you are. I've been waiting for so long for you to tell me."

His form began to dissolve, dissipating into the smoke and flames. The corridor around me fell silent, the roaring inferno extinguishing as suddenly as if a giant had blown them out, leaving only darkness and the lingering scent of burning.

"Come back!" I demanded. "Aren't you supposed to be the scary demon in this nightmare?"

But there was no response, just the oppressive silence and the fading echoes of my own voice. I stood alone in the suddenly dark corridor, my heart pounding.

"Hey, come back!" I called again, but he was gone, and of course, there was no answer.

Instead, I jolted awake, the remnants of the dream clinging to me like cobwebs.

The confines of my casket felt suffocating. I flung the lid open with a loud bang and practically flew out, crossing the floor to the window in a few strides. I yanked it open, letting the crisp breeze wash over me, a welcome contrast to the oppressive heat of the dream.

The evening outside was calm and still, the only sounds were the engine of a single car making its way up Swain's Lane, weaving between the East and West sides of Highgate Cemetery, and the faint rustle of the branches of the trees in the wintry garden.

Standing by the open window, I took a deep breath, trying to calm down. The cool night air wasn't helping much.

The dream vampire had alluded to wanting to kill me to stop me from becoming what he was. But why would he assume, or know, that I would become a vampire when I grew up? My turning hadn't exactly been a planned event. What did he know about my fate that I didn't? The questions circled in my mind, along with a sinister whisper that refused to be silenced. "It was better that you die than become one of us."

The car that had been creeping uphill now came to a stop at the gate. The soft pool of streetlamp light illuminated a familiar figure stepping out. It was Lyrica, back from her European travels.

Before the driver could get out to assist her, she had already opened the cab's back door and retrieved a large, battered leather suitcase that looked like it had been around since the Victorian era. In fact, I was pretty sure I'd seen it in the attic the first time I'd explored it. Like much of her wardrobe, it had the aura of another century - though she had at least been practical enough to have it customized with wheels.

Lyrica paused by the gate, glancing up at the mansion. I raised my hand in greeting, and she spotted me, offering a faintly rueful wave in return. Her shoulders were drawn up. Even from a distance, I could see the tension in her posture.

I watched as she began the long trek up the winding path, dragging her suitcase behind her. By the time I made it downstairs, she had just stepped into the great hall, setting her suitcase to one side.

It seemed oddly timed that she should return just a few nights after I'd found Jeremy dead. Lyrica had no phone, so no one could have contacted her to deliver the news of Jeremy Gently's demise. But somehow, it seemed, she knew.

She was dressed in a long black gown that suited mourning, though that wasn't unusual for her. Her midnight-black hair, usually falling in a silky curtain around her shoulders, was pinned back with an antique-looking silver barrette. As she removed both the barrette and her long lace gloves, her gaze shifted to meet mine. Though invisible, I could feel an abyss-black cloud of despair hovering over her.

"Harlan, please tell me that no one has perished?" Her deep blue eyes glimmered with an anxious shadow. "As you can see, I have hastened to conclude my travels. I sensed that something was amiss and feared the worst."

"It's Jeremy Gently." I hesitated. "Maybe you should sit down for this."

Jeremy had been Lyrica's solicitor since 1969 - her only mortal friend, as far as I knew. Though she'd lived in the mansion since her reawakening that year, Lyrica had remained a recluse. Before Sebastian and I came along, Jeremy had been her only link to the surrounding world.

Lyrica's frown deepened, but a flicker of fear darkened her eyes. "What dire fate has befallen him?"

I held her gaze, and she understood before I said a word. After a brief pause, I murmured, "I found him."

"You found him?" She moved, more like glided, over to the staircase, where she sank onto the third step as if suddenly drained of all strength.

I followed her and sat beside her on the wide step. Lyrica's breath came slow and deliberate as she pressed her fingers to her temples. Her long hair cascaded down like a silken veil, half-concealing her face, making her look like one of the sorrowful figures carved into the woodwork of the mansion's balustrades above us.

"I went to his office," I began. "Remember when you suggested I talk to him about how he found me?"

Lyrica nodded, her head bowed. "And you found him dead." Her voice was low and hollow.

"Yes. Actually, it was worse than that." I didn't offer more. She would ask if she really wanted to know.

Slowly, Lyrica shook her head. When she looked up, her eyes shimmered with blood tears that welled up but didn't spill. "I've known Jeremy longer than I've known any other mortal," she said quietly. "He was a dear friend. A rare thing in this world."

"I'm really sorry," I said softly, reaching over and squeezing her hand. Her grip tightening around my fingers.

"When you say it was worse than him simply being dead, what precisely do you mean?"

"I found him gutted. There's no better way to put it. Everything was strewn across the floor. My best guess is that he must have pissed someone off, angered someone. Not someone human, though. I'm no forensic expert, but it looked like someone had ripped him open with his bare hands. Or her bare hands, I guess, but that's probably not the case. I've informed the Society, but they won't let me help investigate. I'm still only handling warrants." I sighed and wondered if I should mention my meeting with Evander Eve. His request to bring Lyrica his love suddenly whispered through my mind.

Lyrica frowned thoughtfully. "It has to be someone with a grudge against you. Or me. Or perhaps the family." She sighed deeply. "Clearly, the the wretch responsible for this heinous act wished to silence Jeremy, prevent him from divulging anything to you."

Releasing my hand and rising from the stairs, she said, "I must reach out to Jeremy's wife and daughters, to see if there is anything I might do to ease their sorrow. And I must, of course, ensure that they do not turn to Gabriel for the funeral arrangements - Jeremy would have absolutely loathed that."

"Lyrica?"

"Yes?" She paused, glancing back at me over her shoulder.

"When are you going to tell me? About how you or Jeremy tracked me down, why you sent my grandparents into hiding, and about Evander Eve? When are you going to tell me what someone killed Jeremy to keep him from sharing?"

Lyrica was upset - it wasn't fair of me to push her to reveal whatever she was keeping locked away right now. But the words had already slipped out, and now they hung oppressively in the space between us.

She froze. "Who told you about all of this?"

"Gabriel did."

"I cannot fathom," Lyrica said, her eyes narrowing, "what Gabriel's motives are, but I know he will say whatever serves his purposes - whatever they might be at this particular moment."

With that, she turned on her heel, her long skirt swirling around her ankles as she grabbed her suitcase and wheeled it away toward the parlor. She had never been so curt with me before. I must have struck a nerve.

I followed her. "Lyrica, don't just walk away like that."

She paused a few steps into the parlor, glancing back at me again, her eyes flashing with anger. Beneath that anger, I could see a roiling storm of pain.

Then suddenly, with a sigh that seemed to deflate her, she abandoned her retreat and let herself sink into one of the high-backed armchairs by the cold, empty fireplace, the leather creaking softly beneath her. She buried her face in her hands for a moment. "I know you are right," she half-whispered from behind them. "I suppose I do owe you the truth."

I slid into the armchair opposite her, waiting for her to speak. The parlor was plunged in darkness - neither of us needed light to see beyond the silvery-blue moonlight casting long, sharp rectangles on the wooden floorboards.

"As you know," she began slowly, choosing each word with care, "I shut myself away in my casket and slumbered in the Thornhill family tomb from 1861 to 1969."

I nodded. I already knew this much.

She drew another breath, as if preparing to dive into something deep and murky. "I shall keep it brief. If you desire a more detailed account, I can provide it another night. For now, I am weary and shall simply give you the gist of it."

Upon my awakening in the summer of 1969, I encountered Jeremy Gently. He was one of the youths who had broken into the tomb and, in doing so, unintentionally woke me. Despite that, he became my familiar - my human servant, my solicitor, and, in time, my friend.

At the time, I had no intention of interfering with any mortal descendants the family might have. Yet, I couldn't resist the urge to check up on them. So, I tasked Jeremy with finding out if there were any left. It didn't take him long to unearth, so to speak, a living branch of our accursed family tree: Alastair Hartenbrook, the last living descendant of Augustine Hartenbrook. Despite the different surname, Alastair was a Thornhill through and through.

I was pleased to learn that Alastair was a happy and healthy man with a thriving wine-importing business and a loving wife, Christabel. By the time I found them, they were expecting their first child.

Under my instructions, Jeremy became their solicitor and would report back to me on how they were faring. Initially, I had no intention of interfering in their lives - they seemed blissfully unaware of the Thornhill legacy.

But then, I started receiving what I could only interpret as death threats - dead foxes turning up on the mansion's doorstep. To this day, I don't know who left them there, but the message was clear. Someone knew what I was and wanted me to be aware that I might be in danger.

Soon after, Alastair and Christabel began receiving similar threats, and worse. It became evident that someone, other than myself or Jeremy, knew of our familial connection. Could it have been Gabriel, Evander, or someone else entirely? Perhaps the same person was responsible for the mysterious deaths of other Thornhills over the years. If you've spoken with Gabriel, as you've implied, you might know that quite a few of your ancestors met untimely ends.

Faced with these escalating threats, I suppose paranoia got the better of me. One night, I appeared in Alastair and Christabel's home. I told them everything - my story, the family's cursed history - and urged them to flee London. I impressed upon them the importance of protecting their unborn child, your mother. I pleaded with them to change their name, to break away from the family. The surname "Thorne," short for Thornhill, but subtly altered, was my suggestion.

They left the country soon after, splitting their time between France and Austria. Per my instructions, they never shared their precise location with me, but I received a few letters over the years. It seemed they had successfully shaken off the shadow that loomed over me and the mansion.

Eventually the death threats that I had been receiving stopped, as suddenly as they had started.

As for my own descendants, because, yes, I do have descendants, if you must know, I was never able to find any trace of them.

I have Evander Eve to thank for this. As you may have already guessed, he and I have, well, a history.

I left him out of my story when I told it to you the first time. And I'm sorry I did. All I can say is that I couldn't bear to revisit it. Perhaps I'm still ashamed of my naivete, or maybe I'm still wounded. Love, as it turns out, can be the cruelest of all curses.

And by extension, I neglected to mention our daughter. Even after all this time, I suppose you could say that my Victorian-era sensibilities, the shame of having given birth to a child out of wedlock, still hangs over me, silencing me whenever I try to speak of it.

I met Evander here, at Thornhill Mansion, in 1858.

Truly, I blame Emily Brontë for how quickly and easily I fell for him. I'd recently read *Wuthering Heights*, and Evander was like Heathcliff come to life - only more polished, more alluring. He was sophisticated, powerful, and daring. A world traveler. I was young and hopelessly naive. He showed a genuine interest in me when there were so many other women he could have pursued. Inevitably, I was drawn to him.

Evander wasn't yet a vampire at this point. Had he been, he would never have succeeded in entrancing me. Gabriel was the first vampire I ever encountered. My instincts picked up on the darkness of vampirism the moment I laid eyes on him. While everyone else melted like butter in his presence, I was terrified of him. That hasn't changed much.

Evander and I never had an official relationship. But I saw him at every event I attended, and each time, he would talk to me as if there was no one else in the room. He knew all my favorite books, could recite my favorite poems from memory. He made me laugh. Over time, I grew comfortable around him, lowering my guards with just a smile or a well-placed comment.

You can easily imagine what happened next. He swore he loved me, but when it came to the point of choosing, he wasn't willing to abandon his life to tie himself to me, or to our child.

Yes, we had a child. A daughter I was forced to entrust to Evander and his wife to raise.

My parents knew, of course. They weren't angry, just concerned I'd ruined my chances of ever finding a proper suitor. Venedict and Octavia knew as well. And Clyde, naturally.

WE SAT in silence for a few moments, her words settling like dust. When it became clear Lyrica had said all she intended to about Evander for now, I quietly added, "I've met him."

"Indeed?" Lyrica's eyes widened. "I heard he still owns an establishment of some description, down by the river."

"Nightside of Eden. I went there recently to deliver a warning - people, mortals, have been disappearing from his club." I grimaced. "He also asked me to bring you his love."

"Well, he can have it back," Lyrica snapped, her voice sharp. "Just as I've returned all his letters and other belated declarations of tenderness."

There was a pause before she murmured, "The last time we spoke in person was in 1860."

"You've been ghosting him since 1860?" I couldn't help but be impressed. Ghosting Aubrey for a few months was nothing in comparison.

"Ghosting? If only," Lyrica replied with a hint of amusement. "Dabbling in the spiritual realm can easily backfire, or cost more than one is willing to pay. No, I've met every attempt at contact with the coldest silence I could muster."

One thing you could say about this family, they knew how to hold a grudge. But I could see why Lyrica felt betrayed by the man who'd refused to marry her when she'd fallen pregnant, at a time when that kind of thing was beyond scandalous.

Then again, it had been over a century. Not that I was defending him, or suggesting he deserved a second chance. After meeting Evander and sensing his dismissive attitude to his missing patrons, he wasn't someone I felt any urge to defend.

"If I see him at the Games and he asks me to pass along his love again, I'll tell him exactly where to shove it," I promised her.

"The Games?"

Now, I was the one who had some explaining to do.

FIFTEEN

E ve Hall was nestled within the rugged beauty of Dorset's southeastern coast, near Burning Cliff and several hiking trails, but far away from any neighboring buildings or villages. Its location was coincidental, but Evander's ancestors couldn't have chosen a better spot for a vampire's lair.

According to records I'd found in the Van Helsing Society's archives, the Eve family had amassed a fortune during the Industrial Revolution, and prior to that, they'd lived the high life as feudal lords and ladies for generations. Aside from the infamous double murder of his wife and brother in 1868 - and the subsequent suspicion that led to his exile abroad - Evander had never known anything but unbridled privilege. Overall, I didn't feel too guilty about my complicity in Gabriel's plans to persuade Evander to part with a few of his properties.

The approach to Eve Hall was nothing short of majestic. An allee, lined with ancient trees whose leafless winter branches formed a natural canopied archway, led to the heart of the estate. It gave way to a gravelly driveway and then to the Hall itself, which was illuminated from below by several colorful projector lights. In the middle of the driveway, a fountain glowed red, lit from beneath by submerged lights that created the illusion that the fountain was filled with blood. Nice touch.

If I had to venture a guess, I would say that the main building was easily five centuries old. Constructed of stone, its facade was well-kept but inevitably weathered by the coastal winds and rain that had swept over it for centuries. The architecture was Gothic, featuring plenty of intricate detailing and grand arched windows overlooking the sprawling and beautifully maintained grounds. Here and there, I even spotted a few gargoyles, some of them serving double duty as drainpipe exits.

The estate grounds stretched the length of a football field in every direction, except behind the main building, where the land dropped away abruptly into a sheer, dizzying cliff, plunging straight down into the vast, dark expanse of the English Channel below.

I had opted to drive myself to the Games. Arriving solo would send a better message than showing up with either Gabriel or Csilla. Besides, Venedict had been in an impressively sulky mood while I packed my car, and I didn't want to make it worse by having either of his undead exes roll up to the wrought iron gate to pick me up. Both had offered.

As I lugged my large hardshell suitcase down through the mansion, Venedict had sidled up to me, bombarding me with questions about the Games. I'd pointed out that it wasn't too late for him to change his mind, that there was plenty of space in the car if he, and maybe Octavia, wanted to come along after all. I knew for a fact Octavia wanted to go - she'd told me as much - but she felt obliged to display loyalty to Venedict by staying behind. Needless to say,

Lyrica was also refusing to go and was utterly aghast that I had backed myself into owing Gabriel a favor.

"How dare you suggest such a thing?" Venedict had shouted at me, his voice echoing through the grand hall before he turned on his heel and stormed up the grand staircase to his turret. "The last thing I need is to watch Gabriel and Csilla rubbing shoulders with the Count and gossiping about me! You should be more sensitive to my needs. I bared my soul to you, and for what?"

Circling the driveway in front of Eve Hall, I bypassed the valet who stood waiting. I wasn't about to hand over my car keys with the boot full of stakes, knives, a crossbow, and a gun. The valet's eyes followed me with both curiosity and annoyance as I parked the car myself. I wasn't going to let anyone near my arsenal.

In addition to the valet, another inconvenience was Lord Eve's security staff at the entrance. They were welding metal detectors, and I guess it was a sensible precaution to ensure that the sanctity of Eve Hall remained intact.

I'd have to leave my stakes and knives in the car, at least for now. But before I stepped out, I angled the rearview mirror towards me, lifted my tongue, and placed three razor blades under it. A few razor blades could hardly count as weapons, could they?

The razor blades I preferred weren't the flimsy type you get from breaking apart a regular razor - they were traditional stainless steel, sharp and sturdy enough to slit a throat through to the bone. I had done it before. And once, I'd shoved one into a vampire's eyeball. I can still recall the sickening wet sound it made.

I killed the engine and stepped out into the cool, crisp air. It carried the scent of burning wood and the sea's briny tang from the nearby cliffs.

Evander's security team insisted on running my luggage, including Algernon's haunted mirror, through a scanner. At least they didn't open and go through my suitcase.

Once I had slipped through the security checkpoint, I discreetly removed the razor blades from my mouth and transferred them to my back pocket.

The foyer gave way to a grand hall with a high arched ceiling, an ostentatious winding staircase, and church-like stained glass windows. A profusion of potted ferns and tropical looking flowers that I didn't have names for hung suspended from chains from the ceiling at different heights. They filled the air with a flowery, slightly musky scent that seemed to fit the space. Everything was beautifully lit, a blend of soft atmospheric lighting and bright pools of blood red neon. Evander knew how to set the stage.

The rooms and parlors beyond the hall were already abuzz with voices, laughter and the rustling of movement. Music drifted out into the hall, the same strange blend of harpsichord and something electronic that the DJ at Night-side had been playing, only now the harpsichord elements were by far the most dominant.

How many vampires were already here, and how many more were coming? A hundred, maybe more. I suppressed a shiver. I knew logically that I was one of them now, but I'd never been in a place with so many bloodsuckers gathered under one roof. It was setting my teeth on edge.

The count himself stood at the foot of the stairs to greet all of his guests. He was flanked by two younger dark-haired, gray-eyed vampires that I figured had to be members of the Eve family.

Evander, smartly dressed in a black silk suit, was gesturing animatedly as he spoke to a group of three sisters, all with long, corn-gold hair and nearly identical shimmering black dresses. After a few minutes, the trio disappeared into a vast parlor visible through an open door.

I hadn't seen the count since I brought him his warning at the club, and he had seemed ambivalent about me then. Now, though, he gave me a warm smile as he caught sight of me.

"Harlan Thornhill," he announced. His handshake was firm as he clasped my hand and then clapped me on the shoulder with a friendly vigor. "Welcome, welcome. Let me introduce you to my niece, Holly, and my nephew, Roderick."

Evander gestured to indicate each of them.

Holly had soft, youthful features, and long, nearly black hair that cascaded down her back in tight curls. She wore a gossamer peach gown and greeted me with a shy nod.

Roderick, dressed in a midnight-blue suit woven with subtle silver threads, had his dark brown hair neatly parted in the middle, framing his boyish good looks. Despite his clean-cut appearance, his eyes, which met mine evenly, sparked with an intensity that manged to be both playful and menacing at once.

"Roderick," Evander suggested, "why don't you show Harlan his accommodations? And explain about the green-stemmed glasses. I want you back here in five minutes to greet the Northwoods."

Roderick gave his uncle an obedient nod. His demeanor was polished, but the crooked smile he flashed me and the slightly fevered gleam in his eyes hinted that the polish didn't filter down to the deeper layers.

Roderick led the way up the windy stairs and down the dimly lit corridors of Eve Hall and I followed, eager to get away from the buzz of vampire activity downstairs. I could sense them, in the parlor just behind the great hall, like an overly intense cloud of static energy.

"I better explain about the glasses," Roderick said, casting a glance over his shoulder as we made our ascent up the grand, winding marble staircase. Its filigree wrought-iron railing hinted that it must have been installed much later than the rest of the building. It had probably replaced a much older, wooden staircase, similar to the one at Thornhill Mansion.

"There will be servers downstairs circulating with glasses on trays - you can well imagine what the glasses contain. The green-stemmed glasses are for vegetarians, so to speak. Means the blood is sourced from a hospital and isn't freshly brought in from the kitchen."

"What goes on in the kitchen?" I asked.

Roderick chuckled. "Given your profession, I cannot tell you."

We reached the third floor and moved along the corridor, its ancient stone walls lined with original paintings - mostly landscapes of the local coastline, including several depictions of Eve Hall throughout the centuries. Beyond the tall, narrow arched windows, the landscape rolled on in endless waves of green.

"This place is gorgeous," I said sincerely.

"I'm well aware of it," Roderick replied, turning slightly to flash me a grin. "My ancestors built Eve Hall in the late 16th century, and we've managed to hold onto it ever since."

We passed a large family portrait set on the grounds outside. It featured a slightly younger Evander standing proudly in front of the stately building, with a beautiful strawberry blonde woman in a long, flowing white summer dress beside him. Three little girls stood around them, the eldest clinging to her father's hand.

"Uncle Evander, Aunt Tessa, and their daughters: Emmeline, Victorine, Felicity." Roderick indicated each in turn, as if he were a tour guide who'd given this spiel a million times.

"And here we are," Roderick announced, opening the door to my accommodations. The suite was grandiose, a masterpiece of Gothic design, with a bedroom dominated by a four-poster bed crowned with a carved wooden canopy. There was also a casket, so I had options. An adjoining parlor was filled with dark, ornate furniture, and the Gothic arches of each window were framed by rich velvet drapes that just about masked the rolled-up blackout curtains. My suitcase and Algernon's black-shrouded mirror were already neatly placed by the door, courtesy of Evander's staff.

"All the heads of the bloodlines are on the fourth floor," Roderick continued. "Gabriel has the corner suite at the right end of the corridor. Csilla is next door to you, and Elizabeth - Gabriel's sister, the one he claims to have heroically retrieved from a plague pit - is next door to Csilla. Uncle says she's studying to become a surgeon, or some such thing, so he had the bright idea to let her get some practical experience as a medic for the Games. Uncle is much in favor of the concept of women doctors. Well, it is a shame none of the other Thornhills could come. I would have liked to see them."

Roderick walked over to one of the arched windows overlooking the grounds before turning around to face me, framed by the window's arch.

"Just a point of curiosity," he said, his gaze locking onto

mine. "Is it true that Gabriel killed you?" He tilted his head slightly, studying me.

"It's true. With a bit of help from his brother. He wouldn't have managed it on his own."

If Thomas hadn't blindsided me, I would have put a knife through Gabriel's heart. And then, I would have decapitated him. I wasn't sure how to feel about that now. Ambivalent, I guess.

"And yet here you are," Roderick observed, "competing on his behalf. I know Gabriel can be persuasive. He's talked me into a few things over the past century and a half, including," he added with a raised brow, "some that I really do not care to recount. But this? Well, it boggles the mind."

His eyes were sharp, expectant as he leaned forward, waiting for some intriguing explanation. The silence stretched between us, and when it became clear that I wasn't going to offer more, Roderick pushed away from the window. "Very well, should we head back downstairs? Uncle will be most exasperated with me if I am not there to greet the Northwoods." He sighed. "The Northwoods are insufferable, the lot of them."

As we reached the main hall, the sound of laughter and clinking glasses floated through the air. The guests had started to gather. The Northwoods were among them - five in total. There were a man and a woman, and three children, a pair of little twin girls and a slightly older boy. They all had the same gaunt expressions, dark eyes, and prominent noses, hinting that they were an actual, traditional family unit consisting of a father, mother, and children. All they needed was an undead golden retriever to complete the picture.

Roderick went over to greet them while I continued next door.

The grand ballroom at Eve Hall was alive with energy. Crystal chandeliers hung from the ornate ceiling far above, scattering shimmering light across the walls and the crowd below. From one corner, the rich, timeless melodies of a live classical ensemble filled the air, while from the other, the industrial beats of Lord Eve's favorite DJ pulsed. Somehow, the two genres merged into a soundtrack that felt perfectly fitting.

Conversations ebbed and flowed around me as I weaved through the throngs beneath Count Eve's expansive roof. The women wore gowns that ranged from modern styles hugging them like second skins to elaborate, historical pieces that swept the floor in cascades of velvet and silk. The men were dressed in tailored suits, some cut in modern fashion, others in aristocratic styles from centuries past, complete with velvet coats and silk cravats. I was beginning to understand why Gabriel had insisted on making my wardrobe choices for me - left to my own devices, I would have been hopelessly underdressed. Now I wasn't, but I still felt out of place.

I could feel the pings of attention as many pairs of eyes found me or followed me - I was both a newcomer to the blood and the vampire hunter whose presence, I knew some had protested.

For a fleeting second, I thought I spotted Sebastian somewhere in the crowd, and the sight nearly froze me in place. I blinked, and he was gone. It was just someone who looked like him - pale skin, blue eyes, and raven-black hair swept back from a tall forehead. Sebastian wasn't here. And he wasn't a vampire.

I stopped abruptly when a small group of vampires closed in around me just a few steps into the room.

"You must be Harlan Thornhill," said the female

vampire standing at the forefront. "I am Dolores Pender-gast. Gabriel hasn't failed to mention you. I am delighted to meet you. These are my friends, Darius Marwood and Tibor Beauchamp."

Dolores. I was pretty sure she was the friend Gabriel had mentioned gifting him the two undead dobermans.

She looked to be in her late forties or early fifties when immortality had claimed her, with long copper hair threaded with silver and vivid cornflower-blue eyes. She wore a black dress that highlighted every curve and cascaded to the floor, the fabric shimmering with dark red metallic patterns.

Darius appeared to be around sixty at the time of his turning. Distinguished, with silver-gray hair and eyes the same color, he wore a black-on-black velvet suit with a starched white collar, complete with a cane tipped with a jackal's head. He looked perfectly suited to the mid-2020s but would have been just as at home in the mid-19th century.

Tibor appeared to be around my age. He was a big guy, both tall and slightly chubby, with an impeccably groomed pencil mustache and chestnut brown hair pulled back into a short ponytail. He wore a deep burgundy velvet blazer over a black shirt, and his nearly black eyes glinted sharply as he regarded me.

"Darius Marwood," said the older vampire, clasping my hand firmly. "There are those who oppose your presence here, but I would like you to know that I am not among them. Rather, I am intrigued - most intrigued. You are not what I would have expected based on your reputation. Though I see you bear the scars of your vampire-slaying past." His gaze lingered on the scars threading up my collarbone to my neck.

Darius withdrew a black-and-white business card from his breast pocket and offered it to me. "Should you ever need a lawyer - one who understands, shall we say, the peculiarities of our condition - you need only reach out to me."

I accepted his card without comment.

"I have heard a few things about you," Tibor interjected, his tone clipped. "From Valentina Clark and others. Is it true you killed her husband, Nolan?"

"I did," I replied. "But it was a work thing, nothing personal."

Tibor's expression only soured further. Something told me he had been among the detractors urging Evander to ban me from the Games.

"How do you reconcile being a hunter with being one of us?" Dolores asked, shifting the conversation. "I mean no disrespect - I am genuinely curious."

"That's easy," I said. "I was a hunter first. I've only been a vampire for a few minutes by comparison."

"Did you bring stakes here to Eve Hall?" Darius asked. His eyes gleamed, and his tone was almost hopeful.

"I did," I answered honestly, "but I had to leave them in my car because of the security check."

A stunned silence fell over the small group. For one drawn-out moment, no one knew how to react, but then Darius and Dolores erupted into laughter. The sound was rich and melodious, dissipating the tension that had hung in the air moments before. Tibor chuckled softly, but his eyes remained stone-cold, boring into me.

The conversation moved on, but I wasn't paying any attention. I'd caught another glimpse of Sebastian's doppelganger in the crowd. This time he was in profile, engaged in an animated discussion with a snow-haired vampire wearing a boxy pinstripe suit. This was bizarre. He looked too much like Sebastian for it to be a coincidence.

My mind was already piecing together a theory as to who the Sebastian lookalike was: Clyde, Lyrica's long-lost brother, once Octavia's briefly wedded husband, and another one of Venedict's fledglings. I tried to hold back from jumping to conclusions, but who else could it be?

"Excuse me," I mentioned to the others before I began navigating through the crowd.

As I made my way through, I caught sight of Roderick attempting to catch my attention, signaling for me to join his group. When I declined with a shake of my head, he theatrically tilted his head back and swept his hand slowly across his throat in what was either his peculiar sense of humor, a dark promise, or a bit of both.

I sidestepped a largeish, animatedly gesturing group of vampires and stood in front of Sebastian's mirror image.

"Clyde?"

He turned to face me. It was like looking at Sebastian but with subtle differences. Eyes like deep pools of midnight blue and elegant, narrow features set in a complexion that could have rivaled the marble-like pallor of his undead existence even in life. Long raven black hair, slightly curly and swept back from a high forehead completed the picture. He wore a simple yet elegant black ensemble, the sharp lines of his tailored blazer contrasting against the crisp, snow-white shirt beneath.

Only the crowd was billowing and moving behind him while he stood still as a statue, rooted to the spot. Then his mouth opened slightly.

"Clyde Hartenbrook," he said, confirming it. His eyes narrowed as he tilted his head slightly to the side. "And you are... Harlan, is it not? I heard you would be here, but I am afraid that is just about all I know about you. Let me take a guess - Venedict escaped the confinement that Lyrica and I subjected him to, and he turned you, hoping to, perhaps, complete the family?"

Clyde being out of the loop made sense. Lyrica had mentioned that he ventured off to the US in 1861 shortly after becoming a vampire, and she had barely heard from him since.

"It was something like that," I replied. He looked so much like Sebastian that I had to restrain the impulse to pull him into a hug. But something about his aura told me that he wouldn't want me to.

I held my hand out to him instead, palm up. He hesitated before taking it, giving it a quick squeeze before letting go.

"Well," he said, his brow furrowing like a passing cloud. "I'm sorry you've been dragged into all of this, into this family. I've heard from a few here tonight that you were a vampire hunter, so I imagine it must have been doubly difficult for you, trying to come to terms with the curse." Clyde paused, his eyes briefly scanning me from head to toe before narrowing. "You couldn't have been much older than twenty-five when you were turned. At least half a century of life, stolen from you."

"Realistically? I might not have made it to thirty," I admitted. "Hunting is a pretty hazardous job. And I had, well, still have, a reputation for being a little reckless."

"Reckless?" Clyde said thoughtfully. "I see. A well-known Thornhill flaw." His gaze lingered, a mix of pity and disdain.

Based on Lyrica's glowing account, I had expected Clyde to be a little more approachable. But standing here with him, I found him cold and aloof, and it was hard not to take his standoffish attitude personally. For Lyrica's sake, though, I did my best to curb my knee-jerk response of disliking him.

"So why are you here?" I asked, trying to shift the topic. "Are you competing in the Games?"

"Oh no," Clyde chuckled, a note of surprise in his laughter. "No, I am merely here as Lord Eve's guest. He extended a very gracious invitation. You could say I am here to reconnect with some old friends after spending more than a century abroad. Afterward, I plan to visit Thornhill Mansion to catch up with all the family. Naturally, I'd appreciate it if you kept my planned visit a secret from Lyrica - or anyone at the mansion, for that matter, if you happen to speak to them."

"Sure, I can keep it zipped if you're aiming for a surprise," I agreed. Lyrica would be beside herself to be reunited with her long-lost brother, and Sebastian would be intrigued to meet his Victorian-era doppelgänger. I wasn't too sure how Venedict and Octavia would react, but I offered anyway, "You're welcome to ride back with me after the Games, if you like."

"I'd prefer not to," Clyde replied curtly. Then, without another word, he turned and disappeared into the moving throng of guests, letting the crowd swallow him up.

CHAPTER
SIXTEEN

I wasn't going to let him simply walk away from me. The doors had barely whispered shut behind Clyde when I pushed them open and followed him into the adjacent parlor.

The room was steeped in shadows, lit by the soft, crimson glow of glass chandeliers that hung from a ceiling lost in darkness. Ghostly white sconces clung to the wood-paneled walls, while large windows framed a dramatic night view of the estate's beautifully illuminated fountains and pathways.

Several groups of vampires congregated around the room, their low murmurs barely reaching my ears as I focused on the main attraction, a large, ornate poker table dominating the center of the space. A handful of the self-crowned elite of London's vampire society were gathered under the watchful eye of a grand portrait of some ancient Eve ancestor. Evander sat directly beneath the portrait, likely to emphasize his status. What a self-important prick. He was flanked by Holly and a male vampire with short-cropped, grey-peppered black hair.

The only other familiar faces were Gabriel's and Csilla's - I hadn't seen either of them arrive, but here they were. Both had pulled out all the stops, dressed to impress. Csilla was stunning in a black silk dress with daring lace cutouts and long lace gloves, a diamond-encrusted choker glinting at her throat. Gabriel wore a well-tailored emerald suit, a dark silver tie pin shaped like a coffin, set with tiny emeralds, gleaming against a black silk tie.

Clyde stopped just a few paces into the room and stood motionless, his shoulders visibly tensing up.

"Gabriel," he said frostily.

The expressions of the vampires at the main poker table had ranged from intensely focused to mildly entertained as they laid their cards down - now the game paused, everyone's attention drawn to Clyde. I stopped a few paces behind him, waiting to see where this would go.

"Clyde, what a surprise. Snazzy suit." Gabriel rose with a flourish, extending his hand, though Clyde pointedly ignored it. "It has been quite some time. Are you not in the least pleased to see me?" Gabriel's cordial smile made something in Clyde's jaw twitch involuntarily.

"And why would I be?" Clyde retorted.

"Perhaps," Gabriel gave a nonchalant shrug, "because you owe your immortal existence to me. That is no small thing."

"Indeed," Clyde said. "I suppose I should thank you for the eternal journey you've thrust upon me. If not for your meddling with Venedict, I might have enjoyed my mortal life, lived it fully and happily." His words dripped with resentment for a path he clearly regretted.

"Would you really have preferred that?" Gabriel's voice was laced with skepticism. "Do you not remember the myriad dangers of that era? The pestilence, the accidents that could claim a life unexpectedly, and often did?"

"You know I am a man of science," Clyde said, ignoring Gabriel's questions, stepping closer, his voice tight with barely contained anger. "But do you know what has been the primary - nay, the all-consuming - focus of my research for the past century and a half?"

"I can tell you're bursting to tell me," Gabriel remarked dryly. "Indeed, I doubt I could stop you if I tried."

Holly giggled, as if Gabriel had said something unimaginably clever.

Ignoring Gabriel's thinly veiled sarcasm and Holly's laughter, Clyde continued, "Vampirism. I have been delving into both the known universe and the realms beyond, seeking a cure for vampirism, a way to purge the poison you introduced into my lineage."

"Any luck?" Gabriel asked, feigning politeness.

"None whatsoever. Zilch. Zero. I have reluctantly concluded that this curse is permanent, irrevocable. Final."

"Well, that is a relief. Now you have eternity ahead of you to do something actually meaningful."

Clyde's restraint shattered. With a blur of supernatural speed, he rushed forward, vaulting over the poker table - eliciting gasps and a delighted shriek from Holly - and landed on the other side, seizing Gabriel by the lapels, his expression blazing with fury.

A flicker of annoyance flashed across Gabriel's face. The room fell into a hushed silence, the poker game momentarily forgotten as every vampire in the room was captivated by the unfolding drama. The only sound was the faint crackle of the fireplace at the far end of the parlor.

I was faintly aware of Evander's bodyguards beginning to edge out from the shadowy corners of the room, but they didn't intervene, at least not yet. I felt torn between the instinct to intervene - I didn't want Clyde getting himself into too much trouble - and the urge to let this play out.

"Meaningful?" Clyde spat, his grip tightening. "Do you even understand what you have done? What you have condemned me to?"

Gabriel's lips curled into a mocking smile. "I understand perfectly well, Clyde. But perhaps these are concerns you should discuss with Venedict - he, not I, turned you into this. I am not sure if you recall."

"But it all comes back to you," Clyde insisted, his voice trembling. "I told you, all those years ago, to leave Venedict alone." His voice dropped to a tense near whisper. "I pleaded with you, I *warned* you."

My eyes widened - this was news to me. Had Clyde known what Gabriel was, and what he intended to do before it happened?

"I recall," Gabriel responded, a hint of admiration in his voice. "You were onto me, and you were very brave to stand up to me. I mean that, genuinely."

"And yet, you didn't listen."

"No," Gabriel conceded, "of course not. But I appreciated the effort you put into it."

"And so you chose to condemn my entire bloodline." Clyde's voice broke, the pain evident. "You tainted my lineage with your vile gift, your poisoned blood, over your obsession with Venedict."

Gabriel remained calm, though a glint of malice flickered in his eyes as he began prying Clyde's fingers from his lapels with an air of quiet contempt. "You speak of obsession, but what about your own? A century and a half spent chasing some imaginary cure. You see vampirism as a curse only because you are weak. You wallow in self-pity, blaming me for your misery. It's all so tedious, and frankly, so predictable I could weep."

Clyde's voice dropped, his grip tightening as he yanked Gabriel closer. "You *will* weep, Gabriel. Mark my words - you will pay for what you have done. Perhaps sooner than you think."

"Gentlemen, gentlemen," Evander cut in, his voice ringing clear above the simmering resentments as he rose from his seat at the poker table. He placed a calming hand on both Clyde's and Gabriel's shoulders. "Why not channel this marvellously combative energy into the game? Clyde, Harlan, why don't you join us at the table? Harlan can stand as Csilla's lucky mascot, and Clyde, you can do Gabriel the honor."

The chandelier above the table flickered slightly, as if sensing the hostility coiling in the air below it. Or perhaps Eve Hall had its own ghosts.

Clyde, still tense but visibly reigning in his anger under Evander's influence, gave Gabriel a long look before reluctantly moving towards the table. Gabriel, for his part, smoothed the front of his jacket and offered Clyde a slight, provoking smile as he took his place opposite Csilla.

Csilla, who had been watching the scene unfold with a smirk, patted the chair next to her, her eyes gleaming with mischief. "Come, Harlan. I was just about to send all these boys to school. But I could use a bit of extra luck, and I suppose you owe me some."

As I approached the table, Evander clapped his hands theatrically. "Excellent! Now that we're all here, let's proceed with the game. Remember, gentlemen, and lady," he nodded at Csilla with a half-smile, "this is all in good fun."

The clinking of chips on the plush velvet of the table

and the gentle rustling of cards filled the parlor and started to replace the tension.

I focused on Csilla's whispered advice, trying to absorb her tactics, which seemed to hinge on pure luck and plenty of sly, knowing smiles intended to throw off her opponents. Now that I knew her a little better, the way Csilla played poker seeemd quite revealing about her overall philosophy towards life.

The same might be true for the others at the table. Gabriel maintained a serene, impenetrable expression, his eyes briefly scanning the table before returning to his cards. Benvolio Torrero, seated between me and Evander, played with intense focus, his stern face like a general deciding which soldiers to send into battle. In contrast, Evander's play was full of exuberance, dramatic gestures, broad smiles, and playful eyebrow wiggles.

Seated between Benvolio and Evander, Holly wasn't playing. She simply watched, her cloud-gray eyes frequently drifting towards Gabriel.

Clyde seemed to withdraw into himself, his earlier fury cooled into a simmering resentment that he couldn't quite mask. His eyes briefly met mine, and I caught a fleeting glimpse of something raw and achingly painful. Then his expression clouded over, becoming deliberately unreadable.

Clyde and I hadn't exactly hit it off from the start, but Gabriel's contempt toward my cousin still rubbed me the wrong way. Clyde had been out of line, sure, but was his hatred for Gabriel really so unreasonable? My temper flared, and I impulsively kicked Gabriel's shin under the table.

His head snapped up, and his eyes, initially widening

with surprise, quickly narrowed into slits of dark amusement. "Careful, Harlan," he murmured.

About fifteen minutes later, I did it again, harder this time.

I was filled with instant regret when Gabriel's hand darted under the table like a striking viper and caught my ankle. I quickly tried to retract my leg, but it was too late; his hold only tightened until my eyes watered.

His eyes met mine, glinting with both amusement and challenge.

"Gabriel," I sneered, my voice thick with warning, glaring at him in silent command to let go. But he didn't. Instead, he suddenly yanked me forward, leaving me teetering precariously on the edge of my seat. Any more, and I'd be pulled right onto the floor. He casually placed the heel of my boot on his knee, his fingers still gripping my ankle in a firm, confining hold. Then, without missing a beat, he continued playing poker one-handed, acting as though nothing at all was out of the ordinary.

I was sure I could wrench my leg free with enough force, but any abrupt move to pull away would mean knocking against the table or kicking someone else. I didn't really want to do either, not with an audience.

Csilla's eyes were already shifting between us with a look of what I could only describe as overt glee, and the way Evander's eyes crinkled as he took in my frustrated expression hinted that nothing escaped his notice.

The noise of the poker game filled the room as I twisted my ankle, attempting to slip out of Gabriel's grip using a technique from my martial arts training. But he seemed to sense what I was up to, and every time I tried to shift my position, he changed his grip in response, just enough to keep me from escaping.

Sighing with frustration, I finally saw no other option but to resign myself to the deadlock, waiting for him to be off his guard. I eased back into my chair as far as he would let me.

I was just getting my head back in the game when I noticed his vise-like grip was morphing into something else. His fingers traced a slow, teasing path from my ankle up my calf, sending a faint electric current threading up my leg.

With a sharp, irritable movement, I pulled my leg away, finally managing to free myself without causing a scene.

LATER THAT NIGHT, back in my suite, I unpacked my things and checked on Algernon's mirror. As I unwrapped the black cloth, I found my forefather already there, gazing back at me as if he'd been waiting.

"Well, good evening, son," he said, his low voice echoing slightly, as if it was travelling from the other end of a long corridor. "Have you enjoyed your evening? Though I must insist you spare me the details of mine. I find myself relegated to a state I can scarcely describe as existence - a half-life confined to this accursed mirror."

"Fascinating, Algernon. So, you're going to be there tomorrow night, ready to take me to the other side and back? That's all I want to know."

"You have my word of honor," he said, a little gruffly. "Though I must say, I don't appreciate your tone."

"And you won't try to pull some sneaky trick, like closing the portal behind me?"

"You are only asking me this because it's what you would do," he shot back, a glimmer of amusement in his eyes. "You're a sneaky little weasel, just like Venedict. I, on the other hand, am a man of my word. I will make my presence known, and I will impress all of vampire high society, which, I must point out, overlaps somewhat with the Victorian elite I am accustomed to. I have no doubt that more than a few will recognize and remember me. Csilla and I will keep them entertained while you venture into my realm. Indeed, I rather look forward to my appearance, and I assure you, I will ensure your return, though the journey may come with its own surprises."

How reassuring.

I started to close the wardrobe's doors, but Algernon protested, "Wait! It's awfully dark in here. Can you not place me out in the room? In the corner would be quite suitable."

"I don't think so," I replied, shutting the doors firmly. Almost immediately, there was a knock at the door. It was probably Csilla, wanting to be reassured that Algernon was still game for tomorrow night.

But it wasn't her standing outside in the corridor. It was one of Evander's security staff.

"Lord Eve wishes to see you," he said, his expression unreadable.

Lord Eve wanting to see me could only mean trouble. I regretted mentioning the stakes in my car; it was likely that was already coming back to bite me.

"Sure," I said, feigning nonchalance. "Do you mean right now?"

"No better time than the present, is there?"

I followed the guard through a labyrinth of corridors, ascending several stories up a broad wooden staircase. The sound of voices occasionally drifted through the doors we passed, and we crossed paths with a few vampires navigating the halls. Finally, we came to a stop outside the library on the top floor. It seemed no other guests were up here.

If Evander wanted me to disappear, he could easily make it happen. He commanded enough people, and they were all vampires, leaving me without any real advantage.

"I take it you're unarmed?" the guard asked.

"Completely," I replied.

He still frisked me before allowing me to enter, though his search was half-hearted. Since I was already here and my luggage had been checked upon arrival, he treated it more like a formality, just a box that needed to be ticked.

I pushed the library door open and stepped inside.

"Harlan Thornhill, please, come in." Evander rose from a plush leather chair by the window, surrounded by several others just as luxurious.

The library of Eve Hall consisted of three interconnected rooms with tall, arched ceilings. The central room was adorned in a rich, deep red, while the flanking rooms were painted in a dark, elegant teal. Dark wooden bookshelves, brimming with volumes, extended almost to the arched ceilings. The space was softly lit by contemporary orb-like lamps that cast a warm glow throughout. Scattered among the rows of books were glass jars containing various wet specimens, including a two-headed calf and an impressively large cobra preserved in formaldehyde, which occupied a significant portion of one shelf.

"Evander. Mind if I drop the 'Lord'? It grates on me a little," I said, stepping further into the room. "I can't take you seriously if I have to call you that."

"Certainly, Harlan, be my guest." Evander replied with an amused smile, gesturing toward the plush chair beside his own. The windows behind them framed a panoramic view of the dark, restless sea beyond. "Call me Evander."

I settled into the chair across from him. "So, Evander, tell me why I'm here."

He spread his hands in a gesture of openness, his expression earnest. "I'd like to talk to you. Given the circumstances under which we met, and the things Lyrica may have told you about me, I fear I might have made a less than favorable impression."

I raised an eyebrow, leaning forward slightly. "And why would you be worried about what I think?"

"Our world is small," Evander reasoned. "You'll notice that soon enough. You'll be around the same people for centuries. Whenever possible, I find it's better to get on than to harbor animosities. That's one of the very reasons I created the Games, so we can let it all out and leave each other in peace the rest of the time."

"Like the Purge but for vampires," I remarked dryly.

His lips twitched into a reluctant smile. "I'm not sure I like the comparison, but I suppose I see the parallel. The Games could serve as a suitable arena for channeling energies that might otherwise become... well, potentially destructive."

"Are you talking about Roderick?" The question escaped before I could think.

"Well..." Evander hesitated, watching me, a little guarded. "My nephew can be a little intense, that is true. I suppose you may have heard a few things about him. Yes, I suppose the Games are a healthy outlet for him."

He paused, then added, "I am quite familiar with your family and your bloodline, at least with some of them."

"With Lyrica," I prompted.

"Yes, with Lyrica in particular," he admitted, his expression growing wistful. "And contrary to the impression she might have given you, I did love her. In fact, I think I still might." A cloud passed over his expression. "Alas, Lyrica is slow to forget and even slower to forgive. How any woman can be so soft, so gentle, and yet so cold and unyielding when she wishes to be is beyond me. I suppose this seeming duality is part of the attraction, part of the magic that surrounds her."

His words baffled me a little. They were flowery, sure, but the way he said them made them sound sincere, his voice tinged with genuine emotion.

"She hasn't talked about you," I said, watching his reaction closely. "Or barely."

"How cold." He leaned back, a shadow of pain shimmering in his eyes. But then he straightened up again, the cloud passing. "Well, perhaps that is not such a bad thing. It means I get to tell you our story without competing with her version of events." After a brief pause, he added, almost as an afterthought, "I will be brief."

"Usually when vampires say that, it means it'll take about three nights," I pointed out.

Evander chuckled, the sound rich and genuine. "I promise, I will not prattle on for three nights. I simply want you to know the story from my perspective."

CHAPTER
SEVENTEEN

I was born in 1829. I am a decade older than Lyrica, more or less exactly to the day. Our lives never overlapped until one fateful spring day in 1858. We met at Thornhill Mansion, of all places. That is not really so strange - where else would we have met? Lyrica's family at Thornhill Mansion were the only link she had to the world I inhabited.

I cannot now recall the occasion. An easter soiree of some description, a little gathering of some of Algernon Thornhill's business associates and a gaggle of Lords and Ladies. I intersected both of these categories, of course. Algernon was going through one of his jovial phases and had been nothing but a generous and gracious host throughout the afternoon. Of course, as the evening wore on and he kept emptying his wine glass, his voice rose and his energy crested and bristled in that way of his that set everyone on edge. Even so, the overall mood was light and exuberant, with that undercurrent of threat emanating from Algernon like a low electric hum.

Lyrica was in attendance with her brother Clyde and

their parents, Harold and Emma Hartenbrook. At twenty-nine I was already married, but I had come alone. My wife, Tessa, was too preoccupied carrying on her affair with my brother behind my back to be interested in attending social gatherings like this with me. Despite both of us being in our late twenties, Tessa and I had no children at this point, which was rather unusual. Perhaps she was infertile - perhaps it was me.

As you can probably easily picture, Lyrica had brought a book and was carrying it around all evening. Now and then she would vanish into one of the mansion's many other rooms to read for a few minutes before returning to the party. Her behavior struck me as delightfully peculiar, and of course she was very beautiful. The dark blood wrought its fine magic in her, as it does in all of us, but she had all of the raw materials for it to work with. Such a delicate, stormy-eyed little creature. I must say I was drawn to her straight away.

I wasn't planning on doing anything about this attraction, of course. I was married, I had a reputation to worry about, and despite being nineteen, an adult, Lyrica seemed so very young and innocent. Like pure untrodden snow. Yes, I am probably guilty of describing her in ways that seem antiquated, even reprehensible from a modern perspective, but this is my truth, this is how I saw her.

The book Lyrica was so engrossed in that she found it necessary to leave the room several times during the evening was Wuthering Heights by Emily Brönte. You probably know the one - it has become an enduring classic and was of course a big hit, particularly with young women, in the 1850s.

Well, I have always been a voracious reader, and I had read the book. When an occasion arose, I asked Lyrica what she thought about it. This led to a riveting discussion not only of Wuthering Heights but of other literary works that we both admired. It delighted me that this young girl had devoured and loved some of the same books I counted among the guilty pleasures on my own shelves including Mary Shelley's Frankenstein.

Lyrica was a little nervous around me at first. I was after all a Lord, and she was merely fortunate to be here because she was related to the Thornhills. But as soon as our conversation was flowing, all of those differences became irrelevant. She became animated when she spoke and gestured, her eyes and cheeks glowed. The music, chatter and general commotion around us faded into nothingness.

When I left later that night I was already inconveniently and inappropriately in love with her. Alas, falling in love doesn't seem to happen for me very often, but when it does it happens hard and fast. I then will attempt to reel myself back in, to backtrack, but I have never once succeeded in backtracking anything.

I told myself that I would not pursue her.

But that was a lie. I saw her again as soon as I could. I knew about Hartenbrook Trade, ostensibly owned by her parents but largely funded and controlled by Algernon. I'd often send my maids there to get things like coffee and sugar, but now I started going myself, usually on my way to or from a business meeting, a dinner, or some other occasion. All so I could tell myself that I wasn't going specifically to see her.

Another thing I tried to convince myself of was that I simply enjoyed talking with her, simply her company. So what if there was also an element of physical attraction? It was nothing I couldn't suppress and eventually let go of.

But then, one rainy summer afternoon, something came

over me and I invited her to Shakespeare's Globe theater on a whim. She was supposed to be looking after the shop on her own for the rest of the afternoon and said that she would feel guilty if she said yes and abandoned her duties. I dissolved her resistance by arranging for two of my footmen to come around the very next day to purchase more than enough to make up for the early closure.

And so off we went to the Globe to see *A Midsummer Night's Dream* in the light misty drizzle. In retrospect, the afternoon we spent together at The Globe was the point of no return. Up until she took my hand in the crowded theater I could have turned around. Probably. Conceivably. But not after that.

Well, you can probably imagine more or less how things evolved from there. I find it necessary to mention that I never pushed or coerced her into anything. Given our uneven standing, I know I easily could have, and that you might assume that I did. And admittedly there have been plenty of scenarios throughout both my life and afterlife in which I have used my power and privilege to my advantage. I'm not ashamed to say so. With Lyrica, it was never like that.

Of course we had to be very discreet, particularly when we were seen in public together. You know how it is. When two people are romantically involved, there is an invisible thread of tension there that others are liable to sense, sometimes even when deliberate care is taken to conceal it. That cord of attraction between Lyrica and I was certainly so strong that it is a miracle not all of London could tell.

There were rumors, of course. But there were many rumors back then, about everyone. You know, we didn't have reality TV, social media, any of that.

Of course in 1858 which eventually spilled over into

1959, touching a woman you weren't married to was of course considered a great taboo, not to mention a grievous sin. I was well aware of that. I knew most of my family would be ready to condemn me if they found out about my infidelity. This by the way included my wife Tessa and my brother Everett, who were carrying on their own affair, a badly kept secret in its own right. Still, I was the older brother and expected to set a good example. It was always like that in my family. Everett, though only minutes younger than I, missed out on the title and the family seat, but let us just say, the amount of slack our dear parents were always willing to cut him was in direct proportion.

But enough about the Eves. I may tell you more about them some other night. An interesting bunch, to be sure.

Dawn isn't far beyond the horizon, and much as I would like to invite you to stay up with me to watch the first rays dance over the waves, we both know that would be a rather bad idea. I have watched my share of sunrises from these windows, some of them with Lyrica.

I'd bring her here to Eve Hall on occasion, when I knew that no other members of my family were going to be around. This is the Eve family's stronghold, if you wish, and while my parents were still alive, it was their primary residence. They however were very fond of travelling and often went abroad for months at at time to Italy, Switzerland, Greece and so on.

When we were here, far away from London and anyone who may observe and judge us, Lyrica was always at her most free. As was I, for that matter. We would play the grand piano downstairs madly for hours, roam the grounds, read by the fireplace, and well, all sorts of other things that I will leave up to your imagination.

What eventually ended up happening is probably

rather predictable. Lyrica fell pregnant, despite the precautions we took. Suffice it to say that Victorian era birth control methods weren't all that sophisticated, so I suppose it was inevitable.

I should have thought ahead and considered what I was going to do if this happened. But I had, quite optimistically, pushed the possibility out of my thoughts and consigned it to part of the uncomfortable reality that my relationship with Lyrica was such a welcome reprieve from. I suppose mine and Tessa's mysteriously fruitless marriage had accustomed me to not have to think about the possibility of pregnancy. And I suppose, deep down, I expected the problem was with me.

Despite my own fidelity, up to a point, Tesse had displayed a shocking disregard for our marriage vows all along. She was a beautiful creature, phenomenally so, and she seemed determined to reap the rewards in full. She seduced every man she felt drawn to, and because I adored her, I tolerated it, for years.

In retrospect, I wish I had ended my unhappy marriage with Tessa. But at the time, the pressures and expectations that rested upon me made it seem like an impossibility.

I do not wish to attempt to paint myself as a saint here, but many men in my position would have simply distanced themselves from the young woman they had lured into trouble. This, of course, was unthinkable, but I admittedly did suggest that the best solution was to terminate the pregnancy.

Trouble was, abortion procedures and methods at the time were highly unreliable in their effectiveness, not to mention dangerous to undertake. The options ranged from ingesting herbal remedies or poisonous substances to grueling procedures carried out by questionable medical professionals.

The thought of Lyrica being subjected to this was unbearable, yet, so was the alternative.

At least I had the means to call upon the best professionals available, and through my network of connections they were not hard to find. Unsurprisingly, many of my friends had found themselves facing this very same problem.

After consulting with the various doctors and herbalists that my friends put me in touch with, we decided to attempt it, while avoiding the most dangerous methods. I went through it all with her, as best I could. But really, holding her hair while she was throwing up and cramping or sitting beside her holding her hand while a surgeon attempted to scrape the fetus out of her with a curette seemed terribly inadequate. Of course Lyrica suffered infinitely worse than I did, but it was also painful for me.

I recall one particularly grueling procedure, performed by an American doctor whom Lyrica had managed to track down. I didn't fully trust him - no one had heard of him, and he was only passing through. The timing was also problematic, as the appointment coincided with my trip up north for a family friend's funeral. Despite my reservations, Lyrica was adamant about going ahead, and I reluctantly agreed, on the condition that she wouldn't see this questionable doctor alone.

Octavia volunteered to accompany her, and we decided that I would arrive during the procedure to take care of her afterward.

After a day's journey, I reached the reassuringly elegant residence near Regent's Park just half an hour after the procedure was supposed to begin.

A maid welcomed me and led me to a back bedroom that offered views of a verdant garden. This room had been transformed into a makeshift clinic by the American doctor, with the help of a young nurse who might have been one of the household maids temporarily drafted into this new role. The doctor's eclectic assortment of instruments was displayed on a serving tray covered with a white linen cloth, now marred by bloodstains, placed precariously on the bedside table.

I was not supposed to be in here, of course, and I could hardly bear the sight.

Lyrica lay on the bed, her complexion ghostly pale, her expression a mix of terror and irritation, as the doctor worked diligently at her bedside, half hidden behind a bloodstained sheet for discretion, his nurse passing him the tools upon request.

Octavia was stationed in a wicker chair on the other side of the bed, clasping one of Lyrica's hands with both of hers while sobbing theatrically into her puffy sleeve as if her cousin had already passed away or was guaranteed to do so at any moment.

"Evander, get her out of here, please," Lyrica implored me, "I cannot stand any tears as well as this. I have asked her to go next door, but she refuses."

"Octavia, come here," I said, waving her over to the doorway where I lingered. "There is no need for you to stay here."

She stood up from the chair, releasing Lyrica's hand with evident reluctance. She then trailed behind me into the hallway, leaving the doctor and nurse to exhale sighs of relief.

"What that doctor is doing to her is appalling!" Octavia

declared the moment we were in the adjacent parlor and the door closed behind us.

With that, she suddenly delivered a hard smack to my face. Then she stormed off, the sound of her footsteps soon retreating down the hallway towards the front door. I took a deep breath and pressed a handkerchief to my bleeding nostril.

And, as it turned out, it was all in vain. Our daughter, Emmeline, really wanted to live, and she survived every attempt made on her burgeoning life and consciousness.

One day Lyrica had had enough. She declared that she had decided to carry the child to term no matter the social consequences. I didn't argue with her decision, of course not. Indeed, I was quite relieved. I hated seeing her in pain. At this point she was about five months into the pregnancy and it wouldn't be long before she would no longer be able to hide it.

I suggested that she come and stay here at Eve Hall for the remaining four months of her ordeal, and this is what we agreed on. Only a select few members of my staff, a doctor, a midwife and a couple of nurses were going to be around, and of course I would visit whenever I could. Lyrica's parents and brother, and any other family she felt comfortable enough letting in on her secret were more than welcome, too. But the rest of London and its gossip mill were going to be shut out of it.

Once the child was born, it would be up to Lyrica what was to happen. I suggested that I raise the child, since I knew I would be able to provide a suitable upbringing.

Tessa reacted badly when I confessed and explained the entire situation to her. Rather hypocritical, if you ask me, considering her own infidelity which preceded mine by several years. But there you have it. At least she agreed to keep the secret, finding other ways of venting her frustration and wielding my indiscretion against me.

Once the decision was made to cease the attempts at terminating Lyrica's pregnancy, the rest of it went relatively smoothly. It is rather peaceful here, and four months is really not such a terribly long time to wait.

I worried that Lyrica would die of boredom in the countryside, so I traveled up from London frequently, always bringing new books and other gifts to hopefully alleviate some of the tedium of countryside living. I had my coachmen drive her family members up to visit as often as they wished.

Needless to say, Lyrica's parents, and her brother, were not happy with me. But at least they could see that I was making some attempt at conducting myself with integrity in how I dealt with the consequences of my own actions. Still, they never warmed to me and that's entirely understandable.

Venedict and Octavia visited several times. They both seemed to be of the opinion that their cousin's four month stint in the countryside was a terrible punishment for her indiscretion, and they conscientiously supplied her with more gossip and other delicacies from London than she would have ever wished for.

I rather liked them, the Thornhill siblings. Spoiled brats as they were and undoubtedly still are. Unlike my family, the Thornhills belonged to the nouveau riche. They had all of the wealth and much of the privilege enjoyed by the old guard social elite to which I belonged, but they had none of the stuffiness about them. I grew up surrounded by stuffiness, suffocated by stuffiness, so I liked their lack of filters and manners. Simply the way they would sit in my overstuffed, obscenely expensive furniture as casually as you are now, with your legs folded up under you, would amuse me with its unselfconscious casualness. I was so used to my guests sitting on the edge of the seat, so very prim and proper. The Thornhills irked many among polite society, but for the most part I found them refreshing.

On a few occasions Octavia visited alone after their father had sent Venedict off to Bedlam, hoping to get him cured of something or other.

There were a couple of times when she was being very flirty with me. She must have had the impression that I was not above showing interest in a teen girl, but Octavia was only fourteen at the time, and that really would have been a bridge too far. Not to mention that I was still terribly in love with Lyrica and nurtured some small hope that we would have some kind of future together, despite our current predicament.

When I remained unmoved by her fluttering eyelashes and other little advances Octavia seemed to get in a strop and didn't return to Eve Hall for well over a month. But then she must have gotten over it because her nearly weekly visits resumed, and during them she treated Lyrica all the more warmly and generously.

It isn't for me to speculate, but Octavia had no mother, no older sister, no older female figure at all in her life who could have given her some kindly advice about how to deal and how not to deal with men. And while I wasn't one of them, there was no shortage of men at the time who would have loved to take advantage of a girl like Octavia - too brash and too beautiful for her own good. At least the fact she was from a wealthy family would have made most potential predators think twice. Nevertheless, I found myself worrying for her.

Emmeline was born on October 23 1860, right here at

Eve Hall. And while the leadup to her arrival had been fraught with stress, her birth was uncomplicated and she arrived healthy and perfect.

Giving her up for adoption was never on the table, but Lyrica also couldn't raise her. Not only did she have responsibilities to her parents and their business, but having a child would also severely hamper her otherwise excellent chances of marrying well. That was the unfortunate reality of things back then.

Lyrica and I agreed that Emmeline would grow up knowing her birth mother, grandparents and extended family and that she would see them often, but that I would raise her. In public, Emmeline would be known as mine and Tessa's daughter.

Emmeline looked so much like Lyrica right from the start. While Tessa was strawberry blonde and had a rosy complexion, Emmeline's hair was obsidian black, her eyes electric blue and her skin nearly as pale as a vampire's. But so be it.

The fact that Emmeline looked so much like Lyrica only made it easier to love her, and I did, from the moment I first held her. She is the only child I had before I stumbled into immortality. I decided to bestow the dark gift upon her, though I waited until she was an adult. If she had ever taken critically ill or been grievously injured at any point during her upbringing, I would have brought her over then. Fortunately, that was never necessary.

There was an interesting overlap during which I raised my human daughter while I was already a vampire. But that is a story, or perhaps several stories, for another night.

I am conscious of dawn drawing near - I sense its approach across the horizon. Soon, it will rise above the waves, chasing all of the shadows away, including you and

I. But before it does, there is one last aspect to this story that I must not neglect to mention. I am rather certain that you would appreciate knowing. Gabriel has told me that you have been asking about your family, what he knows. And you found your way to Thornhill Mansion - I can only conclude that you are trying to trace your roots.

Well, I already mentioned that my darling Tessa was rather the free spirit - even if her free-spirited attitude only applied to herself. She had a particular fondness for young men. Of course, hovering on the precipice of thirty, I was still a young man then myself, but I mean younger than that. She preferred her lovers to be in their late teens, early twenties at a stretch. She picked them with the discernment of a jewel collector. Whenever we attended functions together and there was a gorgeous teenage boy present, I found myself worrying that Tessa might set her sights on him.

At one point in the summer of 1861, I became aware that Tessa was embroiled in several concurrent affairs - one of her young lovers being Clyde Hartenbrook, Venedict Thornhill another. Clyde seemed smitten and would be around Tessa at the slightest excuse. Unfortunately for him, at 23, he was already at the upper limit of her age preference.

In the autumn of 1861 - indeed, around the same time that your entire family, minus Augustine - became vampires, it became clear that Tessa was pregnant. She was seething at the discovery. At this point, we already, ostensibly, had a daughter, Emmeline. Tessa did not want to feel encumbered by a child, but nevertheless, she tolerated the pregnancy and in the spring of 1862 gave birth to twin girls, whom we named Victorine and Felicity.

You must remind me to show you a daguerreotype of my little family. Tessa and I, and our three daughters.

What was clear to me from the moment Victorine opened her eyes was that she was a Thornhill. She had those tell-tale amber eyes. Her younger twin, Felicity, however, had eyes like the midnight sky, and as she grew older, she came to resemble Emmeline far more than she resembled her own twin, Victorine.

My theory, naturally, is that Victorine and Felicity had different fathers - Venedict and Clyde, respectively. Yes, yes, I know how this must sound to you. But consider the evidence.

Neither of the exceedingly young fathers knew, of course. Clyde disappeared to the New World soon after, and as for Venedict... well, as I've come to understand it, he was imprisoned in a casket deep beneath Thornhill Mansion. I assure you, I was not aware of this. Otherwise, I might have intervened. No, I would have intervened.

Truly, I did not blame either of them for their fleeting affairs with my wife. As I saw it, they were merely among the many young men she fancied for a time. I felt for Clyde, who seemed hopelessly smitten with Tessa. As for Venedict, I suppose he was a little troubled, burdened as he was with a difficult father, managing the Thornhill empire amidst Algernon's destructive temper and habits, and being peri-odically sent off to Bedlam to be *cured* of the various maladies of the mind that Algernon seemed prone to projecting onto him.

I loved Victorine and Felicity as if they were my own daughters. I always did my best not to treat them any differently, or lesser, than Emmeline, their older sister. I would have turned them both as well as her, but alas, fate had other plans.

Victorine died in a tragic accident in 1868 when she was just six years old. There's a lake here on the property, and unfortunately, she drowned in it during an early morning swim. She was alone when it happened. I had, of course, admonished her many a time to never swim alone - but Victorine was headstrong and all of her short life, she did as she pleased.

I was the one to find her. I cannot convey the depths of devastation I felt - but my troubles only increased when Tessa blamed me and gradually began to openly accuse me of drowning Victorine, whom I considered my own daughter. She claimed it was because I suspected that Victorine wasn't mine by blood.

My own dear brother was quick to back her up. At this point, Everett and I were both forty-three and had aged hopelessly of Tessa's sphere of interest. I suppose Everett's enthusiasm in accusing me of drowning Tessa's daughter was his last-ditch attempt at winning her over once and for all. Together, Tessa and Everett managed to turn Felicity against me, convincing her that I had killed her sister and might be just as inclined to take her life as well.

The situation spiraled into chaos, leading to several tragedies within my family. The most horrific was the murder-suicide, where Everett killed Tessa and then himself, staging it so that I appeared to be the guilty party.

This catastrophe was the catalyst for my exile in Paris, my losing contact with Felicity, and, ultimately, my arrival at immortality's door. But all of that is truly a story for another time.

EVANDER'S GAZE drifted distantly as he looked out over the moonlit waves beyond the window. A deep sigh escaped him before his attention refocused on me.

"Where is Emmeline now?" I asked. "You said you turned her."

Evander sighed again, a soul-deep sound, as his fingers traced a restless pattern on the armrest of his chair.

"I did. And yet, Emmeline is no more. She fell at the hands of a vampire hunter, someone she was... involved with, despite my repeated warnings. This tragedy occurred just a few short years ago. She must have attempted to turn him, underestimating his vehement opposition to our kind. You may recognize the name of the hunter in question: Ramsay Fairweather."

I sat in stunned silence, trying to process Evander's words. Now I finally understood how Ramsay had become a dhampir, a half-vampire. It had happened during an aborted attempt to turn him into a full vampire. I wasn't sure how I'd imagined it had happened, but this wasn't it.

Evander spoke again, his expression grave. "Emmeline made me promise, not long before it happened, that I would never, for any reason, harm a hair on his head. That is the only reason I have not sought vengeance. Though," he added, his voice threaded through with strains of grief and unresolved anger, "I have certainly contemplated it. Even now, part of me still entertains the thought of seeking him out, taking his life in repayment for hers. Alas, it wouldn't fix anything. It would not bring her back."

I opened my mouth, about to tell him that Ramsay's death was something Csilla and I had taken care of. But that would lead to explaining how, tomorrow night, I was going to reverse it. I decided not to get into all of that. Not now.

"I'm sorry about Emmeline," I said quietly. "About all of your daughters. I would have liked to meet them."

Evander gave me a melancholy half-smile. "They would

have liked to meet you, too." After the briefest pause, he added, "I'm sure you can see why I am so attached to my niece and nephew, why I chose to turn them once they reached adulthood. They are the only children I have left."

"Did Emmeline have any children?" I asked, though I already knew the answer - at least one.

"She might have, before she accepted the dark blood," he replied, "though she never told me. She kept her distance during her early to mid-twenties, likely to remove any temptation I might feel to turn her descendants. And I don't truly blame her. If I'd known where they were, I would have."

CHAPTER

EIGHTEEN

I got up early the next night and got ready for my journey to the other side. I threw on tonight's ensemble, a silk blazer and trousers spattered with blood-red cherry blossoms, and pulled on the same steel-capped ankle boots from the previous night.

Carrying Algernon's mirror under my arm, I headed down through Eve Hall to the parlor where tonight's conjurations were slated to go down.

On my way, I crossed paths with Roderick, Holly, Tibor and a fourth vampire I hadn't been introduced to yet, heading in the opposite direction. The five of us paused on the landing beneath a tall arched window that framed the starlit grounds outside.

Roderick's eyes sparkled like polished crystals in the soft light. "You have met Holly and I," he said, a strange smile playing about his lips, "but have you been introduced to our friends, Tibor and Zachary?"

Tibor wore a classic black-and-white ensemble, far more formal than last night's getup, while Zachary - who must have been in his mid-twenties when he was turned -

had opted for a pewter suit, the blazer straining over his broad shoulders. He towered over the rest of us, his sharply chiseled features framed by short, neatly styled chestnut hair. His dark, piercing eyes locked onto me.

"Harlan Thornhill," he declared, letting my name roll off his tongue as if it left a sour taste. "The vampire who hunts vampires."

"That's me," I confirmed, giving him a smirk.

"Zachary's maker was killed by a hunter," Tibor informed me. His words made a complex emotion flicker across Zachary's face, somewhere between pain and hatred, as he continued to stare me down.

"Correct," he said, his tone clipped. "In 1979. It still hurts."

"Expecting an apology?" I asked as I tried to move past them.

Before I could get far, Zachary stepped directly into my path, blocking my way. His eyes gleamed with something hard and sharp.

"Don't be in such a rush. I just want to have a little chat, get to know you better. After all, you're both a hunter and a Thornhill, so you'll have to forgive me my curiosity."

His voice was deceptively polite, but there was an undercurrent that made it clear this wasn't about curiosity.

I carefully set down Algernon's mirror against the wall. They clearly weren't going to let me just walk by, and I wasn't about to risk damaging the mirror - even if, on some level, I was tempted by the idea of it shattering and thwarting Ramsay's return to the living. The problem with that possibility was that Csilla wouldn't regain her powers. Venedict would be furious with me, and it might spur him on to strike an even worse agreement with his father in an attempt to help her.

The moonlight streaming through the tall window on the landing painted Zachary's face in shades of silver and shadow as he began to circle me. "I must admit," he drawled, "to feeling somewhat underwhelmed. When I heard the last Thornhill descendant was a hunter with an impressive kill count, I expected, well, a little more. You know what I mean." He punctuated the remark with a shove to my shoulder - just hard enough to be both taunting and menacing.

My jaw tightened, but I couldn't let him get under my skin that easily. I especially couldn't lash out. I was a guest here, a controversial one at that. I needed to at least try to be on my best behavior, which, admittedly, wasn't my strong suit even on a good day.

"I'm not leaving," I told Zachary, "just because you're having a crisis of confidence. You know that, right?"

"You seem to think that you are welcome here," Tibor spoke up, clearly feeling brave now that Zachary had thrown the first stone. He stepped closer, his eyes narrowing with contempt. "After slaying our kind for years before becoming one of us, do you truly believe you can switch sides just like that, without any backlash? That everyone is prepared to welcome you here with open arms?"

"Uncle certainly is," Roderick added, stepping between Zachary and Tibor, leaning in slightly as if confiding a secret. "He insists that we 'accept and embrace' you. Whatever he meant by that is, of course, open to interpretation."

I tried to sidestep, but Zachary moved in a blur, slamming me against the wall. The mirror behind me rattled violently in its frame but, thankfully, didn't shatter. The impact reverberated through me, but I held onto my composure. Disappointment flickered in Zachary's eyes when he realized I wasn't rattled. His hand snapped across my face, and the coppery taste of blood pooled between my teeth. Slowly, I turned my head back to meet his gaze.

I flashed him a broad smile. "Are you done?"

"Zachary, please don't," Holly pleaded, her voice tense. "Uncle made it clear - no fighting or violence outside the Games.""

Zachary held me pinned against the wall, holding my arm in what he seemed to think was a secure grip. A quick twist and a knee in his midsection or groin, and he'd be on the floor. The problem was, Zachary wasn't alone.

With my free left hand, I reached behind my back and slid two of the razors hidden along my arm into my palm. I had a feeling I might need them soon.

"Once the Games are over," Zachary said, addressing Roderick - whom both he and Tibor seemed to defer to - "he'll be back out there, hunting our kind. This might be our only chance to show him how we feel about a traitor, while he's here, unarmed."

"Well, we mustn't hurt him too badly." Roderick's voice was casual, but I saw something dangerous flicker in the depths of his eyes, something sharp that had been hidden beneath the surface and was now pushing through, like jagged cliffs emerging from the receding tide.

He turned to me. "You must understand that I'm making a considerable concession by tolerating a hunter under my roof."

"Under your uncle's roof, you mean." I wasn't about to let this immortal trust-fund baby intimidate me. His grin faltered slightly.

"This may be my uncle's roof, but not everything goes according to his wishes." Roderick's tone tightened, his expression souring with petulance. "One of the drawbacks of immortality is that unless you're the head of the house-hold, you're always waiting in line. And since Uncle Evander killed my father, I'll always be waiting. Sometimes I wonder, why should he be the sole decision-maker forever? Don't you think I should have a say in some matters too?"

He sighed, casting a sidelong glance at me as if implying I should feel some sympathy for his predicament. "Uncle has an impressive collection of hunting knives in the game room upstairs. We could show you a few of them up close. As a hunter, I'm sure you'd appreciate their, well, craftsmanship." His suggestion hung in the air, ominously open-ended.

No, thanks. My plans for the evening didn't include being corralled into the game room like cornered prey.

I twisted out of Zachary's grip, ducked beneath his arm, and shoved him hard against the wall. My other hand shot up, seizing a fistful of his chestnut hair. With a savage yank, I slammed his head into the stone. The jolt ran up my arm, but I didn't stop. I did it again, harder each time.

Zachary's body began to crumple, sliding toward the floor as blood streamed from his nose and mouth. Holly's horrified scream tore through the air, but I only slowed when Roderick and Tibor closed in, one of them wrenching my arm painfully behind my back.

Even so, I managed to slam Zachary's head into the wall a few more times before they dragged me off. My hand came away slick with his blood as they forced me to release my grip on his hair.

Zachary had collapsed in a heap but soon staggered to his feet, blood dripping from his mouth. His eyes burned with fury, and to my satisfaction, he spat out a tooth - though not one of his fangs, unfortunately.

"Perhaps we should simply kill him," Zachary muttered, wiping the blood from his mouth. "No one would have to know."

"I decide our course of action," Roderick said firmly. "We cannot kill him. But I'm not entirely opposed to giving him a proper welcome. In fact, I think it might be wise."

He turned on his heel, gesturing ahead as he added in a lighter tone, "Gentlemen, let's not waste any more time. To the game room!"

Tibor and Zachary, already gripping my arms, dragged me up the short flight of stairs and through the doors Roderick held open with a triumphant smile.

Holly followed at a distance, visibly distressed. "I don't like this," she whispered - but did nothing to stop it.

The game room was bathed in the soft glow of overhead lights, illuminating an array of mounted hunting trophies and polished firearms displayed high on the walls above the glass cabinets that lined the room.

The cabinets were filled with an impressive collection of rifles, pistols, and gleaming knives. The air carried the scents of oiled wood, cold metal, and old blood, making it feel heavy.

Roderick strolled over to one of the cabinets, his eyes roving over the contents with an appreciative expression, as if he were selecting a fine wine for dinner. Meanwhile, Tibor and Zachary maneuvered me deeper into the room.

They forced me into a chair, Zachary looping his belt around my right arm and pulling it tight against the armrest. I still had the razor blades - my last-ditch weapons. They were something I could only use in a surprise attack once.

"Doing anything to him could get us into serious trouble," Holly's voice floated from the doorway. She lingered there, pale and fidgeting, as her brother calmly slid aside one of the glass cabinet doors and reached for a blade. "Uncle will be furious. And what about Gabriel?"

"Uncle may very well be furious," Roderick conceded, shooting his little sister a dismissive glance over his shoulder. "But you know as well as I do that he'll forgive me in an instant. He always does." He plucked a knife from the display - a hunting knife with a wickedly curved edge. "As for Gabriel, you needn't worry about him. I know he has a soft spot for me. I can wrap him around my finger as easily as a particularly beautiful woman might wrap me around hers."

The blade caught a flash of light as he turned it, sending a shiver of reflected brilliance across the room. Holly flinched back as Roderick advanced on me, the knife dangling from his hand, casually graceful.

"This," he said, holding the knife up, "is typically reserved for gutting larger game. But for you, Harlan, I'll make an exception and be oh so precise. You should feel honored, truly - this is a family heirloom."

He stepped closer, the blade now inches from my face, and I could see the delicate etchings on the steel, a twisting latticework of thorns and roses.

When I flinched it made his eyes glow with something close to excitement. His smile widened, exposing his fangs. He was enjoying this.

Fury simmered in my blood. I met his gaze with a steady glare. "I'm beginning to see why they threw you in Bedlam."

"Meanwhile," he said, leaning in closer, letting the knife's tip trace invisible patterns near my face, "I'm utterly baffled. So many scars, yet your face remains untouched. How typically sentimental of our kind." He tilted his head, his eyes narrowing as if weighing a crucial decision. "But here's my take on the matter - a Chelsea smile might suit you. It could even make my Belladira think twice before finding you too distracting. You know how women are - their attentions can be fleeting. And Belladira, well, she certainly knows how to keep me on my toes. Surely, you can sympathize."

"You can't be serious."

"Oh, I am very, very serious." Roderick adjusted the angle of the blade, suggesting he was considering making the first cut.

"Put the knife down, Roderick. I don't want to hurt you." My voice was steady, but it was a lie. Tension coiled in my muscles, and anxiety made my pulse hammer in my throat. He'd better leave my face alone.

Through all the hunts I'd been on, I'd made damn sure nothing happened to my face. It wasn't just vanity, it was the irrational thought that I could live a vaguely normal life outside of work as long as I didn't look too obviously damaged.

Suddenly and brutally, Roderick jammed the tip of the hunting knife between my teeth. The blade wedged tightly, leaving no room to maneuver as I clamped down hard, locking the steel in place.

Roderick's eyes flickered with frustration as he realized his mistake. With the knife trapped between my fangs, he couldn't drive it into my cheek.

"Work with me, Harlan," he sighed, trying to wiggle the blade. The tip scraped from side to side, just above my tongue. "If you don't cooperate, this could slip down your throat, and that would truly complicate things for you. Trust me, it is exceptionally sha-"

Before he could finish, I jerked my head back sharply, wrenching the knife from his grip.

I sprang up from the chair, still tethered to it by Zachary's belt. Using it for leverage, I swung the chair around with all my strength, striking Roderick hard behind the knees. The impact made his legs buckle, and he collapsed into the chair, which spun back toward me.

I quickly freed myself by bringing the hunting knife down on the belt, severing it. Roderick's eyes widened in confusion, his shock barely registering before I was on him. The razor blades gleamed as I drove them into the corners of his mouth. His lips parted in a soundless gasp, and I followed the motion, slicing upward and carving the jagged grin he had so eagerly described onto his own face. The blades tore through skin and muscle, stopping only when they met the hinges of his jaw.

The room froze. The chair's spinning slowed to a stop, and silence settled. Zachary, Tibor, and Holly stood paralyzed.

I could have stopped there - should have, maybe - but I needed them to know that they should never try this again.

Without a word, I yanked the razor blades from Roderick's cheeks and let them drop onto his blood-slicked tongue. His mouth quivered as I pressed the hunting knife beneath his chin, tilting his head back, pinching his nose shut. Blood gurgled in his throat.

"Swallow."

Terror flared in his eyes. He shook his head frantically, refusing, but then the sound of him swallowing the razors echoed through the stillness, a hideous, wet gulp.

I released him, stepped back, let the tension snap like a frayed wire. Holly rushed forward, dropping to her knees beside Roderick, her eyes wild with disbelief and fury as she looked up at me.

"How could you? Roderick didn't mean any harm!"

I didn't bother to respond, just shot her a dark look as I turned to leave, the knife spinning in my fingers. I didn't mind them seeing that I knew how to use one of these.

Tibor, having helped himself to another of Evander's knives, hesitated, his gaze flicking between me and Roderick, who sat trembling in the chair while Holly frantically begged him to cough. Uncertainty flashed across Tibor's face as he weighed his options. Wisely, he stepped back, unwilling to push his luck. Zachary, now hovering by the door, scrambled to press himself against the wall as I approached.

He, Zachary and Roderick had just proven something to me that I already knew - most vampires aren't inherently tough, they just seem that way because of what vampirism gives them.

I paused in the doorway, pointing the blade first at Tibor, then at Zachary. "If either of you wants a smile like Roderick's, now's your chance."

There were no takers, so I left the game room, letting the door swing shut behind me.

I had only made it halfway down the stairs to the landing where the ornate mirror still stood when I ran into Elizabeth.

She was the youngest of the Graves siblings. I wasn't sure how old she'd been in 1665 when her mortal life ended, but I guessed around fifteen. There had to be a significant age gap between her and her brothers - more than a decade, maybe closer to two.

Elizabeth's silky blonde hair, the same pale gold as Gabriel's, fell straight down her back, cut just above her midriff. She had adopted the vampiric version of the old-money aesthetic Gabriel favored, rich velvet and silk, but in sleek, modern cuts. She wore a short emerald green skirt, a crisp white silk shirt, and calf-length velvet boots. A dark emerald glimmered at her neck from a bolero tie.

I lit up at the sight of her, but her expression was less than amused when her eyes were immediately drawn to the hunting knife in my hand.

"Harlan, why do you have that?"

"Roderick and his friends insisted on showing me his uncle's game room. Elizabeth, I think he might need some help."

Her pale brows knitted in suspicion. "What happened to him?"

"It's easier if I just show you."

I led the way back to the game room and nudged the door open. The scene inside was both grotesque and oddly comedic. Holly, Zachary, and Tibor surrounded Roderick, who was doubled over on the floor, making horrendous retching noises as the others desperately tried to coax him into purging the razor blades. Roderick's newly acquired Chelsea smile was bleeding profusely, the crimson staining his white shirt, his hands, Holly, and the plush carpet beneath them.

Elizabeth shot me a glare that could rival one of Gabriel's finest. Without waiting for an explanation, she stepped into the chaos, taking command like a seasoned ER chief. In mere moments, Roderick had expelled the sharp blades onto the carpet, and Holly dashed off to fetch Elizabeth a needle and thread for sutures.

I figured Roderick wouldn't want to see me right now, so I decided against re-entering the game room. Instead, I let the door swing shut behind me, neatly severing the view of the pandemonium inside, like a curtain falling after a chaotic scene in a play.

Standing alone in the quiet corridor, my heart continued to race wildly - a cacophony of anger, adrenaline, and an unexpected whisper of sadness. I was making enemies faster than I was making friends, and the night wasn't over yet - far from it. A quick glance at my watch confirmed that my journey to the other side to retrieve Ramsay was scheduled in just half an hour.

CHAPTER

NINETEEN

I returned to my suite and tucked the count's hunting knife away between the loveseat's cushion. I suppose I just liked the idea of being prepared in case any of my new pals felt like paying me a surprise visit.

I went into the bathroom to assess the damage. I had a split bottom lip and a purple bruise had started to blossom across my cheekbone. My hands and shirt were stained with blood, but I don't think any of it was my own.

I had to quickly wash off the blood and change into a clean shirt - Gabriel's vision of seven costume changes a night was starting to seem like a real possibility.

I'd just tossed the blood-spattered shirt on the floor and was furiously scrubbing Roderick's blood from my hands and face in the bathroom when a sudden knock sounded on the door of the main room. Csilla's voice followed, "May I come in?"

Without waiting for a reply, she did. The door opened, no footsteps sounded, and then she appeared in the doorway behind me, her eyes meeting mine in the mirror without flinching. Venedict had described Csilla as

216

assertive for a 18th-century woman - I simply found her assertive, full stop.

"What have you been up to?" she asked, eyeing me and then the blood now diluted pink and swirling down into the white marble sink.

"Just a little disagreement with Roderick," I replied, reaching for a towel to pat my face dry.

A crooked smile appeared on Csilla's lips. "I brought you something. Just in case you haven't had enough blood for tonight."

She set down a green-stemmed wine glass filled with blood on the bathroom's marble counter. I snatched it up almost reflexively and drained it in one swift gulp, then returned it to the counter. I hadn't had blood since early last night just before leaving the mansion. I'd forced myself to gulp down the last dregs of the pig's blood in the fridge. It'd nearly made me gag with disgust.

Csilla remained in the doorway, observing me with her eyebrows subtly arched. She cradled another glass in her hand - this one with a clear stem. The slight fogging on the glass suggested it was still at body temperature. Fresh blood. I was tempted to snatch it from her hand and drain it for her, but I resisted the urge. Instead, I kept my hands busy by putting on the new shirt I'd chosen and buttoning its delicate mother of pearl buttons.

"What are you doing here, anyway?" I asked. "You didn't come just to make sure I wasn't starving, did you?"

"No. I need to ensure you're fully prepared for what we're about to undertake," she responded.

With that, she turned and glided back into the main room, settling gracefully onto the velvet-upholstered loveseat. "In a minute," she called back, "I'll need you to bring the mirror downstairs."

"Yes, I was working on that," I replied, following her into the room while slipping on the black silk blazer patterned with blood-red cherry blossoms that went with the trousers I already had on.

Ties and even ruffled cravats seemed to be standard attire for the men at Eve Hall, but not for me. Gabriel seemed to have intuited my hatred for the things, and he had included only one among the things he sent me. That one slim black silk tie came in handy now as I wrapped it around the hunting knife I'd taken from Roderick. I then swapped out the steel-capped Alexander McQueen Chelsea boots for the lace-up ones, and secured the blade beneath the laces. It wasn't the ideal setup; I preferred my combat boots with built-in knife sheaths, but those weren't an option right now.

When I looked up from what I was doing, Csilla was giving me a mystified look.

"What?" I asked. "I'm not heading to the other side without at least one weapon."

"Who knows," she replied, leaning forward with her chin resting lightly on her hand, "your instinct might be right. The law of correspondence could apply - if you stab someone there, it might have real effects. If you die in the underworld, you die in reality. For all I know."

"You really don't have this figured out, do you?" I asked laconically.

She shook her head, her bob's blunt ends swaying against her sharp cheekbones. "Barely at all," she admitted. "But I certainly know more than you. Venturing to the underworld is no picnic - even if, coincidentally, when you arrive on the other side, it appears to be one. Algernon Thornhill may not be the king of the underworld - of course, he isn't - but will have some degree of control over the particular part of it you'll enter. Finding Ramsay and bringing him back through the same portal you entered is all you need to do, and all you should be doing. Otherwise, I cannot say what the consequences might be."

"Have you ever been to the underworld, Csilla?" I asked her.

"I have," she confessed, a barely perceptible shiver running through her slight shoulders. "I got stuck there, once, when I was in my early teens and my powers were first roaring to life. That's why I am so adamant about you staying focused. If you fail to exit before Algernon decides to close the portal... well, without my powers, I wouldn't be able to help you." She paused briefly before adding, with a slight smile, "No one would."

COMFORTABLE, ornate sofas, armchairs and chaise lounges had been arranged along the walls of one of Eve Hall's grand downstairs parlors. The middle of the room had been cleared to make plenty of space for tonight's spectacle.

I'd brought Algernon's mirror down, wrapped in its black cloth. I placed it carefully leaning against the wall. It wasn't practical for me to be standing around holding it until it was Csilla's turn, but once the parlor filled with chattering vampires, I'd remain nearby in case someone got the brilliant idea of toppling it over.

So far, it was just Csilla and I in here - well, it was almost just us. There was also Ramsay Fairweather's eerily abandoned body, propped up in an antique armchair in the front row. Two of Evander's security guards had brought it down from Csilla's suite in the casket in which she apparently kept it. Kept him. It. Urgh.

This part needs some explaining - Csilla had to go over it three times before my brain halfway accepted what she was telling me.

Apparently, Laburnum Quint, Csilla's apprentice, was a man of many unusual talents. Among the more unsettling ones was his ability to temporarily inhabit other bodies, without any need for ectoplasm. Because of this, Csilla had allowed him to keep Ramsay's body as a kind of spare, rather than discarding it whatever way he usually got rid of bodies for Csilla.

Algernon had specified that Ramsay's soul would need a body to return to - preferably his own. Well, there it was. Just seeing it there stirred mixed feelings in me about the prospect of Ramsay's imminent return to the physical realm. At least while he had been gone, I hadn't had to stress about him possibly wanting me dead or definitely trying to get me kicked out of the Van Helsing Society for good.

Who knew what kind of mood Ramsay would be in when he returned? I mean, if the roles were reversed and he had been responsible for my death, only to then resurrect me, I'd still be furious. I'd be out for revenge. I could only hope that Ramsay was a better person than me. But honestly, I wasn't too confident about that.

There was also the potential problem of Evander. If Ramsay had slain his daughter, he might not be so pleased to welcome Ramsay under his roof. As soon as I returned from the spirit world with Ramsay in tow, I'd better get him out of here before he was dead all over again.

The double glass-paned doors at one end of the parlor swung open, and a stream of vampires began trickling in, Gabriel and Elizabeth at the forefront. Gabriel's gaze locked onto mine across the room and the slight tightening around his eyes made it clear that Elizabeth must have already clued him in.

I flashed a grin, hoping to disarm him a little, and was caught off guard when it actually worked. His lips twitched into an involuntary smile before he could stop himself. Just as quickly as it appeared, the smile vanished, his expression snapping back to a mask of calm severity.

At the opposite end of the parlor, another set of double doors opened, admitting another wave of vampires. Zachary and Tibor entered among them, both casting dark looks my way as they slunk back to a corner of the room. There was no sign of Roderick - I guessed he needed a little lie-down.

"But what have you got there?"

I turned and found myself eye to eye with one of the most stunning women I'd ever seen. She had appeared beside me as if materializing from thin air, clad in a deep cut, floor-length black velvet dress, her gold-and-copper hair cascading like a mermaid's over her bare shoulders. Her eyes were a peculiar shade of violet, framed by thick dark lashes. She was nearly as tall as me.

"A mirror, for Csilla's conjuration."

"Who, or what, is she planning on summoning?" Her eyes sparked with curiosity, and her elegant eyebrows knitted together.

"A demon," I replied, only half-joking. "Maybe two."

"I am Belladira Pendergast," she introduced herself.

"Harlan Thornhill."

"I know," she said with a cryptic smile, then glided away into the crowd. I couldn't help but follow her with my eyes as she moved towards what I assumed was her blood-line. She half-turned, her half-smile reappearing. Roderick's completely unhinged jealousy was starting to make a bit more sense to me.

The last few vampires were making their way into the parlor, including Evander, who was deeply engrossed in conversation with one of his security staff and failed to notice Holly rushing to catch up. She looked like she was itching to tell her uncle something - and could imagine what it was - but his attention was fully absorbed by his discussion.

Once everyone had entered and settled into their seats, Evander stepped forward and addressed the assembly, welcoming us to the second iteration of the Grim Games and issuing a reminder for contestants to ensure that anything they summoned was kept contained within a triangle. While Evander spoke, some of his staff were moving around the room, lighting candles in candelabras and sconces all along the walls.

"I believe those of you who attended the seance here in 2000 will recall what happened to Rebecca Highsmith. I am certain none of us would like to suffer the same fate."

This comment resulted in scattered laughter and applause. Whatever had happened to Rebecca Highsmith in 2000 had clearly been hilarious, as well as a shining example of something not to be repeated.

I was only distantly aware of Evander announcing that as well as Csilla, the other contestants were Holly, Belladira and Tibor.

"Csilla," Evander addressed her, "you'll be a tough act to follow, but why don't you go first? Let the game start with a bang!"

Declarations of agreement and a scattering of applause rose up under the high stuccoed ceiling.

"Love to," Csilla said, stepping forward. I took this as

my signal to bring Algernon's black-swathed mirror into the middle of the cleared floor space. Csilla indicated the exact spot where she wanted it, and I unwrapped it, facing upwards.

"My contribution to tonight's game will be a triple feature," she announced, her voice carrying through the room. Csilla carried herself with her usual air of confidence, but I could sense her nervousness cresting underneath it. "Act one: I will conjure the spirit of Algernon Thornhill, a figure well-known to many of us here from the 1800s. To some, he was a friend, to others, a business associate - or even a tormentor. Act two: My lovely assistant, Harlan Thornhill, will vanish through this mirror - his ancestor's favorite - into the spirit world. Act three: Harlan will reappear, bringing with him the recently departed spirit of Ramsay Fairweather, who some of you will recognize as a prominent member of the Van Helsing Society."

The mention of the Van Helsing Society triggered a few audible boos and jeers from the crowd. Csilla paused, allowing ample space for those inclined to express their disdain. "And then, the spirit of Ramsay Fairweather will return to its original body, unoccupied for months." She gestured towards Ramsay's body seated in the armchair in the front row, prompting a few amazed gasps from the audience.

"Before I begin," Csilla added, "Anyone who wishes is more than welcome to reassure yourself that Ramsay Fairweather's vessel is currently, for all intents and purposes, abandoned. Unoccupied by any spirit."

A few took her up on the invitation, some rising promptly while others did so more hesitantly. Soon, Ramsay's unconscious form was surrounded by a small group of vampires, each checking for a pulse and heartbeat that weren't there. When no one could find evidence to dispute Csilla's claims, they all returned to their seats.

As if in response, the lights went down, leaving only the light flames and the moonlight flooding through the vast windows overlooking the grounds, while the space was mostly steeped in darkness. There were perhaps forty or fifty vampires gathered in the parlor, but thanks to the mirrors scattered here and there on the walls it felt like we were twice as many.

The mirror on the floor looked like a glittering pond. I stood behind it, facing the room. The tension cresting in the parlor's atmosphere was so thick you could slice it with a knife.

Csilla removed a small pouch of white powder she had been carrying somewhere, probably in her bra, since I really don't think the blood red couture dress she wore had pockets. The powder would have looked extremely suspicious in the context of a nightclub, but it was probably salt, and she used this to draw an oval circle big enough to include Ramsay, me, herself and the mirror, carving out the space and simultaneously cutting us off from the rest of the room.

The assembly of vampires had fallen completely silent, including me. We were all watching Csilla's movements.

Csilla knelt in front of the mirror and knocked upon its shiny cold surface once, twice, three times. In response, the already age-stained mirror darkened further, as if dark cloudy shadows were gathering just below its surface. I stood close enough that it was easy to see it.

Quiet murmurs swept through the crowd, but if anyone had dropped a needle we would all have heard it clatter to the floor.

"Algernon Thornhill," Csilla said in a clear, steady voice. "I am here with a group of friends. We would all rather like to speak with you, and to see you. Appear to us, Algernon. Appareo!"

Now the entire surface of the mirror appeared completely black, and if you looked carefully, you could see something moving or coiling in its depths. I had the uncanny feeling that the mirror had turned into a doorway going straight down to hell, or something like it, and that what we were looking at were the actual writhing forms of the inhabitants of that place. My mouth felt dry. If Algernon was doing all of this, or much of it, it was certainly impressive.

Csilla knocked on the mirror's surface again, three times, rapidly. There was the sound of glass shattering as the mirror's surface cracked under her first. Csilla sat back, her hand bleeding where the glass had cut her.

Slowly, a black cloud of mist started rising through the cracks.

"Welcome, Algernon," Csilla said, her voice still calm, but quiet.

Gradually, Algernon's outline took shape in the mist. Initially just a shadowy form, it soon began to reveal the details of his favorite three-piece suit, the one he wore in his portrait back at the mansion, the brown of his hair, tinged with gray at the temples, and the amber glow of his eyes. Slowly, he let his gaze glide around the room, turning this way and that while seemingly remaining bound to the mirror. He appeared to be cut off at the ankles and his feet weren't visible - wherever they were, they were still below the mirror's surface.

"Good evening," Algernon spoke, his voice resonating powerfully, effortlessly enveloping lord Eve's parlor. "Have you all gathered here solely to honor me? I am truly flattered. Though, that's hardly surprising. Many of you have graced my home, mingled with me in life, undoubtedly driven by your own nefarious motives. Perhaps I should call some of you out?"

Algernon was clearly in a bit of a confrontational mood. This was evident not just from his words but from the playful, challenging twinkle in his eyes as he swept his gaze across the assembled guests, pinpointing individual vampires with precision, like a marksman choosing his targets.

"First I should probably acknowledge Lord Evander Eve." Algernon executed a bow tinged with sarcasm towards Evander. "The man responsible for dishonoring and impregnating my betrothed, and, of course, your esteemed host for tonight's soirée. A man known to more than a few of us, I'm sure, for seizing his desires and then evading the fallout of his actions."

"It's a pleasure to see you again, Algernon," Evander said with a slight bow of his head.

"And who else do we have here?" Algernon spun around, scanning the room, his semi-transparent neck stretching to survey his audience.

"Ah, Benvolio Torrero. A gentleman, by most accounts. Though, I'd advise against conducting business with him if you'd like to maintain that illusion. And do not even get me started on Gabriel Graves. Here is another who saw it fit to interfere with my family. Always so charming, so well mannered in public. But behind closed doors- well, I am getting ahead of myself. Before I get too carried away, I have another matter to attend to first, do I not? The matter of making my descendant, my son, disappear."

Algernon had trailed as far as the elliptical circle Csilla and drawn would let him - but now he turned to me abruptly, his amber eyes glowing with expectant intensity.

He floated directly towards me, as tangible as I had ever seen him. Our captive audience behind him was only faintly visible through the nearly solid-looking woven fabric of his coat.

I fought the instinct to take a step back - if I backed up much, I'd be outside the circle. Besides, I had an audience. I couldn't let anyone sense that my murderous rapist of an ancestor made me really freaking nervous. I didn't even want to admit it to myself.

"Are you ready to visit my realm?" he asked. He had stopped right in front of me, his nearly solid face inches from mine. We were exactly on eye level. His voice echoed both in the room, and seemingly inside my head. "Are you ready to disappear?"

His voice in my head was so distracting that I wasn't sure whether I answered him out loud or only in my thoughts when I gave him my defiant yes, are you?

"Well, then," Algernon said, stepping aside and revealing the mirror now swirling with what appeared to be billowing, rain-filled clouds. When they parted, they revealed a vista of Octavia's old bedroom, now my bedroom. What I was looking at, what all who were close enough to see were looking at, was the view from Algernon's mirror from its usual position, mounted on its ornate stand back home at Thornhill Mansion. The only thing that was different were the colors; they were greyscale and slightly blurry, like an old photo or maybe a daguerreotype that had sustained water damage. Algernon finished his sentence, "step inside."

I stepped closer to the mirror, wondering how exactly this was supposed to go down - was I just supposed to step into it as if it were a regular doorway? I looked over at Csilla, hoping for some guidance. She responded with a subtle nod, as if to say there's no rulebook or specific instructions for this. It's always reassuring when the centuries-old immortals around you seem just as clueless.

I knelt down next to the mirror, much like Csilla had done. Tentatively, I touched its surface. It still felt like the reflective surface of a mirror. I wasn't purely spirit; I figured I needed a more obvious entryway to cross over.

I stood back up and delivered a deliberate stomp to the mirror's surface, causing it to splinter and shatter further, fragments flying across the floor like icy raindrops.

This time when I touched the surface, it felt like a slightly rippling membrane. Deciding to go all in, I lay down on it, and it framed me like a custom-made casket. It was a strange sensation, like floating on cool water that wasn't wet. For the sake of the audience, I crossed my arms over my chest like a vampire in an old movie might do. Gradually, I began to sink through the surface.

TWENTY

I focused on my breathing to keep from panicking as I disappeared fully below the mirror's surface. The feeling was of a syrupy sort of gravity clinging to me, until it suddenly released its hold and I stumbled backward out of the haunted mirror and into my bedroom at Thornhill Mansion. Glancing into the mirror now, all I could see was the stuccoed ceiling in Lord Eve's parlor. I vaguely wondered if anyone close enough to glance into the mirror would be able to see me, in real time, in this spirit world version of Octavia's old bedroom.

I swept my surroundings with a glance. The room looked like itself, only it was nearly greyscale and looked like it was painted with slightly bleeding watercolors. All of the shadows in the room also seemed somehow blacker.

Everything was in place, as far as I could tell. There was the ornate four-poster bed with its cherubs and roses carved into the bedposts, there was the red-lacquered antique desk with my iMac stationed on top. I supposed this explained how Algernon was able to read my emails and text messages - if an item was at Thornhill Mansion,

Algenon would have a shadow copy of it here on the other side.

Octavia's old wardrobe and my backlit weapons cabinet were still there, as was the copy of Mary Shelley's Frankenstein - a book I was finally making my way through based on Lyrica's recommendation. It lay on the bedside table, a bookmark holding my place at the halfway mark. Outside, the garden's branches swayed gently, and in the distance, an ashen, shadowy version of Highgate Cemetery West formed the backdrop.

Drifting up from one of the lower floors, the sound of Lyrica's old gramophone playing a tune from the '50s or '60s reached me. The saccharine lyrics were unmistakable and took on an undeniably ominous tone as they filtered through the floor: "Tonight, tonight/Won't be just any night/Tonight there will be no morning star/Tonight, tonight/I'll see my love tonight/And for us, stars will stop where they are."

Was this the kind of crap Ramsay listened to, or was this Algernon's choice? Or, was this simply what was on offer on the other side?

I felt tempted to have a little look around since I was here, but Csilla's warning not to let anything distract me from the goal of finding Ramsay and returning through the portal was still fresh in my mind. Resisting the urge to rummage through my drawers to see what spirits in this realm might access, I decided to follow the music instead - it felt like a guiding sign.

I reached down and closed my fingers around the knife's handle, drawing it out of its makeshift sheath I'd made using a tie and shoelaces. I wasn't sure it would prove very useful, but I felt better with it drawn.

I stepped into the familiar hallway and moved toward

the source of the music. As I passed the library, curiosity got the better of me, and I nudged the double doors open, sweeping a glance over the ceiling-high bookshelves. Everything appeared as it did back at the mansion, except for the pile of large, black, leather-bound tomes on the carpet - Venedict's collection of occult literature.

Was Ramsay trying to pass the time or to piece an exit plan together? If he was, he wouldn't need one now that I was here.

I continued past the library and descended the stairs. With each step, the music intensified. Occasionally, the needle would snag, causing the record to slow or replay a stanza.

As I passed the family portraits hanging in the stairwell, I didn't feel the usual sense of being watched that I often experienced in the real world. Perhaps here, the portraits functioned like one-way mirrors in interrogation rooms, with all observing happening from this side.

In the middle of the great hall's black-and-white marble floor lay a gaping black void. Trails of the same opaque darkness streaked from the hallway toward the front door, resembling the claw marks of some wrathful demon. It occurred to me that these dark markings could signify where Helen and Algernon met their ends; the larger void possibly marking where Helen fell - whether she slipped or was thrown by Algernon (depending on the version of the story you believe) - and the dark streaks might indicate where Venedict beheaded Algernon, dragging his body across the floor with Octavia and Lyrica's help.

I managed to suppress a shiver.

Pausing briefly outside the parlor doors, where the music - now much louder - clearly came from, I took a deep breath to steady myself, then flung the doors open and stepped inside.

I halted just inside, my gaze immediately finding Ramsay. Like every other room in this shadowy rendition of Thornhill Mansion, the downstairs parlor overlooking the garden was bathed in near ashen greyscale.

Ramsay, too, was rendered in greyscale and sat on the upholstered chaise lounge in front of the fireplace, which held only shadows instead of flames. He wore the same tailored outfit he had worn when he vanished in October, only now it appeared charcoal gray instead of navy. His head snapped up from the book he was reading - one of the rare occult books from the upstairs library, as far as I could tell. The usual cool, icy blue of his eyes was now a light ash gray. The book tumbled from his grasp to the floor, its thud muted by the gramophone's croon.

"Harlan!" he exclaimed. He was crestfallen - Algernon could not have told him I'd be dropping by.

"Missed me?" I asked, my tone light and teasing. Normally, this would have flustered and provoked him, but instead, Ramsay's expression showed only a flicker of uncertainty.

"Harlan, have you... have you died?" He rose from the chaise lounge and took a tentative step toward me, then halted abruptly.

Realizing I was still holding the hunting knife, I quickly sheathed it beneath my boot's shoelaces to ease the tension. I could see how throwing Ramsay to the lions (Csilla) then turning up on the other side brandishing a hunting knife might not come across as particularly reassuring.

"No, I'm still alive," I clarified. "Or, you know, undead." And he must have noticed. Despite my vampiric pallor, the vividness of my eyes and hair, and the bright crimson cherry blossoms embroidered on my clothes marked me as just a visitor in this realm.

"Then what are you doing here?" he asked, starting to recover from his initial shock.

"I've come to take you back with me," I replied, giving him a slight crooked smile. "Don't you miss being alive?"

"More than anything," he replied. "But how?"

"You just have to come with me and do as I say."

Ramsay let out a deep, resigned sigh. He didn't like the idea of that, but what else could he do? His options were thin on the ground as far as I could see.

I let my eyes sweep around the parlor again.

"Listening to this eerie, saccharine stuff isn't exactly lifting the mood," I commented, walking past him to the gramophone by the window. It stood on its customary ormolu table, spinning a record labeled 'Jay and The Americans: Tonight' slowly beneath the needle. Beneath the table, a stack of records was piled up - mostly Lyrica's rock albums from the '70s.

Since my arrival, the song had ended and seemed to have started over, with the ensemble's smooth-voiced singer leading the melody and the rest of the group echoing the word 'tonight'. 'Oh, moon, grow bright (tonight, tonight)/And make this endless day, endless night (tonight, tonight).'

As I reached to lift the gramophone's arm and halt the music, Ramsay snapped, "Stop! Don't touch that."

I paused, my hand frozen mid-air.

I frowned, puzzled. "What's the big deal? You really that into Jay And The Americans? What's wrong with you?"

But Ramsay shook his head. "It's not me - it's Algernon. He insists on playing this record and few others like it repeatedly. Over and over and over. And over. You can't stop the music - it sends him into a rage like nothing else. He can be quite menacing when he's angry, as you've probably noticed, and let's just say he's not exactly stable. It seems to be a family trait."

"Thanks for that," I muttered.

But I stepped back from the gramophone. If Algernon wanted to eternally loop 1950s crooners in the spirit world, that was his prerogative, I suppose.

"Let's get out of here," I suggested, turning towards the hall.

When I reached the doorway I froze in my steps. The dark, swirling chaos portal - for want of a better word - had expanded significantly since I entered the parlor. I couldn't have been in here much longer than five minutes, but apparently, that was enough for the dark edges of Helen's fall print and the scene of Algernon's beheading to bleed together, forming one large chasm that took up most of the great hall's available floor space.

"It seems to expand and contract like a tide," I heard Ramsay's voice behind me.

Then, gesturing towards the book that had fallen on the floor, he added, "What do you think I've been doing with all of the time I've been forced to spend here? Whenever Algernon isn't around, I have been searching for a way out. I mean, another way out than that black swirling chaos portal."

"Portal?" I asked. "I thought it was some sort of, I don't know, trauma scarring."

"It might be that, but it seems to function like a portal," Ramsay said. "I've watched several spirits disappear into it, most of them the souls of the cops Octavia seems so fond of killing. But they don't return." A visible shiver passed through his shoulders - he wasn't able to hide it.

"So if someone dies at Thornhill Mansion, their spirit arrives here - and some of them pass through that dark portal in the main hall, never to be seen again, while others linger in the mansion. Is that how it works?"

"As far as I can tell."

I wondered what determined whether a spirit would pass on to the great beyond or remain here.

"I'll answer that," Ramsay said, his voice tinged with bitterness. "It's sheer determination, and what I know about the spirit realm from extensive reading on the subject. I wasn't ready to die when you handed me over to a soul-sucking vampire. I refused. And fortunately, Algernon allowed me to stay here. And so, here I am."

"If you truly didn't want to die," I countered sharply, "you shouldn't have come at me with a werewolf. It was a pretty stressful situation you put me in. You forced me to act."

"Are you actually blaming me for my own death?" His tone was incredulous.

I whipped around to face him squarely.

"I am, a bit, yes."

He was the one who flinched and looked down.

"Don't make me regret coming here for you. I'm only doing this once. If I have to end you for real, there won't be a second rescue. I don't like this place, I don't like the music, and all in all I'm just not coming back."

"Alright, Harlan, I get it. I understand." His eyes flashed with something that was either hurt, anger or shame. Maybe all of them.

"Okay, let's go, then. But you go first. Just in case you

get the urge to push me into... that," I said, nodding towards the dark, swirling void in the floor.

"Where are we going?"

"Upstairs," I replied curtly. I didn't tell him the rest. I needed him to need me to show him the way.

Now that I was actually here, guiding Ramsay through the corridors of the mansion, I felt even more ambivalent about bringing him back. Was it really wise to resurrect someone who might still harbor resentments and hidden agendas? I just wasn't sure it was a good idea.

"Go on, walk," I said. We didn't have all night.

He did, tentatively.

I followed close behind, watching him navigate around the gaping maw of the void. Each step he took was measured and slow. I maintained a distance of a few meters behind him, cautious in case he decided to try anything unexpected.

As we ascended the grand staircase, I kept my gaze fixed on Ramsay's back, aware of every slight movement, every hesitant pause. The trust between us was as fragile as the cobwebs draping the corners of the stairwell. At best.

Reaching the top, Ramsay paused and turned slightly to glance back at me. The weak light from the hall below cast his face in partial shadow.

"Almost there," I said, more to reassure myself than him. If he tried anything, I was prepared to push him into the void. And if he attempted to cling to the edge, I'd cut his fingers off one by one. I'd prefer not to, but I'd do it.

I let Ramsay lead the way down the corridor until we reached the door at the end, which opened into Octavia's room. He pushed the door open, and we both stepped inside.

My eyes immediately sought out the mirror - relief

washed over me when I saw that Eve Hall's elegant stucco ceiling was still visible through its surface.

Ramsay followed my gaze. "This usually looks out onto your bedroom," he remarked.

"It's a mirror," I responded smugly, "it can be moved. Right now, it's at Eve Hall in Dorset."

"Eve Hall?" An uneasy expression flickered across Ramsay's face.

"Yeah, that's what I said. But it's better than staying here, don't you think? If you're ready to get back to the real world, and back into your body, that mirror is your gateway."

He looked at me skeptically. "When I first got here, I tried all the mirrors - and even the portraits that Algernon uses as doorways. None of them worked."

"This time it'll be different," I assured him. "How else do you think I got here, body and soul? I don't know how he's doing it, but Algernon is keeping the portal open, somehow."

When he didn't interrupt again, I continued, "When you step through, your body will be right there, the first thing you see. You'll be surrounded by a bunch of vampires, but don't let that distract you. Just focus on getting back into your body. I'm not exactly sure how it works - I guess it's just one of those things where you'll just have to trust the process."

I gave Ramsay what I hoped was an encouraging smile.

Ramsay nodded. He stepped towards the mirror and tentatively placed a hand on the glass, then pushed forward. The surface rippled like water beneath it, and he stepped through, disappearing from view.

Taking one last look around the spirit realm version of my room, I paused to absorb the eerie silence that had suddenly enveloped the space. The music from the gramophone downstairs had stopped, leaving a heavy quiet in its wake. There was only one way to interpret the sudden silence; it was time to get out of here.

There was just one final, little thing I had to do first. To test the idea of correspondence between realms, I took the hunting knife and made a sharp cut in the palm of my hand. My fingers clenched reflexively around the wound as I drew a sharp breath. It felt real; if it was still there when I got back to the other side, I'd at least have learned something. A single drop of crimson fell to the floor.

I was tempted to take something from the room to see if it could travel back with me - but who knew what surprise consequences might come with it? Deciding against it, I took a deep breath and plunged into the mirror. The sensation was disorienting, like stepping into a cold stream. The chill enveloped me, drawing me forward through the viscous, glassy barrier. The world around me twisted.

Then, suddenly, I was back in the parlor at Eve Hall, lying on my back on the mirror's surface, just as I had been when I first passed through. I blinked a few times to clear my vision, then sat up, letting the details of the parlor snap back into focus around me.

TWENTY-ONE

Algernon hovered a few centimeters above the floor and a few meters in front of me, facing the audience. He was still captivating them, judging by the murmurs rippling through the crowd.

"I certainly count you, Evander, among the old friends who might have stayed in touch but have instead neglected even to visit my grave on occasion," Algernon was saying. "But of course, you consider yourself too busy, even with eternity at your disposal. Of all of you, only Gabriel occasionally passes by my tomb - but not, as one might reasonably expect, to pay respects, or to express remorse for being a corrupting influence-"

I shook my head to clear the last dizziness from going through the mirror.

Suddenly, Algernon seemed to sense my presence, because he turned abruptly towards me. "Ah, but there he is. Welcome back to the realm of the living, and of the undead, son."

"Thanks, Dad," I responded, my voice dripping with irony.

"Finally, you acknowledge that I am your father. That wasn't so difficult, was it?"

In a flash, Algernon transformed into a void of black mist and vanished back into the broken surface of the mirror, turning it solid black, like a computer that had been switched off. He passed through me on the way, and a shiver of cold ran down my spine.

Or perhaps it was the sight of Ramsay coming back to life that sent that shiver through me.

From its previously slumped position, Ramsay's body suddenly jerked upright with an audible gasp. His fingers tensed around the armrests as his eyes flew open, wide and wild, like someone startled awake from a deep and unsettling dream. They'd been gray in the spirit world; now they were back to being bright icy blue.

As Ramsay regained his bearings and took in his surroundings, a mix of incredulity and relief played across his features.

Unsure how to feel about this, I stood up and swiftly began collecting the scattered shards of the mirror from the floor, gathering them into the black cloth which I then tied into a knot.

To be honest, part of me hoped Algernon might have managed to escape the mirror altogether and was now roaming free around Eve Hall, never to return to Thornhill Mansion. But banishing him for good was likely not that simple. What I knew for certain was that I needed to deal with him soon, tonight, because now that Ramsay was back and Csilla's powers were presumably restored, Algernon would be expecting his reward. If it was up to me, the only thing he had coming was a hole in the ground.

I was peripherally aware of Ramsay getting to his feet, unsteady at first but quickly regaining his composure as he turned to survey the room. His gaze swept over the gathered crowd before landing on Csilla, who met him with a broad grin.

The room fell silent, the audience hanging in suspense, unsure if the performance had concluded. To signal the end, Ramsay gave a half-bow. It might have been tinged with irony, but it still elicited a wave of enthusiastic applause.

With the applause still ringing, Ramsay walked out of the parlor. He pushed through the double doors at one end of the room and disappeared as Csilla began to wrap up the event with characteristic flair. I quickly followed Ramsay, slipping through the doors just before they swung shut.

"Ramsay, wait!" I called out.

He stopped and turned back towards me. We were alone in the corridor.

"What is it? Don't tell me you expect my gratitude for bringing me back. It would be very like you." His voice was weary but carried a sharp edge. "You can count yourself lucky, both you and Csilla, that my appreciation for this second chance outweighs any thirst for revenge."

"I don't expect you to thank me. Just... I'm sorry if I overreacted. You know, back in October."

Ramsay stood frozen, giving me an incredulous look, as if he was trying to tell whether I was being serious or not.

"You're sorry if you overreacted?" He repeated. "You offered my soul to a soul-eating succubus, or whatever she is. My soul, Harlan!" He shouted that last part.

"I think we'll just have to move past it," I said in a clipped tone. Couldn't he acknowledge that I'd just given him an unreserved apology? Ungrateful prick.

When he didn't respond at first I added, "You're the one

who came at me with a werewolf and at least the shadow of intent to see me dead. You should be sorry, too."

"I told you, I had no intention of harming you," he insisted. "I only wanted to shake you up, and you took it incredibly badly. You were seeing shadows on the wall and mistaking them for reality."

"You know what I think? I think you were undecided, that maybe you were letting fate make the decision for you. The situation got out of control, because you let it. But you didn't want to admit that to yourself, or to me. You still don't. You fucking coward."

Ramsay flinched, glancing down and away from me.

Then, he seemed to regain his composure, fixing me with a sullen expression, as if he had just bitten into a particularly bitter lemon.

He didn't address what I'd just said, but finally, his shoulders lowered and he said, "I'm sorry, Harlan. I let it spiral out of control. But you have to understand how infuriating it was that the elders welcomed you back with open arms, vampirism and all, while they revoked my license for less. And I'm a Fairweather."

Ramsay always believed his family name made him superior to everyone else. I frowned. "I don't have to understand it, Ramsay. And I don't."

He sighed, frustration evident. "Alright, then. Maybe this will interest you. Considering my recent misadventures on your bad side, I think I'm ready to take you up on that offer of friendship."

"Really?" I replied, my tone dripping with skepticism. "You're not just playing me?"

"Really," he assured, his voice softening. "This is not a trick. I am simply tired of being dead. I'm tired of the animosity. Let's try something different," he said, extending his hand toward me, palm open, in a gesture of peace.

I took his hand.

Now it was my turn to flinch. I grimaced and looked down - the cut I'd made in my palm in the spirit world was still there. It was already starting to heal, but my blood was on Ramsay's palm, like some kind of metaphor, or a premonition. Something about it chilled me.

"If you really are sorry," Ramsay said, "there's something you can do for me. You said we're in Dorset - and there are way too many vampires around for my comfort level." He made a vague nod in the direction of the parlor we had just left. "Drive me up to London like you said you would. It's just after 4 AM. We don't have much time before sunrise, but I know how you drive. As long as you don't crash, we'll make it just fine."

I smiled involuntarily at the backhanded compliment. "Alright. But give me a minute, I need to go back and get something."

I tossed Ramsay my car keys and asked him to wait for me outside while I quickly returned to the parlor and retrieved the bundle with Algernon's mirror. If I was heading back up to London tonight, or rather, this early morning, Algernon was coming with me. I had a plan for him.

"What is that?" Ramsay asked, perplexed, as he saw me toss the bundle into the Stingray's backseat.

"Oh, just my ancestor's haunted mirror," I replied nonchalantly as I started the engine. "I need to take it back to London with me. Don't worry about it."

As I turned the key in the ignition, the car's speakers

came alive with the last track I had been listening to before arriving at Eve Hall. It was "Spillways" by Ghost - a theatrical sort of heavy metal that, judging by Ramsay's disgusted expression, was definitely not his cup of tea.

I let it play, the staccato chords and pounding rhythms of the music filling the car as I swung out of the parking lot, maneuvered down the allee and out onto the main road. The music seemed a fitting soundtrack as we raced against the sunrise.

"Is this what you listen to?" Ramsay asked, his voice overflowing with barefaced contempt.

Instead of giving him a civilized response, I cranked up the volume and began singing along to the chorus with unrestrained enthusiasm.

"It's the cruel beast that you feed/It's your burning, yearning need to bleed/Through the spillways/Through the spillways of your soul."

Ramsay looked mortified. He had had the sort of upper-crust upbringing where the only acceptable music was probably from piano recitals so stuffy and quiet you could hear a pin drop.

"Sing with me, Ramsay," I encouraged. I wasn't sure whether I was hoping to lighten his mood or was just teasing him. It was probably both.

At first, he just sat there, his frown deepening as he endured my performance. But when the chorus looped back around, his stoic resistance began to melt. The final time the chorus came, he sang along with me.

"All your faith, all your rage/All your pain, it ain't over now/And I ain't talking about forgiveness."

After we'd listened to the song twice, I decided to show some mercy and turned the volume down.

"What do you think, Ramsay - is this our song?" I joked as the last chords faded. "Now that you're back from the dead, we should probably pick one."

He let out a deep, resigned sigh. "If you think it fits."

Ramsay might not fully share my taste in music or appreciate my sense of humor, but it felt to me like we'd just shared a moment of healing.

I refocused on the road ahead, the headlights slicing through the darkness, making the road ahead look like a dark ribbon unfurling before us. Ramsay sank into a thoughtful silence, his gaze lost in the passing night landscape.

I vaguely considered whether or not I should seize the opportunity to grill him about Emmeline Eve, but he looked so deep in thought that I decided against it.

I tossed him my iPhone instead. "Call Denise if you want," I suggested.

Denise, Ramsay's fiancée, was an archivist for the Society. She came off as overly privileged and wholesome, which I couldn't really relate to, but I suppose that's what Ramsay liked about her; she represented the human side of himself, or something like that.

There was barely any traffic on the roads, and we made it to London in record time. Ramsay asked to be dropped off outside an upscale mansion block just around the corner from Regent's Park, its facade a blend of old-world elegance and modern opulence.

"What are you going to tell the elders?" I asked as he stepped out of the car.

"An abbreviated version of the truth," he replied, leaning down to meet my gaze from the sidewalk. "I'll tell them I needed a holiday, far away from you. We both know it wouldn't be in either of our interests to attempt to explain the full story."

He added in a low tone, "If there's anything you feel you need to make up to me, then show the elders you're the exemplary vampire hunter they expect. Show them that a vampire can be trusted and clear the path for me to regain my own license."

"I'm on it," I replied. "And Ramsay?"

"Yes?" His eyes narrowed slightly.

"We have to try to get along. Because next time, one of us is going to end up dead for good."

He nodded. "I'm well aware of that."

I flashed him a fanged smile. I really hoped our attempt at friendship was going to work out because if he ever crossed the line again, I'd drive a stake through him, and there would be no more chances.

As soon as he had closed the car door behind him, I pulled away, steering the car towards Highgate. It was 6:30 AM, an hour and fifteen minutes to sunrise. I had enough time to carry out the plan I'd conceived of for Algernon.

I sped up the now familiar curve of Swain's Lane and brought my car to a screeching halt in front of Thornhill Mansion's imposing wrought-iron gate. The first time I'd stepped through it, it had been rusty, its black paint frayed and peeling. Now it gleamed in the early morning gloom.

The garden was still overgrown, and as always as I made my way up the gravelly path towards the mansion's front doors I had the feeling that the various statues hidden in the tall grass were following me with their unseeing, moss-covered eyeballs. It was a feeling I'd gotten pretty used to.

I pushed the front doors open, not sure whether I would

find anyone home. Thornhill Mansion never felt empty, even when it was. Too much history, too many ghosts.

I went down the windy stairs that Sebastian had discovered during our first visit to the mansion. How strange that that had been less than six months ago - it already felt like an entire reality ago. The scent of dust and earth rose into my nostrils and into my lungs as I descended into the corridor below ground. The circular chamber at the end of the hallway was where I knew I'd find the shovel - the same one I'd had to use a few times to bury Octavia's unfortunate victims in the dirt floor. She seemed to have a bit of a thing for cops.

The circular room with its dusty red velvet drapes and caskets was, objectively speaking, a pretty eerie setting. But now that I was a vampire myself, it seemed normal.

I grabbed the shovel, which stood leaning against the ancient stone wall, and went back upstairs. Here, I dislodged Algernon's favorite painting from its place on the landing - a vantage point from which it overlooked the great hall and had a clear view of anyone coming and going into or out of the mansion.

The painting, of course, was a priceless antique, but this had to be done.

Carrying the painting and the shovel, I made my way down through the dimly lit garden, its shadows elongated by the moonlight. Returning to my car, I picked up my knives, just in case, and the bundle containing Algernon's haunted mirror from the backseat. As a final touch, I slipped my headphones over my ears, the opening bars of Vivaldi's "La Folia" filling the silence around me as I marched off in the direction of the cemetery. Gabriel had had this tune on in the background when I visited and he told me about the family history. Vivaldi isn't always a bad thing, I suppose, it's just that I thought there was a time and a place for the classical stuff.

It was time to commit what remained of Algernon Thornhill to the ground. I could have played him a requiem - but the prospect of dispatching him for good was far too uplifting for something so somber.

TWENTY-TWO

T he tall gates intended to keep out of hours visitors out of Highgate Cemetery West loomed ahead. With the painting secured under one arm and the shovel in my other hand I leapt up onto the top of the gate, then dropped down on the other side, landing among the shadows of Victorian tombstones, stone angels, and creeping shrubbery that made up the landscape of Highgate's western part.

The air was cool and filled with the scent of damp earth as I walked deeper and deeper into the dark cemetery, passing ivy-clad Victorian tombstones and stone angels with time-worn features and wings unfurled as if ready to ascend.

I paused when I reached a secluded nook, shaded by a towering ash tree with multiple trunks and roots snaking through the soil. This quiet corner seemed like a suitable resting place for Algernon, far enough from both the mansion and the Thornhill family tomb in the Circle of Lebanon. It was an interesting coincidence that the spot I'd chosen was at the far end of the cemetery, directly across from Deep Graves. The thought of Algernon potentially wandering over to pester Gabriel post-burial brought a smile to my face.

I began to dig, the shovel slicing through the cold earth. The hole widened quickly as the soil piled up beside it.

I paused between shovelfuls when my headphones suddenly malfunctioned and Vivaldi's La Folia was replaced by a scrambled cacophony. Then I heard Algernon's voice in my ears, as loud and clear as if he had been standing right next to me, but on both sides.

"Not so fast, son. I don't appreciate what you think you are about to do," his voice echoed, sending a shiver down my spine.

I straightened up and removed the headphones. The absence of music left a void.

The cemetery was silent now, the only sounds the rustle of leaves and the distant call of a night bird.

"I'm finishing what I started, Algernon," I said into the stillness. "You think you can tell me what to do? No one can."

I resumed digging.

"You're going into the ground, Algernon," I announced. "See if you can stop me."

There was no response - I guess there just wasn't a damned thing he could do.

Once the grave was deep and wide enough, I kicked the painting and the bundle containing the mirror into it. I did it demonstratively, to provoke him, in case he was watching.

"I'm going into the ground, am I?" His voice, laced with both anger and amusement, but definitely more anger, seemed to come from everywhere and nowhere.

Before a snide retort could even form and roll off my tongue, I was overcome with a sensation unlike any other. It was as if an invisible, buzzing presence had launched an assault directly on the back of my skull. The feeling was intense and violating, like claws frantically trying to burrow into the base of my skull and into my consciousness.

I dropped to my knees, dropped the shovel and instinctively covered the back of my head with my hands. I had no idea whether this would have any effect at all against what was happening to me, but the instinct to protect myself still kicked in.

"This is how you thank me for welcoming you into the family?" Algernon's voice thundered in my mind, unbearably loud. "This is how you repay me for aiding you, for praising you, for loving you?"

"Is this the kind of creepy shit you used say to Octavia when you raped her?" Seemed like it would be.

"I would never demean the tender moments I shared with my daughter by calling them rape," he replied, the words chilling my blood. "But yes, if you must know, I did assure her of my love. I never allowed her to doubt it."

My eyes were open, I think, but I could see nothing. The world had dwindled to the cold earth beneath me, the oppressive sensation of a dark mass looming above me, bearing down on my skull with the intensity of an ice pick, and Algernon's voice echoing in my head, accompanied by a maddening buzzing like a swarm of flies.

The buzzing intensified to a deafening hum, but Algernon's voice still cut through loud and clear, "You know of my desire to live again, to inhabit an immortal body. Venedict's would have sufficed, but I must admit, I find yours preferable. Just a little more height and muscle than his dainty form offers wouldn't go amiss. Have I not had ample opportunity to observe you since your arrival at the mansion?"

I had secured the hunting knife in a sheath on my arm before heading to the cemetery. Slowly, ever so slowly, I moved my right hand toward it. Algernon had no physical form to attack, but the cut on my palm was proof that there existed a tenuous connection between the physical and spiritual realms. A slim chance, but worth a try.

"Until five minutes ago," Algernon continued, "I would have settled for your assistance in securing my hold over Venedict's body once he relinquished it. But since you seem determined to thwart my plans, you leave me with little choice. I shall simply have to take yours. Do you doubt my capability?"

As he spoke, my fingers wrapped around the knife's handle, drawing it silently from its sheath.

"You may believe I require ectoplasm to achieve my goal, and while that would be ideal, my methods of posses-sion have become rather... refined over the past century and a half of being discarnate. What we have working in our favor, you and I, is our shared blood, or DNA, as you might call it. Mine is tied into yours with a double overhand knot, which makes your defenses weak against me."

With Algernon's incessant chattering echoing in my head, I lifted the knife, positioning it behind my head where the pressure on my skull was most intense.

"And here's something else that might thrill you to hear," he continued, his voice low, quiet, like he was confessing a secret, "Venedict has unwittingly laid the groundwork for my approach. While he was locked away in his casket, he spent years chipping away at your psychic defenses by trying to reach you, speak to you, and summon you. In doing so, he paved the way for me. I've been wandering the corridors of your mind for some time now. Your recent, careless spilling of blood in my realm gave me yet another way to anchor myself to you. You belong to me now as surely as Venedict and Octavia do - perhaps even more so. Delightful, isn't it?"

I swung the knife through the air behind me. As I did, I felt the curious sensation of cutting through a dense fog.

Suddenly, there was a lightening, a release as if I had severed something tangible. The insidious buzzing, that oppressive presence attempting to worm its way into my consciousness, ceased as abruptly as if a switch had been flicked.

Algernon's voice, so loud and self-assured moments ago, faltered as the oppressive weight dissipated.

Could it really be this simple to fend off a spirit's attempt at possession?

The cemetery around me came back into view. I found myself sprawled on the ground in front of the grave I had dug, clutching the hunting knife in one hand and still pressing the base of my skull with the other. My entire system was flooded with adrenaline.

I knew I had to finish what I had started. I managed to sit up, still gripping the knife. I spat out a few grits of dirt that had somehow made their way into my mouth.

With Algernon's attempt at possession now behind me, I lowered myself into the open grave. "I said, try to fucking stop me!" I called into the void. This time, there was no response, only the eerie silence of the graveyard.

The painting was lying at the bottom of the grave beneath the shattered pieces of the mirror. These were the symbolic remnants of Algernon and I felt a deep instinctual need to destroy them.

I plunged the knife into the canvas, dragging it first

downward and then across before repeating until I had reduced the portrait to so much antique shredded confetti.

With the painting out of the way I turned my attention to the mirror's shards, stabbing and scraping at them with the knife. The glass crunched under the blade, the sound sharp in the enclosed space of the grave. I kept going until the shards were all opaque, transformed from pieces of mirror into bits of dull, shattered glass.

Once everything was destroyed I finally stood up and glanced at my watch. 7:17 AM. About twenty minutes to sunrise. Thank heavens for those late January sunrises.

When I climbed out of the grave, covered in dirt, I was greeted by the unexpected sight of Thomas Graves lounging against a nearby tombstone. With his blond hair, green eyes, and angular features right down to the narrow grecian nose, Thomas resembled Gabriel a great deal. The most obvious differences were his slightly shorter stature, more solid build, and the darker, more saturated hues of his eyes and hair. The paling moon in the sky above the cemetery wasn't full, but he was unmistakably human. How come? And for how long had he been here?

"Morning, Harlan. Engaged in a little redecoration?" His tone and expression were both casual and slightly amused, but underneath, there was a hint of skepticism. Thomas was not exactly born yesterday. He knew there had to be more to the story than me fly-tipping an old painting and a broken mirror in the cemetery.

I tried to mask my surprise, smoothly disentangling a piece of canvas caught on my knife before letting it slide back into its sheath and shaking the dirt from my hands. "Hey, Thomas. Actually, you could say I'm doing a bit of redecorating. Is that a problem?"

"Oh, I don't know," he said, his tone measured, "is it?"

"You're human," I said, steering the focus away from what I was up to.

"I am indeed," Thomas confirmed, pushing off from the tombstone and walking toward me with a confident, relaxed gait. It was clear he wasn't looking for a fight, but even if he had been, I liked my odds. Thomas might have more muscle, but he was a mere mortal.

"I thought you only shed the tentacles on full moons," I commented, arching an eyebrow.

He stopped just a few feet away from me. "That has been the case for the past few centuries. But it is no longer so," he replied, a touch cryptically. I could tell from his smile that he enjoyed keeping me guessing.

"Has the curse... worn off?" I asked. I didn't know the first thing about how Thomas's form of lycanthropy worked.

His silence seemed to affirm my suspicion.

"Do Gabriel and Elizabeth know?"

"Not yet. I expect they'll both be rather surprised when they return from Eve Hall - where I thought you were supposed to be this weekend."

"I got homesick."

"Hm," Thomas's muddy-green eyes narrowed slightly. "If you say so."

"Sunrise is soon. I've got to tidy this up and get back to the mansion." I gestured towards the still-open grave behind me. The shovel lay where I had dropped it.

"I've filled in a lot of graves in my time, so why don't you leave it to me?" Thomas suggested.

"If you're sure you don't mind," I said, picking up the shovel and planting it in the dirt. "But you don't get to ask me any questions about it."

"I've got no questions," he promised with a hint of a smile.

Why was he being kind to me? It puzzled me a little, but maybe I should just accept it for what it was and try to appreciate that not everyone was out to blackmail, attack or attempt to possess me.

I left him to fill in the grave and began my ascent back to Thornhill Mansion, whose spiky silhouette rose above the cemetery. I could sense dawn approaching, and birds had already started singing in the filigree of branches above me.

Crossing the threshold into the dim quiet of the mansion, I noticed a large hardshell suitcase and a number of black leather bags next to the door. Sebastian was back, and in a considerate gesture, he had drawn the blackout curtains across every window in the mansion, shrouding the world it held in protective darkness.

I didn't have time for a shower and didn't want to fill my own casket with the gravedirt I was covered in, so instead of heading upstairs I went back down into the crypt and climbed into Venedict's old casket. The chains Lyrica and Clyde had used to bind it were still there, severed and trailing on the ground.

I let myself sink into the same threadbare velvet uphol-stery that had cradled my distant brother, and uncle, for 160-something years. A chill ran through me as I closed the lid, cutting off the dim, graying light beginning to creep in under the crypt's door. Sleeping in Venedict's casket was bound to give me nightmares, but I had to sleep some-where, and with dawn flooding the world outside, it was too late to even think about an alternative.

After dealing with Algernon in the cemetery and

listening to his boastful confessions about having 'double-tied' himself into my DNA, I couldn't bear the thought of sleeping in Octavia's old room where, presumably, the transgressions he seemed so pleased about had taken place.

I closed my eyes and slept like the dead.

CHAPTER
TWENTY-THREE

My alarm went off at 4:46 PM and I sat up in Venedict's casket with a start, flinging its lid open. The sound it made reverberated in the silence of the crypt.

I still had the remnants of last night's venture clinging to me. I needed to shower and get dressed at warp speed, then drive back to Eve Hall.

I hurried upstairs, my steps echoing up the old wooden staircase and through the mansion's seemingly empty corridors.

No ghosts followed me as I burst into the ensuite bathroom with the ancient copper pipes and faded tiles attached to Octavia's old bedroom, and to my relief, no shadowy form attempted to start a conversation from the mirror as I turned on the shower, twisting the knobs until the water temperature bordered on scalding. It felt like Algernon really was gone.

The hot stream and water cascaded over me, sluicing away the layers of grime and graveyard dust that had dried in my hair and on my skin.

After the shower I dressed rapidly in a dark, fitted ensemble and descended down through the mansion.

As I reached the landing between the ground and first floors, where Algernon's portrait had left behind an empty square on the wall, I barely missed bumping into Sebastian, who seemed to appear out of thin air. Or, it was probably me who appeared out of nowhere, my supernatural speed a blur in the dimly lit space.

"Harlan!" he exclaimed, his midnight blue eyes lighting up. "I thought I heard you come back early this morning." He stepped forward and enveloped me in a tight hug. I'm usually not one for hugs, and I'm not above sidestepping or ducking to avoid them, but this time I let him. It had been nearly a month since we'd last seen each other.

He finally released me and stepped back with a playful grin. "You left a trail of dirt leading down into the crypt. Wild weekend at Eve Hall?"

"You could say that," I replied, "and it isn't over yet. I'm actually headed back there now. But why are you back here so early? I thought you and Irene still had more places to go."

His smile faded slightly, and he let out a deep, theatrical sigh. "That's just the thing. Irene and I have run our course. I had an epiphany, and it's over."

"An epiphany?" I repeated. After all the effort Sebastian had put into winning Irene back, suddenly breaking up with her now seemed a little impulsive.

Sebastian nodded somberly, his expression shifting into one of resigned acceptance. "I've realized that we just aren't meant to be. With all the twists and turns my life has taken recently, especially now being part of this family, our paths no longer align. I think I'm meant to be with a vampire. I've already started meditating on it, manifesting it."

What do you say to something like that? So I didn't.

"Harlan, why that grimace?" Sebastian sounded a little hurt. "Manifestation works. I've used it plenty of times to attract things I want into my life. Including Thornhill Mansion, that Vogue Italia commission I've landed, and you."

"Listen, I'm deeply fascinated and I'd love to hear the entire saga. But right now, I've got to get back to Eve Hall."

Sebastian nodded, a wistful smile playing on his lips as he leaned against the banister. "I get it. And honestly, that's exactly why things with Irene can't work. She's just not part of the world I'm stepping into. You know, there are all kinds of ways to become a vampire. Love can turn you - or death, like it did for you. I know it's only a matter of time before I'm turned, and I think the immortal flame will come to me as a gift of love."

"Sounds romantic." I glanced at my watch. "But I've got to run."

"Just one thing. I haven't told Venedict or the others. I'm not sure they'd be able to wrap their Victorian minds around the concept, but you should know. I want to get this off my chest. Venedict's plan for me to deliver an heir to the family? It's not happening because, well," he lowered his voice, his eyes darting around as if worried one or more of our undead cousins might be eavesdropping, "after growing up in foster care, I wanted to make sure I'd never have kids. So, I had a vasectomy."

"What, when?" I was aware of Venedict's demands, but this was news to me.

I could understand Sebastian's decision not to have kids. I hadn't wanted any either, but I hadn't gone as far as a surgical solution to make sure it wouldn't happen. A vasectomy seemed a bit extreme to me - what if things were, you know, impacted? But Sebastian was a braver man than I was.

"Years ago," he disclosed, his voice dropping conspiratorially. "So you and I really are the end of the line. There'll never be another Thornhill."

Sebastian wasn't technically a Thornhill by blood, but right now wasn't the time to break it to him.

"Sebastian, you know I don't care about the family having heirs, right?" I said, looking him in the eye.

He nodded, a faint smile playing on his lips. "That's why I feel I can tell you. And you have to help me tell Venedict, or at least be present when I tell him. He's going to be mad about it."

"Well, that sounds super awkward. But sure, I promise. I really have to run now."

"Alright," Sebastian said. "We'll catch up properly when you're back. And don't forget me at Eve Hall, will you? Keep an eye out for the perfect vampire girl for me."

"Sure, drop me your criteria, and I'll keep my eyes peeled for your undead dream girl," I replied, my tone dripping with sarcasm as I turned and hurried down the remaining stairs. Sebastian missed the sarcasm completely and called out as I stepped onto the ivy-covered steps in front of the mansion, "Great idea. I'll text you!"

I drew the doors closed behind me, leaving Sebastian standing under the darker square left on the wall where Algernon's portrait used to hang. With it gone, the air in there seemed a little lighter, a little less gloomy.

I climbed into the Stingray, the engine roaring to life as I gunned it back to Eve Hall. I wasn't sure what awaited me, but after my altercation with Algernon in the cemetery, it couldn't be that bad.

Lord Eve's security team hadn't checked when I left Eve Hall last night with Ramsay, but on the way back in, they insisted I go through their scanner again to ensure I wasn't armed - fortunately, I'd left my knives in the car.

I'd barely stepped through the door of my suite when there was a knock.

I turned around and opened the door for Csilla. She was dressed in a short black velvet dress that hugged her figure, a bright red velvet choker encrusted with tiny, sparkling rubies, and stiletto boots adorned with star constellations in rubies. What a showoff. But she rocked it, and the self-satisfied expression she wore along with the outfit indicated that she knew it.

"You are like a tomcat that strays and gets into fights," she observed with a twinkle in her eye, "but at least you haven't come back with a missing ear, yet."

She walked in without asking and shut the door behind her with a decisive click before locking it with my key left in the door.

"You disappeared so quickly, you didn't even remain to find out whether we won the conjuration game."

"Well, did we?"

"Alas. Holly managed to conjure the ghost of Victorine Eve in one of the mirrors on the wall. Her appearance was nowhere as vivid as Algernon's, of course, but the count was moved to tears, and that moved everyone else, and that sealed the deal."

Csilla swished past me, making her way to the antique dark wood and velvet settee in the middle of the room. "What you also missed was the count's spectacular downfall under Gabriel's hypnotic spell."

"That's just too bad. I had to drive Ramsay home - you know, to appease him so he won't tell the elders I'm responsible for his death." And then I had to fend off Algernon's attempt at taking possession of me, but it seemed too convoluted to explain.

"Well, I suppose that's a good enough reason," Csilla conceded with a playful tilt of her head.

With a graceful sweep, she sat down while at the same time unfurling what appeared to be two rolled-up maps that she must have been carrying somewhere on her person. She smoothed out their creases across the low coffee table before glancing up. "Well? What are you standing there for? We don't have all night. I brought you a gift."

"You got me two old maps? Csilla, you really shouldn't have."

She flashed a mischievous grin. "While Evander was still dazed, I took the liberty of borrowing his keys to the map room. One of these is a detailed map of Eve Hall's underground foundations, the other a map of the maze. If I am not mistaken, the two final games will involve navigating through them." After a beat of silence she added, "No doubt Roderick, and perhaps one or more of the others, already know their way around. I deemed it necessary to even the odds a little, to thank you for helping me."

"I did it for Venedict," I pointed out. But I could feel the corners of my mouth twitch upwards in a smile.

I crossed the room and let myself plop down next to her on the plush, antiquated Victorian settee. The map on top showed an underground cavern, replete with plenty of spindly, curving corridors fanning out from a central space, with several staircases ascending from the depths of the earth and emerging within the bowels of Eve Hall. I lifted it and glanced at the map below, showing the maze on the grounds outside. The maze looked just as tricky as the underground foundations, with pathways and passages deliberately designed to confuse and mislead. In the middle of the maze was a lake - presumably the one in which Venedict's and Tessa's daughter had drowned. No wonder Evander had built a maze around it, hiding it from view.

"See if you can commit these to memory before I return them to their rightful place," Csilla instructed. "Knowing where the dead ends are might help you not only win, but keep you safe." Her voice dropped to a near murmur. "Given the new grin Roderick has been sporting since your little skirmish, something tells me he may be as interested in settling scores with you as he is in winning."

"You've seen Roderick since Elizabeth stitched him up?"

She gave a slight nod.

I wanted to ask her how bad it was, but when I opened my mouth, it was a more pressing question that came out. "You think he'll try to trap me down there and take revenge?" I indicated one of multiple dead ends shown on the map.

"Of course. And I would admittedly prefer it if nothing terrible happened to you."

I spent the next few minutes absorbed in the blueprint of Eve Hall's deeper layers, paying close attention to how the passageways and staircases connected, and marking the dead ends in my mind. Once I felt sure I had it all fairly well pinned down, I studied the map of the labyrinth, noting where one of the cavern's pathways exited. When I was done, I looked up.

"Got it memorized?" she asked.

"I've got it."

As soon as I confirmed, Csilla rolled up the blueprints

and stood to leave. She moved to the door in a blur of movement, unlocking it with a fluid grace. Pausing in the doorway, she turned back to me, her eyes dark with something unreadable.

"Harlan, I really do appreciate you going to the other side for me - even if you did it for Venedict. I... there is no pleasant way to put this." She glanced down, as if searching for the right words. "My powers appear to be back in full force, and I had a vision as soon as I woke this evening. It's about you and Ramsay - you're going to regret bringing him back. Because he is going to hurt you," there was a crack in her voice, "badly."

A chill ran through me. "Csilla, what's going to happen?" I demanded. "Just tell me. I'd rather know."

She let out a deep sigh, a sound tinted deep blue with sadness. "Remember, my visions don't always come true - they're an indication, not a guarantee."

I nodded - I remembered her telling me that. Not that it made me feel much less uneasy.

"Well, this vision was a sensation with no visual component. Sometimes, it is only one or the other." She placed one hand on her chest above her heart and the other against her temple, her expression was serious. "I felt it here, and here. A sharp pain."

The room seemed to darken around us. Was Ramsay going to shoot me in the head and put a stake through my heart - kill me like he would any other vampire?

So much for hoping he and I could put all of the mess behind us and learn to tolerate each other.

"I wish I could give you more specifics," she said, her voice barely above a whisper. "If anything more comes to me, I promise I will let you know. Whatever the future holds for you in regards to Ramsay, I doubt it is going to happen quite soon. And that might mean there is time to change the outcome. Even so," she added, her voice soft, "please be careful."

With that, she turned and disappeared into the hallway, likely on her way to return the blueprints to Evander's study.

TWENTY-FOUR

Accdording to Evander's blueprint, three of the underground passageways led to hidden trap doors on the ground floor of Eve Hall and one continued upwards inside a turret which rose above the rest of the building. There were also two outside, one exiting on the terrace inside the maze. Which one would prove to be the best exit was going to depend on where in the underground cavern I might find myself in when I needed one, so to cover my bases I decided to check out all of them.

The one located in the turret was easy enough to find - it was connected to the third floor's main hallway by an unlocked door. Simple.

The three on the ground floor all had to be hidden, probably covered up by rugs, because I hadn't noticed any trapdoors in the floor.

Instead of joining all the others in the parlor, I opted for moving through the ground floor's various chambers, opening and closing doors, and peeling back rugs in my search for the hidden passages.

The first ground floor exit I discovered was ingeniously integrated into the main entrance hall's elaborate art nouveau flooring. When you looked closely, it was possible to make out subtle discrepancies in the tilework. Lines that delved slightly deeper than their surroundings outlined a trapdoor adorned with the same petite tiles that covered the surrounding floor.

I found the second ground floor exit under a small threadbare Persian rug in what seemed to be a small reading room, overlooking the grounds and the frothing sea through thick-paned windows.

The third one was supposedly through an unused fireplace in the adjoining library, which was a vast circular room, practically overhanging the sea. A low bench lined the crescent of the window, and if you were sitting there reading a book and happened to let your gaze drift a little further than the last word in the row, you'd be looking directly down into the waves. The entire space was covered by a clear glass dome so that the night sky with all its stars was easy to see.

The library featured three grand fireplaces, each an overlarge masterpiece of intricately carved marble, with a sort of baroque elegance. They were seamlessly integrated between the floor-to-ceiling bookcases. I ducked and stepped into the first one.

The inside of the fireplace was about three feet by three feet, spacious enough to stand comfortably. It didn't seem to have any hidden staircases, doorways, or openings but instead housed an iron-caged lift that fit the space perfectly. The lift's brass control panel had unmarked buttons. I was just about to press one, eager to see where it would take me, when I heard a faint sound.

Stepping back out of the fireplace, my gaze landed on a

figure standing in front of the fireplace on the far wall, brushing soot from his shirt. It was Clyde. Ice-cold cousin Clyde, who bore a striking resemblance to Sebastian. The likeness was uncanny, almost incomprehensible, making it even harder to understand why he couldn't be a bit nicer.

His entire posture grew tense the moment he realized he was no longer alone in the library.

"Evening, Clyde. Did I startle you?" As I walked over to him, he straightened his shoulders and arranged his face into a carefully neutral expression.

"Harlan," he greeted me. "I thought you would be in the parlor along with everyone else."

"Yes, clearly." I let my eyes linger on his face as I stood in front of him. "What are you up to?"

"Nothing remarkable," he said, a little too hastily. Then he seemed to think better of it and added, "Merely enjoying the moonlight and the waves. I was looking for a book to read. I'm not particularly social, as you may have noticed. Not much of a people person - not much of a vampire person, either." He sighed. Then he turned away from me and strode over to a nearby dark wooden bookcase and started pursuing its shelves.

"So you didn't find any interesting books inside the fire-place?" I asked innocently, my hands clasped behind my back.

Clyde turned abruptly towards me, something gleaming in his eyes. "You seem to think that I owe you something, perhaps because of our shared blood. Well, I am not sure whether anyone has been telling you in my absence, but you and I share no connection, no familial bond. The only blood we unfortunately have in common is the cursed variety that stems from Gabriel."

I could feel my eyes narrow and my jaw going all tense.

I didn't like Clyde, but damn it, I was going to try to at least be neutral about it, for Lyrica's sake.

But he wasn't making it easy.

"You're a Thornhill," he lamented. "A family mine should never have become entangled with. Dear Aunt Helen was never mad - it was always the Thornhills who were mad, all of them. And that poisoned blood, it's radiating out of you. Algernon's various curses, tragically tied into your DNA more thoroughly than you can imagine."

"Is that my fault?"

"No one said it was your fault," Clyde conceded, but his tone remained dismissive as he walked over to stand by the window, looking out over the dark waves far below. "It's just the way things are."

"Why do you despise the Thornhills so much? You can't blame Algernon's flaws on everyone else. You especially can't blame me - I spent two and a half decades of my life without even knowing about any of them."

Lyrica hadn't treated me like this, like a stranger. She considered me family before she even met me.

Clyde's eyes narrowed, and he looked at me with unbridled skepticism. "If that isn't exactly what a Thornhill would say."

"I clearly can't win with you. I promised myself I'd try to get along with you for Lyrica's sake, but I'm starting to change my mind."

"I can see that. A decision shallowly rooted. You are so very like them. It is remarkable how you have even got Venedict's restless pacing down pat. Of course, you must have a lot of Octavia in you, too. All of her childish, entitled, power-loving tendencies."

Clyde didn't seem to appreciate what the pacing was for - it was to keep myself from acting on the acute desire to punch him in the nose. Of course, if I did that, he was going to wield it against me, and after what I'd done to Roderick, I'd better not get into any more scrapes this weekend.

Besides, I could see what he was trying to do; distract me from what I might have discovered by walking in on him.

"What were you doing inside the fireplace?" I demanded, pacing back and forth along the length of the floor and turning fluidly each time I reached a bookcase with his eyes tracking my movements.

"Oh, nothing. Nothing that would interest or concern you. Are you always this nosy?"

"Always. Get used to it."

"Well, I did have a little look at Lord Eve's wine cellar."

"Thought so."

He could tell that I must know about the underground tunnels, or at least that I knew about this one, so he wasn't really giving anything much away by admitting this much.

"Lyrica told me, a long time ago, about the underground tunnels and passageways that burrow through the rock below Eve Hall. I merely wanted to have a little look. Curiosity got the better of me, you might say. And how do you know about the tunnel?"

"Someone told me."

"Lyrica?"

I shook my head. "Doesn't matter. But you found it - it's through the fireplace?"

"Just right through. It's deeper than you might think."

I felt a little calmer now and stopped pacing. It would be sunrise soon and the sky was growing pale. Clyde stood outlined in silhouette against the paling sky and the waves. It was water behind him, not fire. And still, his outline, the set of his shoulders, the outline of his jaw, the long black hair that fell behind him, it suddenly overlapped with a hazy memory I had.

Past and present blurred into one and all I could see was the outline of the vampire on the staircase of my childhood home, flames dancing behind him as his laughter filled my ears.

I stood rooted to the spot, struck by lightning.

"Harlan? You look like you have seen a ghost."

"I think I am."

"Listen, dawn is near at hand. We should both retire for the day."

"I'm not tired, Clyde. It isn't dawn yet."

Clyde turned sharply and walked, almost ran, out of the library. I followed him down the corridor and as he burst out onto the patio.

"I know you probably don't want to talk," I said, "but we've got to. I've realized something. You seem to know an awful lot about me, but I know very little about you."

"I know many of our fellow undead cannot resist an opportunity to relay their long-winded life stories, but I am not among them," he said curtly, regaining his composure. We were of even height, and that made skewering him with a probing stare all the more effective. He shifted slightly under the intensity of it.

"I don't recall inviting you to join me here on the patio," he said after a beat.

"You know vampires don't need an invitation, right?"

"And you know very well what I mean. For the time being, this is my domain, and I do not want you here. Hasn't Lyrica already told you plenty about me? She told me in her most recent letter - and yes, I do receive her letters. Sometimes I respond to them - that she intended to relay her life story to you and to the last heir of our bloodline."

"Sebastian," I said, and Clyde nodded. "Unlike the Thornhills, we Hartenbrooks do have a mortal heir remaining. Of course, Venedict is of the mistaken belief that Sebastian is a Thornhill. And it is true, he shares Venedict's blood, but only through Helen."

"There's something that doesn't make sense," I said, realizing it as I spoke. "When Lyrica first invited me and Sebastian to Thornhill Mansion and told us her story, she allowed me to get her DNA tested. When the results came back, they showed that Lyrica, Sebastian and I are all related. I must have some Hartenbrook blood in me, from somewhere."

Clyde took a step back from me, as though my words were barbed wire I'd used to lash him with.

"Well, I cannot account for that," he said, but something in his tone suggested that he could. There was something he didn't want me to know. There might be a whole lot he didn't want me to know.

"And now, Harlan, I'd like you to take your leave."

"I don't think I will."

"Have you no manners?"

At least he'd finally asked instead of just assuming. He sighed - he seemed exasperated.

"Maybe your own manners leave something to be desired - but I wouldn't really know. I don't know you and would like to. You were engaged to Octavia, you could start there. She says you were never romantically involved. Is that also how you see it?"

"I've told you to leave politely. I truly do not owe you anything." His irritation was showing through quite clearly now - it was like muddy water rising through a field in spring, impossible to contain.

"Or maybe," I suggested, taking a step closer, leaving

him to take another step back, "you'd rather talk about the more recent past? Like, I don't know, twenty years ago. I don't know about you but that was a very interesting time in my life."

"I am not certain what it is you are insinuating or perhaps accusing me of, but whatever it is, you are quite wrong."

"The funny thing is, Clyde, I think I remember you."

I wasn't sure, but Clyde didn't know that. It's possible I had my wires crossed and that my brain had simply made an explosion out of ingredients that really had nothing, or very little, to do with each other.

Clyde had been getting increasingly uncomfortable during our conversation and had gradually backed away from me. Now he bumped into the french doors leading into what appeared to be a music room.

Clyde's expression suggested that he felt trapped, but I had no intention of easing that feeling for him. I was watching out for any signs of aggression, though, just in case. Not that Clyde seemed like a fighter. He wasn't built for it, and I knew from Lyrica's description of him that he was more of an intellectual, bookish type. A man of science, in his own words.

In an abrupt movement, Clyde spun around, simultaneously yanking the door open and stepping quickly inside. The door swung outwards, meaning all I really needed to do was press my palm against the pane as he tried to pull the door shut behind him. He released the door, abandoning his attempt at closing it.

Admittedly, I was being a complete jerk - unless, of course, he had actually killed my parents. If he had, my behavior felt more than warranted. It was just a gamble I was going to have to take.

"Harlan!" Evander's commanding voice was a surprise. I turned to look in the direction it had come from and saw him leaning out of a window on the same floor, not far from the patio.

"Is pestering your cousin Clyde really how you relax?" There was a slight teasing note in his voice.

"Why wouldn't it be?" I shot back.

"I woud rather you come here, please. I have something I'd like to show you, something you do not want to miss. You can return to - well, whatever it is you seem to be doing - afterwards."

This was technically true, but it was difficult to tear myself away. I'd been just about to corner Clyde, and I could think of a few ways to try to wring some of his secrets out of him. But it might take more than an hour. If Evander had something important to show me that couldn't wait until afterwards.

I hesitated, but then I pushed the door open and strode across the room to get to the hallway. Clyde stood beside a dark piano, his arms crossed and his gaze following me, his expression caught somewhere between disdain and disbelief.

I paused in the doorway. "I'll catch you later, Clyde," I said, and meant it.

I left his room behind and made my way down the corridor to where I assumed Evander would be.

As I reached out to try the door, it swung open, revealing Evander who graciously held it for me. "Please, come in. Welcome to my map room."

The room was spacious, with every available inch of wall space covered in maps. More were carefully laid out on several large tables or illuminated in glass display boxes at the room's four corners.

In the center of the room stood a grand oak table, and above it, a brass chandelier cast a warm light.

Tonight, Evander wore a sharply tailored suit in deep midnight blue. The cut was modern, but there was an unmistakable Victorian influence in the velvet trim along the lapels and in the high-collared, buttoned-up shirt that seemed to mimic the high neck styles of the nineteenth century. The ones Venedict had described as 'all the rage.'

"Interesting place you have here," I commented as I stepped through the door and glanced around. I quickly returned my attention to Evander. "What is it you wanted to show me? I hope it's something interesting - I was just enjoying my catchup with Clyde."

"It certainly looked that way." Evander said with a smile. "And yes, as a matter of fact it is."

He led the way over to the oak table and opened a large leather-bound folder. From within it he produced a blueprint - the blueprint of Eve Hall's foundations. I kept my expression as neutral as possible while he laid it out on the table in front of us.

"There is a network of subterranean tunnels below Eve Hall," Evander revealed in a low, confidential tone of voice. "My family's wealth didn't come only from the land and from industry. My grandfather, Lord Wilbur Eve, was a rather enterprising man. Making the most of Eve Hall's advantageous positioning right by the sea. And so, smuggling various goods and substances became one of his most successful business ventures, all of these illicit goods brought in directly from the ships to the bowels below the Hall."

"Fascinating," I said, letting my eyes follow the stairwells and passageways of the blueprint.

It matched up with the blueprint Csilla had shown me,

well, for the most part. But there were some notable differences. Csilla's version had outlined five exits, emerging at various points around Eve Hall: three on the ground floor, one in the turret, and another somewhere in the maze outside. This blueprint only showed a single exit through the fireplace in the ground-floor library.

Other details stood out as well. Some of the looping corridors that Csilla's blueprint had marked as dead ends were now shown to circle back to the main cavern, and in one case, even lead to the fireplace exit. Strange.

"Thanks for showing me this, Evander," I said, keeping my tone pleasant. "You really didn't need to."

He glanced at me with a glimmer in his eye. "Well, I figured you shouldn't be at too much of a disadvantage. Roderick, it has to be said, is in a bit of a mood after your altercation. Which, by the way, I will choose not to address any further. I know you have been flaunting my rules by bringing in razor blades, but Roderick was, admittedly, out of line. So in this case, I am willing to let it go. Just refrain from doing it again."

"Of course. It was a one-time offense."

Honestly, I was only halfway listening to Evander. My thoughts kept pulling me back to Clyde. He wouldn't have wiped out my parents and grandparents simply to eradicate the Thornhill blood he seemed to despise. He wouldn't have wanted me dead to prevent me from ever becoming a vampire.

Would he?

TWENTY-FIVE

T he following night I was in my car, making the final adjustments to my ensemble. I'd dressed in my hunting gear - what I wore when I expected a bloodbath. Not that I expected things to go *that* far off the rails, but it was best to be prepared for any eventuality. I wore all black: tight-fitting, no straps or zippers that could catch. My knee-high combat boots housed hidden knives in their custom sheaths, and fingerless gloves ensured a solid grip without sacrificing dexterity.

I was about to step out of the car when my phone rang. It was Aubrey on a video call. In the whirlwind of this weekend's events, I'd almost successfully managed not to think about her.

The timing was bad, but I answered her call anyway. I owed her that. The thought of the impending game didn't make me half as nervous as speaking with Aubrey after nearly tearing out her artery. A second ago, I didn't have a heartbeat. Now, it was pounding like crazy.

"Aubrey, hey," I said, aiming for a tone of nonchalance as I wedged my phone against the steering wheel. "I didn't think you'd call." *Ever again*, I almost added, but bit it back.

"I'm nervous, can you tell?" Aubrey was in her hotel room, the rain-soaked streets of central London visible in the background, the city lights casting a hazy glow against the window behind her. Soon she would be heading off to Sadler's Wells to prepare for her performance, much like I had just prepared for mine.

"Not at all," I lied. But of course, I could tell.

"I know you think you've scared me off," she continued quietly. "But you haven't. I miss you more than I'm afraid." She took a deep breath, like it hurt to say it aloud. "That's the truth. I'm probably broken."

"I wouldn't care if you were. That would just mean I have some company."

We both fell silent, the sound of rain tapping softly against the window filling the space between us.

"Does that mean I can visit you at the mansion again?" she asked.

The answer had to be no. Being around her, I'd only run the risk of killing her. Could a vampire and a mortal ever have a relationship that wasn't inherently fatal, one way or the other? I hadn't seen any other vampires manage it. I needed to be mature, reasonable, and just let her go.

"If I come to the show on Monday," I said instead, "would you want to come back with me after?"

By the time I'd ended the call with Aubrey, the drizzle that had drenched London seemed to have moved here. The moment I stepped out of the car, the rich, earthy aroma of the rain-soaked earth greeted me, and a mist of rain hung in the air.

Pools of vivid red light washed over the estate's towering masonry and Gothic turrets. Elegantly dressed figures - contestants and spectators alike - had begun to gather on a grand terrace overlooking the sprawling grounds, with its vast maze shrouded in mist. It was nearly time for the evening's game.

As I moved closer, the buzz of anticipation seemed to ripple through the crowd. I scanned the sea of faces, looking for Clyde, but there was no sign of him.

I joined the other contestants lining up on the terrace near a massive, scowling gargoyle. Evander was obsessed with gargoyles. I wondered how many of them dotted the grounds of Eve Hall in total.

My gaze shifted to Roderick, who had already zeroed in on me. His eyes burned.

I couldn't really blame him. Up close, I could see Elizabeth's handiwork layered over the mess I'd made. The corners of Roderick's mouth had been sliced clean through, stopping just shy of the hinges of his jaw. Elizabeth's stitches were fine and neat, pulling the edges of the wounds together perfectly. Both cuts looked symmetrical, healing quickly thanks to Roderick's vampiric blood. But no matter how well they healed, there might always be a slight unevenness.

Speaking of Elizabeth, she appeared suddenly from the crowd, slipping silently beside me. Without a word, she pressed something cool and smooth into my palm. I closed my fingers around the objects, hiding them from view.

The shapes felt like glass pearls, each one a different size. I was pretty sure I knew what they were - smoke bombs. Gabriel had used something just like these when he whisked Octavia away from the Thornhill tomb. I could still picture the thick, emerald smoke that had blanketed the Circle of Lebanon in a swirling fog.

Elizabeth caught my eye and gave me the slightest

smile before turning and melting back into the throng of onlookers.

I slipped the pearls into a hidden pocket just as Evander's voice cut through the murmur of conversations, the last few stragglers finding their places among the assembly. "We seem to all be here," he declared, clapping his hands together with a loud clap, a gesture I'd already come to think of as a signature one of his.

The terrace lights converged upon him, casting his chiseled features in stark, theatrical relief. Tonight, he was really leaning into the whole vampire count persona. Dressed in a dark, well-tailored silk suit with oversized lapels, he even wore a black and crimson cloak that billowed softly behind him as he moved. He balanced his tongue-in-cheek outfit with a humorous gleam in his eye.

"As we all know, tonight marks the third and final game. The contestants are," Evander's voice boomed across the gathering, "my nephew, Roderick Eve, Tibor Beauchamp, Zachary Winterfield, and Harlan Thornhill." His tone took on a hint of challenge as he added, "The black sheep of our gathering."

Each of us received a smattering of applause, mine mixed with loud, enthusiastic jeers that rang out from the crowd.

"The objective," Evander continued, undeterred, his voice crisp in the slightly misty air, "is to retrieve this." With a snap of his fingers, one of his staff stepped forward. I recognized him from my first visit to Nightside of Eden; thankfully, he wasn't here to do any frisking. I would have been screwed.

Instead, he handed Evander a chalice, which he raised high for everyone to see.

The chalice appeared to be made of solid gold, with a

handle on either side and a large ruby set into the base, like a grape-sized drop of fresh blood.

"The rules for tonight's game are simple," Evander proclaimed. "Return the chalice to the ground-floor library, where we will all await the winner. Once you locate the chalice, you'll find several hidden smugglers' tunnels leading back up to the Hall. You may use any means necessary to stop your opponents and seize the chalice for yourself."

A mischievous twinkle sparked in the count's eyes. "But do be careful - make sure it's the right chalice. This-" he rapped his silk-gloved fingers against the cup, producing a soft metallic ring, "is merely a replica of a replica. Down in the watery caverns below the estate, you'll encounter quite a few of these. While each imitates the appearance of the Holy Grail, none is the mythic original. However," he added with a smile that was equal parts charming and cunning, "one is made of real gold and set with a genuine Burmese ruby. That is your trophy. Return with the real one, and victory is yours."

Evander's gaze swept over each of us in turn.

"Well then, it seems we are ready to commence." This was met with enthusiastic applause and cheers.

Evander stepped forward and touched a concealed mechanism on the gargoyle. The stone beast groaned and shifted aside with a grinding sound. As the gargoyle moved, turning its back on us, a surprisingly broad staircase descending into the smuggler's waterways beneath the building was revealed. Eve Hall, it seemed, was full of hidden layers, peeling back like some endless gothic onion.

The staircase was carved from the same ancient stone as the terrace, the steps worn smooth, the descent into darkness pierced here and there by bright pools of blood-red neon light. The way the red neon glowed made it look like we might be about to descend into hell.

Evander paused, letting the murmurs of excitement swell, before pulling an antique revolver from his jacket. "When this sounds, the game begins," he announced, firing into the air.

The gunshot echoed off the estate's stone walls, spurring the contestants into action. Roderick, Zachary, and Tibor all darted across the terrace and vanished into the dark stairwell, where cool, musty air wafted up to meet them. Roderick disappeared into the shadows first, with Zachary and Tibor close behind, hot on his heels.

I let them rush ahead. I figured I didn't need to lead the charge if it meant becoming a prime target for a push or a well-aimed trip.

As I took my first steps down, the world above disappeared as the flagstones and gargoyle slid back into place, sealing me, Roderick, Zachary, and Tibor in the bowels of Eve Hall. I won't lie, it gave me an uneasy feeling.

The stone steps felt slick underfoot, and the scent of earth and dampness rose in my nostrils as the air grew cooler and heavier. I kept a distance behind the others, careful not to let them get too far ahead. At least, the intermittent pools of red neon light was more than enough to see.

After a long descent, the staircase opened into a vast underground cavern, partially flooded with seawater. I knew from checking an app that the tide was supposed to be out, and I couldn't help but wonder how much of this space might be submerged when the water surged back. The place reminded me of the cavern beneath Villa Graves, but it was much larger, deeper, and connected to the sea.

Shadows clung to the far corners, and the darkness seemed to drip from the high, uneven ceiling.

Suddenly, stage lights flickered on and off, illuminating various rock formations scattered throughout the cavern. Each flash revealed a chalice perched on a jagged ledge, nestled in an alcove, or shimmering beneath the water's surface. Hundreds of chalices blinked in and out of view with each pulse of light, all of them seemingly identical.

"Damn you, uncle!" Roderick shouted. "Which is the real one?" Of course, none of us could riddle him that one.

Roderick, Zachary, and Tibor fanned out, each heading for a different illuminated chalice. I hung back for a moment, surveying the scene. The flashing lights highlighted the chalices like props on illuminated stages, as if a play were about to begin. The thought sent a shiver through me, but I brushed it aside and began to move, carefully navigating the slick, seaweed-covered rocks.

I wasn't sure what my strategy should be, other than trying not to let Roderick trap me and hoping for some luck. As for finding the real chalice, I had a feeling it wouldn't be in an obvious spot, and that the lights might give me some clues. There's always a pattern, a game with rules you need to figure out.

I decided to focus on a chalice tucked away in a deep alcove on the right side of the cavern, partially obscured by shadows and the flickering lights. The cold, damp air seemed to press in as I reached for it.

It wasn't the real one, of course. The weight was wrong, too light in my hand, and when I tilted it, no ruby glinted at the base. Even so, I kept it. It seemed like the kind of thing that could be used to knock someone out with, if I had to. I wasn't planning on flashing my knives around if I could help it, but if any of the others got too close, I wasn't above knocking him out cold with this.

Glancing around the cavern, I saw the others working their own strategies. Tibor had taken to scaling the walls, seemingly convinced the real chalice must be hidden in the hardest-to-reach spot. Zachary was wading through the seawater, collecting chalices and stacking them methodically on a nearby rock like a grim archaeologist, determined to sift through each one. Roderick, on the other hand, was moving erratically, grabbing at whatever caught his eye. I watched him yank a chalice from the water just as the light highlighting it flickered out, plunging him into darkness.

Then I saw it. To my left, near a dark tunnel where seawater flowed in and out of the cavern, a chalice suddenly bathed in several converging blood-red lights. While all the others had only a single light marking them, this one seemed to draw the lights in, glowing with a vivid, ominous hue. Red neon, just like on the descent here, and like the garish lights of Nightside. It seemed Evander had a thing for both neon and gargoyles.

My gut tightened. I had a feeling about this one.

The icy tide tugged at my ankles as I splashed toward the glowing chalice. I reached the rock formation without any of the others having noticed, the chalice glinting invitingly in the flickering light. When I lifted it, the weight felt right. Heavy and substantial. And there, at the base, a faint glimmer of red. A ruby.

As soon as I lifted the chalice, the cavern plunged into darkness, and the rock formation I stood on was illuminated like a stage under a single, glaring spotlight.

A cascade of gold and silver confetti burst from above, raining down on me in a mocking celebration of my supposed victory. The festive debris clung to my wet clothes, landing in my hair, shimmering in the stark light, turning me into a glittering, unmistakable target.

Let's just say it didn't take long for the others to catch on. Zachary, closest to me when the lights went out, was closing in fast. His eyes locked on the chalice in my hand, expression ravenous. I tightened my grip, bracing for what was coming. The confetti continued to fall, absurdly theatrical.

"Hand it over, Thornhill," Zachary demanded, his voice low, almost a growl.

I glanced around, noting Roderick and Tibor maneuvering through the water, closing in from different directions. My mind raced, calculating the odds. Up on the rock formation, I had a slight advantage in height and stability. They were more vulnerable in the water, their movements hindered by the rising tide. That was about it.

"Of course, Zachary," I called out. "Catch."

I hurled the fake chalice straight at him. His eyes widened as the heavy object sailed toward him. He barely had time to react, ducking underwater just a second too late. The chalice struck his temple with a dull thud, sending ripples of blood through the dark water, flecked with shimmering golden confetti.

Zachary resurfaced with a snarl, clutching his head where the chalice had struck. "You'll pay for that," he spat, voice thick with venom.

Roderick and Tibor hesitated, their eyes flicking between Zachary's injury and me. The tide was rising, water already lapping at their waists and sloshing more aggressively against the rocks.

"Back off," I commanded, adrenaline zinging through me. "I'm leaving, and none of you are stopping me."

"Harlan, don't you think you ought to let me win after

what you did to my face?" Roderick demanded, his voice laced with a warning. "It's the very least you can do. Show some remorse - throw me the chalice."

"No," I said flatly.

Roderick's jaw tightened as Zachary and Tibor sidled up beside him, forming an unspoken alliance. "I have grown weary of your disrespect," he said.

"And I've grown tired of yours," I fired back, scanning my surroundings. They were closing in fast. I had to move. The nearest exit tunnel, deeper into the cavern, would take me up into the turret, and from there, I could enter Eve Hall and make my way to the library with the chalice. I could still win. Maybe even without using my weapons.

Then again, maybe not.

Roderick suddenly pulled out a knife, larger and far more menacing than the one he'd brandished back in the game room. This one had a cruel, curved blade, almost like a scythe.

"This is your last chance, Harlan," he said, almost jovial. "Surrender the chalice. If you do, I might stop at giving you a smile to match mine. Then we'd be blood brothers. I wouldn't have to hate you so much."

"Tempting as that sounds," I replied. "I think I'm gonna go with no fucking way."

Roderick sighed, disappointment creeping into his tone. "Then I fear something bad might happen to you, because I'm feeling quite resentful."

When I didn't give him a different answer but started backing away instead, his expression darkened.

"You don't wish to be blood brothers with me?" His tone hovered between disappointment and disbelief as he gave the knife a lazy spin. Its blade caught the light momentarily. He followed this with a deep sigh. "I'd be truly heartbroken if you were to refuse."

"Sorry to break your heart," I said, taking another step back. "But I'm just not into that idea."

"But being my blood brother would be an honor - can't you see? You needn't worry about the pain, it'll be fleeting. And Elizabeth will attend to you immediately once we're back upstairs. She's remarkably skilled, look how well she did with me."

Zachary and Tibor closed in, forming a tightening circle. Roderick, the knife now clenched between his teeth, began pulling himself onto the rock, too close for comfort. Instinct kicked in. Before I could make a conscious decision about it, I surged forward and drove a sharp kick into his face.

The force split Elizabeth's careful stitches as Roderick tumbled back into the water, blood streaming from his mouth and dispersing in crimson clouds around him. The others froze, shocked for a moment, just like in the game room. I knew it wouldn't last.

Now was the time.

I grabbed one of the smoke bombs Elizabeth had given me, one of the larger ones, and hurled it onto the rocky ground. It cracked open with a snap, releasing a thick, scarlet cloud of smoke that quickly obscured everything around me.

I was barely able to make out the outlines of Zachary and Tibor as I slipped past them. As soon as I was clear of them, I sped up, leaping from rock to rock with my heart pounding in my chest and the smoke swirling around me, obscuring everything.

The exit tunnel was just ahead, a faint outline of the stairs leading up. There was no time to look back. I reached the tunnel entrance, the seawater now up to my chest, and hurried up the steps.

Emerging from the tunnel, I found myself inside a night-lit greenhouse. Glass walls and ceilings were illuminated by soft, amber lights that cast a warm glow over the lush greenery inside. Rows of neatly potted herbs - rosemary, thyme, basil, and lavender - lined the wooden benches, filling the air with a calming scent, half earthy, half floral.

The glass panes were covered in a delicate lattice of ivy, and moonlight filtering through them created shadowy patterns on the cobblestone floor. The atmosphere felt serene, but I knew it was an illusion. Roderick and the others might find their way here - I wasn't sure if they'd seen which exit I'd taken.

The cool night air hit my face as I burst out into the greenhouse. According to the map Csilla had shown me, the greenhouse exit was somewhere near the center of the maze.

I needed to get back to Eve Hall and dump this damned chalice in the count's lap so this twisted game would be over. I figured I'd cut through the maze, circle around to the front of Eve Hall and enter through the main doors. Or I could use the chalice to smash one of the library's stained glass side windows for a dramatic entrance.

The night was silent except for the distant murmur of the sea, and the air was crisp and cool. The recent rain had turned the ground beneath me into a treacherous, muddy mess.

I twisted through the narrow paths of the maze, the air filled with the fragrant scent of the sea and of the muddy earth. I was moving quickly, but my eyes darted around trying to work out where the hell I was. I couldn't remember every path I'd seen on the map, and they all looked so damned similar.

Slipping through an arched gateway of greenery, I descended a series of broad, worn stone steps and found myself standing in a carefully tended hidden garden, constructed around a small lake. The lake - it had to be the one where Tessa and Venedict's illegitimate daughter had drowned. This place wasn't marked on the map.

Surrounded by statues and small water features, the garden was a sight to behold, even in winter. Only a few hardy perennials dared to show their faces against the season's chill. The air was completely still. This little sanctuary, or shrine to Victorine Eve, was sunk into the ground, sheltered from the merciless coastal winds.

I cut through the memorial garden, aiming for the stairs at the other end that would take me back up to level ground and the other side of the maze.

The moss-covered statues peeking out of the flowerbeds reminded me of those in the tall grass of Thornhill Mansion's garden. Odd timing, but I had a sudden, intense pang of homesickness.

"You can't run from me," Roderick's voice suddenly called out behind me.

Glancing over my shoulder, I saw his silhouette at the top of the stairs I'd just descended.

He was wild-eyed, dripping seawater and blood. Even from a twenty feet distance, his face was shocking as he stared directly at me, his cheeks slashed open from ear to ear, his teeth visible through the gashes. If the Chelsea smile had looked bad before, it looked much worse now. My heart sank. How were we ever going to get past this?

"Harlan," he shouted, pointing at me with the hunting knife clutched tightly in his hand, his entire energy field radioactive with fury. "You could have taken my offer of friendship, but instead, you chose this. You've only made things worse for yourself. So much worse."

I believed him.

I reached for another smoke bomb, a large silver one this time. I tossed it onto the ground between us and a ghostly haze rose between us.

I sprinted, the dark water of the lake turning into a blur on one side of me, the rows of plants and bushes and statues a blur on the other. I needed to direct my entire focus on where I was going.

Suddenly, I collided with something solid, the impact jarring through me, and a sharp pain radiated from my shoulder. I stumbled back and realized I had run straight into the arms of a stone angel. Before I knew it, Roderick was upon me.

I felt a cold, metal handcuff snap around my wrist, chaining me to one of the angel's outspread arms. I clearly wasn't the only one who'd turned up to tonight's game with some hidden surprises up my sleeve. I yanked at the cuffs, but they held firm.

"Got you now," he hissed, a wild, triumphant gleam in his eyes.

TWENTY-SIX

"Roderick, this is insane. Let me go," I sneered. I still had one arm free, and I reached for one of my hidden knives.

Roderick laughed, a harsh, grating sound. "You had your chance to make this easy. But you wanted it to be difficult."

The chalice slipped from my grasp and fell to the muddy ground. Ignoring it, I reached for the knife in my boot, pulling it free and holding it out to keep Roderick at bay.

"You'll heal - but come any closer now, and I'll make it worse."

Roderick just laughed, not in the least deterred. He started circling me, now and then pretending to lunge, but not getting within my reach. "You really don't want anything to happen to your face, do you?"

I tightened my grip on the knife and tried to keep him in sight despite the stone angel restricting my range of movement. "Don't try to fuck with me. You already know it's a bad idea."

Roderick's laughter grew louder, more manic.

He lunged at me, his blade catching the moonlight, flashing silver. I slashed out, forcing him to step back. His eyes glinted wildly as he narrowed his gaze and lunged again.

This time, I sidestepped and swung out, the blade slicing into his shoulder. Roderick howled, clutching at the wound. Before he could react, I kicked at his legs, knocking him off balance. He tumbled to the muddy ground but managed to roll away, narrowly avoiding my knife as I drove it into the earth where he'd been a split second earlier.

"I'll get you next time," I promised.

Keeping my back to the angel, I switched the knife I'd just used into my trapped left hand and reached for the second blade with my free one. I needed to be as armed as possible. Being chained was a horrible disadvantage, but I had real combat experience. Roderick's fencing skills wouldn't measure up - at least, I hoped not.

He rose to his feet in a single fluid movement, as if someone was pulling him up by a string attached to his crown.

He took a step forward, and then he lunged again with a sudden burst of movement, his hunting knife aimed low. I deflected his strike with the blade in my right hand, forcing him back again.

Just then, a shadow moved in the periphery of my vision. Tibor.

"Roderick," he called out, taking a few hesitant steps towards us. I wasn't sure what he was up to - was he going to try to help me, or was he just going to take the chalice from the mud?

Roderick's eyes flickered toward Tibor, a flash of annoyance crossing his face. "Do not attempt to get in the middle of this, Tibor. This is between Harlan and I."

Tibor took a cautious step closer. "Roderick, what is it you intend to do? The count has asked me to keep an eye on you, to ensure you do not take things too far."

"Yes, that does not surprise me," Roderick replied, voice dripping with scorn. "Uncle has been controlling me for well over a century - I am getting tired of it. I have to assert myself. Otherwise, how can anyone take me seriously?"

"We all take you seriously," Tibor assured him. His eyes flickered towards me with a sense of desperation, silently pleading for my support.

"He doesn't!" Roderick waved the knife at me. "He rejects my friendship as if it were nothing."

"Then give him a smile to rival your own, and leave it at that." Tibor took another cautious step closer. His hands were held out and open in front of him, like he was trying to appease a wild and furious animal - which, in a sense, he was. "Take the chalice, leave him chained up here."

Roderick's expression darkened. Before I could warn Tibor, Roderick let the hunting knife slice through the air before sinking it into Tibor's abdomen. Tibor's eyes widened as he staggered, clutching at the wound, blood seeping and then gushing through his fingers as the knife sank deeper.

"No!" I shouted. Goddammit. I yanked at the chains with all my strength, but they held fast as Tibor sank to his knees in the mud, just out of reach.

Roderick, holding the knife, let it slice upward, splitting Tibor open from navel to sternum. A splash of blood hit me across the cheek as Roderick pulled the blade free, then drove it into Tibor's left eye socket, burying it to the hilt. His hand, slick with blood, gripped the handle tightly.

He proceeded to unhurriedly withdraw the knife with a wet, sickening sound, the pressure releasing like a valve. Tibor shuddered violently, his hands grasping at the empty air in front of him, as though fending off some vengeful spirit only he could see.

"Did you hear what he said?" Roderick demanded. "Keeping an eye on me for uncle. What nonsense!" Then he stood up, wiping some of Tibor's blood off his own face with the back of his hand.

"It's just you and I now," he said in a soft, quiet voice. His attention and the knife's sharp point were now aimed at me again. "You think you can fend me off, chained up like that?"

"I know I can." I tightened my grip on the knives as he began to circle me again.

Roderick leapt at me in a sudden blur, the metal of our blades clanging as I parried him. But the angle was awkward, and my chained wrist made it difficult to maneuver. He knocked me off balance by slamming me against the stone angel and I slid down, the knife in my left hand slipping from my grasp as my arm got pulled by the cuff.

Before I could react, let alone get back on my feet, Roderick kicked the other knife out of my hand and it landed just out of reach, where he picked it up.

I kept my eyes locked on him while I fumbled in the mud behind the stone angel, trying to get hold of my other knife. Where the hell was it? Panic tightened in my chest. "Roderick, listen. This is enough." I nodded toward Tibor, who was curled up on his side, groaning softly in the mud.

Slowly, Roderick shook his head, like he wished things could be different.

I tried to scramble back, but with the angel looming behind me like a specter of death, there was simply nowhere to go. My back was already pressed against the cold stone. "Roderick, come on. You have to stop. We can still get Tibor help - but we have to put everything else aside."

"Stop? No. Not until I feel at peace with you." With a sudden, violent motion, he drove the knife - my knife - into the mud between my thighs. The blade sank deep. He leaned in closer, his eyes gleaming as he twisted it free from the earth.

I really didn't like where this was heading. I swung at him, but he deflected my arm with the knife. The blade sliced through the fabric, and a sharp sting flared as it grazed my skin, forcing me to lower my arm.

"Stay still," he instructed in an incongruously soft tone, the knife hovering dangerously close to my face now. Droplets of muddy water ran off the blade and fell onto my cheeks like tears.

I sucked in a sharp breath, struggling to quell the rising tide of panic. Our eyes locked, and for a long, tense moment, neither of us moved.

"Roderick, please, stop."

He let the tip of the knife trail down my cheek before pressing it beneath my chin, forcing my head back. The cold metal bit into my skin, sending a jolt of fear through me despite my best efforts to suppress it. "Yes, you're anxious now. Quite understandable," he said, almost soothingly. "Stay still. If you struggle, you'll only make me more on edge, and then I truly don't know what I might do."

Fear and anger pounded through my veins as I stared at the blade, the tension between us thick and suffocating.

"Now, where shall I start?" Roderick mused, the knife's sharp point less than an inch from my eye. "Here? Or perhaps..." He slowly moved the blade downward. "Somewhere else? You're much too cocky for your own good, Harlan. Maybe I should castrate you. Do you think that might settle you down, make you more amenable to listening?"

A cold shiver ran down my spine. "What? No."

I wanted to believe he was joking, but the gleam in his eyes suggested otherwise. Given what I knew about his past, and what he'd just done to Tibor, I couldn't put anything past him.

Instinctively, I drew my legs up in front of me, clamping them together as if glued. Not that it would stop him - he could still plunge the knife down if he wanted to.

I had to find a way out of this, preferably one that didn't leave either of us seriously injured.

Probably reading my thoughts, he said, "Well, I am not saying that it has to happen, only that it is an option. Behave, and it might not be necessary."

"None of this is necessary."

Ignoring me, he let the blade slide lower, down my abdomen, pausing just above my groin. The knife tip dug in slightly. "Once our score is settled," he reassured me, "we can move past this. After I've taken what I need from you, we can be true friends. Blood brothers. You'll see. So where should I start?"

My heart pounded in my ears, the world narrowing to a crimson haze. In a single, instinctive motion, I lashed out and captured Roderick's wrist, wrenching the knife from his grip. With my other hand I pulled him closer, twisting his neck sharply. Then I sank my fangs in deep, rupturing his artery.

A choked gasp escaped Roderick's lips as I quickly pushed him down into the mud, pinning him beneath me. He hadn't expected this, but he should have. His pulse thudded against my teeth, the warmth of his blood flooding my mouth. I didn't need his blood. I didn't crave it - this was pure self-defense.

Roderick struggled, his body writhing as he tried to push me off, but the more he fought, the deeper I sank my fangs in until I sensed the fight leaving him.

When his thrashing grew weaker, I released my grip and pulled back slightly to gaze down at him. He looked up at me, eyes glazed and half-closed.

"Guess we're blood brothers now," I said.

He was too dazed to respond, but he actually nodded weakly in agreement.

Despite being barely conscious, he seemed to register my words, so I added, "Alright then. Don't ever try anything like this again. I didn't exactly appreciate your threats."

He managed another nod, his eyes fluttering shut.

The keys to the handcuffs had to be in his pocket. I reached down and found them in the first place I checked - his inner pocket. With a click, the cuff fell away from my wrist, and I snapped it around Roderick's instead.

He struggled a bit, but the handcuffs were already in place.

"Roderick!"

Turning around, I saw Belladira standing maybe ten feet behind us, her long, silvery dress billowing around her in the moonlight. Her eyes were wide with horror as she took in the scene. Roderick and I both smeared with blood and mud, the ground beneath us soaked with the same gruesome mixture, Tibor's lifeless silhouette near us.

Belladira took a step forward, her hands outstretched, trembling, her breath catching in her throat.

"Belladira, I'm sorry, but you need to stay back. Don't get too close right now. I'm a little wired." Whether it was adrenaline or Roderick's blood, I wasn't sure, but there was definitely too much energy surging through my veins.

She nodded, and made no move to come any closer. "Are you both - are you alright?"

"Alive," I said, after checking that Roderick was actually still breathing. Saying he was alright might be pushing it.

I scrambled to my feet, my knees weak and my heart thundering.

Roderick's bloodied, mud-caked face lit up at the sight of Belladira. "My love!" he exclaimed.

"Oh, Roderick," she sighed, her tone threaded through with both sorrow and frustration. "What have you turned this into?"

"You know how it is," he replied, as if that explained anything.

As I stepped away, I picked up the two extra knives from the mud, their blades glinting dully in the moonlight. Belladira went and knelt beside Roderick, his head resting on her thigh as she ran her fingers through his muddy hair. The sight of them together, the tenderness in her touch, made my stomach churn with guilt.

"I worry," Roderick said in a small voice, "that you will never look at me the same way again after what he has done to me."

"That is unfounded," Belladira replied, very softly. "I love you."

But Roderick wasn't listening. His eyes were distant, haunted. "Do you indeed?"

"I am entirely yours. You know that," Belladira said soothingly as her fingers kept gently combing through his matted hair.

"Sometimes," Roderick said, "uncertainty overtakes me, and I feel compelled to act out, to do terrible things."

"I know, my darling. I don't love you any less for it - although, I wish you wouldn't. Deep breaths."

Roderick drew a deep ragged breath. Belladira put her cheek against his, against his jagged bleeding mouth, her golden-copper hair flowing over both of them. They breathed together until Roderick started calming down, his tension slowly ebbing away. Or, to be fair, maybe he was just passing out from the bloodloss.

"Belladira?"

She lifted her head to look at me, her eyes filled with sadness. It couldn't be easy, being with someone so disturbed. Why had anyone ever thought it was a good idea to let him out of Bedlam?

"Give it five minutes before you use these, if you love him." I dropped the keys to the handcuffs in the mud, the metal sinking slightly into the mire.

Then I picked up Roderick's bloodied, sable-like hunting knife, my own two Japanese steel blades, and the chalice from the mud. As for Tibor, there was nothing I could do for him right now, if at all. I stepped over him, and without another glance, I turned away, leaving Roderick and Belladora to it.

Before reentering Eve Hall, I dropped by my car and left my two knives underneath it, to be picked up later. No need to risk disqualification for bringing weapons. No one would have to know that anyone other than Roderick had decided to flaunt the rules. His blood-stained hunting knife, I planted in the gravel in front of the broad stairs leading up to the front door.

About a minute later, I pushed open the heavy wooden door of the library at Eve Hall.

The large circular room buzzed with the murmur of gathered vampires. The low bench lining the window, which offered a sweeping view of the sea, was fully occupied, as were the opulent armchairs that had been gathered from various corners of the building.

Above, a light drizzle began to fall against the clear glass dome of the ceiling, the sound of tapping fingers drowned out by the rustle of fine silk and velvet, the occasional clink of glassware, and the soft, sibilant whispers of countless voices. Large, roll-down projector screens displayed real-time images of the cavern below the building from multiple angles.

I stood in the doorway, drenched in mud, rainwater, and blood. The scents of iron and wet earth bleeding into the rich aroma of the library's aged paper, leather, and wood as a hush gradually fell over the crowd. Too many pairs of luminous eyes were fixed on me.

My eyes scanned the room for familiar faces - Gabriel, Csilla, and Clyde, who slouched in a threadbare velvet loveseat by the fireplace, the same one I'd seen him emerge from last night. Elizabeth knelt on a settee beside a gloomy-looking Zachary, deftly stitching up his cheek. I did a double-take - Zachary sported a half Chelsea smile. Roderick had been busy tonight.

At the center of it all sat Evander in a high-backed leather chair. As I approached, his eyes narrowed with unease.

I dropped the chalice at his feet with a metallic jangle. Evander glanced down at it, then back up at me. "It seems you have emerged victorious," he said, his voice low. He could see from my expression and the blood on me that the victory had been hard-won.

"Where is Roderick?" he asked, tension tightening his voice.

"Roderick is in the maze with Belladira and what's left of Tibor," I replied hoarsely. "He's injured. Thought it might be a good idea to bring a knife. But I'm sure you've already worked that out."

Just then, the doors swung open again. Belladira entered, supporting Roderick, his arm draped heavily over her shoulders. His face was a muddy, bloodied mess, and I had to look away.

A sense of unease rippled through the crowd, the air thickening with tension like dark clouds gathering before the first clap of thunder.

Evander rose from his chair, his calm facade beginning to slip. Belladira gently eased Roderick into an armchair, where he slumped against the burgundy velvet, barely responsive, his head lolling to the side.

The count rushed to him, kneeling beside his nephew, clasping his hand in both of his. "Roderick, are you hurt?" His voice was almost pleading as he added, "And what have you done?"

"I am not hurt in the least. When does the ball commence?" Roderick replied, completely detached from the gravity of the situation.

Evander nodded to two of his staff, who moved swiftly to his side. They carefully lifted Roderick, who protested in a barely audible voice. A few other staff members slipped away in the opposite direction, presumably heading to retrieve Tibor from the maze.

Whispers rose beneath the ceiling as Roderick was carried through a side door. Elizabeth, who had just finished stitching Zachary's cheek, rose from the settee and followed, her medical kit in hand, ready to assess and repair the damage I had inflicted. Again. Belladira followed closely, her long, mud-spattered dress trailing behind her like a spectral presence.

The atmosphere was thick with uncertainty as the door closed behind them, leaving a heady tension in the air.

Evander raised his voice, commanding everyone's attention. "It is clear that tonight's game has come to an end." His gaze swept over the crowd, lingering on me a second longer than I liked. "And I think it might be fair to say," he continued with a touch of irony, bending to pick up the chalice I'd let fall, "that the Graves bloodline takes the prize." He held the chalice out. "Gabriel? I believe this belongs to you."

I'd put myself - and Roderick - through a bit of hell for Gabriel to win this damn trophy. Now he stepped forward to claim it, and I had to fight the urge to rip it out of his hand and send it crashing through the window and into the sea.

My skin prickled beneath the weight of the many judgmental, glowing eyes fixed on me. Roderick was the one who had injured and possibly killed Tibor, but I felt like the blood-stained pariah. Not that anything had really been lost - no one had wanted me here in the first place, except for Gabriel, so I could handle his dirty work.

Evander's voice sliced through the murmurs. "I propose we reconvene in two hours in the grand ballroom," he announced, though the fury roiling inside me nearly drowned him out. "We will host a ball, a peacemaking event to celebrate our alliances in the spirit of-" blah, blah, blah.

I'd had enough. I was done with this place and every

last bloodsucker in it. I suddenly felt a desperate pull to get back to Thornhill Mansion.

As I turned to leave the library, my gaze met Gabriel's. His expression softened and he took a step toward me, opening his arms. The unexpected gesture sent a jolt of confusion through me. Was he really offering a hug?

I wanted to laugh, maybe make a cutting remark, but instead, I froze. All the tension, fear, and anger from the past hour crashed over me like a tidal wave.

"Harlan," he said, his voice low and inviting. "Come here."

The murmurs around us faded. Gabriel's open arms seemed to emit a gravitational pull, as if he were willing me to move closer. Maybe he was.

And it almost worked. I took a hesitant step forward, my heart pounding in my chest.

But then I remembered - I wasn't about to let anyone think Gabriel had some kind of hold over me. With a tight, ironic smile, I stepped back from the edge of his embrace and turned on my heel, fleeing the library. The heavy wooden doors slammed shut behind me. The need for comfort gnawed at me, but that was just too bad.

TWENTY-SEVEN

I reached my quarters, closed the door behind me, and leaned against it. Finally alone. It was a relief being away from the whispers and stares. Apparently, I'd left the balcony door open earlier, and the night air wafting in was fresh and clean.

I just stood there for a minute, breathing, glad to be alive. Undead. Didn't matter.

I peeled off my mud and blood-soaked clothes in the shower. The fabric clung to me like a second skin. Blood and mud swirled down the drain. Apart from a small but deep cut on my neck, a long but superficial cut on my arm, and another tracing my inner thigh - all three already beginning to heal - I was unscathed, physically at least. I felt like crying, but I wasn't sure whether it was from sadness or relief, and either way, I didn't want to spare the time.

I got dressed quickly in a simple black outfit, packed my things, and left my suitcase and duffle bag by the door. I rinsed the mud off my boots in the sink, put them on still damp, and laced them up tightly.

I was intent on heading back home to Thornhill Mansion tonight, but there was still something I needed to do before I could leave Eve Hall for good.

I was itching to pick up my earlier conversation with Clyde. Evander had interrupted us, but now, Clyde was going to tell me everything - the whole truth, everything he knew - whether he wanted to or not. I'd hold a knife to his throat if I had to; I wasn't in any mood to be told no.

I headed down to my car to collect my knives. Eve Hall was eerily quiet; I imagined the other vampires had withdrawn to their rooms to talk trash about me and get dressed up for the ball.

I found the long steel blades underneath the car where I had left them. I picked them up, wiped them off, and slid them into the concealed sheaths in my boots' shafts. Next, I sat in the car, strapping two shorter knives into harnesses on my upper arms before throwing a blazer on top to conceal them. I was done making any attempt at complying with Evander's policies. I'd be out of here soon, anyway.

I needed to avoid the scanners at the main entrance, so I let myself back in through a red and blue stained glass window in the now-empty library. I'd already popped it off its hinge from inside, and it opened easily. The library, which had been buzzing with tense energy just half an hour ago, felt long-abandoned. Inky shadows pooled in the room's corners and under its arched roof, from which crystal chandeliers hung like the crystalline bones of some died-out species.

I passed a few vampires on the way up through the Hall, their gazes flickering toward me with curiosity or remnants of judgment, but no one tried to speak to me or stop me.

I was pretty certain Clyde didn't want to talk to me, but when I tried his door, I found it unlocked.

The door swung inward to reveal his well-appointed suite, an echo version of mine on the floor above. Most of the furnishings and tapestries in mine were red, while his were blue. The room was mostly cast in shadow, with only a couple of warmly glowing electric lamps standing on a few of the suite's ornate coffee tables.

Clyde was nowhere to be seen at first, but probably hearing the sound as I shut the door behind me, he emerged from the bathroom, looking surprisingly calm and welcoming, as if he'd anticipated me. I suppose he had.

"Harlan," he said. "I apologize if I have been a little hasty in my judgment of you."

He gestured toward the armchairs by the window. So now he wanted to talk.

Considering that his attitude towards me up until now had been nothing short of ice cold contempt, and that he hadn't been able to get away from me fast enough earlier when I dropped in on him out on the balcony, his sudden change of heart made me a little suspicious.

"You mean it?" I asked, making no attempt at keeping the skepticism out of my voice.

"Most assuredly. It is true, I can be a little...cold at times, a little aloof. I am a scientist. It is a common trait among us, or so I hear. And I suppose I still feel rather attached to the old family history. I am not someone who forgives easily. Regrettably, immortality comes with the luxury of being able to hold onto old grudges for a lifetime. Longer, in fact."

He turned and walked over to the window, taking a seat in one of the high-backed armchairs, placing his elegant hands on either armrest. "Well? I have decided, despite not owing you this, that I wouldn't mind so much sharing a few highlights from my journey through the latter part of the nineteenth century, the twentieth and the twenty-first, as far as it has unfolded. For Lyrica's sake."

"Sounds grueling when you put it like that," I commented, following him to the window where I let myself sink into the other armchair, mirroring his posture. "But I'd like to hear it."

"Well then," he began, his eyes gliding up to the side, as if he was pulling a dusty tome from a high-up shelf in his memory. Then his gaze returned to meet mine. His vivid blue eyes were shockingly like Sebastian's, but the moonlight falling through the tall arched windows and fell on half of his face traced a squarer jaw and fuller lips. And he had the whole vampire thing setting him apart, of course, with flawless marble skin and a certain presence that mortals simply lack.

"You already know about my upbringing, well, at least in essence. Lyrica has described it quite vividly, or that is the impression I've gathered, so I shall skip over most of it lightly. You know that I grew up in Kentish Town in London, a mere stone's throw from Highgate, from the cemetery and from Thornhill Mansion where my aunt, uncle and cousins lived. They had the money and the power that came with it, but the Thornhills belonged to the nouveau riche. I would quite like to point out that by contrast, both of my parents - and my mother's sister, Helen, who as you know was married to Algernon and is the mother of Venedict - hailed from significant landowning families. Good breeding, some might call it."

The expression was cringey, but I didn't comment on it. Mostly everything out of my mind seemed to bother Clyde, so it was probably best to say very little and to just let him talk. I'd start asking my questions where he might seem to be leaving things out.

"No doubt," he continued, "you're well aware of how entangled my family were with the Thornhills. Algernon's investments were irrevocably embedded in my parents' business, Hartenbrook Trade, and Lyrica and myself were frequently tutored at Thornhill Mansion by the same tutors Algernon had enlisted to attempt to educate his own unruly offspring. Inevitably, Lyrica and myself grew up somewhat close to our Thornhill cousins. We shared in a few of their privileges, thanks to Algernon, but they shared none of our troubles. Venedict and Octaiva were always both horribly spoiled and entitled. The concept of real problems was unfamiliar to them."

"Didn't they have their own troubles?" I couldn't resist asking, referring of course to Algernon's violent temper, the incident in which he'd killed Helen by pushing her from the mansion's third floor gallery, his substance abuse and his sexual abuse of his daughter. Those weren't financial problems, but they seemed like real problems to me.

Clyde waved a dismissive hand. "I am not denying that the Thornhills had problems - but they were undeniably above the mundane problems, such as speculations about financial security, that hovered like an ever-present dark cloud over most families at the time. What I am getting at is that we shared their world on occasion, but only on occasion."

AND OF COURSE, there was always something lurking there - something dark and destructive. Algernon always insisted that the capricious instability that plagued his own mind, and, it has to be said, the minds of his children, was introduced through Helen's blood. But it never was. It came from him, and whatever twisted lineage must have brought him into existence. It destroyed Helen, and eventually, it destroyed the entire family.

Venedict was always as mad as his father. Worse, in some ways, because he grew up with money. He had no concept of not getting what he wanted. And this will perhaps be news to you - he wanted immortality, long before Gabriel appeared to bestow the vampiric curse.

I cannot tell you precisely when my cousin's unseemly obsession with the occult first began, but I would say by the time he was in his mid teens. At first, it seemed to be a mere interest, a point of curiosity. But it grew.

At first, his aim seemed to be to summon his mother, to conjure her presence. And, well, I can only supposed that he might have succeeded in accomplishing something in that regard, because ghostly presences seem particularly active and vivid at Thornhill Mansion. Part of that may be due to the ley lines criss-crossing both the estate's grounds and the cemetery, but there could be more to it. These are merely my thoughts.

Now, by the time Venedict was in his late teens and I in my early twenties, it was a full-blown obsession, and the things he was attempting to make happen were more... elaborate. For one, he wanted to resurrect his mother, using a corpse from the cemetery.

I am not proud to admit that I assisted him in this unhinged endeavor. I was a medical student at the time, attending The Royal College of Surgeons. I was eager to put the things I was learning to the test, and I shared in the same general feeling of optimism that pervaded the Victorian mind, for all of its restraints and suppressions; the feeling that science might be able to answer any question, achieve any feat or miracle.

Venedict would insist that I attend funerals with him, with the aim of spotting suitable corpses and where they ended up buried. His requirements were a corpse that resembled aunt Helen and was of a similar age to how she would have been, had she still been alive. Because Helen was only sixteen when she gave birth to him, we were looking for a corpse in her early to mid 30s. This was the Victorian era, of course, and there was no shortage of women dying at that age, in childbirth or from various disasters or diseases.

Whenever a suitable specimen came along, we would return to the graveyard in the dead of night, usually on the same night after the funeral had taken place, to dig it up. Naturally, most of the digging fell to me. Venedict had never done a day of physical work in his life, and it was clear that he appreciated the sense of forbidden adventure much more than the hard work involved.

As a wealthy heir, Venedict would not have needed to procure bodies in this manner - not when Victorian London was teeming with body snatchers, grave robbers and resurrectionists that could be paid to deliver corpses according to one's exact requirements. But he liked the thrill, and to be perfectly honest, so did I. Whenever we slipped into Highgate Cemetery with shovels in hand to gather our material, I felt like Victor Frankenstein, poised on the brink of some equally marvelous and catastrophic breakthrough.

The same could be said for when we had a corpse hooked up to electrodes writhing and twisting on the dining table at Thornhill Mansion. Never with lasting effect, it must be said, but a few times, between high voltage electric currents and occult incantations and powders, we did manage to make the corpse open her eyes, sit up, and attempt to speak. Whether Helen ever attempted to embody one of these unfortunate, putrefying experiments, is not entirely clear to me.

Securing new life for his murdered mother wasn't Venedict's only objective, however. He brought me various recipes, torn out pages and old leather bound tomes that he procured from obscure sources, asking me to put the ingredients together in the correct way. A few times we would test these makeshift elixirs and substances out on some of the briefly resurrected corpses. This never resulted in any of them acquiring immortality, however - quite the reverse.

What I am getting at here is that Venedict had a hunger for...unnatural things, horrible things, long before he found his way into vampirism. And after the loss of his mother at such a young age, he seemed determined to not let any of the rest of the family depart the world without his say so. Except, of course, my parents, whom he never seemed to consider of any importance or interest. That's Venedict Thornhill for you. I am certain he will have told you nothing or only very little about any of this. He is full of rotten secrets.

One of them is that he had the nerve to seduce the woman I loved, Tessa Eve - and to make matters worse, he was quite boastful about it, at least in my presence. I suspect he was simply amazed that he had succeeded in getting it up for a woman, thereby, by his own estimation, proving his father wrong.

Tessa was not, however, a game or a conquest to me. She was the love of my life - though she was quite unwilling to concede her true feelings for me.

Octavia was only slightly more sympathetic than her brother, and in my world her presence felt increasingly troublesome. She and I were engaged as part of a scheme to mask Algernon's misdeeds - a plan I agreed to with great reluctance, primarily to secure the futures of my parents and Lyrica. As I have already mentioned, my heart and soul were already devoted to another woman. In my eyes, Octavia was merely a child, and a petulant, spoiled one at that, showing little understanding of or empathy for the altruistic motives behind my pursuit of medical science.

Our betrothal was among the many doomed events that took place in 1861, the same year Venedict murdered Uncle Algernon, Gabriel appeared like a demon summoned from the darkest realms of hell, and Venedict dragged all of us down to the bottom with him, forcing the immortal blood down our throats in the most literal sense and forever cutting us off from all of life.

CLYDE PAUSED MOMENTARILY, his eyes flashing, as if with lightning. It was anger. The same anger that was also evident in the tense set of his jaw.

Clyde spoke again, breaking the momentary silence. "Becoming a vampire very nearly broke my spirit. You would think, after mine and Vendict's Frankenstinian ventures, I would perhaps find the concept of vampirism fascinating and grisly alluring. And from a scientific perspective, this is the case. In terms of first-hand experience, however, I never had an appetite for becoming one of the monsters." A brief, sudden and bitter burst of laughter escaped him. "Very unlike Venedict, who stepped into vampirism with his arms open, ready to be swallowed up by the darkness. My dear cousin always had this recklessness, this destructive drive, same as his father. Same as you.

At least you, for a while, attempted to turn that darkness into something constructive through your efforts as a vampire hunter. I suppose that is something worth noting." He said it with a slight nod as if he was conceding something.

IT WAS only thanks to Lyrica's persuasion and insistence that I still had a place in the world, that I may still achieve accomplishments and do good in the medical field that I became convinced that my new life - my unlife, my afterlife, call it what you will - was still worth living. And two of us did what we could to stop Venedict's monstrous rampage. Who is to say where it would have stopped? We did the best thing we could have done, short of piercing his heart with a stake and severing his head. We wrapped layer upon layer of sturdy metal chains around his casket, preventing his escape.

Did I toy with the idea of taking the other approach - the approach involving the stake? Yes, of course. It would have been the only certain permanent solution. But I suppose I lacked the tenacity, at the time. And Venedict was my cousin, whom I had known most of my life. I simply lacked the final ounce of conviction.

There was also Gabriel to consider. He might be furious with my cousin, but I still sensed that I might encounter dire consequences, should I dare to do away with his favorite toy boy of the century. That wasn't something I was particularly willing to risk. I have never been the confrontational type.

The best solution, then, seemed to be to put the whole mess behind me. The whole bloody ruined mess. And so, I took my leave of Thornhill Mansion, of the family and of London, heading instead for the New World with its promises of freedom and renewed hope. I wondered if these things also applied to vampires.

And I wondered - as you may have sensed, I have always been possessed of a curious mind - whether the scientific exploits I planned on pursuing in America were going to lead me to the ultimate solution; a cure for vampirism.

Throughout the 20th Century I encountered both highs and lows in my search, which took place in a variety of labs and hospitals scattered throughout the states. Fortunately, my medical training made it easy enough to gain access to medical equipment and facilities.

I attempted all manner of things, as you can well imagine. Draining every drop of blood from my immortal body, only to give myself a full blood transfusion with mortal blood in an attempt at refilling my veins with mortal life. Injecting myself with various questionable elixirs in order to test their effects - and in rather desperate moments, resorting to rather crude methods such as removing my own fangs with pliers, only to have them grow back again in time for the following night's battle against the bloodlust.

I was the subject of most of the experiments I carried out - though admittedly, I have also experimented on other vampires over the years. Always with the same discouraging lack of result. Vampirism, it seems, is utterly resistant to reversal. It is incurable. As incurable as most believe the human condition to be.

~

CLYDE LET OUT A SOUL-DEEP SIGH, his shoulders hunching slightly as if he was overcome with a sense of defeat.

"I chased this illusion," he said in a near whisper, "this sadly impossible hope of one day regaining my mortality, my humanity. But as evidenced by my sitting here right now talking to you, fully conscious of the hours ticking away before sunrise, I have not achieved the one scientific breakthrough that eclipsed all others in my mind. And now, at last, I have given up. I shall always be a vampire."

Despite their obvious personality differences I was beginning to see parallels and similarities between Clyde and Lyrica - something about the melancholic Victorian-era poet way they both expressed themselves. This made me appreciate Clyde a little more.

But he still had things to answer for; my unanswered questions.

I was about to open my mouth and speak, when he got in there first with a question. "Tell me, Harlan. Now that you are one, do you... enjoy being a vampire?" he asked it sort of cautiously, as if he was worried that the question might offend me.

"It's complicated," I told him honestly. "Trust me, I don't want to like it. After being a vampire hunter for a decade, and being raised by one for another decade before that, liking being a vampire isn't something I can really admit to." I paused briefly before admitting it anyway, "But, in many ways, yes, I do like it. I even love it a little. Except for the bloodlust. I'm still struggling with that."

Clyde looked as if he was contemplating what I'd said, his raven's wing eyebrows knitting in a slightly concerned frown. "I do wish you didn't love it in the least." he said, with a note of wistful regret.

I shrugged. "I want to be honest. Since we're having an

honest conversation." Tonight had already involved me being more honest and more open than I usually am in a year, but why not keep it going? Tomorrow night, I could always revert to deflecting attempts to get me to open up with sarcastic comments and brooding silences.

"Yeah, the bloodlust aside, I love being a vampire. I enjoy feeling powerful and I like knowing I'll never grow old. And I'm completely unconcerned about whether it's unnatural or not. That's the honest truth. How could it not be?"

Clyde's eyes glided to the side, and didn't return as he chewed his lip, skillfully without piercing it with his fangs, and pensively let his fingers dance on the armrest in restless rhythm.

"Clyde," I said - my turn to ask him a question - "since you resent vampires so much as a species, what are you doing here, surrounded by them? Why subject yourself to a vampire weekend? It doesn't make much sense."

"Well," Clyde responded, shifting slightly in his armchair, "I have my reasons. I am not here for the company, or the entertainment."

"That much is clear," I conceded. "That's the only thing that's clear."

"As I have already hinted at, I have some things to settle with Evander."

"Is this to do with Lyrica and his relationship?"

Clyde shook his head, "That is only part of it. I mentioned that I was interested in another woman while I was engaged to Octavia; Tessa Eve. Ironic, is it not? Both Lyrica and I got entangled with one of them. Entangled in their games. As you may have noticed, Evander is fond of playing games."

I'd noticed alright.

"So have you settled your score with him?"

"Not," Clyde replied, the moonlight gleaming off his fangs as I saw his smile for the first time, "quite yet."

As I faced him, sitting there in the high-backed victorian chair, I had that strange feeling of an overlay with that terrible dream, the one that had been haunting me for two decades, most of my life.

"Clyde," I said, letting my voice coil through the air like a silk ribbon laced with an edge of steel. I imagined it trying a slipknot around his mind as I commanded, "Look at me."

He couldn't help it - he glanced directly at me and our eyes locked. His eyes widened as I concentrated on establishing the link, imagining a sharp gleaming hook sinking into his energy field.

"What is this?" Clyde demanded sharply, jerking his head back. Immediately, he was onto what I was doing, and of course. Hypnotizing a fellow vampire, and someone who had been around for a century or two longer than I, wasn't going to be easy.

But I was intent on putting Clyde under and getting him to talk. I would have preferred to take a more subtle approach, but since he was onto what I was up to, well...

I rose swiftly from my chair and in another split second I was kneeling before Clyde's armchair with my hands against his temples, pulling him forward until we were eye to eye.

He attempted to pull back, but I held firm.

"Harlan, I don't appreciate what you are trying to do! Is this how you thank me for my generosity in opening up to you, by pulling this dirty vampire trick on me?"

"Uhuh. Talk to me, Clyde. Why are you here at Eve Hall? Tell me the truth."

"I will not be subjected to this, I refuse to be hypnotized!" he declared, and attempted to push me aside, and of course he was stronger than he looked, but it wasn't enough.

In a sudden motion I maneuvered Clyde to the floor. I pinned him beneath me, my knees immobilizing his arms against his torso, while my hands pressed firmly against his temples, both to keep him stationary and to help the ethereal connection along.

"Clyde, won't you tell me the truth? Wouldn't that be a relief?" The gentle tone I used contrasted with the physical restraint as he squirmed, trying to escape my grasp and get away from me, but I was determined not to let him.

I wasn't letting him close his eyes, either. Positioning my thumbs just above his eyelids, I forced them to remain wide open.

"Clyde, listen to me. You're hiding a lot of things. You're carrying such a burden. Don't you think it would feel better to just release it all?"

As I felt the thread of the vampiric hypnotic connection finally latch into place, I tightened my mental grip on it.

I had him securely now, though he still thrashed like a fish trying desperately to slip the hook.

"Clyde, you can be completely honest with me. You can tell me all of it. Tell me what you're doing here at Eve Hall."

"I- I am here to settle scores." His voice sounded drowsy, distant. I'd managed to do it.

On some level I wanted to reach for my iPhone - where was it, in my back pocket? - just so I could record this to show off later in case anyone doubted that I'd managed to hypnotize a nearly two centuries old vampire. But I recognized it as a stupid impulse and shoved it aside. I had something much more important to do than showing off.

"Clyde, keep talking. What scores - are you talking

about your score with Evander? And with Gabriel? Or are there other scores to settle, too?"

"There are other scores to settle, other problems that have to be...dealt with."

"Am I one of those problems, Clyde?"

"Yes."

TWENTY-EIGHT

"How do you intend to deal with the problems you mentioned?" I coaxed, gently but firmly. I was still pinning his arms to his body, but I'd let go of his temples. He was no longer resisting my line of questioning and keeping him restrained like I was was just a precaution.

"You're all vampires, all predators, and should be put down like the rabid dogs you are. Of course, I include myself in this. I, too, will die at dawn," he declared, "though not quite as soon as you."

My blood ran cold at his words.

"Elaborate. Which vampires need to be put down like rabid dogs?" I pressed.

"Everyone, every last one. You, Evander, Gabriel, Csilla, everyone here under this roof when the sun rises. And then, everyone at Thornhill Mansion. Even Lyrica, yes, even her," he responded, his voice a monotone echo. "Even I, in the end."

"Why does that need to happen?" I asked.

"It is the only way. After all my scientific explorations and my ponderings, it really comes down to the simplest, sweetest thing. Only the healing light of the sun can cure vampirism. If Venedict can turn our entire family tree into what Aunt Helen once described as a tree of death when we summoned her in spirit form in the parlor of Thornhill Mansion, then why should not I do the same, in reverse, taking as many others with me in the process as possible?"

"What if we don't want to be cured? I'm pretty sure no one under this roof tonight wants to be cured in the way you describe. Shouldn't we all have a choice?"

"I had no choice!" Clyde's voice echoed under the high, stucco ceiling. "No one offered me any choice. Did you have a choice?"

"No," I admitted, the word heavy on my tongue. "But I'd have been dead without Venedict's intervention. I thought I told you this before."

"He could have done the merciful thing and let you die the mortal man you were supposed to be," Clyde retorted, his tone dripping with both accusation and sorrow.

"What if I'm supposed to be a vampire?"

"No one is supposed to be a vampire." Clyde's voice grew colder, more clinical. "But this is one of the very problems with the condition; believing that vampires are not unnatural predators. You used to know the truth, but after a few short months of being a vampire, you have lost sight of it. You no longer consider vampires simply the monsters that we are." His laugh was bitter.

He wasn't wrong about that; it was an uncomfortable truth. But this conversation wasn't supposed to be about me.

"How do you intend to pull all of this off? How do you intend to expose everyone to the cure?"

Clyde's laughter morphed into sobs, his voice breaking as he spoke. "Well, I may not have discovered a scientific cure for vampirism, and though we seem to be exceptionally resistant to most substances we ingest or inject - apart from blood - my experiments over the years have yielded some results." His voice trailed off into a ragged breath. "The most notable is a muscle freeze formula that, I must say, works quite effectively on us." After a brief pause during which he fought to get his laughing sobs under control, he resumed, "Tonight, just before sunrise, I shall make my way from room to room to inject everyone with a suitable dose, leaving every casket open and every curtain drawn to welcome the sun."

His words hung between us, making the air feel heavy like the air before a lightning storm.

Clyde had essentially just laid bare a mass murder plot - one that he intended to execute tonight.

"Then tomorrow night," he continued, "I shall repeat the process at Thornhill Mansion. Afterward, I plan to take one of the armchairs from the parlor, place it out on the portico, and sit there, watching the sunrise over the gravestones from the east."

"Clyde," I asked sharply, digging deeper, since we were here, "Did you know my parents or grandparents? Did you kill them? Have I seen you before?"

"I didn't know them - but yes, I did kill them." His laughter echoed through the room again, a sound devoid of any joy, bitter and hollow. "Oh, it was terrible. And terribly necessary. Your mother was pregnant, at the time. It made it more difficult to kill her. But I managed it. I feared - and rightly so, as it turned out - that Venedict might one day escape his confinement and attempt to lay claim to any remaining mortal descendants of his bloodline, and perhaps of mine, which of course, is also his. He is Helen's son, after all."

"Why didn't you kill me, then?" I demanded, my voice biting. The urge to strike him was overwhelming, but I restrained myself. I needed him to keep talking, now that he was finally revealing the truths I had needed to hear for so long. He was slowly revealing himself as the missing puzzle piece in my life's mysterious history, the key that made much of the rest click into place.

"I intended to. But you were so young, so small, that it made me hesitate. And then a vampire hunter appeared on the scene, as you know. Instead of confronting him, my softer instincts - or perhaps it was just cowardice - took over, and I fled without harming you. But not before setting everything on fire to eradicate any trace that might link you to Thornhill Mansion, its dreadful history, and to the family." He paused, his voice both remorseful and resigned. "As it turned out, I was quite successful. You grew up, blissfully unaware of your true heritage. For a while."

"Killing my family wasn't the same as not harming me," I pointed out, my voice calm, sort of, despite the storm of emotions inside me. "I grew up without parents, without any family. You took that away from me."

"Sometimes," Clyde offered his opinion, "it is better to have no family than to belong to the wrong one. And don't you, in a way, have a father in the vampire hunter who found and raised you? That was fate giving you the best chance to escape the darkness that had enveloped Thornhill Mansion and its occupants. And it worked, for two decades. You had the chance to grow up, to make a positive impact in the world - to the extent that your Thornhill blood would allow, of course. But, inevitably, the family curse caught up with you. It is... most tragic."

"How do you know anything about my life and my work - did you get that info from Jeremy Gently?" After a beat of heavy silence, realization dawned on me, chilling and sharp. "Whom you also killed."

"Yes, yes, yes." Clyde's voice was laced with exasperation as he brushed off my accusation. "Oh, I am feeling rather dizzy," he added, pressing a hand to his forehead as if trying to steady himself.

"And you killed Sebastian's family, too - your own lineage," I stated rather than asked.

"Yes. But I deliberately left him alone, placing him in an orphanage to give him a chance at life. He resembled what could have been my own son, and I couldn't bring myself to end him, unlike how I might have ended you. And as I will indeed end you. You are no longer the innocent mortal child you once were. You are one of the monsters now, and that will make it a little easier for me." Clyde's voice grew colder again, more detached. "And that is needed because, as much as the echo of Venedict that I see in you makes me dislike you, it also makes the prospect of harming you more uncomfortable. Your features are so familiar; you look like family. "

"I am family," I retorted.

I got up and started pacing. The movement helped me think, and with Clyde a disheveled mess on the floor, he wasn't going anywhere. His gaze followed me, clouded and a little uncertain.

"Well... but it has to be done," he rationalized, lying on his back and gesturing weakly as he spoke. "Ultimately, I must prioritize my own bloodline. Surely, you can understand. Eradicating you, the other Thornhills, and as many vampires in the vicinity as possible gives Sebastian the best chance to escape the darkness. He alone deserves to survive. He alone can carry the Hartenbrook family forward."

"There's a piece missing from your view on things, Clyde, something you still haven't addressed. I'm related to Lyrica, and to you. How do you explain that? The DNA test I had Lyrica and Sebastian take proves it."

"That," he countered, his voice weak but stubborn, "I cannot explain. Perhaps the sample was flawed. Or perhaps..." His tone darkened with realization, "Augustine, that insidious child of Octavia and Algernon, seduced Emmeline Eve during their overlap in Paris. Yes, I supposed that's possible. Either way, it doesn't change your fate. You are just trying to confuse me."

"You don't have to go through with this, Clyde. So far, no one knows about this. Only I know. We could still get you help," I offered, stopping my pacing to look at him directly. I had no idea what could help him, but I was sure I could figure it out.

"Get me help?" He laughed bitterly. "It's far too late for help. My plans are already in motion. They have been in motion for years, decades. I've developed the formula at great cost and with considerable difficulty, and I've brought it here, risking discovery and any vicious punishment that might befall me as a result of it. After faltering so many times before, intending to eliminate at least the Thornhill vampires, I will not waver again this time. Now, I have my supply, ready in syringes, secreted somewhere within this manor that no one will stumble upon at random."

What was I supposed to do with all of this? I obviously wasn't going to let Clyde just go ahead with his crazy plan.

Annoyingly, my first impulse was to ask Gabriel. Gabriel would know what to do - the problem was that his solution was likely to be both effective and result in there being no

Clyde to try to fix after all was said and done. The other problem with involving Gabriel was that I just didn't want to have to deal with him right now - particularly not in the context of asking for his help with anything. He'd enjoy that way too much.

I could ask Evander, but after his trickery with the map, my trust in him had worn a little thin.

If only I could get hold of Lyrica, she might be able to talk Clyde down from the ledge, but I had no way of reaching her.

I could try Sebastian; he was the only one Clyde didn't seem interested in killing, and he might be able to talk some sense into the family's prodigal mad scientist. He might do great with talking to Clyde, or he might get all flustered and fuck it up. It could go either way.

After a moment's wavering, I decided to do what I usually do when I'm in over my head. I called Eli.

It was just after midnight, but he'd still be up. He was a night owl, particularly when he was working on a case - and lately he'd been branching out into more and more poltergeist cases, and that entailed a lot of late nights.

It wasn't long before he picked up. He was at home, at the desk in his study, its surface covered in stacks of papers and books and folders. A steaming mug of black coffee was leaving dark rings on the desk's surface.

"I'd like to say I'm just checking in, but really, I need your thoughts on something. I'm having a bit of a crisis."

"A crisis?" Eli's eyes narrowed slightly, leaving crows feet in the tanned skin at the corners of his vivid blue eyes.

"A minor crisis, I think. It might have escalated into a major one if I hadn't caught it in time." I looked over my shoulder. Clyde was still on the floor, now dozing off.

"I don't recognize where you are - is this related to work?"

I walked over to the balcony doors and pushed them open, eager to let in some fresh air after my tense and surreal conversation with Clyde.

"Not work, no. I'm at this event called the Grim Games."

"Grim Games?" Eli raised a quizzical bushy eyebrow. "Sounds uplifting."

"It's a vampire thing," I explained, "that Gabriel black-mailed me into attending. Imagine something between a Victorian tea party and the Hunger Games, hosted at an old country manor crawling with the undead."

"Isn't this Gabriel Graves the same vampire who has troubled the Thornhills for over a century, and who killed you?"

"Yeah, that's the one."

"And you wonder why I sometimes still worry about you?" came Eli's response, his expression somewhere between amusement and concern. Then, after a deep breath, "And if I'm correct, none of what you've just described is the crisis you're calling about?"

"No, the Games aren't a crisis. Or at least, that's a different crisis and they're over now. This crisis is that I've run into Clyde. Clyde Hartenbrook. I mentioned him to you. Lyrica's brother, the scientist who went to the states in the 1860s. Apparently, he's been pursuing a cure for vampirism ever since."

"Yes, I recall. I'd like to think I'm doing a good job keeping tabs on the who's who of all the vampires that have flocked into your life."

"Clyde never found a cure, but he did develop what he

calls a muscle-freezing substance that affects vampires. He's turned up here at the Games, at Eve Hall, planning to inject everyone with it and then let the sun do the rest at dawn - to 'cure' us all of vampirism in one go. Including me, Eli. Then he wants to do it all over again tomorrow night at Thornhill Mansion and take himself out too."

I stepped outside on the balcony, letting the fresh, chilly night breeze wrap around me as I continued explaining to Eli, "I've managed to heavily sedate him with hypnosis, so he's not a threat right now. But I'm kind of stuck on what to do next. I guess I'll just lock him in his casket and tie it up to keep it closed, but what then? If I tell any of the other vampires here, I think they might kill him for plotting something like this. I don't really want that for him."

"The first thing you should do, before anything else," Eli suggested in his calm, authoritative voice, "is to lock him up in a casket, like you've already thought of. Make sure he can't escape. That's crucial. You don't want him running loose."

"I'll pop him in the casket to be on the safe side, but he's already incapacitated. I've completely overwhelmed him with hypnosis, Eli. I've gotten really skilled at it - you'd be surprised. He's essentially comatose."

"Harlan, I don't doubt your prowess with this new vampire ability you're honing. But right now, don't waste any time angling for praise, alright? Go get your cousin Clyde locked up. Even if you think you've put him deep under. Let's get that done, and then we can figure out our next steps."

"Okay, I'm on it. I'll call you back in five."

I hung up on Eli, turned around and went back into the suite. Angling for praise - that's not what I'd been doing.

But Eli could at least have seemed a little impressed that I'd managed to hypnotize a nearly two centuries old vampire. It's not something any fledgling vampire can just do.

I froze just inside the door.

The space on the floor where Clyde had been comatose minutes earlier was empty. He was gone without a trace.

TWENTY-NINE

W hat now?

Clyde couldn't have made it very far, could he? He'd seemed completely bleary, nearly unconscious. Then again, perhaps he'd pulled the kind of thing that I would have pulled by pretending to be more affected or wounded than was the case, just to gain an edge of wiggle room to make a surprise move. Fuck.

I threw the door to the hallway open and looked in either direction. No signs of Clyde. The hallway was lined with doors to other rooms - about ten on this floor alone. There were way, way too many places he could hide.

This was bad. I'd gone and done it again; assumed I'd carried something off with a little more finesse than I actually had, and I'd not wrapped it up properly, and now the consequences of my carelessness could turn out to be catastrophic.

Now might be the time to admit that I was really in over my head. Now was probably the time to swallow my pride and go tell Evander, as the lord of the manor, that we had some trouble brewing.

But maybe it wasn't too late for damage control. If I was still in time to contain this burgeoning disaster before anyone noticed, I would.

Already on my way down through the manor, I made a silent promise to myself that I had five minutes to test the theory that had formed in my mind. I had one theory about where Clyde might have gone, where he might have decided to store his supply of muscle freeze stuff.

When I'd walked in on Clyde emerging from one of the defunct fireplaces - the wrong fireplace, the one that didn't turn into a tunnel going down - I'd thought that he had been looking for the library's tunnel exit. But in light of his confessions, it seemed much more likely that he had been hiding something in there.

As I hurried down the stairs, I passed a few vampires who paused in their conversations, their heads turning almost in unison to track my rapid descent. I whipped past them at a speed that caused a ripple of air to flow through the staircase, making their long, dark hair billow dramatically. Their piercing eyes, glowing faintly in the dimly lit hallway, followed me as I vanished from their view.

I reached the ground floor breathlessly, stormed down the hall and into the library. There were no immediate signs of Clyde being here. The library seemed vast and empty, the only light the ambient glow of the moon glancing off the waves outside.

I went over to the fireplace I'd seen Clyde step out of, and ducked under the mantlepiece, finding myself standing in a small square space, the stone walls blackened by ancient soot. But there was no sign of anything in here, other than the bare walls. I let my hands brush over them quickly to check for any loose stones. Nothing.

Time to admit defeat?

Nearly time. On a whim, I decided to check the other fireplace. Since I was here.

Crossing the room, I ducked and stepped into it. It was like the other, except that one wall had an opening, a doorless doorway, and a windy, narrow stony spiral of a staircase going straight down.

Standing completely still and closing my eyes for a second, I was able to make out the faintest sound of something moving, further down the stairs. It was nothing but the distant sound of a few loose pebbles falling as one of Clyde's shoes must have stirred them from their customary resting places in the dark.

My pulse quickened. I didn't always have one these days, but right now I did.

Taking great care to make my descent completely soundless, I started descending the spiral, the fingertips of my left hand lightly brushing the ancient wall. With my right hand, I withdrew one of my knives from its sheath on my left arm, grateful to myself for deciding to ditch Lord Eve's no-weapons policy for the evening.

So it was down here, somewhere, in a hidden nook or behind a loose stone that Clyde had decided to hide his stash. Well, probably. It was possible that he had simply decided to flee, now that he'd found himself in the bad position of having unintentionally revealed his plans - but something told me it was more likely that he was still intent on carrying them out. He was gonna give it his best shot.

Too bad for him that he was up against me. I'd been careless, nearly letting him get away. But that wasn't happening again. I just needed to be careful - he might have some of that muscle freeze stuff on him right now, and I didn't particularly want to be the first to get loaded up with a dose.

A few times, Clyde seemed to stop and pause, possibly to listen out for any signs of pursuit. Each time it happened, I stopped too.

After a few minutes, Clyde stopped being quite so careful - he sped up his pace and didn't seem to worry so much when he kicked up pebbles and loose small stones here and there.

The spiral stairs finally ended, giving way to what appeared to be an old wine cellar with a high arched ceiling. Large, ancient wooden barrels covered in centuries of dust stood on plinths along the walls. There were several doorways along the walls, supposedly leading off into other storage rooms or tunnels. The wall at the opposite end from where I stood was missing, revealing a view of broad stone stairs going down into Eve Hall's watery underground cavern.

I imagine that, back in the day, smugglers would have brought their barrels from ships anchored just outside, allowing them to bob through the underground cavern along the water's surface, guided by oars or long poles. The Eve family's staff would be waiting at the bottom of those broad stone steps, ready to carry the goods up directly into the underground wine cellar for storage.

Clyde stood at the top of those broad stone stairs, outlined in silhouette against the subtly moonlit waters of the cavern behind him. Eerie, watery patterns danced across the arched ceiling.

He hadn't seen me, and it was best if he didn't until I was right beside him. The best way to accomplish that seemed to be to make my way along the wall, between the wall and the barrels.

I did, moving as silent and light as a shadow.

The barrels had the dual effect of mostly blocking me from Clyde's line of sight, should he decide to turn around and look over his shoulder, and blocking him from my view as I approached. And as I reached the end of the long wine cellar and started making my way along the side of the final wooden barrel in the row and the top of the stairs came into clear view once more, Clyde had vanished from the top of the stairs.

Where was he?

He must have been able to work out that I'd come after him. The question was, had he seen me?

Suddenly, his face appeared around the edge of the barrel, just a couple of feet ahead of me. His hands were hidden from view behind his back as he stepped forward. Not a good sign, in my experience.

"Oh, hello," he said calmly, as if he was greeting an unexpected guest who'd decided to pop by, "I thought you might decide to follow me down here."

"Hi Clyde. I thought I'd come get you. I think it's best if we head back upstairs. But first, show me your hands."

I held both of my knives aimed at him, the watery moonlight gleaming in their blades.

"I would rather not," he declined, reasonably, taking a step forward. "You don't really want to use those knives on me. What would Lyrica say if anything were to happen to me?" His expression was one of benevolent concern, as though he was more concerned right now for me than for himself.

"You're wrong. I've stabbed countless vampires with these."

"Indeed, you have. But I am not just any vampire - I am

family. You said so yourself," he reminded me. He took another small step forward.

He was close enough now that I'd be able to make a swift lunge forward and pierce him with one of the blades, and I did.

Ramming the point of one blade quickly followed by the other through his chest, I pinned him to the barrel like an insect. I'd avoided the middle of his chest, avoided piercing through his heart or lungs, anything that might seriously harm him.

Still, he didn't seem to appreciate the great care I was taking with him. His mouth opened and he let out a furious, agonized wail. His white shirt was already darkening with blood.

His arms flailed as I took two gun-like instruments from his hands. They looked similar to injector guns, made from metal and glass, and instead of gun barrel openings they had thick hollow needles. They were loaded with a thick, clear liquid that I squeezed out onto the ground before throwing the syringes over my shoulder, into the water where they sank.

"Lyrica should never have salvaged little Augustine that night in the chapel," Clyde hissed through gritted teeth, "It would have been better for all concerned if she had let Octavia drain her newborn son - at least the Thornhill bloodline would have ended then and there. And we would never have come to this moment."

"Sure. Come on, Clyde, let's head back upstairs."

There was a bit more angry flailing, and then he finally seemed to relax, realizing his defeat.

Once he seemed calm enough, I pulled the knives out of his shoulders, all ten inches of each glistening with his slick dark vampire blood. He was hurt, but this is the kind of injury that a vampire will easily recover from.

I kept my eye on Clyde as he let himself slide down to the cold, damp stone floor where the clear muscle freeze liquid had been spilt. He covered his face with his left hand as he drew a ragged breath.

"I know, I know. It's been a tough night. You'll be okay, though," I said as I wiped both of my knives on my sleeve, then put them through two of my belt loops so they were within easy reach.

"Well, at least the bloodline has come to an end," he mumbled, his face still hidden behind his hand, "with you. And now that you have gone and gotten yourself turned into a vampire, there will be no more Thornhills. None at all."

"Yeah, that's true. Take some comfort in that, huh?" I held my hand out to him, offering to pull him to his feet. "No more Thornhills."

Clyde took my hand. But instead of our palms meeting, his hand went under mine, his fingers closing around my wrist.

"You're the last one," he said, "and the first one I intend to do away with."

I felt a sharp sting and looked down at my hand. Clyde must have kept a third hidden injector gun full of muscle freeze liquid somewhere, because there it was, its stinger in my palm. He was pressing the plunger.

Instinct took over as I closed my hand over Clyde's, quickly pulling the injector gun backwards and withdrawing its hollow needle from my hand.

I threw it behind me and heard it clattering down the stone steps. I wasn't sure how much he'd injected me with, but it wasn't a full dose. I should have checked, but I'd acted too fast for thinking.

The sting from the injection site had sent a jolt of alarm through my body, but that sensation now gave way to something far more terrifying. A creeping coldness began to spread from my palm, seeping into my veins like icy water.

"Clyde, what the fuck?"

The chilling sensation was already creeping up my arm, stiffening my muscles and tendons.

I wasn't sure what was going to happen now, but I could already tell I wasn't going to like it. I needed to subdue him quickly.

Clutching the back of his head with both hands, I drove my knee into his face. I hoped the force would be enough to knock him out. There was a horrific crunch as something in his face gave way. I let go, and he collapsed onto his side.

With the coldness invading my shoulder and fanning out across my chest I scrambled on top of him, rolling him onto his stomach. I grabbed both of his arms, pinning them behind his back, and pressed upward, intending to break them. I wasn't ready to die. Let's see how far he'd get with both his arms and legs broken.

There was just one problem. Clyde's muscle freeze was swift, its effect chillingly efficient. I was shivering, teeth chattering from the icy grip of the stuff he'd injected me with.

Breaking his arms like this shouldn't have been too difficult, but it was. I pushed harder, but couldn't put enough force behind it. Meanwhile, Clyde wasn't even trying to fight me off - perhaps he was that confident that he wouldn't have to.

"How are you feeling, Harlan? A little cold, perhaps?"

Clyde inquired, his voice calm as he twisted his head to glance up at me. His face was covered in blood, the bridge of his elegant nose shattered.

As if on cue, the room seemed to tilt and swirl. The edges of my vision seemed to be frosting over as I felt for my knives at my waist. I was going to have to slice his throat, wasn't I?

I brought both knives under his throat, the cold steel making him flinch.

"You would really do this to me?"

If one of us had to die in this place, it wasn't going to be me. I tightened my grip and sliced upwards with both blades. But in that same split second, Clyde reacted with surprising agility, twisting sharply and throwing me off.

I tried to get my legs under me, to stand so I could create some distance between us, but my legs just wouldn't obey. My vision was blurry. Panic surged within me, racing just ahead of the spreading cold paralysis.

"Don't worry, Harlan. I know it isn't pleasant - enough of my test subjects have told me that, and I have even tried the substance out for myself." Clyde's voice echoed distantly, as if coming from the end of a long, dark tunnel.

His face was a blur above me. Far above me, it seemed. Everything was distant.

"I can't very well carry you back up the stairs in case anyone sees us," Clyde mused, talking to himself as much as to me. "I think I shall have to leave you down here. But not before injecting you with the rest of your dose, of course. I will not be taking any chances. I have made my plans much too carefully for that."

He grabbed my legs and began to drag me across the rough, stony ground toward the stone steps and the moonlit water. There wasn't a damned thing I could do about it. The muscle freeze had reached my throat and neck, robbing me of the ability to even speak. I was painfully aware of my body's stillness - no heartbeat, no pulse, and my breathing was so faint it was almost nonexistent. If I had been mortal, I would have been dead.

"You know," he said, "what I said earlier about you looking like family making it harder for me to kill you was true. But it also makes you the perfect practice before the big finale at Thornhill Mansion."

Soon we'd reached the stairs - I felt the bumps as he pulled me down them. The stairs themselves were cold, wet, and slippery, coated with a thick layer of algae.

"And," Clyde continued as he paused briefly at the final stair to reach into the water and retrieve the injector gun that had come to rest there, "it is also very true what you said, about it not being your fault that the Thornhill blood is in you. It just happens to be in you, regrettably."

Positioned as he was, dragging me, Clyde now stood in front of me, his legs submerged in silvery water up to his thighs.

"I think," he said, tilting his head to the side as he regarded me with a thoughtful expression, "perhaps I should drown you, like an unwanted kitten. As you hinted earlier, you're not, alas, particularly interested in being cured of your vampirism. Perhaps you would prefer this dark, watery grave?"

Not really. But I wasn't in any condition to weigh in on it.

Suddenly, I felt faint tingles of sensation returning to my limbs. The chilly water lapping around my waist seemed to be helping a little, breathing a desperate energy back into my body.

Clyde was so absorbed in his macabre contemplations that he failed to notice the slight movements of my fingers, the underwater flexing of my wrist.

As he lifted the injector gun and placed it against the side of my neck, I mustered all the strength I could gather and struck his arm, knocking the injector from his grasp.

I grasped for it from where it fell on one of the steps just below the water's surface. Although the effects of the muscle freeze had lessened, they hadn't completely dissipated, and I was shivering, moving sluggishly. I accidentally knocked the gun down another step, panicked that it might slip away into the watery depths. But then I managed to close my fingers around it.

Submerged in the chilly water, I pressed the injector against Clyde's thigh and pushed the plunger all the way.

Clyde gasped, his eyes widening in shock as the rapid onset of paralysis froze him in place. Of the two of us, he had received the larger dose by far. He attempted to speak, but the muscle freeze silenced his voice. Slowly, he sank to his knees in the water before me, his expressions frozen into a mask of horrified stillness.

I fucking love these moments when the tables turn on my opponent. I live for them.

A peal of laughter burst from me as I, still weak and trembling, grabbed a handful of Clyde's hair and yanked him forward. His chin rested on the stair just below the water's surface, his nose above the waterline, allowing him to draw labored, bubbling breaths through water and blood.

I managed to lift my legs out of the water and curl up on my side on the stair above Clyde, still clutching a fistful of his gleaming black curls to keep him anchored in place until I recovered enough to move again.

For the first time in a long time - for the first time since I'd become a vampire - I felt that rush of peace that used to envelop me after a hunt. Everything around me stilled, and the dark roaring chaos that always lurked somewhere in my mind was nowhere to be found.

THIRTY

After a while, the effects of the muscle freeze began to subside enough for me to be able to move. I realized I would have to move for both me and Clyde - he was still completely paralyzed, thank heavens. The only signs of life from him were the bubbling breaths he drew through his broken nose.

I lifted him out of the water by hooking my arms under his and dragging him backward up the slippery algae-coated stairs.

Clyde might finally be thoroughly subdued, but I was done taking chances for the night. I secured his arms behind his back using his own black leather belt, just in case he felt like attempting any surprises. I love surprises, but only when I'm in charge of delivering them.

I still felt a little unsteady on my legs as I collected my belongings: my knives and my iPhone, which lay on the stony ground with its glass screen shattered. Peering through the spiderweb of cracks, I checked the time: 01:03. This entire episode with Clyde had taken about an hour.

Several missed calls from Eli also showed up on the broken display.

Letting my fingers fly over the cracked glass, I shot him a quick message. The smashed screen was stuck on the caps lock so it came out shouting in all capital letters: GOT HIM!

I didn't want Eli to worry that I hadn't managed the situation. I could fill him in on the details later. After a moment's hesitation, I followed my first message with another: I GOT THIS. DON'T NEED HELP.

"Clyde," I said, crouching in front of him, not sure whether he'd be able to answer, "where'd you put the rest of the injector guns? I'm guessing you have one for every vampire in this place, at least. I know they're somewhere down here."

He glared at me, his eyes darting to the left, probably involuntarily.

I followed his gaze but saw nothing obvious.

"Over there somewhere?"

Clyde let his eyes dart around some more in an infuriating attempt at confusing me. But I hadn't missed his initial sort-of answer.

I grinned at him, rose to my feet and started searching along the left side of the wall behind the barrels, my fingers brushing against the rough, cold surface. There was a nook in the stone, empty except a bunch of rolled-up rusty chains with hooks attached that, once upon a time, had probably been used to haul smuggled wares. I followed the wall until I found another nook that held an old rotting crate. Badly concealed just behind it was a newer, sturdier one.

I pulled the newer crate out of the nook and used one of my knives to pry off the lid. Inside was row upon row of injector guns, neatly arranged, ready for use and gleaming ominously in the faint light filtering through the cavern.

I picked up one of them, and threw it against the ragged stone floor where it smashed with a satisfying sound of breaking glass. I glanced over my shoulder and savored Clyde's expression of helpless rage as he watched me destroy his plans.

One by one, the injectors went on the ground where they shattered into thousands of pieces. It didn't take me long to reduce Clyde's whole murderous plot to nothing more than a useless pile of shards, scrap metal and twisted, broken needles. I used the crate's lid to scrape the shattered pieces across the uneven floor, past Clyde, paralyzed and furious, down the algae-slick stone steps, and into the cavern's watery depths. A mental image of the count taking a swim down here and stepping on a rusty needle made me chuckle darkly.

I'd saved only one injector - Clyde had only had about three-quarters of a dose, after all. I stepped toward him with the needle gleaming in my hand. "What do you say, Clyde - you want some more of this?"

Clyde's eyes widened, darting from the needle to my face. His breath came in shallow, rapid gasps, but he was helpless to stop me when I swept down beside him and injected the last remaining dose into his neck. His eyes rolled back as soon as the freeze hit his bloodstream, and I winced - it didn't look pleasant.

I hoisted a now unconscious Clyde over my shoulder. If I were still mortal, carrying a grown man soaked in sea water up a fifty-foot spiral staircase and down various corridors would have been a daunting task. But now, it was manageable. If Clyde couldn't see that being a vampire had its advantages, he was simply being stubborn.

On impulse, I grabbed some of the rolled-up metal chains I'd found and draped them over my shoulder. Then I climbed the grand staircase to the library, carrying the chains and Clyde's limp body, leaving behind only a trail of seawater dripping from his hair.

I spotted the hidden cage lift inside one of the old fireplaces and hastily dragged Clyde inside. My fingers fumbled over the brass buttons, hoping one of them would take us upwards without drawing attention.

The mansion buzzed with activity as preparations for the ball were underway. The main staircase was not an option. Running into anyone would raise too many questions, and explaining why I was carrying an unconscious, seawater-soaked Clyde was impossible. Even if someone understood it was family business, there was no guarantee they wouldn't alert the count. I couldn't risk it.

The lift rattled and groaned as it ascended through the dark, narrow shaft. We finally emerged into a forgotten, cobwebbed linen closet on the top floor. I pushed the door open cautiously, peeking out into an empty corridor. The view from the windows indicated we were one floor above where we needed to be.

Rather than risk another uncertain button press in the lift, I decided this was close enough. Lifting Clyde again, I slipped out of the linen closet and made my way down the flight of stairs at the end of the corridor to the correct floor.

I reached my suite without incident, kicked the door shut behind me and dropped Clyde into the casket next to the bed. He was still unconscious, his face frozen in a furious grimace. He was breathing faintly - holding my hand above his slightly open mouth confirmed it.

I rummaged through my suitcase, retrieving two extra belts to secure him with, a set of dry clothes, and the steel-capped Alexander McQueen ankle boots - the only pair of dry shoes I had left at Eve Hall.

Quickly, I changed into the dry clothes, stuffing the wet ones into the suitcase. I then tied Clyde with the extra belts, securing his arms against his torso, so that he wouldn't be able to break free even if the freeze wore off.

With that done, I sat on the edge of the bed and called Sebastian. He answered on the first ring, almost as if he'd been waiting for my call.

"Sebastian, sorry to call you this late. Or early. Whichever it is."

"Harlan, I just had this insane dream. You won't believe-"

"You won't believe this," I cut him off. "We have a bit of a family crisis here, and I need you to get involved."

"A family crisis?" He asked breathlessly. "I've been waiting to get involved in a family crisis my entire life!" I could practically hear the lump forming in his throat, and it was easy to visualize the excitement twinkling in his eyes.

"Perfect, because this one is epic. Buckle up."

I quickly summarized the situation, omitting none of the important details. I concluded with, "I need to get him out of here before anyone else finds out what he's been up to and decides to kill him."

"This is wild," Sebastian said in a quiet voice. "But what can I do?"

"You can hurry down here. And bring a hearse."

"A hearse - why?" I could tell from his tone that he wasn't immediately sold on the idea.

"Because," I said, "if anyone finds out what Clyde was up to, he's dead. I want to head back to London tonight, and we need to transport him somehow, hidden. The best way is in a casket. When the freeze wears off, something tells me he is going to be a little agitated. It's probably best to keep him boxed up until he calms down. I figured we could put him in the basement when we get back to the mansion. You know, where he and Lyrica put Venedict."

"But we can't leave him there for two centuries," Sebastian protested. "It wouldn't be ethical."

I rolled my eyes, grateful that Sebastian couldn't see it. "No," I said, with as much patience as I could manage, "of course not. We'll find a better solution, but right now, I just want to get him out of here. We can think about everything else later."

"But where am I going to get a hearse from in the middle of the night?" Sebastian sounded infuriatingly anxious and overwhelmed. I was already questioning my decision to call him instead of Jed or Carmen. They would have helped, and they both knew how to keep their cool.

"Deep Graves," I replied.

There was a pause, the line silent for several seconds. Then he asked hesitantly, "Is Gabriel okay with that?"

"Probably not, but that's why we won't ask."

"Harlan, I'm not sure about this. Maybe we could ask Thomas?"

"We don't have time for that, and we can't afford to risk being told no," I replied. "I know how to pick locks and hot-wire cars, and I'll guide you through it. It's really not that difficult. And we're not stealing anything, just borrowing for a couple of hours."

"But, isn't there another way?" I could hear the internal struggle, the cogs turning in Sebastian's head, creaking with resistance.

"I'll take full responsibility if anything goes wrong," I assured him, "which it won't. I promise. There's always a hearse parked right outside Deep Graves, you know, right at the bottom of the cemetery. That one is vintage, easy to break into. And Gabriel is here at Eve Hall, so you don't need to worry about him. Just don't park right in front of the place - that would be tempting fate, just a little. Park outside the gates and call me when you get here."

After a beat of silence, I delivered the killer blow, "Do you want to be involved in this family crisis or don't you, Sebastian?"

With a sigh, he surrendered, "I want to be involved. Of course I do."

"That's the spirit. I know you'll do great. All my break-in tools are in the black satchel in the hallway. Don't mix it up with the one Venedict uses for business school. Hurry up."

Sebastian swallowed hard. "I'm on it."

"I owe you, Sebastian."

I hung up and breathed a tentative sigh of relief. Maybe, just maybe, no one would have to die tonight. I mean no one apart from Tibor.

The realization that the shadowy veil of mystery surrounding the first years of my life would never be fully lifted stung like a bitch. Everyone who had known me, who had loved me back then, had been dead and buried for over two decades. I finally knew how my parents had died, knew why, and knew who had done it. I had dug as deep as I could into the event that had shaped my entire existence. My life, in any conventional sense, was over. But I was still here. What the hell was I supposed to make of that?

I was about to shut the casket lid when the sight of Clyde's shattered nose made me hesitate.

Eli had taught me how to set bones, made me practice on roadkill and eventually on my fellow hunters at the Van Helsing Society. I'd popped more than a few shoulders back into place and broken arms back together in haste on missions. A nose, though, is more delicate work. I would have preferred for Elizabeth to handle this, but if I brought her here and let her in on even a fraction of what was going on, she was probably going to say something to Gabriel. I didn't want to take the risk.

Clyde's nose wasn't completely pulverized - his nasal bone had broken cleanly and been squished to the side, making it look worse than it was. I leaned over the casket and, gingerly, lifted it back into place and pressed its aristo-cratic bridge into position with a wet click.

With that taken care of, I shut the casket lid, wrapped the long chain I'd taken from the subterranean nook tightly around it, securing it with the hook attached, sealing Clyde and all the chaos away inside.

THIRTY-ONE

G abriel's suite was perched at the corner of Eve Hall, a floor above mine, just as Roderick had described. I hoped to catch him before he headed downstairs for the ball, where I imagined he'd be floating around on a cloud of victory-inflected self-importance.

Sebastian had managed to start the hearse, and as I made my way upstairs, my phone buzzed with a message from him saying he had cleared London and was on the highway. He promised to call me when he arrived.

I checked that the volume was all the way up before slipping my phone into my pocket. I couldn't risk Gabriel seeing even a hint of a message from Sebastian that might give away what we were up to.

I knocked on the ancient, arched wooden door, which creaked open to reveal Gabriel in a black silk and velvet ensemble with a pattern of poison-green dragons. His light blond hair was brushed behind his ears, falling gracefully over his shoulders, his eyes glowing faintly, like a cat's. Soft strains of a piano piece floated from the room behind him, its melodic pull as subtle and pervasive as the tide.

"Harlan," he remarked, one pale eyebrow arching slightly. "You slipped from my grasp earlier. I was just about to go hunt for you."

"I'm the hunter, remember?" I brushed past him into the parlor. "I'm out of here, but I want a quick word."

"Certainly." Gabriel closed the door behind me with a soft but distinct click.

The space was opulently furnished, with gilded-framed paintings on the walls and antique mahogany and velvet furniture. Tall, pointed-arched windows offered an uninterrupted view of the coastal landscape, the ocean stretching endlessly, its surface shimmering like silvery skin. The air was heavy with the intoxicating scent of lilies. I spotted several large bouquets of those waxy, ghost-white flowers, just like the ones I'd seen at Deep Graves and Gabriel's villa. It wouldn't have surprised me if he insisted on fresh lilies in his suite, like some eccentric immortal diva.

"We're even," I said, turning to face him with a look that dared him to argue. "I don't owe you anything anymore. So don't expect me to jump at your beck and call the next time you want to play Monopoly with your rich, centuries-old pals."

"I wouldn't dream of it," Gabriel agreed, though the gleam in his eyes was far less reassuring than his words.

"You have no idea," I said, my voice tight with frustration, "what I've had to deal with tonight to secure this absurd victory for you and keep everything from falling apart." That was the understatement of the century.

I stalked over to the luxurious Victorian settee in the center of the room and sank into the plush red velvet cushions, folding my arms across my chest. Couldn't Gabriel show me a little appreciation, even if I'd backed myself into this mess?

"Would telling me about it perhaps ease your mind?"

I shot him a withering look. "No. Talking about it won't make a blind bit of difference."

It was tempting, though - to let it all spill out. Roderick's threats, Clyde's freezing formula and him killing my parents. The disorienting realization that my destiny as a hunter might have run its course, leaving me suspended in mid-air. And why not mention Algernon's attempted possession, the fear that Ramsay might still be vengeful despite his words, or my barely acknowledged fear that I might end up killing Aubrey - and that I preferred that risk to pushing her away.

It was a lot. My chest tightened just thinking about it. But if I shared it with Gabriel, he would twist it, turn it into something he could use against me. Or at least, he would see it as weakness.

And there was Clyde to consider. I had to keep quiet about him to protect him. What the hell was I going to do about him, anyway? Sebastian was right - locking him in a basement forever wasn't a real solution. Should I get Malcolm involved, see if he could help with Clyde's mental state? Then again, Malcolm hadn't exactly been much help with me. Every time he tried to pry into my emotions, I either shut down completely or laced my words with so much irony that my true feelings got lost in sarcasm. How could he possibly help Clyde, who was far more broken?

I shoved the thoughts aside, just in case Gabriel was silently rifling through my mind. His expression remained inscrutable, impossible to read.

"No," I finally said. "Talking about it won't make a blind bit of difference."

But the silence lingered, pressing down on me, and before I could stop myself, I heard myself say, "I used to agree with Clyde - vampires were just monsters. But since I grew these stupid fangs, I've realized you're, I mean, we're, people." I exhaled sharply. "Maybe I'm kidding myself, thinking I can be both a vampire and a hunter. Maybe being a hunter should've ended when my mortal life did."

I'd never voiced any doubt about being a hunter before, because I'd never felt any. Everything I'd just said felt like a betrayal leaving my mouth, and I immediately wanted to take it all back, but it was too late.

I stared down at my hands, half-expecting to see them stained with the blood of all the vampires I'd slain without a second thought. But they were as clean as if none of it had ever happened.

"What if," I whispered, the realization striking me, "I didn't become a monster when I turned? What if killing vampires made me one a long time ago, and I just didn't realize it? What then?"

I looked up. Gabriel had taken a seat on the piano bench across from me, his expression unchanged. "Yes, what then?" he echoed. His calm, unruffled tone made the question seem almost trivial. "If you insist on considering yourself a monster either way, should it really matter when exactly it happened?"

He paused, then added with a faint smile, "At least you make an exquisite monster, if you'll forgive the observation. And doesn't that make it rather more bearable?"

I tried to summon one of my usual ironic smirks - something to deflect both the compliment and the awful vulnerability creeping in. But I couldn't. Instead, a sob clawed its way up my throat.

I clenched my jaw and looked away, but the blood tears had already begun to well up, sliding down my face in silent, unstoppable streams.

The tears should have been my cue to get up and leave, but instead, I drew my knees up tight, wrapped my arms around them, and buried my face against my legs, shutting everything out while I wrestled my emotions back under control.

I sensed rather than saw Gabriel move closer, settling beside me. "Shh," he murmured. "There is no need for tears."

His fingers grazed lightly at the nape of my neck, so delicate, so fleeting, I could have imagined it. Almost.

I turned just enough to shoot him a glare through the red haze of tears. "I don't need-" I started, but the rest of the sentence trailed off as his hand settled at the back of my neck. Slowly, his fingers traced a line up to the base of my skull, the spot where Algernon had attacked me, as if he somehow knew.

"No, of course you don't," he replied, his voice almost too soft, too understanding. His fingers drifted back down my neck, down between my shoulder blades, leaving a faint shiver in their wake.

Letting Gabriel comfort me like this felt like a potentially bad idea, but his touch drained the fight from me as quickly as it welled up. I wiped at my eyes, frozen, caught between the urge to push his hand away and the strange pull to let him continue.

"You don't have to fight me." His voice was low, coaxing, as if calming a skittish animal. "I have no intention of harming you - well, not anymore. And this is tolerable, isn't it?" His fingers traced little circles along the back of my neck.

It was more than tolerable, and he knew it.

I didn't answer, but I felt my muscles gradually unwind, tension giving way to a reluctant surrender. He wasn't using any supernatural influence on me, just a quiet persistence that was nearly as disarming. I let my arms fall from around my knees, uncurling from my defensive position.

Sensing the shift, Gabriel slid an arm around me, cautiously at first, almost experimentally, as if testing whether I might bite. When I didn't, he drew me just a little closer. Every muscle in my body tensed in resistance - but the tension didn't hold. And the moment I eased, even slightly, he took it as permission, closing the last sliver of distance between us.

But then we reached a standoff as he started to guide my leg over his, as if he actually thought I might let him pull me into his lap. The thought made my jaw clench harder than the memory of him killing me.

"I can't. This is too fucking weird." But my voice wavered slightly. We were already here, and now I finally just wanted the damn hug.

"Okay, but Gabriel?" My tone turned deadly serious. "If you get a boner, I'll know - and I'll kill you. Then I'll bring you back to London in my suitcase and feed you piece by piece to Faust and Mephistopheles."

"I can vividly picture it," he assured me, the smile in his voice subtle but unmistakable. "And I assure you, I have both self-control and a strong preference for remaining in one piece."

Reluctantly, I let him pull me onto his lap, my arms hovering uncertainly before I finally gave in and wrapped them around him. I leaned into him fully, resting my head against his shoulder.

On any other night, the thought of curling up like this in another man's lap would have made me recoil. But tonight wasn't any other night, and it was too late to pretend we weren't already in this surreal situation.

Besides, it was just for now.

"This doesn't, you know, mean something," I mumbled.

"It means precisely what you say it means," he agreed quietly.

A pause settled between us, almost comfortable. But the awareness of just how close we were never fully faded. And as the last remnants of my sadness dissolved, it became impossible to ignore the way his touch lingered - the press of his fingers along my spine, the slow tracing.

I shifted, unsettled, irritation creeping in. Just then, his hand drifted up my thigh, agonizingly slow, before retreating like the tide, slipping back to safer ground. Testing. Seeing where the boundary lay.

"Gabriel," I warned.

"Yes, Harlan?" His voice was almost a purr. "Did you not want me to show you some appreciation? I caught that in your thoughts earlier. I certainly could, if only you would let me."

His hand resumed its ascent, slipping dangerously high between my thighs, his fingers pressing just enough to draw a sharp gasp from me, perilously close to a moan.

He made a low, satisfied sound in response.

"Gabriel," I hissed, yanking back just enough to meet his gaze. His eyes were bright with thrill and provocation.

"Cut it out."

"This is novel for you, I understand," he acknowledged, his hand lingering rather than advancing, tracing slow, idle patterns that sent an unwelcome shiver through me. "And yet, you might find that you are capable of enjoying my attentions. If only just this once."

He watched me closely, the same way he had when he placed that cursed glass of blood in front of me. Waiting. Expectant.

"You needn't be frightened."

Frightened?

After more than a century of his shadow looming over my family - after killing me, after blackmailing me into this twisted weekend - now he was toying with me, provoking me, as if I were fragile enough to be intimidated by this.

He knew I might have killed as many vampires as he had mortals. He had seen me stand at death's threshold without so much as a flinch. How could he think I was so easy to rattle?

"Don't insult me, Gabriel. Nothing about you scares me."

Then, I made a mistake.

Before I could second-guess myself, I grabbed a fistful of his hair, yanked his head back, and crashed my lips into his. I poured every ounce of frustration, anger, and defiance into that kiss - maybe even a sense of triumph. That despite everything, I was still here. Still intact. I wanted to stun him, throw him off balance, take back control.

Instead, I just felt out of my depth.

His lips curled into a smile against mine, as if my sudden aggression amused him, as if he'd been baiting me to cross this line. He kissed me back with equal intensity, but slowly, forcing me to match his pace.

I hadn't meant for it to be a real kiss, but that's what it became.

His hand slipped up the back of my neck, fingers tightening in my hair, and his other hand slid higher. I hadn't expected him to just go for it like that - but here we were.

Heat pooled in my core faster than I could make it stop, and I had to fight the urge to lean into the sensation. Maybe, just for a second, I did - letting my tongue melt against his as I pressed closer.

Then, regretting it, I twisted my head away. But the moment I did, he sank his fangs into my neck.

My body froze instinctively as he clamped down. All I felt was the sharp, searing pain and the pressure of his hand sliding over me, unhurried, savoring.

My own hand shot up to his chin, my fingers digging into his jaw. I could pry him off me, but I didn't.

It felt so good, I wanted to die. At this rate, Faust and Mephistopheles would be feasting on me before Gabriel.

As if granting me one last chance to escape before things spiraled hopelessly out of control, Gabriel retracted his fangs.

I slid off his lap in a blur, scrambling backward until my spine collided with the velvet armrest of the settee. My heart hammered, wild and erratic, like a swarm of bats trapped inside my ribcage, desperate to break free.

Our eyes locked, his still gleaming with that same provocative challenge. But there was also something much softer, something alarmingly close to tenderness.

"Don't ever," I said, voice low but cutting, "touch me like that again. And don't freaking bite me."

Instinctively, I reached for my neck - a trickle of blood ran down, just a few drops. He hadn't even drawn much blood. The bite had been about something else, and the thought made my skin crawl.

"I'm not a stand-in for Venedict. And I'm not into whatever the hell you think this is."

"Well, that is a shame." Gabriel's fingers brushed lightly against my ankle, a teasing echo of our tug-of-war during the poker game. "Because I have a feeling you could entertain me far better than anything occurring downstairs."

"I'm flattered," I said, grimacing, "but I'd rather poke my own eyes out with a stake."

My phone, which had somehow ended up on the floor near the settee's lion-clawed foot, started ringing. It had to be Sebastian.

"I need to get that." I yanked my leg to my chest and scrambled to my feet, relieved as the last remnants of the spell shattered like fragile glass.

IT WAS 3:27 AM when Sebastian called to say he had arrived and was parked outside the gates, just as I'd instructed. I had to focus on that - getting Clyde out of here and back to London. But as I stomped down the hall from Gabriel's suite, slamming the door behind me with a reverberating thud that I hoped conveyed my feelings, that strange, vulnerable moment I'd let myself get drawn into clung to me like invisible tendrils.

I knew I wasn't interested in men - not even a little. But I'd been in an unsettled headspace, and Gabriel had seized the opportunity to nudge, provoke, and slip past my defenses further than he should have. Now, a lingering trace of heat still flickered in my core, refusing to fade.

I paused on the grand staircase. Did I have a few minutes? Truce or no truce, maybe I should go back, beat the crap out of him, or drain his blood, making it crystal clear that he should never touch me again, or mess with anyone in my family.

No, I didn't need to do that. At least, not right now. I forced myself to keep moving before I made any bad decisions. Just a few months into my undead existence, I'd already made enough of those to last me another century or so.

Back in my suite, I checked on Clyde. He was still paralyzed, but now conscious, seething with rage. His teeth were clenched so tightly I half-expected them to shatter, and his midnight eyes burned with fury as soon as I cracked the lid open. I snapped it shut again, rewrapping the chains for good measure before dragging the heavy, chain-bound casket out onto the balcony, overlooking the darkened grounds.

Music already drifted up from below - guess the night's festivities were kicking off.

I took a deep breath, tipped the casket over the balustrade and began lowering it, link by link. I had to get it all the way to the ground from the fifth floor without drawing any attention, then drag it through the grounds to the gate. My suite was on the far end of Eve Hall, away from the ballroom, so my chances seemed, if not great then at least reasonable. But there were about a hundred vampires gathered downstairs, and even one pair of eyes on me would be too many.

The chain rattled, the sound echoing very faintly off the stone walls.

As the chain extended, guilt gnawed at me. Would Venedict be upset if he knew about this whole episode with Gabriel? Should I tell him?

I probably should, before Gabriel did - and he definitely would. To be fair, that was likely a big part of his motivation. He knew it would rile Venedict, fuel his jealousy, and maybe even sow discord between us. And like an absolute idiot, I'd let myself get swept along, at least for a moment.

How was I going to spin this? *I climbed into his lap, he provoked me, so I made out with him. Then I regretted it, and he bit me.* That didn't sound good, did it?

When the casket finally touched down on the flagstone, I tied the end of the chain to the balcony's banister and began my descent after it.

Everything went smoothly until I was about halfway down. A sudden burst of light and music flooded the darkness as a double window flung open just inches from me. Roderick leaned out, his face hovering alarmingly close to mine. The room behind him was a swirl of shadows and warm, golden light.

The sight of his face stopped me cold. He was dressed in crisp, clean clothes, his dark hair neatly parted in the middle. Elizabeth's stitchwork was flawless, but the damage I'd done to his face had left it twisted, splintered. There was still symmetry and beauty there, beneath the scars, like a grandly structured building covered in cobwebs and creeping ivy.

"Harlan, fancy catching you here," he said, his voice surprisingly calm. Whether he was here to settle a score, to watch me squirm or to take revenge was anyone's guess.

"Roderick. Hey."

"I see you're making off with one of uncle's caskets," he remarked, his tone still nonchalant.

"Couldn't find my suitcase," I replied dryly. "Hope you don't mind."

"Not particularly. I was hoping to ask you something, before you leave. Would you be my best man at Belladira's and my wedding this summer? I would consider it an honor."

"Don't you- I mean, don't you hate me?"

"Why would I hate you?" His tone shifted to mild exasperation, as if he were explaining something to a particularly slow child. "I told you, did I not? That we could be friends, blood brothers. And now it's happened. Granted, not quite the way I envisioned, but even so - the resentment is gone. I feel connected to you."

Are you insane? I wanted to say, but I clamped it down. Given Roderick's stint at Bedlam, it probably wasn't the best question to ask.

"Sure," I heard myself say. "Okay."

Roderick's face lit up with a smile, though the expression made him wince as the fresh scars tugged at the stitches.

"But," I added, "you'll need to tell the guards to open the gate in about a minute. I'll have a hard time getting the casket over the fence."

"Consider it done."

"And no knives," I said pointedly. "Let's be done with that."

"Naturally. I'll never threaten you again." He tilted his head. "May I have a hug?"

I hesitated. Was he up to something?

I let my eyes sweep over his hands, sleeves, waist, anywhere a knife could be hidden. I came up empty-handed; there were no glints of metal, no signs of deception in his posture.

"I swear to you, I am guileless."

Reluctantly, I let go of the chain with one hand and leaned in. Roderick wrapped his arms around me in a tight hug, but he didn't try to stab me or pull me off the chain to make me fall. It was just a hug.

"Thank you," he whispered and released me.

Still baffled but oddly relieved, I lowered myself the rest of the way to the ground. As soon as my feet hit the flagstone, I looked up to see Roderick vanish back into the building, closing the window behind him.

Grabbing the chains, I started dragging the casket around the side of the building, through the slick, muddy grass, heading toward the parking lot. A hesitant sense of relief began stealing over me - I was getting away with this, wasn't I?

I glanced over my shoulder, just to be sure. No one was watching me. No one was following.

When I reached the car park, I tied the casket to the Stingray's exhaust pipe using the chain. I'd never tried towing anything with my car before, and I knew it wasn't built for dragging coffins. But hopefully, it'd work.

Sliding behind the wheel, I turned the key, and the engine hummed to life. My luggage was still upstairs, but that was a problem for later. Maybe I'd ask Evander to send it to Thornhill Mansion, or just write it off as collateral damage.

The gravel crunched beneath the tires as I rolled toward the tall wrought iron gates at the edge of the property, the casket trailing behind me in the gravel. By the time I reached them, I found them wide open.

I'd told Sebastian to park out of sight - couldn't risk any of the other vampires finding him first. Now, as I turned right onto the road, I spotted the black hearse limo with its D33P 6RV vanity plate. Its sleek body gleamed under the moonlight and its lights were off. It looked like some oversized, ghostly insect.

Sebastian stepped out, his pale face animated, his eyes feverish. "I feel alive!" he proclaimed, throwing his arms skyward. All that was missing was a flash of lightning illuminating the sky behind him.

"That's great, Sebastian. Let's keep it that way - let's get the hell out of here."

He'd been a nervous wreck when I walked him through boosting the Deep Graves hearse, teeth chattering and hands trembling, but he'd pulled it off. I felt proud of him. He'd never make a good vampire hunter, though.

He eyed the casket on the ground and asked in a whisper, "Is Clyde in there?"

"The one and only."

Together, Sebastian and I loaded the casket into the back of the hearse. There was an extendable bar the casket had to rest on so we could slide it in, and a fiddly chrome piece which needed to be slotted into two precise holes and tightened to stop the casket from rattling around.

"I should drive this," I told Sebastian once we were good to go. "You know, just in case. Let's not risk a horror movie ending where Clyde wakes up, breaks through the chains, and drains your blood while the hearse flies off a cliff."

"I don't particularly like the idea of that, either." Sebastian agreed.

We swapped places, and I tossed him my car keys.

The hearse's interior was all premium leather, sparkling chrome and lacquered mahogany trim, almost like the vehicle was trying to distract from its grim purpose. I flipped down the rearview mirror. Gabriel's bite marks were twin crescents on my neck, still faintly visible.

I slammed the mirror back into place so hard that it broke off in my hand. I tossed the shattered pieces into the backseat, trying to shake the unsettling feeling that Gabriel had marked me.

Turning the ignition, the hearse purred quietly to life. As the headlights flickered on, Beethoven's *Moonlight Sonata* began playing softly through the speakers, the haunting melody feeling like a fitting soundtrack to the strange procession we'd become - me driving the hearse, with Sebastian ready to trail behind in the Stingray. I left the music on, pulled away from the curb, and started back toward London.

EPILOGUE

The time on the hearse's digital display blinked 05:26 as I reversed through the wrought iron gates of Thornhill Mansion. I left the engine idling, the soft strains of classical piano filling the cool air. The mansion grounds were thick with mist, swirling like ghosts around the hedges and statues. It was good to be home.

I swung open the hearse's rear door, grabbed the casket's cold handles, and slid it out before giving the lid a knock.

"Clyde? We're home."

Silence.

Up the winding path, Sebastian hurried to make sure the doors to the crypt were open. The once-white marble steps of the mansion glowed in the mist.

When he returned, we carried the casket through the garden - well, I did most of the lifting while Sebastian balanced the back end a bit - across the grand hall, and down the narrow staircase into the heavy, musty air of the windowless, velvet-draped circular chamber beneath the mansion.

We placed Clyde's casket beside Venedict's in the circle of caskets. The rusty chains clattered as we transferred them from one casket to the other. After everything that had nearly gone wrong tonight, I wasn't taking any chances.

Sebastian went off to see if he could rally the others for an early morning family meeting - there was much to discuss about Clyde's unexpected return to Thornhill Mansion after 160-odd years.

I lingered, alone with the casket.

"Clyde?"

Still no response. The freeze must not have worn off yet. But even though he couldn't talk back, I knew he could hear me. I'd been able to hear him and his mad rambling just fine when I'd been subjected to the freeze.

"I know it probably doesn't feel like it right now," I said, "but we'll figure this out. Everything's going to be okay. Maybe you could see this as a fresh start? Once we let you out, it could be the beginning of something new. Maybe it's as easy as that."

A dry, muffled voice drifted from inside the casket. "That, I believe, is the most flippant suggestion I've heard since... 1858, at least."

The sound of his voice surprised me.

"Yeah? Well, maybe you should try being a little more flippant. Some levity wouldn't kill you."

"And you - will you not kill me?"

"No. I probably should, but I'm not going to. I'm trying to be less of a monster than I could be."

Clyde fell into what I hoped was a contemplative, rather than sullen, silence.

I found Sebastian in the library, his silhouette framed against the tall windows as he lowered the blackout curtains one by one, the thick fabric pooling on the floor like dark water. The room smelled faintly of old books and candle wax, the air still and heavy beneath the high ceilings and glass dome.

Overhead, a recently installed solar-blocking panel slid into place with a soft hum, preparing to block the light that would otherwise begin streaming through the dome at dawn and form a warm, golden circle on the threadbare carpet below. I remembered standing in that circle my first morning at the mansion, bathed in sunlight. That felt like a world ago. A sharp little pain seared through my heart like a bullet.

I would never see sunlight again, that was true - but at least I wasn't doomed to be alone in the dark.

"Sebastian?"

He turned toward me, a grin spreading across his face. He looked completely wired. "I had a look around for the others, knocked on their doors - none of them seem to be home."

"Perfect," I said. "Do you still want to become a vampire?"

He froze, his expression shifting ever so slightly. At first, it seemed like he thought I might be joking.

"But hasn't Venedict forbidden it? I thought you agreed with him - that I should stay mortal."

I shrugged. "I've changed my mind. I think you should join the rest of the family as a vampire. And frankly, I don't think you should wait around for some cute vampire girl to sweep you off your feet. One thing, though - you've got to explain the whole vasectomy situation to Venedict. Make him understand nothing's been lost. You weren't going to continue the bloodline anyway. That's the only reason he's against you turning."

Sebastian's smile slowly returned, wider this time, understanding dawning in his eyes.

"And there's something else - the bloodlust. I might've given you the impression I've got it under control. But I don't. Not really. I don't think I can teach you how to suppress it." It sounded more vulnerable than I liked, but I had to be honest.

Sebastian nodded quietly. "I understand. I don't expect you to."

"Not everything's gone according to plan this weekend," I continued, stepping closer. "But we can still end it on a high note."

"You mean... you'll turn me now?"

"Unless you'd rather have six months to get in the best shape of your life?"

He let out a chuckle, a nervous energy rippling through him. "I'm already in great shape. I like the famished poet look."

I smirked at that. "So, you're ready?"

"More than ready. Wait-" He suddenly reached up and touched his face. "I need to shave. I'm not about to rock a five AM shadow for eternity."

"What about your hair? If you want it snipped, I'm good with a knife - I can probably wield a pair of scissors."

"No," he replied with a tone of sharp finality. "You're not touching my hair."

I raised an eyebrow, amused. His raven-black hair was tousled and slightly wild, falling nearly to his shoulders, and that was clearly how it would stay. "Alright, suit yourself," I said, watching as he left the library to handle his pre-turning grooming ritual.

The door swung shut behind him, and I checked my watch: 05:51. There was still a solid hour before sunrise - plenty of time to turn someone into a vampire and then coast the hearse downhill to Deep Graves before anyone would miss it. Or maybe I'd crash it into the fence, you know, to send Gabriel a message.

I moved to the love seat, the same one where Lyrica had sat when she first unraveled the story of her life, the Thornhill family saga, and how Sebastian and I were connected to it all. I had just settled into the cushions when the outline of Helen Thornhill flickered to light in the semi-darkness, standing right in front of me. She wore her long, white wedding dress, her long black hair billowing gently around her, as if stirred by a wind sweeping through another dimension.

I started slightly; Helen had never appeared to me directly before.

But I supposed this was a special occasion. After all, I was about to fulfill her prophecy.

In a few short moments, I would corrupt the bloodline's last pure soul. The family tree would finally be complete, but it would be a tree of death, forever suspended in darkness, just as Helen had foretold in 1861. But was that really such a terrible thing?

"Helen," I said, feeling slightly guilty, like she'd caught me at something I shouldn't be doing. "Are you angry with me?"

She smiled, but it was melancholy. Slowly, she reached toward me, her ghostly fingers brushing against my temple with a faint coolness, like she was trying to tuck an errant strand of hair behind my ear. I reached up and did it myself, my eyes locked on hers.

"I don't want to disappoint you," I said quietly. "But I'm

trying to do what's right for the family. I think the family should be complete."

She nodded silently. She might not approve, but she seemed to understand.

Also by Lucius Valiant

Dark Roots (The Thornhill Vampire Chronicles Book 1)

Deep Graves (The Thornhill Vampire Chronicles Book 2)

Foul Moon (The Thornhill Vampire Chronicles Book 3)

Grim Games (The Thornhill Vampire Chronicles Book 4)

About the Author

Lucius Valiant is a Danish-British author.

The first real book he recalls reading is Bram Stoker's "Dracula." And that, as the saying goes, was that. There would be no turning back.

Lucius's literary inspirations include classics of Gothic fiction, such as Mary Shelley's "Frankenstein" and Oscar Wilde's "The Picture of Dorian Gray," as well as horror, supernatural, and speculative fiction by writers such as Anne Rice, Poppy Z. Brite, and Stephen King. He also draws much influence from Britain's rich history, folklore, and legends.

All of these influences shine through like glittering, dark fairy dust in his writing, which readers have described as vivid, visceral, and cinematic, with a sprinkling of wry humor.

Visit his linktree to learn more, join the mailing list, and be kept in the loop about upcoming releases and secret subscriber treats: https://linktr.ee/luciusvaliant

Author's Note

Writing this book was much like wrestling a stubborn, slithering, writhing creature, dragging it up from the depths of the abyss by its tail. The story shifted constantly in my hands, morphing beneath my fingertips, trying to get away from me. But I didn't let it.

The *Thornhill Vampire Chronicles* are far from over - but this will be the last book with Harlan Thornhill as the narrator, at least for a while. There are several other characters in this expanding, interwoven tapestry of fates whose skin I'm itching to take you under.

Lucius Valiant, October 2024